To Touch The Sun

☉

Laura Enright

*To Lisa,
Thanks for being such
a positive inspiration*

Laura L. Enright

*Dagda
Publishing*

Copyright © Laura Enright, 2014
Cover Design Copyright © A D Warr, 2014
Book Design Copyright © A Popa, 2014
Edited by R J Davey

First published in Great Britain in 2014
by Dagda Publishing, Nottingham, UK

First Impression, 2013

ISBN-13: 978-1494740801
ISBN-10: 149474080X

Dagda Publishing
85 St Stephens Road, Nottingham, UK NG2 4JR
www.dagdapublishing.co.uk
www.facebook.com/dagdapublishing
www.twitter.com/dagdapublishing
www.dagdapublishing.tumblr.com

All enquiries: info@dagdapublishing.co.uk

Contents

This book is dedicated to libraries everywhere.
Portals to knowledge and adventure.

Prologue

Reg Jameson squinted one eye, checking the view through the night-scope with the other. The scope was unnecessary; his vision was perfectly capable of picking up the smallest movement even on cloudy nights, but he liked to keep up with the latest in cool toy technology and the scope had been recently acquired through a French arms dealer who he'd dealt with over the years. Many years. Based in Chantilly, the man must be pushing 75 at this point yet remained on the cutting edge of weaponry. He was also very discreet, a trait Jameson prized above all else.

Through the scope, Jameson picked up the silhouette of one of his ferals stepping carefully through the forest, senses alert for its prey. The feral's skin shone a ghastly white in the moonlight filtering through the trees, his features marred slightly by the prominent brow-line and extreme dental anatomy particular to most ferals. But the hair that would have once been snarled and ratty, in a length dictated by the decades, was clean and short, his beard carefully groomed. The feral could pass in normal society provided no one stared too long…and with the energy ferals emanated, people rarely did.

Two flanked him and eighteen others fanned out, their instincts the only thing required for the task. This was their world and no matter how civilised Jameson succeeded in making them, the ferals would always be able to utilise the hunting instincts that had kept them alive long before he arrived.

Reg sometimes marvelled at the ferals. As powerful as he had grown over the decades, his abilities paled in comparison to theirs. And yet, despite their strength, their fractured minds had kept them from re-entering the societies they'd been torn from decades – sometimes centuries – before.

He should have used them first. It would have saved a great deal of time. Instead, he first sent a hunting party of trusted "normal" mercenaries to track down the creature, hoping that it would be weaker in the daylight. The encroaching shadows of night would not harm the mercenaries, but daylight was toxic for Reg and his ferals. The creature, however, was powerful, even during the day which was one of things about it that initially caught Jameson's attention.

A feral (christened "Pierre" with his real name lost to history) stopped and grunted softly, waving a hand low. The grunt with the slightest of whistles indicated to the others that they were close. Yes, Jameson could sense the beast himself. It gave off a very distinct presence.

"This should be interesting," Jameson whispered. His normal hunting party had fared badly and he'd had a devil of a time erasing their connection to him. They understood the risks to both their lives and reputation, which was why their fee was so high. The French police listed them as poachers, their sketchy backgrounds and the high-tech gear they sported backing up this profile. What authorities couldn't explain was what killed the group – breaking their bodies, draining them of blood and leaving them in a horrible heap on the side of the road.

The grisly discovery was made by a young couple out for a hike who would no doubt carry the image with them for a long time.

And that's what brought Jameson to the Amiens area of France. There had been talk of something terrorizing the woods. It started with an attack at a construction site for a new housing development. The gruesome deaths of a few of the workers, found drained of blood, had made international news and Jameson caught sight of it one night on the BBC. Recognizing the area immediately, Jameson quickly speculated what could be terrorizing the area, soon realising that it was something the authorities might never admit to be possible. What led Jameson to become a participant in the hunt, rather than remain a television spectator – what made the prey so important to him – was that the attacks had occurred during the day.

Only a feral could attack with such efficiency that he could bring down five men, drain their blood, then disappear, as it was reported "something" had done on the construction site without the rest of the crew being the wiser. But ferals were hampered by the weakness of all vampires—natural sunlight. The attack happened on a cloudy day, yet the light would still have been paralysingly toxic. Somehow, this feral had built up immunity to daylight.

Who knew how old the creature was? It could be centuries old, buried deep in the ground until an urge… an instinct… something drove it up to the fresh air again. And, if Jameson's suspicion was correct, the building going on in the area had disturbed it. Humans were encroaching on the territory of any number of species, so why should vampires be any different? Perhaps a bulldozer had unearthed it. If it had gone dormant, as many ferals did during lean times, it would wake up very hungry and very determined.

A bit like poking a hornet's nest.

A mutated feral haunting the French countryside was not a good thing for France, but it could be very advantageous for Jameson. He dispatched the human hunters in the hopes that they would be able to capture the beast. That was a bust, and coming on the heels of the carnage at the construction site, it fuelled more interest in the beast. This would complicate any attempt he might make to capture it, unless he was able to do so before a media frenzy began.

This thing was more than likely feral and sometimes fire was needed to fight fire.

His expedition would require special arrangements such as the specially designed mobile "tombs" for his hunters and himself to stay during the day should the effort take more than one night, which, ultimately, it did. Jameson utilised every connection he had both in government and the underworld and was able to make arrangements which would enable them to make a thorough search of the area.

He travelled to France regularly on business, but it had been almost a century since Jameson had last prowled that parcel of land. Of course, the landscape looked very different. Barren, mangled, chewed up by the "war to end all wars." Much like the soldiers struggling to stay alive during it. For a moment, he fancied he could smell the acrid stench of the gun powder that once had hung thick in the air. He could hear the screams of the young men falling around him and feel the dirt and shrapnel bursting forth from the craters made by the mortars pounding the ground. Then there was the horrible shredding of the German bullets that ripped into him; one in his shoulder, one in his side, another burrowing into the meat of his thigh, still another filling his chest with a fire he'd never felt before. He'd been brought to his knees with that agony, before falling flat and still in the mud where he slowly drifted away while the fight raged on around him. He'd been like so many…a war time statistic; never standing a chance, destined to die for "King and Country." Except that his destiny lay in the hands of another.

As his gaze wandered through the darkness of the forest and across the decades gone by, a grin spread across Jameson's face. He could still feel the slit of the blade across his throat before Private Narain Khan descended upon him and pulled the very life essence from him as they both lay dying in "No Man's land." Dying? No. Changing. Khan was no longer the man who had travelled so far to fight in a war that truly didn't concern his country. What had forced Khan to steal the blood of his dead and dying comrades that night had transformed both him and Jameson into something neither could ever have imagined.

The memories remained strong and clear through the decades, for Reg Jameson had never felt so alive as he did when he finally came to his senses and realised the irony of this great gift being bestowed upon him by a greater adversary.

He stifled a chuckle at the memories, not wanting to spoil the hunt. At last, in this, their fourth night, the hunters seemed to be making progress. Jameson checked his watch and noted that in three more hours they'd have to call it a night and return to the security of their well-constructed, windowless caravans driven by "normal" members of his staff who could answer any questions from passers-by during the day while he and the ferals remained safe and secure inside.

Just then the party caught sight of the beast they'd been sensing. Jameson stared, agape, at its size. It was a man with dark blonde hair and a beard long and matted from decades, possibly centuries, of being buried deep within the earth. While his clothes also bore the mark of ninety odd years above and below ground, Jameson could still note that he wore what appeared to be a British military uniform from World War I. Jameson was sure that it was a former soldier, perhaps even one of his own, though so many never made it home from that war that it would be hard to tell.

"Well Khan, you were very hungry that night," he whispered with a grin.

The being rested with his back against a tree, looking like a man lost in the woods, which for all intents and purposes he was. If he had been ripped from dormancy (which would be the only thing explaining the sudden rash of killings) then he had to be confused. If he was a feral, his thoughts would go no further, for as a rule they did not think about much beyond obtaining their next meal.

But what if he were sentient? Reg studied the man's face, which was partially obscured by matted locks of filthy hair. The look the man shot into the sky had a touch of melancholy as well as confusion.

Pierre glanced back for the order and Jameson nodded his head. Gracefully, silently, the ferals assumed a pack and made their way forward to surround their prey. But the man's hearing was apparently exceptional; whether he heard the softest of grunts or the smallest crunch of leaves, something caught his attention. His head snapped in the direction of the noise for barely an instant before he was off, navigating the forest floor with the expert precision that only his condition could produce. The ferals sped after and Jameson followed behind as close as he could.

Sentient or feral, it was a beast, a huge hulking frame, perhaps that of a former farmhand or blacksmith. Perhaps it was much older and had simply borrowed the uniform from one of his victims. The grace he displayed despite his size, however, was amazing as he dodged fallen branches and the outstretched grasp of the ferals gaining on him.

A few sped to the creature's left flank and eventually the rest began to herd the beast toward them. What Reg didn't reckon on was just how strong this man was. When the take down came, it was not easy and did not last. In fact, the ferals had to attempt it twice before the beast stopped and stood his ground to fight.

Ferals fought with little noise; one reason why they were so unsettling. They dove in and out, grabbing, clawing, nipping at the man soundlessly save for a few grunts or gasps. The man screamed unintelligible words at them, grabbing one and thumping it against a tree while shoving another from its other side. They piled on him a few times, but he was always able to throw them off.

"This contest could be an all-nighter," Jameson hissed. The creature had swatted some twenty ferals like gnats. A few of the ferals were grabbed and quickly dispatched, body parts thrown in all directions. No wonder the human hunters had never stood a chance.

Reaching into the breast pocket of his hunting jacket, Jameson pulled out a small case that contained two darts. A tranquiliser that would stop an elephant wouldn't stop Jameson, not to mention this maniac. But Channing had assured him that the solution in these darts, experimental as it was, would stop a feral. He looked up at the battle going on, then back at the darts. This was not your average feral. Too little and the beast might become even crazier.

In the meantime, the ferals were being slaughtered.

Loading one dart into his rifle, he took aim, hoping the beast would stand still long enough for a clear shot. Impatience gripping him, he called out, "Hey!" and took his shot when the startled combatants all looked up. The dart plunged into the being's right pectoral, releasing its drug before the beast had a chance to dislodge it.

Undeterred and furious, the man grabbed a feral and twisted his head clean off its neck with a sickeningly wet sound, tossing it far into the woods behind him. Jameson grimaced, but noted that the creature seemed to be growing lethargic. There was still plenty of fight in him, though, so Jameson took aim with the last dart in the chamber. The dart pierced the being's left side, embedding itself firmly. Taking a few steps back, he being looked down and yanked it from his body.

Deciding it was time to let the drug take its course, Jameson whistled off the feral attack and watched the remaining ferals back away while keeping the beast encircled. The huge being howled, falling to his knees and beating the ground in an effort to fight off the paralysis overcoming him. It was pointless. In a matter of moments he was completely immobile face down in the grass, the only sound being his furious hissing.

Straightening from the crouch he'd been in, Jameson lowered his weapon and ran a hand through his brown hair. "Pierre..." he began before realising that Pierre had been one of the casualties. Frowning, he turned to another feral, ordering, "Declan, get him back to the vehicles and pack him up for shipment. Do it quick, too." He glanced at his watch. "Not a lot of time and I want him secure before sunrise. Oh," he studied the body parts strewn about the forest, "and bring back some accelerant."

By the time Declan had returned with a container of petrol, Jameson had collected the gruesome remains and set them in a pile. Arms, legs, torsos, and heads, twitched with a zombie-like life and could have been pieced back together to recreate their original owners, but time was leaking away and there'd be no time for such handy-work. Jameson couldn't allow them to be discovered either. If evidence had to be found, let it be a charred lump to give the authorities yet another mystery to worry over.

When the gruesome deed was done, he and Declan hurried back to the caravans to make arrangements to leave. A special lorry had been arranged to transport their prize, its reinforced structure able to contain the creature even if it were to escape the specially designed restraints. Jameson had come prepared with more of the paralysing drug so he planned on keeping him as heavily sedated as possible. In the back of the lorry, arms, legs, and abdomen clamped to a shelf, the beast still battled with the agent attacking his system. Or, if Jameson understood Channing correctly, the little creatures inside him did battle with the drug.

The being's face was turned away from him when Jameson came in to check the restraints. Feeling the touch, the man summoned enough strength to turn toward him. It was then that the decades came rushing back to both of them. Eyes wide, Jameson mouthed, "Private Fred Blythe."

Under all that hair, he hadn't recognised him. And the Blythe he'd known during the Great War was nowhere near the size of this giant. There had definitely been some sort of mutated effect over the years. But the eyes told it all. This was Blythe, and his pale blue eyes still blazed with hatred as they gazed up at the man who had tormented him in the trenches another lifetime ago.

Rubbing the back of his hand against his chin, Reg said, "So, old chap...you made it out too, eh? Been a long time." A snarl formed on the creature's face. "Tut tut, none of that. I'm here to help you." He checked the restraints again. "Provided of course you're able to help me."

Chapter 1

"Narain, why are you standing in the dark?"

Dominic Amato had given the door three sets of sound knocks before resorting to his spare set of keys to Narain's condo. Opening the door, he noticed that the lights were off, the only illumination being the city lights of downtown Chicago flowing in softly through the balcony windows. The condo on the 68th floor of Lake Point Towers overlooked Lake Michigan and the festival atmosphere of Navy Pier with its brightly lit Ferris Wheel which, at 264 feet, dwarfed the very first Ferris Wheel constructed for the 1893 World's Fair. The city was running its cycles early to take advantage of the unseasonably warm April weather.

Off to the side of the window, a shadowy figure leaned against the wall, arms folded, pensively watching the twinkling lights of the wheel below. Narain Khan was usually far from melancholy, but the normally musical Indian clip was subdued as he chided, "Oh, there's plenty of light, Dom."

"Maybe for your eyes, Rain, but not mine."

Dominic pushed the light button next to the door and the ceiling fixtures brightened the living room considerably. The home was elegant, but welcoming; the living room, dining room and kitchen all open to create one large living space. The kitchen, Narain's "territory," was offset by a large island with a built in range where he could cook and immediately serve the food he so lovingly prepared for dinner guests sitting around it. The parties had lessened as Sophie grew frailer, but she wouldn't allow herself to slip away easily and the couple entertained whenever possible.

Noting the jeans and black T-shirt his barefoot friend wore, Dominic said, "Did we forget what tonight is?"

"No, we didn't," Narain said, never turning from the view out the window.

"The restaurant is supplying the food for this benefit," Dom said, stepping down into the living room area and taking a seat in a plump grey chair, "I think the owner should make an appearance."

"I have trust in my staff. They can handle things. Besides, you made the arrangements. I think your representation will be more than adequate."

Concern narrowed Dom's eyes as he stared at the figure by the window. His partner, his friend, could be a private person at times with good reason, but Narain didn't shy away from social events, especially when they involved his restaurant. And he had assured Dominic months ago that he'd be willing to attend this event. They couldn't go until after sunset, of course, but he seemed more than willing to supervise the catering of the event. Galas such as this garnered a lot of publicity for the Chicago restaurants that took part in them. While Khan's reputation as a premier restaurant had been solidified years before, extra publicity never hurt. Yet Narain had seemed to be drawing inward for the past month or so; making excuses, avoiding social situations, even staying away from the restaurant during business hours that were convenient for him when normally he would schmooze with the patrons.

Of course, the one year anniversary of Sophie's death must have had something to do with it. Grief had its own expiration date and Narain was not immune to that fact. But Dom had a feeling that it was more complicated. When dealing with the vampire, it usually was.

As if sensing Dom's thoughts on Sophie, Narain said quietly, "I wish I could have attended the funeral."

Dom sighed. "Your situation doesn't exactly accommodate 10am funerals. Sophie understood that. Everyone else just thought you were too broken up."

Narain gave a hollow chuckle. "They were right." Sighing, he pulled himself away from the window and stepped down into the seating area, sitting languidly on the couch. "Really, Dom, I think it'll be fine if I skip this tonight."

The charity benefit went to the back of Dom's mind when he saw his friend's handsome features in the better light. There was a greyish tinge to the rich mocha skin and his olive-brown eyes, which typically sparkled playfully, looked haggard and lost under high arched brows that furrowed in tension. This wasn't just depression.

"Rain, are you okay? When was the last time you fed?"

If anyone had told him ten years before that he'd be asking after the feeding schedule of a vampire, Dom would have laughed in his face. Life certainly had a crazy way about it. What concerned him was that he'd never had to ask the question before, but then before, Narain had Sophie.

Narain seemed reluctant to answer, running a hand through his thick, black hair which sometimes seemed impossible to tame. "I think I had a rat the other night." Dom stared expectantly at him and he shrugged, admitting. "About three weeks ago."

"Well, don't you need that stuff, the human kind, fairly regularly? That's what Sophie told me once."

"Optimally. A couple of months is pushing it, but it can be done, if you supplement with other sources—animals, you know? But I used the last of my reserves about three weeks ago."

"Reserves?" Dom grimaced slightly then caught himself, hoping it hadn't been obvious. "Sophie?"

"Yes. My dear, practical Sophie was always looking out for me. She managed to store up enough for me to live on for nearly a year once she was gone. I'd grown complacent though. Several decades of convenience will do that. I knew I needed to consider the future and find another source, but I just didn't want to think about it."

"Well, can't you go out and, you know, get a quick nip?"

Narain rolled his eyes disgustedly, picking at the fabric of the couch. "It's a bit like pick-pocketing, don't you think? I mean, yes I could do that, and the host need never be the wiser," a wistful look crossed his face, "but I haven't needed to do that for a very long time."

"Well, maybe you can call up a blood bank."

Narain sniggered. "And tell them what? That I need another year's supply?"

"Push comes to shove, we can hire a prostitute. I know they've been asked to do weirder things. Give her a fair wage."

Dom's suggestion brought forth a full-blown laugh from Narain and a bit more colour to his face. Rising, he went over to Dominic and butted his forehead against his. "Dom, you're my friend. I love you like a brother. But the situation is a bit more complicated than that, so let's leave it at that. I'll figure something out. Okay?"

Biting back, "Why am I not surprised," Dom said instead, "Just remember, it's an option. Where are you going?"

Narain stopped near the hallway leading to the bedrooms and turned to face him. "I'm going to get dressed for the benefit. Make sure my staff is performing to its usual high standards."

"Great, and dress nice. I'm sure photos will be taken."

Raising a finger, Narain said, "By the way, have I told you how very robust you're looking? Very pink. Good circulation."

As Narain walked down the hall, Dom said with good humour, "And I told you and Sophie both that wasn't in my job description."

Turning on the TV, Dom settled in to wait for his partner, but he found his thoughts tearing his attention away from the latest Idol show. He missed Sophie, but he'd only known the pair that was she and Narain for about a decade, and was never entirely privy to the special relationship they had. They rarely burdened Dom with the reality of Narain's life, though it did come up from to time in his relationship with the vampire. How could it not, when one of the reasons they had allowed him into their lives was so that he could be Narain's representative during daylight hours? Sophie and Narain had prowled the world together for nearly a century.

He couldn't even begin to pretend that he understood the depths of his friend's loss. Sophie had been Narain's lover, his confidant, his best friend, but she was also his food source. The widower's grief Narain was obviously still going through was only compounded by the reality of his existence and what was necessary for his survival. Dom never understood that part of their relationship but he respected the arrangement that brought such life, love, and health to both of them.

Now, Narain had some difficult choices to make, especially for a man who had fought so hard to have as normal a life as possible. Fishing out his wallet, Dom ticked through the cards in one of the pockets until he came across the card of his cousin

Michael Perelli. As a cop out of the 18th District, if push came to shove, Michael might be able to direct them, discreetly, to the girls who weren't afraid to get kinky.

†

Margot felt her husband's warm hand cup her breast as his left one eased down to rub her inner thigh. Despite the seat belt buckle digging into her right butt cheek, she couldn't help but giggle breathlessly.

"I can't believe you talked me into this," she said, heart racing. "I haven't done this since high school."

Robert's chuckle was throaty as he freed his hands, repositioning himself to pull down the straps of her dress. "Yeah, but it's still a turn-on, isn't it?" He kissed her deeply. "Trying to cop a feel." He kissed her again. "Hoping to go further." He nuzzled her neck. "Hoping the cops won't pound on the window and ruin everything." He laughed. "Of course, I was more flexible in those days."

"Oh, you're flexible enough." She giggled some more and reached forward to undo his shirt; his coat and tie long since discarded onto the floor. It was doubtful the police would bother the car parked deep within the parking garage of Michigan Avenue's Regent Hotel and the tinted windows would keep out prying eyes. But the thrill was still there and it made his body pressed against hers that much more arousing as the scent of his aftershave mingled with the scent of wine on his breath from their anniversary dinner at Khan's. Ten years. Ten magnificent years, when the marriages of most of her friends hadn't made the five-year mark.

Taking hold of his face, she said, "Ten years and I still find you wildly attractive." Then her eyes widened and she giggled more, saying, "Oh, and it would seem as though the feeling is mutual."

They both burst out laughing as he hardened for her, and they worked furiously at removing the rest of their clothing. Upstairs in the hotel the bed in Suite 412 was freshly turned down and waiting for them, but at that moment, the back seat of the Lincoln, and all the memories it entailed, was much more seductive.

As Margot raised her chin Robert's lips investigated the curve of her neck as he moved down toward her exposed breast. Her head fell forward and she sighed, eyes half closed. Stroking the nape of his neck she glanced up, her brows furrowing when she saw a figure outside several yards away staring at the car. Through the darkened windows, his features, hidden by the hooded red sweatshirt he wore, weren't clear but his attention seemed riveted on the car.

"Hey," she whispered, curious but not wanting to break the mood, "are you sure no one can see in here?"

Panting, he replied, "Yeah, why?"

Her head tilted back and she groaned slightly as his hand went back between her legs. "I think someone out there wishes they could."

"Huh?" Robert mumbled turning his head in the direction she'd been looking. There didn't seem to be anyone outside the car, in any direction.

When he pointed this out to her with a chuckle, Margot lowered her head staring out in the direction where she saw the figure standing. "That's odd. There was someone."

"Maybe they went to their car."

"They're fast. The way he was standing there, I thought he'd settle in for the show."

With a sly grin, and the confidence of privacy, Robert said, "Well, let's not disappoint him then."

They writhed together, her hands undoing his trousers as her legs parted for him. What happened next happened with such speed that neither had time to react.

The grating sound of ripping metal echoed in their ears as the rear passenger side door was torn from its hinges and tossed violently into the side of a car parked several spaces down.

The insistent shrill of a car alarm filled the air as a hulking figure forced its way into the back seat, gripping Margot's neck with one hand while pulling Robert away from her with the other. Margot kicked and scratched at the being's arms, but it was as strong as a ram rod, holding her in place against the rear driver's side door. She stopped struggling long enough to see the ashen face which had been buried in Robert's throat turn toward her, its hideous multi-fanged mouth dripping with blood. It stared at her, more cognizant than a beast should be, the black eyes glowing red, then a smile twisted its lipless mouth as it went back to violently feasting off her half-dead husband.

A scream of horror welled up but the beast's hand tightened and the scream died in Margot's constricted throat. Darkness enfolded her as air was denied and her struggles ceased. The last thing her gaze fixed on was the cold dead eyes of her husband as his head was severed from his blood-soaked body.

Chapter 2

Narain Khan did not want to fight with his father, especially now that the decision had been made and there was such little time to prepare. The two were close, father and son, and any argument wounded each deeply. But there came a time when a son had to stand his ground and for Narain, the time was now.

How did a son stand his ground, however, without disrespecting his father?

It was a gorgeous day in the Bengal province. June, 1916. The monsoon season had begun but on this day the sky was still ripe with sunshine that seemed to seep into his very pores. The fields were bright with flowers perfuming the air, and birds seasoned the air with their song. For some reason the walk back from The Viceroy Hotel in town was sweeter today; a memory to be treasured. His mind was filled with music that occasionally escaped through his lips, his smoky voice flavoured the surroundings, and he wondered if perhaps he had been painting problems where none existed. Perhaps his father would understand.

"Narain!" He heard the flute like sound of Ujaali's voice, and his mouth curled into a smile as he saw his little sister bouncing toward him, the braid in her hair swaying from side to side. She ran to greet him every day, relishing the tradition the two had created. Five years before, she had been a surprise for his parents, who thought their child bearing days had finished with his younger brother Zaheer.

"She came with Parvati's grace," his mother said of Ujaali, who instantly became the favourite of the family. Even brother Aziz had a soft spot for her, and his petulance knew no bounds.

As for Narain, she was his flower, her bird-like laughter a constant reminder of the joy of life. He would miss her so very much while he was gone.

She flew into his arms, and he caught her with a deep chuckle, lifting her high as she held her arms up to reach the sun. "Perhaps one day you'll touch it," he said, squinting.

As he lowered her back down to hold her, she said, "No. I can't touch the sun."

"Perhaps one day I will," he said, as she toyed with his shirt collar.

Her soft brown eyes twinkled as she shook her head. "Silly, you'll never touch the sun. You'd be burnt."

He shrugged. "Then, walking in its rays will have to suffice."

They hummed a few strains of a child's song until Ujaali said, "Baba wants to talk to you."

Narain's smile faded slightly. "He does, eh?" His father might want to discuss something entirely different than what he feared they would discuss, he reminded himself.

She nodded. "He and Maa were talking."

"Were they talking, or yelling?" A coy smile spreading across her face giving him his answer.

Well, he had expected this so he could not be surprised. His mother knew of his wishes, had known from the start, and while she didn't want him to go through with it, she promised to support him.

His father was just finding out and was apparently not happy.

"Have you taken leave of your senses!?"

Narain and Ujaali had only just arrived at the front of the bungalow when his father stormed out followed by his mother and brothers, Aziz and Zaheer. His father was short in stature. In fact, at 5' 9" Narain was the tallest in the family. But Mohan Khan matched his son's height in bluster at that moment as he gestured with the packet of papers he had only just seen.

Narain looked at his mother. "I'm sorry, Narain," she said, her eyes wet with tears as she glanced at her husband. "I was reading them and your baba saw me."

Narain blinked. Her story rang false. He looked at his brother. Thirteen-year-old Aziz had been snooping again, and father discovered him. That's what happened, more than likely. Putting down his sister, who ran to his mother, he said, "That's alright, Maa." He straightened. "At least now it's out."

"War!" his father exclaimed running a hand through his mass of grey hair. "You've enlisted in their filthy war!"

"Yes, Baba."

Pacing back and forth, his father said, "They came here, subjugated us in our own country, exploited us and now they wish to take our sons to die in that far away war. I thought I had raised an intelligent son. I thought I had raised a level-headed man. What possessed you to sign this document?"

"Baba, he is a dreamer. You know this." Aziz said, with a spiteful air. The ever placid Zaheer simply looked on.

Narain could never understand the antagonism Aziz showed him. They shared a strong physical resemblance but theirs had always been a contentious relationship, though what fuelled his younger brother's seeming jealousy was a mystery, since their father never blatantly favoured one child over the other. But then parents could never really keep from favouring the first born and the bond Narain and his father shared was powerful. And Aziz with his unfocused energy and penchant for trouble confounded them both.

"Come," his mother said, herding his siblings. "Your bhai and baba have things to discuss."

Aziz sneered at Narain, but left with his mother into the house.

His father said nothing, simply stared at him, the papers still held out accusingly. Narain knew he had to be strong. "Babaji," he started firmly, "You know what my dream is."

"Yes, to cook. And I told you I would support you in this. I will not force any of my children to act contrary to their hearts. What does this have to do with war? In a foreign land? You've never been out of the province, let alone out of India."

"Precisely why I did this." Taking his father's arm, Narain brought him to the porch steps of the bungalow where they both sat down, his father continuing to stare at him for an answer. "I don't want to just be a cook. I want to be a chef. I want to create. To bring joy to people through the excitement of nourishment. I have learned a great deal working for the hotel restaurant..." he began.

"And you are very well respected from what I hear."

Narain smiled slightly at the pride in his father's voice. "But Baba, there is so much more I wish to learn and experience. So many styles, so many tastes...A whole world of tastes!" He shrugged. "I can't learn what I wish to learn here alone. There are amazing culinary schools in Europe, but when would I have the money to even travel to Europe let alone attend those schools?"

"I would find the money."

"Babaji," Narain said in a lightly scolding tone, "on a teacher's salary? Such an amount would be near impossible. You have other children. Besides, I will not let you go into debt for me. This seemed like a good solution. I will serve in the army, perhaps gain some contacts and maybe when my service is finished, they will be kind enough to grant me money for school."

"Those British," his father spat. "They will use you and discard you."

Shrugging again, Narain said, "Well, then I'll get a job in a European restaurant and pay my own way through school. At least I won't have to pay to travel to Europe."

"This cooking has been a passion for you since you were a child." A tear ran down his father's cheek as he softened his tone. "How quickly the years have gone. As if they were stolen all at once."

Sensing his father softening, Narain looked at him. "Babaji, with all due love and respect, I'm not seeking your permission for my mind is firm on this." His voice caught and his father placed his hand behind Narain's neck. "I just don't want you to be angry with me."

With a sigh, his father chuckled and pulled him close so that Narain's head rested on his chest. "I have been frustrated by my children. Sometimes disappointed. Occasionally irritated. But anger is far too strong an emotion to inflict upon those I love. Rather, I suppose, I am proud of a son who wishes to make his own way in the world, yet fearful that the European madness might keep him from succeeding. Or worse, take him from us." He sniffed and laughed, saying, "After all, who will make my birthday dinners? Not even your mother can make kheema bhurjee the way you can. Though don't ever tell her I said that."

Narain laughed with some relief and wiped a tear of his own away. "I will return, Baba. And perhaps I'll have some new recipes for your birthday."

His father said nothing, simply held him and together they sat on the steps in silence for a long time.

†

Narain Khan blinked back to the present, shaking his head slightly. He did not know what had caused thoughts of his father and that conversation to come unbidden to his mind. That strip of memory had taken place so long ago that it seemed almost unreasonable for it to be pestering him now, as he stood near a sweet table in the Winter Garden of Chicago's Harold Washington Library watching glimmering North Shore faces mingle amongst themselves. The Max Baldoni Orchestra played a passionate rendition of "That Old Black Magic" as people glided along on the dance floor or swayed to the music while networking in tightly packed groups.

The fifth annual Reach for the Cure Benefit for Leukaemia Research had proven to be a great success and the moments that Narain had been able to focus on the present and not zone back to the past, he had found it quite enjoyable. He'd dutifully performed the rounds of publicity Dom had arranged, making the statements, taking pictures, shaking the hands of the city's elite, Chicago personalities and politicians, and even the mayor himself. Generally sociable by nature, Narain possessed a playfulness that his sweet Sophie had managed to re-ignite decades ago after those dead years following a painful trip home to India and an aborted attempt to reunite with his family. He so often regretted not going through with contacting them but how would they ever understand what he had become on that battlefield when he didn't understand it himself? He had returned to Europe after visiting his boyhood home, shattered in mind and spirit, existing by chance, not by choice until he had met Sophie and she helped him face life again. Life such as it could be with his strange condition. She would have liked this gala, and any other night he would have taken some elderly Chicago socialite for a spin on the dance floor in Sophie's memory, pretending that the woman he was holding was the woman who had saved his soul so many decades before.

Considering his current state and need though, he felt it best to remain distant. The room was ripe with the warm, exhilarating scent of human life and echoed with the sound of racing pulses that called to his very core, and occasionally he found his vision blurring as he nearly lost himself to the sensation. There were moments, in fact, when the instinctual urge to lower his fangs overwhelmed him and he had to fight to stay focused.

He was perhaps being too stubborn. The fangs tucked behind his canines could be brutal weapons or precision instruments depending on the need. After the transformation, it had taken weeks for the fangs to come in as the structure of entire mouth naturally adjusted to better fit the new dental anatomy. A few back molars fell out, there was no longer a need for chewing, and his upper and lower jaw elongated slightly to provide a better bite radius. It was a change imperceptible to anyone else but Narain knew the change had occurred. The dull, constant ache lasted for weeks; the memory of it lasting even longer. When he used his fangs for the first time, it both startled and disturbed him how natural they fit as they slid down and allowed him to puncture the thick hide of the horse he'd chosen to feed off.

Nearly a century later he could glide through the crowd like a snake, mesmer people with a curious breath technique that had developed with his new life and pierce the delicate flesh so quickly and cleanly that the host need never know that such a violation had occurred. Narain had been walking that path the night he met Sophie, and when they discovered that Sophie could offer the sustenance he needed without fear of her turning, he refused to go that route ever again. He remained grateful he still had the strength to refuse.

Dom was right. Narain had to do something soon. It had been too long since he had the sustenance he required and the time would come when his body would rebel and make the decision for him. It had happened before and he couldn't let it happen again.

"I enjoyed your spicy cashews." A voice scattered his thoughts and he turned to see a woman standing next to him, sipping a drink and glancing up at him coyly, fully realising the innuendo she just spoke. Her long, brunette hair was swept up in a stylishly haphazard fashion and strings of it draped across her bare shoulders. She wore a clingy black cocktail dress and an elegant necklace that hung loosely a few inches below her neck, its small teardrop diamond resting comfortably just above her cleavage. Her features had a rosy fullness to them, with the slightest of under-bites that gave her face an attractively determined look. What really struck him, however, were her eyes. A crystal blue that twinkled with a zest he hadn't seen since...

Sophie. How often had he lost himself in the depths of Sophie's eyes never caring if he ever re-emerged? "But then," she continued, "I imagine few woman would forget your cashews."

Raising an eyebrow, he grinned, replying, "I've also satisfied a few men in my time."

She laughed huskily, the ice cube she was sucking falling back in her glass in a move he found refreshingly uninhibited. "Well, that was fun," she giggled. "I wonder how long we could have kept that up."

"I once kept it up for two days," he said, looking out over the crowd then realising the implication, this time unintentional. His head turned quickly toward her as he clarified awkwardly, "I mean, a conversation is what I kept up."

She laughed at his fumbling and he smiled wide. Focusing her full attention on him, she switched her glass to her left hand holding out her right. "My name is Cassandra. Cassie if you like."

Taking her hand, he felt a curious warmth spread through him. He usually felt something when he shook the hands of others, but he had trained himself to be indifferent to the sensation since it often seemed so very predatory. This time, he allowed the alluring warmth to spread up his arm and fill his body, manifesting itself in a slight glaze to his eyes. It had nothing to do with his current hunger. It was much more. She had a strong, steady pulse that complemented her playful essence. While he yearned to be lost in that essence, he knew better and released her hand, returning to the present.

"My name is Narain," he said.

"Yes, I know who you are. You're responsible for this delicious feast."

"Ah yes," he grinned. "The spicy cashews. I'm glad you enjoyed the food."

"It was nice of you to donate your services."

"Donate?" he shot out. "Nobody told me I was donating..." When she realised it was a put on, she burst out with another round of giggles that entranced him even further. He was enjoying the flirtation. Sophie had taught him how to feel comfortable with flirting again, but since then he had only been interested in flirting with her. With Sophie gone, the desire seemed to leave him. He was glad to find out that it had been a temporary loss.

"Tell me, Narain, do chefs dance? And if so, would you care to?"

Smiling, he nodded. "They do and I would."

Thoughts of other heart beats disappeared as he concentrated only on hers, making it much easier for him to follow her onto the dance floor. He put his hand around her waist and. as they began moving to the Bacharach ballad the band was playing, she leaned a little closer to his left ear, saying, "I have to admit, I love dancing, but I'm not a very good dancer. I can't get rid of the instinct to lead."

He chuckled, noting how she pulled. Shrugging, he said, "Very well, then you lead," and the dancing became smoother.

Impressed, she said, "Not many guys would give that up."

"I'm not like most guys," he said, looking down into her jewelled eyes. "This is a new century, and I've had many years to lead in the dancing."

"Ooh," she said, "a whole what, 28, 30?"

He smiled. "Yes, something like that." Changing the subject, he said, "I'm curious though. Why am I, rather than your date, fortunate enough to be dancing with you?"

For the first time a small look of exasperation crossed her face. "My date, huh?" She glanced around the room then turned the dance in the direction of her gaze. "Do you see that group of people talking by the buffet table?" Narain nodded. "Do you see the buzz-cut blonde gesturing continuously with his drink?"

"That's Dr. Richard Channing. I met him earlier. He's the director of NewGen labs."

"Co-director. He's my partner."

Narain's brows furrowed slightly then he looked at her, realisation on his face. "Cassie...Dr. Cassandra Lambert." He felt a bit sheepish but the fact was that Dominic did most of the arranging and Narain had only met Dr. Channing during the course of the evening. "You're co-planner of this event?"

"Yes, with Richard, who assured me that if I attended he wouldn't leave me alone for long. Now look at him over there, chattering away."

Curious, Narain asked, "Don't you know those people? Shouldn't you be chattering away as well?"

"They're all finances which is, you know, important, but I'm much better with the technical part of the research. Get me going about blood workup and DNA, and I'll talk your ear off. Otherwise, I guess I'm not very social."

He turned his gaze back to her. "You seem to be doing fine now. What is it about me that drew you into my orbit?"

She smiled. "I don't know. I guess you have a friendly face. I feel...comfortable with you. I feel like I know you."

"And let's not forget my spicy cashews."

They continued dancing, jousting with words and relishing each other's company. Regretfully, the evening came to a close when Dr. Channing collected Cassie for some photo ops. He seemed a bit overly earnest when it came to his partner. There was a tight smile to his voice when he chastised her for ignoring her other guests, but Narain couldn't tell if it was from jealousy or sincere concern that the guests felt snubbed. There was a hint of both to his mannerisms.

Cassie rolled her eyes then turned to Narain taking his hand. "Thank you for a great evening." With uncertainty, she pulled him to her and lightly kissed him on the cheek. "Next time, perhaps you can lead."

Then Dr. Channing practically yanked her away, and the two disappeared in the dancing crowd as the band started the first few bars of "That's Amore." Narain stood there enjoying the tingling sensation her lips left on his cheek as couples danced around him. When he was in India, so many decades ago, he had been a romantic. His passion for life heightened his five senses bringing passion into his cooking. That war; that grey, heartless war, began to dull that passion long before the attack on the battlefield left him a different, possibly dangerous man, who feared the consequences brought on by any lack of control. Sophie helped him redefine his condition and saved him from becoming the old creature of habit he could have become. When she began to deteriorate, he began to fear that death would begin to creep back into his own existence. When she died, the thought that anyone could again bring that tingle to his skin seemed impossible.

Dominic found him still on the dance floor a few moments later, contemplating the impossible that became possible. He tapped Narain on the shoulder and said, "Hey, Maggie Stewart from City Life wants to do a quick interview. Maybe some photos. Shouldn't take long."

Blinking, he turned to his friend and smiled. "Dominic, it would seem you were right."

"I usually am," Dom quipped then asked, "About what?"

"About coming here tonight."

"Oh yeah? You have a good time?"

Narain looked over where Cassie was corralled by a group of people and no doubt trying desperately to match her wavelength to theirs. He focused in and grinned when he caught her quick glance in his direction. Then she ran a hand through her hair and smiled, returning her attention to the group. "Yes," he finally answered. "It was nice to feel human again, if only for one night."

Chapter 3

"I'm telling you, Rain, you have to call that woman!"

After a few interviews and some last minute paperwork, Dominic and Narain left the Harold Washington Library, walking down State Street to a parking garage a few blocks away. At two a.m., the cool mid-April lake-breeze against his face left Narain refreshed in a way it hadn't done in over a year. That was when Sophie's tests had come back and the world began to spin away from him again. Grief left him dead inside when she'd gone and it was only now that he felt as if he were slowly resurrecting.

When he told Dom of his encounter with the lovely scientist, his friend seemed even more excited than he was and Narain's insistence that it was a case of "two ships passing in the night" left Dom frustrated.

"Obviously you were attracted to her," he argued. Narain nodded, knowing with some humour that silence would exasperate his friend more. "And she was attracted to you." Narain only shrugged silently, grinning as Dom's gestures became more animated. "What? What does ," Dom shrugged, "mean? She had to be attracted to you. She came on to you."

"She didn't come on to me," Narain clarified. "She asked me to dance."

"My point. My point exactly."

"Coming on to me makes it sound crass. Like she asked me to step into the coat closet for a quickie."

Dom stopped and stared at him. "You know for someone who's lived through two world wars and a handful of police actions, you sure are prudish about some things."

"It's not prudishness," Narain defended, continuing his walk. "It's just...well, perhaps one reason I found it so enjoyable was there was no pressure. We met, we danced, we parted."

"And you'll call her tomorrow night."

"No, I'll treasure the memory."

"Narain."

This time it was Narain's turn to stop. Hands on hips, he said, "You know Dom it means a great deal that our friendship has grown to the point where you can offer me advice on romance as if calling a woman for a date would be the easiest thing in the world for me. Yes I've lived through two world wars and a handful of police actions and aside from a date here and there when I was normal I have only been in love with one woman through all that time. And her discovering my unique condition was an unexpected thing. I didn't have to sit down and reveal it to her one night over a dinner, which by the way, I wouldn't be able to eat."

Dom conceded the point with a nod but before he could retort, Narain raised his index finger, swivelling his head to listen for something. "What is it?" Dom asked.

"I heard a scream," Narain told him, swivelling his head, trying to gauge the distance. He pointed down State saying, "Someone's being attacked," then sprinted off in a shot, disappearing into the night leaving Dom to sigh and follow after.

In a grease-stained alley illuminated by yellow street lights, a man was lying on top of an unconscious woman, hiking up her skirt to rip off her panties. He had followed her as she made her way from the EL station, noting the sway of her ample hips as she walked along the vacant street. He was hungry, and she was just the thing to satisfy that need, so when the time was right, he caught her in his grasp and forced her down the deserted alley throwing her to the ground, anxious to force his way inside her. He hoped she would struggle. He loved it when they struggled. It made it so much more worth the effort when they struggled. And she did, until her head connected with the asphalt. Then she just lay there, quiet and still, pliant to his manoeuvres as he spread her legs.

Silent and swift, something yanked him off her with such force that he spiralled into the side of a nearby wheelie bin, his shoulder stinging from the force of the impact.

Crouching, Narain felt the woman's neck, grateful not only for her steady pulse, but also that her unconscious state would avoid explanation. Gently fixing her skirt, he rose smoothly, stalking over to the dazed, would-be rapist demanding, "What do you think you are doing?"

"Screw this shit!" the attacker spat, and turned to run down the alley only to find Narain blocking his way. Blinking, he scowled and whirled the other way but was blocked again by Narain. "What the hell…"

"Let's wait for the police," Narain suggested calmly.

Furious and desperate, the man growled, "Screw you!" and produced a switch blade, slashing at Narain and slicing a deep gash across his abdomen, followed by a gash across his cheek.

His skin had grown tougher over the years, but a sharp enough instrument could still open it. Investigating the rip the knife had produced, Narain opened his shirt and wiped at the blood on his stomach revealing that, despite the crimson staining his shirt, the deep gash was already beginning to seal up. The man's eyes widened as he noticed that the cut on Narain's cheek was already puckering into what looked to be a scar at least a week old.

Keeping his head lowered, Narain raised only his gaze, right eyebrow arched as he calmly said, "Ouch."

"What the hell are you?" the man stammered, stepping back in shock.

Narain's voice turned cold and the man was sure his eyes glowed red as he said with chilly precision, "I'm someone who can follow you without a sound." Never taking his eyes off him, Narain stepped toward the man who seemed to be struggling against a strange inability to move. The sweet scent of cinnamon perfumed the air as Narain released his mesmer scent, noting the man succumbing to it. "I'm someone who doesn't like to see a woman treated like garbage. I'm someone who could take your life in an instant."

And why not? The closer Narain got to him, the faster the man's heart beat, and the sound of that blood flow was the sound of a rushing river to a man dying of thirst. The fierce vampire teeth concealed behind his canines slid down as Narain felt his own pulse race. No one would miss this disgusting creature; this thing that preyed on innocents. Within moments, Narain could drain the beast and toss him into the bin where he belonged.

His own trance was broken by footsteps nearing the alley and a deep sense of shame overcame him as he realised how close he had come to losing it. Retracting his fangs, staring deep into the man's frightened eyes, the scent of cinnamon ripened again as Narain said, "You'll remember nothing but your crime." Considering this he added, "And that someone is always watching you."

And at last he released the man who crumpled in an unconscious heap at his feet.

Dominic jogged onto the scene, breathing heavily, and studied the picture. Having experienced this situation before, he shrugged, saying, "Well, it looks like my work is done."

Chuckling, Narain said, "Yes, before it began," then knelt down and fingered the attacker's neck searching for a pulse. He felt it, strong and vibrant and for a moment his fingers lingered on the spot as he imagined the blood flowing through the veins. At last, he cleared his throat and pulled his arm away. "He shouldn't be out too long."

"Too bad," Dom commented sourly then glanced at the girl. "At least you got him before he could do anything. But Christ!" Looking around uncomfortably, he then noted how his friend remained on one knee near the body. Any misgivings he had with what his friend was had been dealt with long ago. The whole situation was weird, even when Narain had Sophie to feed off of. Especially when he had Sophie. But life was made up of weird and as long as it was not the malevolent kind, Dom tried not to obsess over it. "Rain," he said, quietly, walking over to him, "No one's around. The guy's a dirt bag. Why not have a quick feed?"

Narain's head snapped up and he focused his gaze on his friend. "What?"

"I'm not saying drain him," Dom clarified, wondering if he'd transgressed some vampire etiquette. "I'm saying jab his arm, take what you need and no one needs to be the wiser."

Lingering over the body as he was, Narain still considered it. He could smell the tang of the man's sweat and hear the tauntingly steady rhythm of his heartbeat. He felt the heat of the need rising up in him but he fought it back down. Standing, he moved away from the attacker and stood near Dom, whose own heartbeat was strong and enticing too, but was safe since it resided in the chest of a friend. "You're always thinking of me, aren't you?" he quipped as best he could with a suddenly dry mouth.

Dom grew insistent. "Rain, look, you need the human stuff occasionally and you haven't had any for a while. Now every so often you play this superhero shit and here's your chance for a reward."

Anxiety showed on the vampire's face. "I can't." He laughed hollowly. "I...uhm...I don't do it for the reward."

"The guy's scum," Dom said, emphatically. "Why not?"

"I have my reasons," Narain replied, his tone sharper as he turned away from the scene.

"But Rain, the guy's a creep. You saw what he was going to do to that woman. Who knows how many he's done that to before?"

"That's why." Narain snapped, staring at the attacker. "It's because of what he is." *What he could become*, he thought but kept to himself. "That's what I want no part of."

Dom blinked, confused, but knew enough to realise that there was more to that response than they had time for right then. "Alright, alright."

Sighing, Narain fought down his anxiety, at last saying, "You'll have to take the credit for this one, Dom."

Dominic grimaced. "Aw, why do you do this? This is the third time in a year."

"Should I just ignore these crimes if I know they're occurring?"

"No, but jeez..."

"Consider yourself that much closer to being named citizen of the year."

Dominic pointed toward the attacker. "But he's going to tell them that it wasn't me."

"Whatever he tells them will sound like it's coming from the mind of a demented pervert," Narain said calmly. "Remember, people like me exist only in films and folk legends."

Knowing it was pointless to argue Dominic pulled out his cell phone and began to dial 911. "One day, it's not going to be so easy to explain," he cautioned waiting for the response on the other end. Once the emergency personnel answered, he began, "My name is Dominic Amato and I want to report an attempted rape. We'll need paramedics, because both the victim and the attacker have been injured."

Smiling, Narain put his hands in his pockets and walked down the alley leaving his friend to clean up. He would be forever grateful for Dominic's willingness to clean up.

Years ago, a young man from Melrose Park met a vampire. Not exactly something someone tells relatives or even trusted friends. Their partnership was beneficial to both. Dominic Amato was never going to set the world ablaze with his culinary skills so he wisely switched his studies from cooking to the business of cooking. He needed someone to take a chance on him.

Narain Khan needed a liaison with the daylight hours. He had the culinary skill and through the decades, thanks in large part to Sophie had acquired more than enough money to bankroll a restaurant. How did a prisoner of the dark do business during the day though? It had been Sophie who matched them up, meeting Dominic through a friend of a friend. After their travelling had slowed, she had convinced Narain to live his dream and open a restaurant and he did with the stipulation that she be his manager. As age crept up on her though she no longer had the strength for the demanding job of an increasingly successful restaurant. Sophie had sharp instincts when it came to people and Dominic had an unflappable nature that she knew would come in handy with some of the things he was bound to see and would need to do.

Narain's initial response to her retirement was predictable. He would sell the restaurant. Money was of no concern anyway and the years he'd been able to wear a chef's hat had satisfied him. She knew it had not. This was his passion – a dream he had fought for against surprising odds. He could not be content going from creating the sumptuous delights he was famous for to simply making her final meals more palatable.

If she had been given the choice to become what he was, she would have turned it down knowing it was her humanness he needed most. But it was that humanness that would eventually tear them apart as he continued on and she withered away.

Dominic could not replace all that she was to him but he could fill in certain aspects. Provided Narain would just agree.

"Narain," Sophie started as they spoke while closing the restaurant one night, "you have trusted me for over seventy years. Why won't you trust me on this?"

She suspected she knew the answer but also suspected he needed to say it out loud.

"I trust you as always," he insisted never meeting her eyes. "But I've considered it and have decided that it's time for a new path. You've said it yourself—the world and all it has to offer is mine. Perhaps it's time to explore again. We used to enjoy exploring. Remember Asia? Africa?"

"At least meet the boy and see what you think."

"I know what I think and I have thought enough on it." His motions were more for busy work than anything else.

At last, she reached out and took hold of his hand. Two sets of eyes stared down at the hands, his unable to note the differences, hers unable to see anything else. Her hands were those of a woman who had weathered nearly a century and his were as smooth as the hands of that young man who became embroiled in the First World War.

She turned his hand over and chuckled, "Whatever it is about you, you've kept me surprisingly youthful and relatively healthy for my age. Still it seems like every time I look in the mirror I see a new wrinkle."

He raised the hand to her jaw and turned her head up to look into her eyes. "I see no wrinkles. Only my beautiful Sophie."

Her eyes became misty as she smiled kissing his palm. "And that's one reason I love you."

His voice became choked with emotion and he sounded rather like a child when he admitted, "I don't want to lose you. You have been my anchor."

"I like the sound of guiding star better."

He laughed and sniffed, placing his forehead against hers.

"Narain, my love, you are going to lose me. Whether it is next year, five years, heaven willing twenty more healthy years—which would really make people talk. It doesn't matter. I'm going, you are staying. I just want to make sure that you won't be alone. I want you to have someone to look after your interests."

"And you think this man can be trusted with what ultimately he must be told?"

She nodded. *"I believe so. I've spoken with him a number of times. He seems charming, honest, good-humoured, down to earth and loyal."*

"So very much like me then," he said, grinning. She giggled. At last, with a sigh, he relented. *"I'll meet with him. I'll promise nothing, but I will meet him."*

Dominic Amato proved to be everything Sophie said he was and more. His stocky frame belied an intensity and energy that would be extremely useful in a partnership with the vampire. He had an excellent mind for business and was a born promoter, his natural charm helped by a cherubic face and puppy dog eyes which no doubt played a part in Sophie's initial opinion of him. And his outward response to proof of Narain's condition was typically implacable, though Narain could sense the increased speed of Dominic's heart registering the shock and concern his face didn't convey. Dominic was a realist though, and as long as no one got hurt he didn't care what Narain was or what he ate for dinner. He even respected the relationship between Narain

and Sophie by never questioning it. In the arrangement, Sophie had the best of both worlds: With Narain she still felt like the alluring young woman who had captured his heart decades before, and with Dominic she could practice her mothering skills, which she did frequently.

No doubt there were times when Dominic, the devoted son of devout Italian Catholic parents, considered his current path with some trepidation. If such moments arose, they never lasted long and after a decade of partnership Narain was happy to call him his most trusted friend.

†

Reg Jameson stared out the cabin window, his thoughts lost in the blackness of the cloudless night sky, as his private plane flew across the vast expanse of the Atlantic Ocean on its way to America. His latest business trip to Germany had illustrated how important the newest research with Blythe was. Had it not been for Piri, it might have been extremely difficult. How did one tell a consortium of Germans, Russians, and Belgians who preferred to meet face to face that he couldn't attend a vital meeting because the 9AM sunlight could very well be the death of him? These people sought the personal touch and Piri, his great niece, was able to conduct the meeting so skilfully that they forgot they weren't meeting with the head of Jameson Enterprises but rather a representative. Reg touched base with all the partners via conference call, assuring them that aligning themselves with Jameson Enterprises would prove a fruitful move for all concerned.

His condition at one time proved occasionally problematic in the business world and Piri McGuire was the solution. Reg's sister Mercedes had married Robert McGuire, a clever Irishman only too happy to go along with the Jameson family's efforts to keep Reg's condition a secret. Money was, after all, money and as queer as Reg's condition was, as long as it kept the family comfortably solvent, which it did, and then some, little else mattered. Robert and Mercedes had three children, one of which, Stephen, married a woman named Keiko, a refugee from the misguided actions of Japan during World War II. Stephen and Keiko McGuire produced John, Michael, Giles and Piri. Within the family, Reg was the head of the estate. His father had died so very long ago, accepting his son's condition, and understanding the benefits that could be obtained because of it. Arrangements were made to make sure that Reg remained in charge throughout the decades and future generations accepted this. Some out of loyalty to the family; some out of fear of what Reg could do to them if they didn't. But the daylight was a curse to him. Through the years he'd been forced to rely on the talents of the other Jamesons; Piri was the latest logical choice for a personal assistant. She had an agile mind, capable of accepting the strangeness of her family secret and had quite a head for the business world herself. Piri was very possibly the favourite relation who Reg had to deal with over the years, mainly because of her cleverness regarding the weirdness of what Jameson was. She was unflappable and that counted for so much in his reality.

So when, as they flew back to America, she came to him with the troubled look on the lovely Asian features inherited from her mother, he knew enough to take it seriously. She sat in the chair across from him and he studied her for only a moment before saying, "Penny for your thoughts."

Sighing, she leaned forward, her glossy brown blunt cut slipping forward as she said, "You're not going to like to this. I think we may have some problems."

"And what, my dear, would force that conclusion upon you?" His tone was blasé but he closed the book he was reading and turned his full attention to her. Piri did not spook easily. That's why she was so valuable. If she even foresaw that there was a problem, there was a problem.

"I have a web service," she began, "internet surfers who will send me items that I indicate might be of interest."

"A digital news clipping service." Reg smiled. "I love the Internet."

Continuing, she said, "I asked to be alerted to any news of strange attacks. Any which were particularly violent, particularly bloody." He grinned at her. "I just thought it might be a good idea. After all, it was a news story that helped you discover Blythe a few years ago."

Always thinking, she was. He smiled. "I bet you get a fair share of crank stories."

"More than," she nodded. "But I just came across some that I think were legitimate." She unfolded a map on the table between them and indicated where she had highlighted certain towns in the western United States. "They've happened with too much frequency and there seems to be a pattern."

Reg inspected the map with deep blue eyes. "These are places where the attacks have taken place?"

She nodded, tracing a pen along a line. "See, I've numbered them. The most recent so far was recorded in south-eastern Iowa. Before that you have two in Nebraska, three in Denver. Trace it all back and it begins...."

Reg scowled, looking up at her. "Just outside of Los Angeles."

"Yes. Now it could be a coincidence but I find it a little troubling. I've had this service for a whole year now and I've never seen anything like this. We have one of the most dangerous creatures housed in the Los Angeles labs and suddenly all these attacks, with similar and mysterious MOs start occurring in the past few weeks." Her green eyes met his. "I think there's been a breach."

"Escape? Surely Channing would have notified me."

"I've tried contacting him. His service says he's gone back to Chicago to attend some benefit."

"Benefit!" Reg snarled, springing to his feet. "What about his staff? Is anyone trying to fix this?"

"Sir, the fact is that I'm surmising here. I haven't been able to get a hold of the lab yet. Too much interference. Hopefully I'm wrong and everything is fine."

"Piri," Reg stared at her, hands on hips, "you are never wrong. At least in situations like this, that's why you're my favourite in the bloodline."

"I just felt you should be prepared."

"Another reason you're my favourite." He cupped her chin and she looked at him basking in his approval. Then he turned deadly serious. "If there has been an escape, what would send Channing to Chicago at a time like this?"

"It might have occurred after he left. He does have the other lab to tend to."

"So, he should go back to L.A. straight away."

"Perhaps he doesn't know. Maybe his staff isn't telling him."

Mouth tense, Reg ran a hand through his hair. "Heads will roll on this, Piri. Quite possibly literally."

She indicated the map again. "There's something else. If all the attacks were committed by the same being, they indicate a definite course."

Reg studied the map. "A beeline...straight to Illinois. Chicago. Where Channing theoretically is."

"Exactly."

Reg threw up his hands and paced, gesturing angrily. "This is the last thing we need. My kind I mean, not only Jameson business concerns. This sort of thing is bound to draw attention to us. That sort of creature isn't concerned with secrets or subtlety of any kind. I need to remain a myth to function to full capacity. Take that legend away and..." he sighed, "Well, I don't even want to think about it. If there is a breach, we need to seal it."

"Precisely why I brought this to your attention. Hopefully, it won't be necessary. But if it is..."

"Keep trying the lab. Once we're in American air space it should be easier. In the meantime, we need to divert our flight plan."

"O'Hare International. Already done."

"Piri, if you ever produce a child as capable as you, he or she has a job for life. Just as you do."

She smiled shyly. There was a slight flirtatious nature to the relationship that both enjoyed. After all, it was at times difficult to look upon the youthful, ruggedly handsome face of Reginald Jameson and think that he was her great uncle. As for Jameson, he found both her face and her brains wickedly alluring.

Continuing his pacing, he said, "Keep trying Channing as well. Cell, e-mail, Twitter the bastard, whatever. Let him know I'm looking for him and I'm not happy." Considering this, he said, "And just out of curiosity, find out everything you can on this NewGen Labs. I didn't mind him serving two masters as long as my affairs weren't slighted. Something brought him back to Chicago and I want to know why he might have hightailed it back there at the worst possible time."

Piri was about to begin carrying out his orders when he stopped her. "Oh, and find out as soon as you can, exactly which one escaped from Los Angeles. That information will be vital in figuring out a course of action."

Chapter 4

"There are still no leads in the gruesome double murder of attorney Robert Anders and his wife Margot. Area 4 police estimate that the crime happened sometime early Saturday morning in the parking garage of The Regent Hotel on Michigan Avenue."

Narain's attention was now fully on the television news report as he blinked in recognition from behind his office desk at the faces of the deceased that were being flashed on the screen. Anders, of course. They came in frequently. He'd created a special anniversary soufflé to be baked that night. That was the night of the benefit. "Such a shame," he commented to himself. They were nice people. He returned his attention back to the files littering the desk while the report showed a reporter asking questions at a police press conference.

"Is this in any way connected with the murders in Wicker Park?" the reporter asked.

The police commander, a hefty man with a salt and pepper moustache and hair to match, shrugged saying evasively, "We won't know until we investigate a bit further. This certainly appears to be similar but right now we'd prefer not to speculate." Another question was offered and Narain, half listening, commented, "He won't tell you, idiot. He doesn't know yet himself."

"Police have released a photo," the news anchor continued, "of the parking lot attendant who has been missing since the morning of the crime. He's not yet a suspect but police are hoping he can provide some clues. Funeral services for the couple are pending the investigation."

While Narain continued looking through vendor receipts, Dominic flew in, bringing with him a slight air of excitement. "Janet told me you left in the middle of paella. That's not like you."

Focused on his mission, Narain mumbled, "I wanted to check something." It was half a lie. In the kitchen, among the exertions of the staff, he had found himself feeling a loosening of control as the anxiety over his hunger grew and he thought it best to be on his own for a bit. This gave him an excuse to do some investigating on a matter he'd been curious about.

Waving his hand, Dominic said, "Well, none of that matters now," then went over to a bank of four security monitors on the other side of the room to scan through the feed from the various cameras camouflaged in the restaurant. "You have to see something."

"Hmm," came the only reply.

"No, Narain, come here."

"In a moment."

"You'll be pleasantly surprised."

As if Dominic hadn't said a word, Narain, finding what he was looking for, slapped the invoice with the back of his hand. "I knew it! Dom, you bought the mushrooms from Jueng Luck Oh."

"Yeah, so?" Dom said, intent on his channel surfing. "We buy a lot from Jueng Luck Oh."

"I told you to buy mushrooms from Mirake."

"They're cheaper at Jueng."

"They don't taste as good. I don't want my paellas spoiled by bland mushrooms."

"What do you mean? They taste the same."

"Well maybe to your cretinous palette, mister 'I put ketchup on a hot dog.'"

"Hey my family always put ketchup on hot dogs. I know it's not popular but that's how I like it. Besides, I went to cooking school too, you know."

"And what is your degree in?"

"Business management," Dom said sheepishly.

"I rest my case."

"Will you forget that and get over here?"

Staring at the receipt, Narain exclaimed, "Five count, Dom?"

"Jueng had a deal." At last he got up and pulled Narain away from the files and over to the security monitor. "Will you forget that please and see what I have to show you."

"I hope it's not people keeling over from the mushroom and spinach casserole," Narain said, reluctantly sitting in the chair and looking at the monitors. "Ah, my restaurant. I am impressed."

"Shut up," Dom said, adjusting the camera angle on one. It landed on a woman sitting at the bar swirling her glass, occasionally looking around while the guy next to her hit on her.

Gratified by Narain's shocked look, Dom commented, "Looks like your Princess Charming has tracked you down."

"That can't be her," Narain said, looking closely.

"Well you'd know better than me. You were the one gazing lovingly into her eyes on the dance floor last week. Besides, she asked to see you, making her agenda quite clear."

Finding it hard to take his eyes off the image, Narain none the less said, "Tell her I'm not here tonight."

"What? Why?"

At last the vampire turned away and rose from the chair, pacing. "I can't allow this to happen."

"Rain, calm down. Maybe she's just here to thank us for helping at the benefit. Go down, have a drink…well, be there as she has a drink, and if something comes from it, so be it."

"I told you, it isn't that simple."

Dom was shocked to see the whites of his friend's eyes flash red as the blood vessels contracted, a symptom of his condition that flared when he was upset or angry. "And I told you to calm down," he said sharply. Narain stopped pacing, sitting on the couch against the wall, arms folded. "You really like this woman, don't you?" Narain's silent glare confirmed this. "Rain, you know this brooding vampire crap isn't you. You have a long, long life ahead of you and when you shut chances like this out it'll only make it a harder, long life. I get that it was easier with Sophie. I get that there are certain particulars about you that make any close relationship difficult. But if you're going to let that stop you from enjoying the sort of interaction a guy with your personality craves, well, then you might as well be dead. I mean really dead."

Staring at the floor, Narain remained still for some moments after Dominic stopped. Then he looked up at him and raised his index finger. "One drink. I'll be there for one drink. Tell her I enjoyed the benefit. Then excuse myself back to the kitchen."

Conceding with a nod, Dom walked Narain to the door. "Jeez, this is like pulling teeth with you. And those are sharp teeth to pull."

"You are an ass," Narain told him, and then waved the receipt in his face. "And we buy mushrooms from Mirake from now on, Renfield."

As he locked the door behind them, Dom said under his breath, "Yeah, well, we'll see."

When they approached the bar, it was obvious that while Cassie was still nodding her head politely, the man flirting boisterously with her was getting on her last nerve. Ted. He was a regular. Nice enough guy until he got a few drinks in him. Then he'd spend the rest of the evening trying to prove, usually unsuccessfully, that he was God's gift to women.

"Here he is," Dom called grabbing Cassie's attention easily. He manoeuvred Narain onto her left side saying, "He likes to hide in the rafters sometimes. We just had to beat him out."

Narain shot him a look that clearly stated, "You're an ass", to which Dom shot him a grin that sang, "I know." He then proceeded to prise Ted away from the bar. "Don't you have a wife waiting for you, Ted?"

After they left, Cassie breathed a sigh of relief. "Well, that was an endurance test," she commented, smiling.

She had a lovely smile. It gleamed as brightly as it did at the fund-raiser and her eyes sparkled in the ambient glow of the restaurant. A sudden urge to run gripped Narain. This dance he sensed they were about to begin was easier at the benefit because he knew, or thought, he would never see her again. It had been about the moment. But her presence here, in his restaurant, felt nourishing and he knew he would want more. That's how it began and then a person just spiralled down into it, lost to all sense or thoughts of consequences.

"Is everything okay?" she asked, made curious by his silence.

Blinking, he said, "Oh, yes, certainly. I apologise. This is a pleasant surprise. What brings you here?"

"You." His heart skipped and she clarified, "I mean, I was in the neighbourhood and thought I'd drop by to thank you again for the help you gave us with the fund-raiser."

"Well, we like to do things for the community whenever possible."

"Well, it's a nice way to be."

"Well, we try to be nice."

An awkward silence blanketed them, magnifying the clinking sound of the restaurant patrons enjoying their meals and leaving Narain feeling somewhat better that she apparently felt as nervous as he did. He had sensed her respiration quicken as he approached and she was still slightly warm from the flush of it. Still, he suddenly began to worry that she might mistake his nervousness for indifference, which was the last thing he wanted to project.

"I like your restaurant," she said at last.

He leaned closer, "What?" having heard her, yet not heard her.

"She said she likes the restaurant," Charlie the bartender said with a teasing smile having witnessed this very awkward interaction as he served a few drinks nearby.

"Yes, well, there may be a change in bar staff," Narain said, and Charlie simply grinned, walking away confident in his job security.

He looked at Cassie's smiling face and suddenly the tenseness melted away as he realised just how difficult he was making the encounter. One more night. Enjoy the night and let it be. Shaking his head, he sighed, "My deepest apologies. I don't know where my mind is at."

"You do seem a bit preoccupied. Kind of like you're expecting the roof to cave in or something."

"I was." He shook his head again, correcting, "I mean I was preoccupied." Extending his arm, he asked, "Would you care for a tour?"

"Very much so," she said, taking his arm.

They walked past contented patrons many of whom smiled and waved their compliments to Narain. He was glad the place was so busy. It usually was, but tonight it was especially vibrant and he felt a surge of pride as he walked her through the dining area.

While the menu was eclectic, and he wanted the ambience to reflect that, he also decided to put a distinctive flavour of India in the décor. The colours were earthy; the colours of his Bengal, as vibrant and rich as the cuisine itself. Statues, furniture and photographs Narain had collected over a century seasoned the restaurant and while he couldn't be explicit about all of them during the tour, he enjoyed silently reliving the memories, occasionally alluding to items passed down by "grandfathers" or "uncles."

They made their way into the very busy kitchen where chefs created dishes with flair while waiters quickly darted in and out to pick up the orders and busboys and dishwashers kept clean plates and glasses flowing. Keeping mindful of stove fires and sharp knives, the staff continued their preparation while acknowledging Narain's presence. He smiled and returned their greetings, keeping Cassie just outside of the busy knot of cooking going on between the stainless steel grills and ranges.

"This is the magic behind Khan's," he said proudly gesturing to the staff. "This is the true reason for my success."

"Can we get that in writing?" a short chef said as she plated a delectable piece of grilled salmon.

"Not in a million years," he replied. "And I'll deny it all tomorrow."

"I've had nights like that," a beefy chef said as he swept past them to get something from the walk-in refrigerator.

"You see," Narain feigned helplessness, "I get no respect. This is Dr. Cassie Lambert. She's the one who held the benefit we catered the other night."

"Oh yeah?" a chef said while sautéing garlic in a pan. "The one where you two spent most of the night on the dance floor?"

Cassie blushed slightly before saying, "I just wanted to tell you all what a great job you did. It was really delicious and helped make the evening very successful."

"Okay, enough," Narain said with a smile. "They'll get swelled heads and they're hard enough to handle." Then he looked at her. "Tell me, are you hungry?"

She shrugged. "I don't think I was till I came back here and smelled all these delicious smells."

"I'll tell you what. I'll make you a special dish. How's that?"

He could see in her eyes that she liked the idea very much but she said, "Well, only if you'll have dinner with me."

"Well, quite honestly, I already had something earlier," he said smoothly. He'd had many years to practice declining offers of dinner. A strange feeling came over him and he looked over at the members of his staff who were all staring at him quietly as best they could while monitoring their dishes. At his look, they snapped back to work. "But, I could always sit with you while you eat."

"Sounds fair," she agreed. "But can I watch you cook it?"

He practically beamed. "Of course." Then he considered it, saying, "But not here. I don't want to get in their way." As he walked her toward the back of the kitchen, he shot back, "They're already handicapped enough without having to cook in the shadow of my brilliance."

A shared groan followed the statement.

He directed her into a small darkened room which illumination revealed was a kitchenette. When he had it constructed, Narain had told everyone that he simply needed a private place to create recipes and they had learned long ago not to question some of the more curious things their boss did. In fact, the kitchenette held a distinctive purpose. It hid the fact that every time he tasted a new recipe during the course of cooking, he had to spit the taste into the sink. With Sophie's encouragement, he had discovered that his taste buds were sharper than before, but his body could assimilate only minute particles of certain foods, so any that slipped down his throat brought only a little bit of discomfort. But should any more find its way into his stomach, the reaction would be violent and painful. As well as disgusting if he had fresh blood in his stomach.

So the only way to sample the dish in mid-creation was to spit the remnant out after his tongue assessed what was needed.

The kitchenette with the door closed provided him privacy when the realities of his condition became inconvenient at work. While they found it odd at first, the staff said little about this. He was, after all, the boss, and if his occasional shyness, as he put it, was so great while cooking that he often needed a place to create in private, so be it. It was his culinary genius that kept the patrons coming in to dine and his name on the pay cheques.

"I find that hard to believe. You being shy," Cassie said, sitting on a stool by a small preparation table a few feet away from the stove. He had just returned with the ingredients for his dinner and gave a truncated explanation for the kitchenette while pouring her a glass of red wine.

"Oh, there's a lot about me that's hard to believe," Narain replied, engrossed in his preparation. "That doesn't make it untrue."

"May I ask what you're making?"

"For you, I'm making kheema bhurjee. It's my take on an old family recipe. I used to make it for my father's birthday until the war."

"You were in a war?"

Catching himself Narain countered, "Well, not really a war. More like a skirmish. There was always one border fighting another in India. I don't like to talk about it much."

He closed his eyes tightly, hoping, then was finally relieved when she changed the subject. "Do you get a chance to go back to see your parents?"

"Well, unfortunately, my parents died some years back."

"And you weren't able to see them before that, were you?"

He was surprised by her perception. Trying to disguise the wistfulness in his voice, he sprinkled turmeric on the onions he was sautéing saying, "I went away to make a dream come true and I never made it back." Then he brightened. "But Baba loved this dish, and I hope you will too."

"It certainly smells good," she commented as he added ingredients to the skillet. The devotion he put into his cooking was apparent in each move he made. After several more minutes he took a plate from a small counter and drizzled it with sauce.

"Someone once told me," he began, plating the finished dish and garnishing it carefully, "that every dish must succeed at being four things: A painting for the eyes, a symphony for the ears, and perfume for the nose."

"And what's the fourth thing?" she asked as he set the plate before her and turned to get the bottle of wine from the counter.

Narain grinned, "The dish must also be a kiss for a lover's tongue."

Smiling, she sampled a bit, her eyes closing as her mouth slowly relished the experience. "Well, my tongue is tingling," she said, then caught herself, and anxiously took another forkful.

"This is amazing." As he poured her another glass of wine, she said, "At least have a glass of wine while I make a pig of myself."

Now this he could do. Nodding, he poured himself a glass of wine and held it casually, occasionally sniffing it and swirling it around the glass. Once in a while he would raise it to his lips, pretending to sip and once he even commented on the taste, but the main thing was to use the glass as a prop while he misdirected his companion's attention with conversation. Of course, Cassie was so engrossed in her food that misdirection was not all that necessary.

She ate with gusto, savouring each bite almost as if she were analysing the flavours in it. It gratified him. So many people simply wolfed down their food, claiming they enjoyed it, but never having it in their mouths long enough to really appreciate the taste. She swallowed the food slowly too, enjoying the feeling of it slipping down her throat. Narain missed the feeling of solid food in his stomach. While he was grateful he could still taste, there had always been something comforting and warm about solid food in the belly. It reminded him of home.

"Would you be interested in becoming my personal chef?" she asked at last wiping her mouth.

He smiled. "I don't know, what does it pay?"

"Oh, no pay," she said with a swallow. "I couldn't afford you."

"Well, if I'm ever in a position where money is absolutely unnecessary, we'll talk."

Taking a sip of wine, Cassie held her hand out. "Okay, deal." He shook it and they both chuckled.

Gazing down at her plate, she pushed around a few remaining onions. Curious by her sudden demeanour change, Narain asked, "Is everything alright?"

Her smile turned shy as she shrugged. "I feel I should be honest with you."

"Is the food not to your liking after all?"

Her gaze shot up. "Oh no, it's wonderful." Her voice grew softer. "It's just that... well, I didn't really come here to thank you for your work at the benefit. I mean, of course I'm grateful but that's not the only reason I'm here."

He couldn't help but grin at her awkwardness. "What is the other reason?"

Again she shrugged. "Well, to see you, mainly."

Somehow, Narain was not surprised but he was none the less flattered. He was also a little concerned at his own inner reaction to her words for he found himself enjoying being the object of her attention.

Without a word, he got up and began washing the skillet he'd used for cooking the kheema burjee. He couldn't help but fear this had been a mistake. He had agreed to have one drink with her, not cook her a romantic dinner and send off a signal that there could ever be anything more.

But damnit! He craved more. That's what unnerved him so. He was like an alcoholic who'd taken that one drink. He liked her. He could very well imagine loving her. And if indeed this were true, how could he think of forcing his reality on her. At that moment, as much as he craved her attention, the lack of nourishment of late left him craving so much more...he felt the need gripping him constantly, which was why he had been avoiding people of late.

How did one weave that into romantic dinner conversation on a third date?

"I'm so sorry," she said uncomfortably, breaking the silence. Pushing the plate away, she said, "I think I've overstayed my welcome."

He raced over to her, faster than he meant to, insisting, "Oh no, not at all."

Taken aback by his speed, she still couldn't hide her obvious discomfort as she explained, "You know, I thought there might be something here," she waved her hands indicating Narain and herself, "but maybe I misread signals."

"Oh, no, there is definitely something here." The words fell out before he could censor them and Narain was surprised to feel a sense of relief, especially when he saw her face brighten.

A bit ashamed, she admitted, "I'm awful at this sort of stuff. I spend so much time focused on microbes and blood samples. You know, I can pick up on the slightest variation in a virus but signals between a man and a woman…I mean, I'm awful when it comes to flirting."

"I'm not complaining," Narain said, shrugging. "Besides, I haven't exactly been smooth myself."

"You've been fine."

Taking her hand, he said earnestly, "Cassie, I've been attracted to you since we danced at the benefit. The thing is I'm shy about entering a relationship. I…well I have some baggage and have had many, many years to collect it."

"We all have baggage."

He grinned, raising a finger. "Not like this. In fact, I think I can safely say that very few people have baggage like this and I suppose I just don't want to inflict it upon you."

Biting her lip, she cupped his chin, studying his face. "You expend a lot of energy shielding people, don't you? That can lead to a great deal of loneliness."

He chuckled, enjoying her touch. "You sound like Dom."

"Well, maybe you should listen to him." They stared into each other's eyes for a few moments before she cleared her throat and glanced at her watch. "Well, I think I'd better be going. Dinner was delicious, thank you." Reaching into her purse, she withdrew a business card, stating matter-of-factly, "Narain, I don't know what is going on or where it's headed but I'm very interested in finding out." She handed him the card. "If you feel you can trust someone else with some of that baggage, give me a call. We'll see if I'm strong enough to help you carry it."

She kissed his cheek, the same one she'd kissed at the benefit, but this time her movement was more confident and he stood there silently as she smiled and left the kitchenette.

†

Tyler rolled along the tarmac before coming to a stop, his skateboard skidding alongside him and thudding into his hip. Spencer and Jared were nearly doubled over with laughter at his failed attempt at an ollie heelflip and their laughter frustrated him even more than the wipe out.

Damnit! He thought, picking himself up off the ground and inspecting the mild scrapes on his arms and hands. He'd been trying to perfect that move since the weather had warmed up and they'd returned to the parking lot of St. Mathias Church in Jefferson Park that they'd discovered last year right before the snow forced them to abandon their boards. The lot was perfect since the church was pretty much desolate most nights and the asphalt was smooth and free of cars. There were also a long flight of stairs and a large cement planter to challenge them.

"I keep telling you you're not doing it right," Jared said once his giggling subsided.

Tyler glared at him. Jared thought he was so cool because he'd figured out the move before Tyler and Spencer. What he didn't get was that Tyler already knew the move—he was experimenting with a variation to outdo Jared.

"I can do it," Tyler insisted, grabbing his board resentfully.

"Then why don't you?" Jared asked in a mocking tone.

Tyler inspected his wheels, then glanced up past his two friends to a figure standing just inside the entrance to the lot. The figure had been there ever since the sun had set, not moving, not saying a word. Just watching, his hands in the pocket of the oversized, red sweatshirt he wore. The hood of the stained sweatshirt was pulled over his head, obscuring his face and hiding any features that might be visible in the glare of the yellow sodium lights.

"It's that kid over there." He indicated the figure and the other boys turned their heads to look. "I don't like him standing there."

Spence shrugged. "He's just watching us skate. Probably wishes he knew how."

"He might know how," Jared countered.

"If he knew how, he'd have a board and would be skating," Spence said, satisfied with the logic.

None of that mattered to Tyler; the kid still made him nervous. He was a lot bigger than them and Tyler was worried that he was some older teen who was considering starting a fight. What if he was waiting for friends who would beat them up?

"Will you stop worrying about him?" Jared demanded.

Tyler nodded then put his board down before taking one last glance at the stranger…Who was no longer there. Tyler blinked, squinted and cast his gaze around the area of the lot where the kid had been standing, but it was deserted.

"Where'd he go?" he asked and the others turned to look at the now vacant spot.

"Weird," Spence commented flatly.

Turning back to their boards, however, all three took steps back as the hooded figure now stood a few feet in front of them, head lowered, only his chin visible in the shadows of his hood.

"Dude, how'd you do that?" Tyler asked, unsure if the kid's trick impressed or frightened him.

The kid said nothing. Didn't move. He never lowered his gaze from them though one could barely see his face for the hood.

Spence stepped a bit closer. "Do you skate?"

The figure remained silent, but with amazing speed, grabbed the board from Spence's grip and ran off, throwing it to the ground and hopping on board.

Any protest the boys were going to make was cut short by the sheer skill displayed by the kid who skated better than Tony Hawk or Shaun White. Eventually it became apparent that he wasn't stealing the board but rather simply joyriding and the tricks he was performing stunned the on-lookers. The three boys let out shouts and whoops and the kid finally shoved the board back to Spencer with one kick before landing gracefully a few feet away. The boys were so excited by the display that even Tyler had lost his misgivings.

"That was awesome!" Spencer exclaimed, retrieving his board from where it had stopped by his feet.

"Where'd you learn to do all that?" Jared asked. "Will you show us?"

"Yeah, show us," Tyler said, stepping forward.

The figure stiffened and stepped back, his head bowed slightly forward so his face remained shrouded by his hood. The nervous feeling crept back into Tyler's gut and he suggested, "You know what; let's go home now. I'm tired."

His friends slowly agreed, equally disturbed by the kid. That's when they heard the eerie squeal of laughter emanating from the shadows of the hood and then watched the boy stepping toward them. As he walked, he slowly reached up and pulled back his hood, raising his face to them and revealing the horror of his disfigurement. His eyes were huge, black marbles, his jaw elongated, and his wide mouth bulged with rows of huge serrated teeth that pressed forward gruesomely.

The boys screamed in horror but by the time they dropped their boards to run, the creature flew at them, mowing all three to the ground and deftly keeping a grip on Jared and Tyler with horrible power as it began to feast on Spencer. Tyler was able to wriggle his arm across the lot far enough to grab hold of his board and when he did, he raised it and brought it down sharply on the creature's head. The board cracked in two and the creature raised his blood smeared face from his victim to stare at Tyler, eyes glowing red. Then it lunged forward and silenced the screams of the last two victims.

Chapter 5

Dr. Richard Channing climbed into the back of the truck and glanced at the dishevelled being strapped to the ledge jutting out from the wall. Parked in the lot of a west side factory abandoned a year previous, the truck had arrived that night in Chicago after a cross country trip from California. It had been a long trip but considering the cargo, using one of Reg Jameson's specially equipped trucks seemed like the safest way to transport it. Had Jameson any knowledge of it, they could have brought the creature to Chicago by plane, but it was Channing's hope that they could clean the mess up before Jameson found out. The vampire would be furious enough with the escape; he would never agree to what Channing had planned. Directing his attention to the attendant in a white lab coat, he asked, "No trouble, then?"

Ken Davidson, an assistant from the Los Angeles lab, handed him a chart, commenting, "He was quiet for the most part, but you're right, he's definitely building up immunity to the tranq. It took 25 percent more this time to get him down."

Channing scanned the chart, shaking his head. "I was afraid of that. The formula may need to be constantly updated since the creature's immune system is forever adjusting to it."

"A unique problem."

"An annoying problem. I don't doubt for a moment though that what worked on him would be useless on Boris."

"Makes control hard."

"Damn hard." Channing chuckled bitterly. "Those surveillance photos you e-mailed me...I mean, I warned Reg what Boris was capable of, but I guess I never realised the sheer brutality."

"And calculating. You were right. Once we got the computers back on line, it was obvious he'd hacked into the system before escaping. He had plenty of time to do it. A whole weekend with the facility to himself once he cut everyone down. Can't really tell what he saw, but I think he saw quite a lot."

That's exactly what worried Channing and why he felt the need to take the drastic step of bringing this creature to Chicago. "Our big mistake was underestimating Boris. Thinking he was pure feral. If he had a conscience before, it's gone now. That part is probably very much feral. But he has all the street smarts he had prior to the transformation. Perhaps even more now that his reflexes are quicker."

Staring at the creature, Davidson asked, "Are you sure this is a good idea, Doctor?"

Channing gave a sardonic chuckle. "I haven't a clue if this is a good idea. All I know is that we've already lost three very capable people chasing Boris across the country, and the others have come up unsuccessful. He's here now, for whatever reason, and this might be our only way to catch him. Sometimes you have to fight fire with fire." Noticing the man's nervousness, he said, "You can wait in the cab until I'm finished."

Gratefully, the man took one look at the figure on the ledge, and then nodded. "Call me if you need help," he added before hurrying from the back of the truck.

The creature didn't speak as he watched Channing studying him. In the past two years the creature rarely ever spoke. Aside from occasionally taunting him, Jameson was certain that the creature's mind had been destroyed long before they found him, but during experiments and exams, Channing always sensed reason behind the pale-blue eyes that stared back at him from under the wild matted hair.

The creature still showed some of the effects of the tranq but Channing could tell it was wearing off. Hands trembling slightly, he began to undo the restraints holding the creature in place on the table. The pale-blue eyes followed his movements but the being gave no indication of attacking.

"You and I both know that there's more to you than Jameson gives you credit for," Channing said firmly, almost antiseptically. "And we both know the sort of pompous ass he can be."

With the restraints off, Channing backed away but not too far, hoping to retain some level of dominance. "I know what you want," he told the creature, "and I can help you get it, but first you have to help me." Pausing to let the words sink in, he then said, "Boris is in this town and he's feasting liberally. Of the hunters we've sent out after him, those who've found him have come home in body bags. He's too strong, and he's too clever. I think you're the only one who can stop him."

The creature sat up with unexpected speed and Channing tensed. But as the creature threw his legs over the table, he simply stared at Channing, unkempt hair framing his face, the pale-blue eyes staring eerily into Channing's.

Slowing his respiration, Channing said, "I need you to do two things for me. In exchange, I will give you what you desire." The being's brows furrowed and Channing nodded. "Yes, I know of a way to accomplish it. But first I want you to hunt Boris down. I think you're the only one who can successfully subdue Boris and do what needs to be done. I mean, if the ferals barely captured you, how will they fare against Boris?" He sighed. "I'm just grateful sunlight affects him or I don't know how much damage he'd be causing. You don't have that consideration, do you? So you have that point up on him."

Silence gripped the inside of the truck until finally the creature mumbled with a gravelly voice unused to speech, "Second?"

It was a question said with resentment. The restraints were off but the creature was still a prisoner of circumstance. Channing appraised him saying, "I want you to protect someone who means a great deal to me. I think I know why Boris has come here and she may be in a great deal of danger. Boris knows she's in the city but he doesn't know where yet. He's clever though and he's hunting." Taking out a packet he handed the beast a photograph. "This is my friend. She has absolutely nothing to do with what Reg and I have been doing with you." He frowned. "In fact, I think it's safe to say she'd be very disappointed in the research we've been conducting. Are you able to read a map?" The creature nodded and Channing took a map of Chicago out of the packet, opening it up on the table next to where the creature sat.

"This is the city and the surrounding suburbs," he explained. "You have no idea what a modern urban metropolis is like. Hell, London was crazy back in your day. Twenty-first Century Chicago isn't anywhere near what you're used to. It's vibrant, fast-paced, in places twenty four hours and in some areas quite dangerous. Be aware of that. It will be culture shock." He pointed at a dot. "In orange highlighter is where Boris has been spotted. In red is where attacks have taken place. I can't swear they're all his. The two bloodiest in the Regent Hotel parking lot on Michigan Avenue and on a playground here. Given the description of the crime scenes, I'd say he was definitely responsible."

The creature studied the map, nodding, then asking, "Green?"

"That's my friend. Her house," Channing pointed to a dot on the map near the lake, then west to the suburb of Hoffman Estates. "NewGen Labs." He sighed, commenting, "Sometimes a second home to both of us. If she's not at one, she's more than likely at the other."

The creature's gaze remained fixed on the map for several moments before he raised it to stare into the eyes of his captor. "I do this," he said slowly, his voice uncertain in its abilities, "and you free me."

Channing couldn't tell if it was a statement or a question and it actually didn't matter. "Yes," he nodded firmly then pointed to a green dot. "That's why we need to protect her. She has what you need."

Without warning, the creature grabbed hold of Channing's shirt front and lifted him easily, Channing's feet dangling ridiculously several inches above the floor of the truck. Shaking his head, he looked Channing square in the face, snarling, "Don't cheat me."

Shivering, Channing tried to stay in control, assuring him, "I won't. I promise."

Without another word, the creature released his hold and darted from the back of the truck, abandoning the map on the table.

Channing collapsed to his hands and knees fighting the nauseating fear gripping him as he watched the creature disappear into the night. From the moment he'd seen him, trussed on a lab table, Channing was sure that this creature had never been a cruel man. Circumstances had transformed him into the hulking creature now capable of so much violence that he could have torn Channing apart without a moment's hesitation and the thought of how close he had come to death left Channing almost paralysed on the floor of the truck. But he was certain that, as far removed as the creature was from the man he once was, he still retained a level of honour and would carry out the mission he'd agreed to.

Not like Boris, who, during his escape from the L.A. lab, simply butchered for pleasure those of the weekend staff that he didn't feed on. The security footage from the weekend of Boris' escape revealed a being killing not for expediency's sake but rather consciously relishing the hunt and the kill. Boris had had a bit of the feral in him even before his "death and resurrection" and the transformation had heightened his abilities but it had deadened his conscience.

At last catching his breath, Channing sat back against the side of the ledge wishing he could make good on the promise he'd just made to the creature. He couldn't though. Once Boris was dealt with, the creature would be wrapped up and shipped back to the lab where more testing would be done. He was just too valuable. Locked inside his body might be answers to questions much more important than those Reginald Jameson was interested in. The creature was the catalyst for the cures of countless diseases, Channing was sure of that, which was why he had to somehow pluck up the courage to bring Cassie in on the current research. There'd been too many secrets between them recently and secrets tended to eat away at any relationship. With her help, who knew what he could accomplish. Then perhaps he might still have a chance with her. He'd never been certain what had doused the passion between them. Collaboration on this project might bring them close again.

But Boris had to be taken out of the mix, no matter what Jameson said. Channing had warned him how unstable Boris was and that any knowledge gleaned from him was not worth the risk of keeping him around. Jameson refused to address the issue so it was now up to Channing to do what needed to be done.

†

On the afternoon of a glorious April day in Chicago, Dominic found Narain seated at his desk in his living room, the specially designed security shades encasing the windows blocking out any harmful rays from the spring-time sun. Depending on the age of a vampire, sunlight could be deadly. As the years rolled by a vampire's tolerance decreased to the point where the being's skin would begin to blister and burn instantly in direct sunlight. Dom had seen it happen to Narain once and the image stayed with him. While the effects of indirect sunlight weren't quite as deadly, just being near it could bring a psychosomatic response sickening the vampire to near paralysis from the panic- induced pain.

The light as the vampire surfed the web on his computer was provided by the chandelier-like ceiling fixture in the middle of the room giving the room a sunny sparkle all its own. Noting the intent with which Narain stared at the screen, Dominic wondered what it must have been like before television, before the Internet, when a being that didn't require eight hours of sleep none the less found himself needing to hide away until the sun went down and it was safe to prowl again. Narain was a remarkably literate man; no wonder, considering how at one time reading was one of the few ways to pass the hours until it was safe to emerge from his cocoon. Sophie had once quipped that they played a lot of board games and gin rummy.

As if making up for all those decades when this was his only escape, Narain now sat furiously scanning the Internet while Franz Ferdinand played loudly through the speakers embedded in the ceiling, and two television monitors tuned to two different cable news stations played stories from around the world. Narain's attention had been flickering between both TVs and computer but when Dominic entered the apartment it was fixed on the Internet site he had wandered onto and was now studying closely. Next to the computer was a pad of paper that he wrote notes on.

"Dom," he called over the music, sensing his friend's presence and greeting him before he could speak. Eyes still glued to the screen, he brought up another window. "I was going over last night's receipts. We had a great night. I thought for sure it would be slow."

Dominic heard him but barely. The decibel level at which the music was being played made holding a conversation with normal human hearing difficult. "Hey, Rain, can we cut some of the noise." The vampire had superhuman hearing. The decibel level was purely to distract an over anxious mind.

Frowning, Narain finally realised what he was talking about, and then smiled at the realisation. "Of course." He raised a small remote and aimed it at a CD player embedded in the wall. The music stopped and the televisions muted when he aimed the remote at them.

Stepping toward the desk, Dominic said, "I'm guessing that piece Maggie Stewart wrote on the benefit didn't hurt the receipts. She particularly liked the spicy cashews though I got the feeling she was interested in more than just your recipes when she was interviewing you." Narain simply rolled his eyes and Dom shrugged innocently. Then he glanced at the pad of paper by the computer, noting the curious words. "Ujaali Chopra? Is that a new dish you're working on?

Narain burst out laughing, saying, "No. It's a name. A woman's name."

Uneasy at his multi-cultural faux pas, Dominic said, "Oh jeez, I'm sorry. Really."

"Don't worry. It's alright. How would you know?"

"Someone you know?"

Narain stared at the name wistfully. "A relative, that's all." He clicked out of the Website. "I was doing a bit of family research, that's all."

Dom paused a moment, then asked, "Do you plan on contacting her?"

Narain pursed his lips in thought, and then said, "No, she wouldn't know me anyway."

Dom studied him, glancing at the protective window shades before returning his attention to him. "You know, sometimes I forget how logistically inconvenient your life can be."

Shrugging, Narain turned his full attention on him, placing his hands behind his head and leaning back. "You look preoccupied. What's up?"

Dom took a seat on the arm of the sofa and folded his arms. "I had something I wanted to talk to you about." He paused, uncertain how to ask the question. The information he had about his partner's condition had been acquired sparingly over the years, usually from necessity, mainly due to Narain's insistence upon living as normal a life as he was able to. "I know you can sense humans. Are you able to sense other vampires?"

Struck by the question, Narain considered his answer. "It depends. I have been able to sense the few I've been around, but really only when they're in the vicinity. From a distance, I don't believe so. My skills may be better than right after I turned, but it seems so long since I've needed them. Sometimes even a vampire can fall out of practice."

"But the other night after the benefit, you knew someone was being attacked."

"Yes," he pointed to his ears, "I heard it going on. Sensing another vampire's presence, or anyone's for that matter, is…well it's a different vibe. Why do you ask?"

Almost reluctantly, Dominic said, "Well, it could be nothing, but you know my cousin Michael is a cop out of the 18th precinct?" Narain nodded. "I was talking to him the other day and he told me about a case that came up. You know about the Anders couple being killed."

"I saw that on the news. Very sad. They still haven't figured out who did it."

"This new case involves three kids; age 12, 14, something like that. Their bodies were found in a church parking lot. From what Michael said, and he's seen some things—you know—this was the worst thing he'd ever seen."

Narain's brow furrowed. "In what way?"

"The violence of it. The blood." Dom grimaced slightly. "He said these kids were pretty much just torn apart like some wild animal got at them. It reminded me of the Anders case and I started thinking…"

"That there might be another vampire prowling Chicago," Narain finished.

"Yeah, basically. I mean, maybe I'm wrong, but killings of that sort just seem sort of coincidental. Michael said that one of the bodies was practically desiccated. The other two were ripped apart, but the blood had pooled as it usually does in dead bodies so it was likely the trauma that killed them. But the third one didn't seem to have much left in it at all. Now, maybe it leaked out, it was pretty ripped up, but like I said, normally it begins to pool after they die, if it's there to pool."

Troubled by the idea, Narain stood up, arms folded against his chest, rubbing his chin with his right hand. "Well, anything is possible. It could be simply some very psychotic killer."

"Yeah, it could. Like I said; just a thought. Believe me, if I hadn't seen the things I've seen, the thought would probably never even cross my mind."

"Well," considering the possibilities, Narain said, his Indian accent becoming thick as it tended to do when he was anxious, "if one were not to rule out vampires, then the attack in the church lot sounds very much more in keeping with an attack by ferals."

"Ferals. What are ferals?"

Narain turned to look at him, smiling slightly. "There's quite a lot I haven't shared with you, isn't there?"

Dominic shrugged. "Hey, it's not exactly like I've asked you either."

Narain took a seat, rubbing his face which suddenly looked very haggard. "Basically, there are two types of vampire. That's as Alphonse figured it, at least."

"Alphonse. The guy who found you after the battlefield, right?"

The vampire nodded. "Despite their research, neither he nor his niece Lucy was able to figure out what caused one person to become feral and one person to become sentient after the conversion."

"Sentient?" Dom thought this over. "I'm assuming you'd be one of the sentient ones?"

"Exactly. You see, a sentient vampire would never cause the sort of mess you describe. I'm not saying they're incapable of sadism or cruelty, but they also know the risks they'd run in carrying out such careless attacks." He stood from the desk chair and began to pace the floor, discomfited by the topic he was discussing. "You don't lose or gain a moral compass simply because of the conversion. However, even the most psychotic sentient would never leave a kill lying around like that. They know what there is to lose if…well if the world discovers we exist."

"But a feral wouldn't give it a second thought?"

"No. It's not in their make-up. If I had become feral rather than sentient I quite simply wouldn't care what happened after the kill. My whole purpose, every thought, for lack of a better term, would be about basic survival. It's possible that during the conversion, a person's psyche is so tested, so tormented, that it might not be able to handle what's happening to him. It shuts down and all that's left is the feral need to survive. Even for a sentient, it takes a particular mindset to…well, to feed."

"So these ferals are kind of like sharks," Dominic commented.

Narain paused his pacing and pointed at him. "Exactly like sharks. Swim and feed." He looked down as an unpleasant memory struck him. "It was a pack of ferals that set upon the soldiers in no man's land during World War I. There was no spark of humanity or compassion whatsoever in their eyes. All that possessed them was the need to feed. Ferals love plagues and war and anything that causes unrest and presents them with the chance to feed. They take what they can then, if food becomes scarce or feeding inconvenient, they may dig into the ground and hibernate. It's only then that the need doesn't grip them. Otherwise it's all consuming, that hunger."

Dom studied his friend, noting the haunted look that came over his face. He saw again how tired the vampire appeared, how dull his normally rich mocha complexion was. He didn't need to ask if Narain had yet fed properly. It was clearly evident that he hadn't. Clearing his throat, he asked, "Rain, this feral nature; are even sentient vampires capable of this kind of extreme sometimes?"

Struck by his friend's perception, Narain turned his head away. His movements became more fluid, fuelled by adrenalin, like a caged cat or a man caught in an untenable situation. At last, he said softly, "It is practically impossible for a vampire to kill him or herself. Sentient or feral, the mind might want one thing, but the body will always choose survival and will do what is necessary to continue that survival even if it means overriding the mind."

An uneasy feeling passed through Dom as he said, "And would killing ones-self include starvation, even if unintentional?" Narain conceded reluctantly with a nod and Dom asked, "Rain, what we talked about the night of the benefit…how serious can this get? I mean, could it get serious like this playground thing?"

"I'll do my best to keep it from getting serious."

"But could it?" Narain said nothing, giving Dom his answer. He had sensed the unease in his friend's tense demeanour only increase since their talk weeks before regarding the subject. Narain was becoming more distant as well, physically and mentally, which made sense. Every movement a person made, every increase in pulse or pressure would no doubt affect Narain like the smell of sizzling meat to a starving man. Narain was dealing not only with the discomfort of his starvation but also with the reality of what could happen should it progress too far. It happened very rarely, Narain tried to keep it so, but every so often the reality of his condition intruded on their relationship, reminding Dom just how strangely different his partner was.

At last, Dom said, "So I'm guessing that I don't need to tell you how important it is to get this under control." He wasn't sure if Narain would resent the chiding tone, but he didn't care. He'd seen too many other people deny the seriousness of their issues—insist that "it was all under control" only to have tragedy follow.

If he resented the tone, the vampire didn't show it. Instead he simply nodded sharply and returned to talk of the playground attack. "I can't say if it was a feral that attacked those kids or the Anders couple for that matter, but it does alarm me to think there might be a feral loose in the city. I can't imagine where it came from. They generally keep to rural areas."

Dom grinned. "With all the building going on, rural areas are becoming few and far between. Hey, we have coyotes climbing into coolers in sub shops on Michigan Avenue. Nothing would surprise me."

"Well it frightens me." Running a hand through his hair, Narain stared at the carpet, eyes unnervingly wide. "Ferals are remarkably dangerous. They're conscienceless ghouls unconcerned with anything but feeding."

Recognizing the look, Dom warned, "Rain, your condition does not make you responsible for every one like you. The world is getting smaller. It was bound to happen that a few others would pop up here."

Narain looked up at him, narrowing his eyes. "If you are correct, I should do nothing when I know what this thing is capable of? I should let it feast off the city?"

"And are you in any condition to do anything about it?" Dom saw the vampire slump slightly as that reality struck him. Gently, he said, "Besides, this was just a theory of my own. I don't know maybe it was some sicko... mortal sicko."

"The same for both attacks?" Narain asked incredulously.

"I don't know, I don't know. I'm just saying let's not go off half-cocked."

They stared at each other, but before anything else could be said, the phone rang. Picking up the receiver, Narain stared at Dominic as he took the call. A smile that spread across his lips stiffened slightly as he said, "Tonight? Of course I can. That shouldn't be a problem. That's rather late though. Is everything okay?" There was a pause, and his smile relaxed slightly. "Very well, then, I'll meet you there." He hung up and looked up at Dominic, a mixture of excitement and anxiousness crossing his face. "That was Cassie."

Dominic grinned. "Oh yeah, huh? She's calling you... that means you gave her your number."

"To be polite," Narain said, brushing off his friend's extrapolations. "We've had conversations since the night she came to the restaurant."

Dominic laughed. "I've been polite to a lot of women, my friend, but I haven't given my number to them simply out of politeness. She's got a hold on you, and you know it."

"Why do I tell you anything?" Narain said helplessly.

"Because you value my opinions and know that, usually, I'm right."

Narain said nothing as he shut down his computer and headed down the hallway toward his bedroom. "Where are you going?" Dom asked.

"To figure out what to wear. She's asked me to meet her tonight." He indicated the beat up T-shirt and jeans he wore. "I can't very well go like this."

"Tonight? Several hours to pick out a suitable outfit? This must be love."

"Shut up," he heard the vampire say from down the hall. "It has been half a century since I had to court a woman."

"Wear blue," Dom called after him. "It brings out your eyes."

Grinning, Narain stepped back briefly, asking, "Dom, my friend, I wasn't aware you noticed. Do we need to re-examine our relationship?"

Dominic rolled his eyes and prepared to leave. "You only wish, pal. Ain't gonna happen."

He watched as Narain chuckled and went back down the hall. Dr. Lambert's call had brought a bit of colour to his friend's cheeks, but Dom knew it would be fleeting. Narain was hurting, psychologically and physically and Dom had no idea how to help alleviate the pain. He could not for a moment think that Narain would be capable of the sort of brutality that had been exhibited in the recent murders in the city. But what if he reached a state where he was no longer in control? Leaving the apartment, Dominic resolved that, despite his friend's stubbornness, he would figure a way to get the vampire the sustenance he needed to survive.

✝

The screams, like church bells, resonated exquisitely through Boris' entire body as he remembered with a smile his latest attack. It had garnered him the laptop he held; the second he'd taken and hopefully this one had a bit more life in it than the last one he'd acquired. He had followed the man to the parking lot after the man had exited the Metra train. The businessman had no doubt just ended a very long working day where last minute details kept him late at the office downtown until he was finally forced to leave or miss the last train.

Boris had been fishing all night at the train station hoping to come across the right person at the right time. When he saw the weary, middle aged man carrying a computer laptop disembarking alone from the train, Boris knew he had found his mark. He let the man walk on for several moments before beginning the hunt. The man had been so focused on his thoughts that he apparently found nothing unnerving about a hooded figure sitting on the benches at a deserted Metra station nor did he bother to check occasionally to make sure that he wasn't being followed.

It wasn't hard to catch up with the man and as he followed at a careful distance, Boris scanned the area for any other late night pedestrians. Traffic on the normally busy street had slowed considerably at that time of night and his heart began to race with the thrill of the hunt.

A silver Honda civic beeped and winked its lights as the man entered a parking lot and raised his car alarm remote, pressing the button to disarm the alarm. Stepping up to it, he put his computer and brief case on the hood and stretched in preparation for the rest of the commute home. Dropping his keys, he bent down to retrieve them and when he straightened, started to see Boris standing in front of him.

This was Boris' favourite part. He loved to scare them shitless before taking them down. Stand silent for a few seconds; let the uncertainty slowly turn into panic. Then pull back the hood and let them see what was in store for them.

The man had screamed when Boris lowered his hood and Boris would have loved to listen longer, perhaps engage in a chase before taking him down as he had the last victim, but, empty as the parking lot was, there were apartments nearby. Someone was bound to be civic minded enough to call the cops after hearing the blood curdling cries of a man being torn apart. So when Boris lunged, he went for the throat first, ripping out the man's larynx and allowing the sweet blood streaming from the carotid artery to flow into his mouth. The man twitched a few times, then shock overcame him and he lay still, bleeding to death.

When Boris was finished, face sticky with the man's warm blood, he wiped an arm across it and stood up. That's when he caught a glimpse of his reflection in the driver's window and he found himself transfixed by the sight. Huge black eyes narrowed as he traced his fingers around the shark-like maw that was now his mouth. He then stared at his hands, with their tapered fingers and nails as hard as iron. Claw-like. As capable as his teeth now were of ripping into flesh.

He had been someone else a long time ago. His mouth had been normal, his fingers…his eyes had been a soft brown – not the dead black they were now. Of course that was their mistake. His captors had thought he was nothing more than what his appearance advertised – a mindless feeding machine. But they hadn't taken away everything he once was.

Turning to the laptop on the hood of the car, he opened it, turning it on and inspecting the function. There were a lot of files regarding projects for the former owner's job – that could all be deleted. A few icons for cheesy, time-waster games. Boris sneered more than smiled. He could keep those.

Reaching into his trouser pocket, he pulled out a flash drive and fitted it into the port on the side of the laptop. He had carried it with him all the way from California. Selecting that drive, he was thrilled when the files began appearing. He had spent a great deal of time downloading files from the California lab's system. It hadn't taken him long to hack into the system once the weekend crew had been dealt with. There was so much information about him, about Jameson's little experiment. He wanted to be able to digest it all properly and there wouldn't be enough time for that over the weekend. So he found some empty flash drives and downloaded what he could. He went straight for Channing's files – that'd be where all the meat was. What particularly caught his attention was information on "a cure." Channing had been trying to duplicate it unsuccessfully but he knew who had it. Boris' cross country rampage had illustrated just how invulnerable his new physique was. The sun still sent him into hiding, but it seemed that very little else could stop him.

He wanted to keep it that way and the only way to do that was by destroying everything having to do with a cure, including the creator, who, based on information in Channing's files, was in Chicago. And so the hunt began. Boris didn't have an exact location but once in the city, tracking down the creator of this cure shouldn't be too difficult. With luck, the files would contain more clues.

The one handicap, aside from the sun, was the insatiable desire to feed. The fact of the matter was that were it not for particular procedures performed on him, he might very well have ended up a simple feral. Now, occasionally the feral warred with the sentient in an almost vampiric ADD and very often his mind was obsessed with thoughts of the next kill.

Switching off the laptop, he removed the flash-drive and closed the lid. The problem was that he couldn't waste all his energy on that endeavour even if he desperately wanted to. There was far too much to do—the destruction of this kill, the elimination of Channing, perhaps even of Reg Jameson, whose sick program had originally snatched Boris off the street and turned him into what he now was. Walking over to a bush, Boris reached in and pulled out a skateboard, a recent acquisition from new found friends in a church parking lot. He had stashed it there before obtaining the computer. It was fun, but cumbersome when hunting. Perhaps once he was done with his tasks, he could switch his focus to things his feral nature might better enjoy.

Chapter 6

It was close to 2a.m. when Narain arrived at NewGen Labs, in Hoffman Estates about 30 miles outside of Chicago. The trip at that time of the morning was relatively smooth, with traffic light on Route 72 going west, but it was a long drive, nearly ninety minutes thanks to a lane closure for several miles. 2:00a.m. was a very curious time for Cassie to want to meet. She claimed that a series of unavoidable off-site business meetings would keep her from meeting him earlier, but Narain didn't mind too much. The late night hour meant that he wouldn't have to explain why he had to wait until the sun went down. He thought it odd she wanted to meet at NewGen. In fact, she sounded rather evasive on the phone, personable, but quick, though she assured him that everything was fine despite a slight urgency in her tone. He had taken Dom's advice and wore a cerulean blue sweater, casual but dressy, settling on this after trying on five other shirts and wondering about a sixth. More than once while preparing for the night he asked himself what he hoped to accomplish, occasionally glancing at photos of Sophie on the dresser as if seeking approval or advice. Now was not the time to start what he desperately wanted to start. He had other things to concern himself with…more pressing matters. He had made the same argument the first time she had called him, yet found himself calling her a few days after that.

The more the argument began to wilt and die, the more conversations they had. He was a moth to the flame in this situation and had been able to override any complaint lodged by common sense.

So, Narain drove with careful speed to Hoffman Estates and pulled onto the carefully landscaped grounds of the NewGen Labs office complex. It was an impressive structure, six stories and taking up half a block on a few acres of manicured land, with large glass windows that revealed only one light on the fourth floor. He figured that would be Cassie's. Noting two cars in the large parking lot, Narain considered the unseasonable humidity as he walked toward the entrance to a gleaming lobby. Something caught his attention and he turned to see a small rabbit skittering under a bush. His pulse quickened and for a few moments he found himself transfixed before shaking his head and coming back to his senses.

Even the few drops found in a rabbit would give him a bit of relief. He sighed. It would not offer what he needed.

The lobby floor appeared freshly buffed, the grey speckled tiles gleaming under ample lighting. Off to the left was a round, black security desk, but it was unmanned, which Narain found curious, as well. If a building such as this was open for anyone to walk into, surely a security officer should be positioned in the lobby. Cassie had told him the floor, she had told him the suite number, but Narain continued to stare at the desk with a frown as he walked to the elevator and punched the call button.

A nervous feeling cascaded down his spine. It was a feature of his condition that he could now sense things that he would never have picked up on before the conversion. Months ago he would have trusted the feeling.

Now, he was uncertain. His lack of sustenance was bringing on increasing fits of anxiety that sent his heart pounding. He felt the changes going on deep within his mind and it was becoming harder to mask and to control. He needed to get a handle on it. He needed to feed, but it wasn't that simple. It had never been that simple. Until Sophie. With her, he no longer needed to depend on those instincts. He could be like a normal human again, despite what he was.

Stepping into the elevator, Narain punched the fourth floor button and leaned against the wall, staring at his hands which shook slightly. This was a mistake, he was sure this was a mistake. "Nip it in the bud now," he told himself. "Go home. Figure a way to deal with that which must be done."

Cassie was waiting for him, though. Let him enjoy tonight. He could deal with it all the next night. He relaxed slightly. Seeing her would help bring him some peace. Oh, the baggage she would have to carry should this romance proceed.

Narain smiled softly and feeling a bit more at ease, walked down the hall toward her office, the glass door, wide open. Stepping carefully in to the darkened room, which was lit only by a few small fluorescent lamps over a long work table and a few tanks of tropical fish near the wall, he called out, "Hello?"

Something was wrong! It had struck him outside the door. He'd felt no sense of Cassie but rather, a sensation he hadn't felt for a long time prickling the hair on the back of his neck and causing his heart to race. Damnit! Had his skills atrophied so much that he couldn't decipher...

"I knew it!" a voice said triumphantly as a figure stepped forward from the side of a tall supply cabinet.

The light from the tanks was more than sufficient for Narain to view the figure's features. They had changed slightly, not aged at all, but the piercing blue eyes still had a glow of anger despite being screwed up in a smile. Narain's stomach flipped. "Reg?"

"You remembered," Jameson said, his accent still reminiscent of the clipped, upper-class British of nine decades before. "How thoughtful. Boys," he stalked around Narain. "I'd like to introduce you to...well, my creator, I suppose. And in this case, blood truly is thicker than water, or at least a lot more satisfying, eh what?"

Two other figures came up on both sides of Narain and each grabbed an arm. He looked at them, both male, hair shaved to a Velcro length, with the unmistakably pronounced eye ridges and jaw lines of ferals. They were passably humanoid, but just barely. One sneered, revealing the row of serrated teeth hidden in his mouth.

Narain blinked in shock, staring ahead. The last time he had seen Reginald Jameson, Captain Reginald Jameson, was when they were both lying wounded on the battlefield…

"And you were feasting off me, weren't you old chap?" Jameson echoed Narain's very thoughts then caught the slight look of surprise. "Not telepathy, just simply deduction. I figured: What would my first thought be if our situations were reversed?" Leaning forward, his smile only grew as he stared into Narain's eyes. "Now, I imagine that when your conscience gets the better of you and you spare me a thought, that you assure yourself that you were helpless to this thing that now controls us both. You were new—half out of your mind. Starving." His smile faded and his voice gained an edge. "That does not negate the fact that you created me. Never forget that." He turned and paced away, hands behind his back. "I haven't. I've been waiting for decades to run into you. Didn't expect you here, though."

Reginald Jameson was dressed in a fashionable black leather jacket rather than the British army brown of World War I, but there was no mistaking that arrogance. It came off him in waves, just as it had decades before, but now there was a danger behind it. Captain Reginald Jameson had been a sadistic buffoon whose only power lay in his rank. The Reginald Jameson that now stood before Narain was infinitely more dangerous. The sadism was no doubt there, but now it was backed by the bizarre power of the immortal.

Shaking off his handlers, Narain waited for them to take a step back after a nod from Jameson, before demanding, "What are you doing here? Are you here for revenge?"

"Good lord, no. I was expecting someone else actually." Reg leaned forward, studying the fish swimming around in a large fish tank against the wall. Off-handedly he said, "Bloody tropical fish are everywhere. What is this infernal fascination with fish these humans have?" Then he glanced up at Narain, as if expecting an answer.

Narain's brows furrowed. "These humans? You are human."

"Well, no actually," Reg said, studying other areas of the lab. "None of us are. Were, once, perhaps, but no longer. Not really. And that's why I wouldn't dream of taking revenge upon you for using me as a midnight snack all those years ago. I mean, look at us, Khan. We are so much more than human now. Yes, there is that inconvenient sunlight issue…" The ferals nodded in complete understanding. "But aside from that we're faster, we're stronger, smarter."

Narain glanced sceptically at the ferals and Reg conceded, "Not all of us, mind you, but these two have come a long way."

The two grunted in agreement and Narain found himself oddly bemused by the weirdness of it all. And confused that ferals were even able to pass themselves off as human, let alone understand a conversation.

"The point is that we have more tricks up our sleeves than we would have had that night in 'No Man's Land' not taken place and we should never regret it. Of course, it wasn't easy. Took me quite some years to get over it. Death and rebirth is not something you get over in one night. Well, surely you yourself know. What might have been had Alphonse not discovered you?"

"Alphonse," Narain stepped forward carefully monitored by the ferals. "You knew of him?"

Jameson whirled to face him. "Yes. Nice old man. Tasty old man." Narain's eyes widened and Reg shrugged. "Let's just say I bit the hand that fed me."

"You killed him!" Narain hissed.

"Well, what would you expect once I came to my senses? I mean, you had him to walk you through it from the start. I had...well I had these two." His voice grew sinister. "And a whole pack of other ferals. They taught me their share, and valuable information it was, but it turned out I was sentient after all. Once I became fully conscious, I found the old man. Bear in mind, this was nearly a decade after that night on the battlefield."

Narain tried to control his fury. Flanked by two vampires with another in front of him, he wouldn't stand much of a chance. Especially when two were feral and Reg... well Reg was black hearted, a trait he possessed before his rebirth. Bitterly he said, "So you came all the way to Chicago to hunt me down?"

Reg scoffed at him. "Oh for heaven's sake, Khan, it's not all about you. I mean there's a whole world out there old chap. So much for me to sink my teeth into."

The ferals laughed and Narain stared at them fascinated at their apparent ability to understand humour, poor as that humour was. These weren't like the ferals he had experienced first-hand. Nothing like those beasts that had attacked the dying soldiers – attacked him – on the battlefield in France.

Jameson's voice brought his attention back as he continued, "It was just a happy coincidence that you happen to be in the very city where I need to be. You know, I saw your pictures in the papers—something about a gala, I told my two friends here, 'That's Private Khan. Surely that's him. *My old army chum,*'" he spat out the last sentence. "Isn't synchronicity fabulous? Gutsy move on the photos though. I mean ten, twenty years from now, how will you explain away the fact that you look no older than you do in that picture?"

Trying to sound more flippant than he felt, Narain answered, "Good genes."

"Yes, well. Not that reminiscing wasn't fun but we do have business to attend to with Dr. Lambert."

Narain tensed. He could feel the anxious energy coming off the two ferals who were not sophisticated enough to mask it. They were up to something. "What is it you want with Cassie?"

"Cassie? So, you know the doctor. Beautiful woman, very charming. The sort of woman who could help you forget...Sophie was her name?" Narain's eyes flashed as he watched Reg pace in front of him. "Yes, of course I've done my homework. I know you two were an item...for a long time. I can only surmise that it was more than sex." His pacing morphed into stalking. "I must say, having a Sophie must make it easier. Your own personal wine cellar. You get what, about fifty, sixty years out of her until the old cow keels over."

"Reg!" Narain snapped at the disrespect, and then eased back as the ferals growled.

Heart beating heavily, he said, "They say vampirism tends to exaggerate certain attributes. In your case, your tendency to be an ass."

Ignoring the comment, Reg looked around. "Well, I feel it's probably time to leave. Looks like I've been stood up." Studying Narain, a grin played across his lips as he put his hands on his hips. "You know though, this has been such a treat to see you again that I would like to give you a little something to remember me by."

Narain stared at him, confused and suspicious, wishing that he and his creatures would just leave. "What?"

"This!"

Pain seared deep into Narain's gut as Reg reached underneath his jacket and deftly whipped out a hunting knife, plunging it into Narain's abdomen and ripping it toward the left. The pain was breathtaking and he stared in quiet shock at his attacker before falling to his knees in agony.

Reg grabbed Narain's hair and forced his gaze up to look at the blade, proudly saying, "The sheath is filled with iodised salt, see. Comes in handy when I deal with our sort." Sheathing the blade again, he slid it out, slashing at Narain's left shoulder, and slicing through his shirt and deep into the skin. Then for good measure stuck the blade into his upper pectoral.

"That's gotta hurt," one of the ferals growled, attempting a levity and pronouncing the words as best as he could.

As Narain clutched at the fresh wounds and fell on his side, his three attackers laughed enthusiastically at the feral's quip.

"A perfect example of too much sodium in one's diet," Reg chuckled. He knelt on one knee and leaned in toward Narain's face saying, "Rather reminds me of the battlefield, eh?"

When Jameson stood up, Narain reached out and clutched his jacket with a blood stained hand, but Reg easily batted it away. "Reg," he gasped, a wave of pain causing his body to contract, "I never meant to harm you."

Head cocked, Reg stared down at him, an odd smile on his face. "You misunderstand, old chap. As I said, you freed me on that battlefield. This isn't for revenge. It's because I truly hate you and have hated you since the moment I met you." With a wink, he delivered a kick to his victim's ribs then glanced at the open drapes before nodding to the ferals. "Come on boys. Whether the salt or the sun, this isn't going to be pretty."

The three vampires walked from the room leaving Narain in agony on the floor. The salt was scalding his wounds. Had his diet not been so nutrient poor the past few months, his body might have been strong enough to at least slow down its caustic properties. But he had starved himself of human blood, the one blood source he needed the most, and his already over-stressed system couldn't fight this attack. Where once the slashes would have sealed in minutes, they remained open and raw, the salt sending shards of pain throughout his body as he tried to stand.

He had to get out of that building. No matter what happened, he couldn't be found there. He couldn't let Cassie find him there. The feral instinct for survival ever present in every vampire began to move to the forefront. If he could find something to feed from on the street, it might hold him till his body could wash away the salt and begin to knit. That could take days. Right now, he just needed to feed.

The desperate ache of hunger threatened to overtake him and flashes of those horrible nights on the battlefield when he became what he was reminded him of just what depravity he was capable of. His hand smeared the glass door with blood as he opened it, stumbling into the hallway. The lab coat he had grabbed from a coat tree and pressed against his abdomen wound helped staunch some of the blood. In the elevator he allowed himself to succumb to dizziness and lean against the wall, but refused to let his knees buckle. Once down, he wasn't sure if he'd have the strength to get up.

Thoughts of Reg filled Narain's mind as he wiped sweat from his eyes with the back of his bloodied left hand. That hateful wretch whose extreme sense of cruelty now resided in an immortal body of amazing ability! What the hell had he set upon the world decades ago? Yes, it was like the battlefield, where the need of sustenance erased everything from his mind including the horror of sucking dry the corpses of his fellow soldiers. Not all corpses though, some, apparently like Jameson, still living even if only barely, infected by the very thing that had resurrected Narain. A spasm of pain wracked Narain and he staggered to retain his feet. How many others did he unknowingly infect that night in France? How many since then?

The elevator bell announced the lobby and he prayed there'd be no late night visitors waiting when the doors opened. He didn't have the strength to deal with panicked normals. Nor could he be assured that they wouldn't fall victim to the hunger gripping him.

Tripping, he fell to his knees on the hard marble floor, splattering blood from his still leaking wounds. Struggling to his feet, his legs felt leaden as he hurried to the door. Then he noticed the security guard behind the desk. The one who hadn't been there earlier and who now seemed to have taken no notice of the bleeding visitor sprawled in the lobby. Drawing closer to the desk, Narain realised why. Chin resting against his chest, the pudgy guard was tied to the chair, his hands behind his back. Shaking, Narain wondered if the man was dead until he sensed the man's sleep induced respiration and realised why he had been left there. In Narain's current state, losing blood, instincts were sharpening. He could smell the warmth of the man. Feel the pulse of the heart. Narain's eyes glazed over as the hunger began to control him.

The guard was a Judas goat, not necessarily to trap Narain, but to torture him. Reg had no idea whether or not Narain was strong enough to make it out of the building but in case he was, he left him a taste of the temptation that Narain wasn't sure he had the strength to deny. Now the struggle was not only with the loss of blood, but with what he was willing to do to replace that blood. Reg knew it would torment Narain, because it wouldn't affect Reg at all. There'd be no second thought. Reg would feast greedily and move on.

Narain needn't necessarily feast. He leaned against the counter staring at the spot on the guard's neck where the carotid pulsed so vigorously. He could see the slightest thumping of the skin and his own heartbeat slowed to match the rhythm of the guard's. Just enough to carry Narain over until he could obtain another source or make it home. His wounds were on fire. The salt had to be flushed out so he could heal. Just enough…He stopped in horror as he realised that he was easing himself over the desk like a panther ready to pounce. Focused on his objective as he had been, the pain withdrew briefly as the feral came out, but sense slammed back into him and he pushed himself away from the desk with a grimace. In his current state, he would never be able to stop. He would drain the guard just as Reg figured he would. He had to leave now, while he still could.

Twisting, he turned toward the door, jogging toward that freedom, but found himself instead ploughing into Cassie who stared down at him as he lay writhing on the floor.

Chapter 7

"Dear God, Narain!" Cassie exclaimed, crouching beside him and uncertain where to touch him. "What happened?"

"A run in with my past," was all Narain could mumble, agony etched on his face.

Cassie delicately opened his shirt and grimaced at the deep slash on his pectoral muscle and abdomen. "I don't understand. Why haven't they healed?"

Panting, Narain said, "Salt. They won't close."

Rubbing her forehead, Cassie scanned the lobby trying to figure out her next move.

"Okay, think, Cassie," she whispered. She couldn't exactly call an ambulance. He needed blood to heal and right now stored blood was leaking away. She couldn't even be sure if any major organs had been affected by the salt. He needed his wounds flushed and bound but his immediate need was blood. Her eyes widened. There were still units of whole blood in the small refrigerator in her lab. That should help until she could get him somewhere safe.

She tried to ignore his howl of pain as she forced him to his feet and back to the elevator. "Come on, Narain. I have to get you to my lab." With his arm over her shoulder, they entered the elevator and she pushed the button for her lab's floor, then leaned back with him against the wall.

Feeling his weight shift a little, she wondered if he had gotten a second wind, giving her a moment to concentrate on her next move. There were at least three units of blood in the lab. That would hopefully hold him. Cleaning his wounds would be too time-consuming to do there, especially with dawn coming, not to mention early morning members of the staff. They were fortunate they hadn't run into anyone so far. She had no idea how the blood all over the lobby floor was going to be explained away.

With serpentine swiftness, Narain's hand shot forward and jabbed the emergency stop button. Shocked from her thoughts, she glanced at the illuminated floor number before turning her attention to Narain, who now pressed his palms against the panel wall, effectively trapping her between his arms.

"Narain," she said, studying the glazed look in his olive-brown eyes as he studied her face. They seemed distant, almost foreign. Not the eyes she had stared into before on the dance floor and in the small kitchen in the restaurant. They were cold, predatory, yet completely mesmerising as the whites slowly turned red and she said nothing as his face moved closer to hers, his lips tracing down from her left temple to her cheek. They were slightly parted, and she detected a soft scent of cinnamon that spread a warmth over her, flushing her cheeks and leaving her skin tingling. Nothing else existed outside the elevator. Nothing else existed outside their two bodies as his lips trailed down her jaw line toward her neck. She tilted her head, almost invitingly, eyes closing languidly, and she whispered, "Yes," in a breath so soft she wasn't sure if she spoke it out loud. His lips hovered over the tender flesh, his breath warming the spot and it seemed a lifetime that she waited for his kiss.

Rather than pierce her flesh, he roared and pushed himself away from her, collapsing backwards in the corner of the elevator. Clutching himself into a ball, he pounded his right hand on the floor as if that would dampen the much more urgent pain of his starvation. Shaking her head, Cassie snapped out of her trance realising what had just happened. Her neck tingled as if slightly blistered. Restarting the elevator, she turned back to Narain, considering the moment. He had her. She was willing and not simply due to the spell he had woven. Why had he forced himself away from the relief her blood would have brought?

The elevator doors opened and she grabbed his arm, dragging him out. As with the lobby and now the elevator, the floor of her lab was splattered with blood and would draw plenty of attention later on, but she couldn't worry about that now. Rather, she directed Narain to a stool by one of the tables then pulled her keys from her pocket, searching for the key to unlock the refrigerator. Within it were samples, medications, and serums and on one shelf, three units of blood. Grabbing them, Cassie went back to Narain, offering one to him. He was barely cognizant as he scanned the room, eyes wild. She called to him and his focus snapped in her direction, his eyes hooded, dangerous, and still so red.

She was about to explain as she held up the bags of blood, but a part of him understood. He snatched the bag, opening his mouth and allowing the retractable razor sharp teeth concealed behind his canines to protrude. Then he bit down and sucked the bag dry, holding it between his hands like a lion held a hunk of red meat between its paws.

Cassie's eyes widened with fearful fascination as she watched him suck the nourishment from the bag, then she shook off the feeling and gave him the second bag. As he fed, she hurried to a first aid drawer and grabbed a wad of gauze and tape. She couldn't close the wounds, but she might slow the bleeding.

When she returned, sense had returned to him as well and he allowed her to bandage the wounds, holding on to the back of the chair as the pain engulfed him. The wounds still looked fresh and raw when normally they'd be scars by then.

"Narain, are you with me?" She asked, closing his shirt.

Head lolling, all he could groan was, "Somewhat."

"We have to leave now."

He nodded and she grabbed the last unit of blood before putting his arm around her shoulder. She could tell by his spasms that any movement brought fresh pain, but he didn't complain as she led him from the lab and back in the elevator.

"Ah, this looks familiar," he mumbled as they entered and she was grateful that a sense of humour was returning to him, weak as it was.

With him partially fed, the ride down was somewhat less tense than the ride up had been, but she still worried over the blood loss. Already the bandages were blood soaked and until the caustic salt was washed out, the tissue wouldn't knit properly.

"Narain, who did this to you?"

"A ghost from long ago," he said ruefully, his words thick and bitter.

They made it through the lobby and she considered untying the guard but realised it might look better if he was discovered bound. Outside of the climate controlled building the unseasonable humidity hung moistly in the air making Narain seem that much heavier to support. She hurried him as much as she dared through the parking lot, hoping the lot would remain empty long enough for them to leave. Easing him into the back seat, she tried to ignore his gasps of pain, then handed him the last unit of blood.

"One for the road," he quipped weakly.

"Yeah, just don't stain my upholstery," she tried to say jovially, looking up and scanning the lot. All it would take was one person walking by.

Once he was secure, she climbed behind the driver's seat and sped the car from the lot. She'd have to be careful. The last thing they needed was to be pulled over for speeding. During the drive, Narain cried out a few times and the sound bit into her since she was helpless to take away his pain. *Every bump and turn must be agony for him,* she thought, as the creatures within him died and the tissue reverted back to what it should have been. Turning onto 72 she glanced at the dashboard clock, wondering when sun-rise was. In his weakened condition Narain's constitution might find even a little sun detrimental.

"Narain, can you hear me?" He mumbled what she hoped was affirmation. "I have to take you to your home. My place isn't exactly vampire friendly." He chuckled softly and she grinned, not losing the urgency in her voice. "You need to tell me where you live."

He cried out again and a bloody hand gripped the top of the seat. When the spasm eased, he said, "Lake Point Towers."

"Lake Point Towers?" On the lake front! It would take over an hour to get there and would be cutting it extremely close. Increasing her speed would be too risky. She couldn't afford to be pulled over with a bleeding vampire in her car.

Pink trails teased the sky by the time she finally entered the garage of the building that stood alone like a sentinel on the shore of Lake Michigan. It had taken a bit of prodding to get Narain to focus on his password. Now the challenge would be getting him into his building without his condition attracting attention. Making sure no witnesses were in the vicinity, Cassie helped him out of the car after parking in a guest space and eased him into a lab coat she had in the back, wincing as he winced. At one point he had to stop before putting his wounded arm in the sleeve and her heart pounded as he gritted his teeth and summoned his reserve. Once it was on a few dots of blood began to show from his shoulder wound and she hoped they could get to his apartment before more leaked through. She took a tissue from her pocket and wiped away some of the blood that stained his mouth. The last unit had been ingested on the way there and the empty bag now rested on the seat in the back.

After a dreadfully long elevator ride, they made it to his floor with only a few stares from some early morning risers out for a jog or bagel or both, and once inside the apartment she began to relax—somewhat. The dawn was blossoming now outside the bank of his windows and she noticed that his head rose toward it. Pulling away from her, he stumbled over to a light switch which illuminated the apartment when he hit it, then reached a bloodied hand to a button next to it, barely noticeable, which caused thick security blinds to lower slowly over all the windows.

Kneeling on the floor and panting, he said, "Seemed like a good idea to get those," when she crouched beside him. "I miss the sun but not enough to fry for it."

A few drops of blood fell on the floor beneath him and she knew whatever energy the units of blood had bought him was also leaking away.

"Narain, listen to me," she said as his body shivered in pain. "We have to wash as much of the salt out of your wounds as possible, so they'll heal. Some of it might be affecting organ tissue."

Looking toward a hallway near the kitchen, he pointed weakly, murmuring, "The shower is down there."

Good, he was still thinking. "Okay, help me get you there."

His muscles stiffened as she helped him to his feet and they stumbled down the hallway to a large bathroom with a shower compartment separate from the tub. Lying in the tub might be easier for him, but the hand held shower head would make it easier to flush the wounds.

Without a second thought she helped him strip and enter the shower, then un-wrapped the bandages, which by this time were soaked with blood, and threw them in the tub where they landed with a splat of crimson. Just as she had thought, his body was dealing with the salt as a dangerous substance and fighting it as an infection. Nasty, green pus oozed from the wounds indicating tissue damage, and the surrounding area was swollen and raw. She just hoped it wasn't irrevocable and that his body could assimilate whatever salt couldn't be flushed out.

Taking off her shoes, Cassie kicked them to the door, then entered the stall.

"Narain…"

"Do it," he hissed through clenched teeth, shivering, knowing what needed to be done and bracing himself by raising his arms and leaning forward against the wall.

She took the shower head from its holder and started the water, waiting for it to warm. The pectoral and shoulder wounds would need flushing but the abdomen was the most serious. She wasn't sure how deep it was but it was wide and the longer the salt stayed in there, the more tissue died. Shivering herself, she raised the shower head and adjusted it to shoot a constant but low stream of warm water. Then she aimed it at his stomach.

Howling in pain when the water hit, he shoved her roughly away and pounded his fist into the wall, breaking a few tiles. Cassie fell sideways hitting the stall's metal frame and cutting her scalp slightly. A thin stream of blood trailed down from the cut as he shook her. Looking up, adrenaline coursed through her as she saw Narain standing over her, the feral-red look in his eyes. The pain was bringing out his base survival instincts just as it had earlier. Standing she faced him squarely, detecting that seductive cinnamon scent again from his mouth. She wouldn't give in to it. Slapping his face hard, she ordered, "You stay with me, Narain. Stay with me!" Then she slapped him again.

She raised her hand a third time but he grabbed it and the light seemed to return to his gaze. Reaching out, he wiped the blood from her forehead with his thumb, his brow furrowing, then he shook his head and released her hand.

"Give me a towel," he ordered flatly and she grabbed a hand towel from a rod near the sink. "The neighbours will think I'm being butchered." Shaking, he put his palm on her cheek softening his expression before saying, "Okay, try again." Then he stuffed the hand towel in his mouth resuming his previous position. This time, when the water met his wound, he struggled not to flinch away, his cries muffled in the towel, but he remained in place while the job was done.

When she felt she had flushed out his abdomen wound as best as possible, she worked on the less serious, yet still nasty, pectoral and shoulder wounds. The blood pooled in the drain at Narain's feet until the water finally ran clear. Blood seeped from the wounds slightly, but nothing to the extent that it had and Cassie took that as a sign that the undamaged tissue was beginning to knit as normal.

Narain's face was beginning to look clearer as well. Allowing herself to relax a bit, she realised that her head was throbbing and remembered the fall she'd taken. That could be attended to after. For now, the vampire had to lie still.

"I don't suppose you have any bandages."

"No need," he groaned hoarsely grabbing the bath towel she handed him. "Or at least there's never been much need before."

Sighing, she said, "Can you dry yourself?" He nodded weakly. "Good. As impressive as it all is, I think I've seen quite enough of your anatomy for one night," and she found herself trying to focus on everything but him as she rummaged around the cabinets.

As if finally regaining consciousness, he blinked realising that he was standing naked in front of her. Oddly bashful, he cleared his throat, quickly wrapping the towel around his waist, careful to avoid contact with the still open wound. He studied it, asking,

"Will paper towels do?"

She looked up at him and started laughing. "It's a good thing you're a chef and not a surgeon."

A sheepish grin crossed his haggard face as he shrugged. "It's been many, many decades since I last needed a surgeon."

His eyes lost their focus and she could see his knees failing him. Directing him to the tub, she instructed him to sit on the side of it. He did so, putting his head in his hands. He was better, but not out of the woods yet. "Okay, I'm sure you still have some salt in you that we couldn't flush, not to mention the tissue damage inside. They're going to have to deal with that. But you've lost a tremendous amount of blood. I can get you more."

His head shot up and he stared at her. "What? How?"

"I can have a connection with a blood bank through my research. But you're going to need to be quiet and still and let your tissue heal and let them build back up."

His head fell forward again, as he was nearing his last bit of strength. "The still and quiet part shouldn't be a problem." His words were becoming thick. "But I need to ask you..." he moved his hand out in front of him, "All this...how...did you..."

"First things first, Narain," she said, helping him to his feet. "You need sleep. A lot of it."

She followed his directions to his room and noted that inside, the blinds were sealed as securely as they were in the rest of the apartment. Narain's room housed a king-size bed with a set of burgundy cotton sheets covered by a matching comforter. The four poster bed was cherry wood, as were the tall and long dressers against the wall. The walls were painted a light Hunter Green. As she directed him to the bed, she wondered if he picked that colour for healing properties. Despite what she knew, it seemed an incongruous thing to be helping a vampire into a soft bed. As he lay back, his body tensed before relaxing slightly, the wounds still bleeding slightly.

Taking her arm, he said, eyes closed, "In my kitchen, lower left drawer near the refrigerator, there are needles and thread." Opening his eyes, he noted her look. "It never hurts to be prepared. Once I wasn't and it nearly cost me a thumb. I learned after that."

In the kitchen, Cassie found the drawer he referred to and by the time she returned to his room, he had passed out. *For the best*, she thought. Though, remembering the shower incident, there was a moment's hesitation before she stuck the needle into his flesh. Thankfully, he remained unconscious and she was able to suture his wounds within ten minutes, despite the fact that it was a bit like stitching leather. It would definitely help his wounds close and heal faster. When she was finished, she took a few moments to stare at his sleeping face. Only weeks ago, she had danced with him at a charity function. Now she was stitching up his wounds.

Stretching her arms up toward the ceiling, Cassie yawned then returned her gaze to his face. Her day was far from over. She would need to get that blood. He would be hungry and would need to replenish the blood. Then there was the mess left at the lab. If it hadn't been discovered yet, it would be shortly. A wave of guilt overcame her as she studied his face and she looked away sadly.

It had been a clinical fascination that drew her to him initially. Several months before the benefit, she had seen Narain Khan on a local news show as he was interviewed briefly in his restaurant and she nearly fell out of her chair. It was him! The man from the photos. Aside from the modern dress, however, he looked exactly the same. The high arched brows, the full lips, the nose, a bit large yet that gave his face a leonine quality. Of course she knew how it was possible for it to be the same man as the man in the photo, but she couldn't help but marvel at a planet so small that it would enable their paths to cross. She decided then which restaurant would be catering the Reach for the Cure benefit if only to have a more plausible excuse to approach him.

Meet him. Get to know him.

She never imagined the sort of sparks that would fly when they gazed into each other's eyes, or the warmth she would feel as he held her close on the dance floor. He was, at first, merely a piece to a very strange puzzle.

She never thought she'd end up falling in love with him.

What had she done? What had she been thinking to involve him? Of course how could she have known that there was history between him and Jameson. But for the sake of one flat tire, she could have gotten there in time to avoid this and perhaps all could have gone to plan. Adjusting the comforter over him, she bent forward and lightly brushed Narain's lips with her own detecting the still noticeable scent of cinnamon upon them; an automatic response, perhaps, from his current need for sustenance. She knew when she had recognised him at the gala, and they had danced, that this wouldn't be a simple thing. She never realised just how difficult it would be, but then she never imagined that the ghosts from his past would still haunt him. Her hand lingered on his forehead before she finally pulled it away, smiling ironically. She'd been so focused on the getting of him she never once gave a thought to what would occur once she had him. She knew one thing – she couldn't be here when he woke up. Brushing his hair back, she bent down and lightly kissed his forehead, then reluctantly turned and left the room.

Chapter 8

Narain raised his eyes carefully, staring at the body-strewn field known as "No Man's Land" lodged between the trench systems of the Allied and the Central Powers. Bird song could be heard in the distance, as could the groans of those men still alive and suffering from their injuries. The air was thick with the stench of gunpowder from that day's raid on the German line, as twilight closed cruelly over them. Narain's head throbbed and his arm had gone numb from lying on it while unconscious. The shrapnel from the mortar rounds found its mark, slicing deeply into his right side and left thigh and yet, he had felt nothing as he fell; barely felt the impact of the ground. Regaining consciousness, he lay face down on the cold, moist ground, the pain of unattended wounds causing his body to contract before the wave slowly passed to a dull, sickening throb in leg and stomach. The commotion of the push over the top had quieted now. There were neither shots nor mortar blasts, just the cries of his fellow soldiers who had streamed over the trenches and the enemy soldiers who raced out to meet them. In a variety of languages, they begged for water or relief. Many begged for death. Raising his head slightly, Narain looked around, trying to get his bearings, which seemed impossible in that featureless landscape of craters and the mounds of dirt blown from them. He tried to get to his hands and knees knowing that there was still danger of sniper fire if he should stand and make too large a target. It was as he groaned and lifted his fevered body that he saw it: a figure, shadowy and strange, threading its way through the bodies. To his right he caught a glimpse of another, and another following behind that. Shivering, Narain willed himself to be still, squinting as he tried to make out what they were. They were humanoid, but they moved with a terrifying grace, not the dazed agony of desperate soldiers. Like jackals, slunk low to the ground, they investigated the bodies they came across and, to Narain's silent horror, fell upon some of them. He counted nine; there may have been more, and what he thought was initially the robbing of the dead turned out to be something much more sinister.

Narain's blood froze as one scrounged by a body near him. Vivek, staring lifelessly, was an arm's length away when one of the creatures began to nose around his body. Easing back onto his stomach, Narain tried to control his increasing panic as the being moved on to the next body. Private Charlie Perkins was not far and Narain could see by the shallow rising of his chest that he was still alive. The creature, up close, was noticeably human but strangely grey, as if all the blood had been drained from him. His head looked slightly mis-shapen, especially around his jaw, as if his mouth wasn't large enough to hold the teeth within it, and his clothes seemed to be rotting off his body. Perhaps he was a poor peasant made homeless and desperate by the vicious war, now hoping to make some money by stealing the effects of the dead.

It is very possible he once was.

But as he lurked around the bodies near Narain that night, the creature was something more. He had crouched near Vivek's cold body briefly, but turned up his nose in disgust. He focused instead on the still breathing Perkins who was beginning to regain consciousness.

"Don't awaken!" Narain mouthed the words, but Perkin's eyes opened as he weakly raised a hand to his temple.

With a squealing growl, the creature dived toward his throat and Perkins screamed, struggling pathetically, unable to dislodge him. Briefly, the creature raised his head, a slightly elongated tongue reaching out to lick the dripping blood from the sides of this mouth. Then he moved back in and reattached himself, Perkins's pointless struggles growing weaker until his arms fell to the ground and he remained still.

Narain's mind was ablaze at the sight of this cannibalism. Swallowing the bile rising in his throat, he tried to take advantage of the fact that the creature's attention was lost in the blood lust and squirmed away from the scene, desperately praying not to attract attention. He had to get away from the horrible sight, the awful wet sucking sound, and the creature's unnerving purrs of contentment.

He passed the bodies of men he had served with; Fred Blythe, Sunil Patel, Captain Reginald Jameson. Half conscious, the captain, face streaked red with blood, reached out to Narain but made no sound. When he felt it safe, Narain took the chance to go from squirming to crawling.

In the distance, he could see the entrance to a forest which stood untouched by the brutalities of modern warfare. It might offer better cover from these beasts or could offer no safety at all. Narain couldn't be sure. He was just certain that he wanted to get away from the fresh brutality happening on the field, already soaked with gore. His own wounds throbbing mercilessly, his mind hot with fever, he decided make a dash for the trees.

He never made it.

✝

Eyes flashed silver in the half moonlight of a cloudless sky.

Mouths watering instantly, there was little hesitation to the wolf pack's scavenging, despite a strange feeling to the clearing; a haunted energy, that raised their hackles a bit. As each one loped onto the field, they took a quick swipe from a nearby body. It was indeed a feast with enough to fill every wolf's belly, so all were allowed to feed as equals with no squabbles over meat. Still in an instinctual understanding for the need to show dominance, the alpha male sauntered from feeding party to feeding party to chase the feeders away before taking a few bites and moving on.

A few of the humans were still alive and groaned pitifully until a fierce ripping of their throats silence them. The fact was that never had the pack eaten so well with so little effort and more than likely never would they have the chance to again.

Still, the field made the leader uncomfortable. There was nothing to fear from the humans scattered around. Even those still groaning didn't possess the strength to pose a threat. He looked at his mate who seemed as uncertain as he was, but they were both too much the opportunists not to take advantage of this lucky find.

A two-year-old raised his head from the shoulder he was gnawing on and yawned. Deciding to sample other dishes, the impulsive fearlessness of youth led to a reckless curiosity that encouraged him to ignore the very same disquieting energy that was making the alpha couple so nervous. While the alpha male might have sensed it, the two-year-old was oblivious to the pair of eyes staring at him hungrily. As he sniffed around three bodies that had seemingly fallen atop each other, the two-year-old was certainly not prepared for what came next.

The yelp of surprise echoed across the field and then there was silence. Raising his head, the alpha male stood stiffly, staring ahead, his ears tuned to any other noises of distress. Licking at his blood-soaked muzzle he sneezed, then walked forward a few paces. The others had heard it too and were testing the air for any foreign scent. He did as well, but all he picked up was the scent of his pack and the delicious meat dotting the field. There was something, though. That strange energy that had been teasing his fight or flight response ever since.

The other wolves went back to their feeding, but the alpha male sauntered on, taking a mental note of each adult he went past. There was one missing. One that had seen only two winters. He moved in the direction the yelp seemed to come from and soon picked up the scent of the two-year-old.

There were disturbing areas to this field that made his hackles rise, as had some of the dry bodies he'd turned away from. Very little frightened him in the forest, but this field terrified him the longer he stayed in it.

Stopping short of a strange pile of bodies, he picked up the scent that indicated the two-year-old had gone closer to it, but a quick circle around the perimeter indicated that the younger wolf never left. The alpha male stood before the pile, staring at it, an occasional soft growl disturbing his panting. Body stiffened, his ears moving back, his lips pulled back in a toothy snarl, but his tail dropped low till it went between his legs as terror swept over him.

Slowly he began to back away, growling what he knew was a futile warning. Releasing a few barks, he turned tail and ran toward the others indicating beyond question that the feast was over. His mate, understanding, rounded up those nearest her, herding them toward the forest. A few of the wolves were reluctant to leave, but the alpha male backed up his insistence with some well-placed nips. Wolves began to follow, ripping a last morsel or grabbing an arm or leg to bring back with them to the den. Once the field was cleared of wolves, the alpha male halted, taking one last look at the scene, torn between the meat that would feed his pack and the danger he knew was there. He would lead the pack far away and never return to this field. Let the rodents and carrion birds feast on the meat and whatever danger resided within.

†

The three bodies piled atop each other began to shift slightly. The sweet coolness of night beckoned and Narain at last felt safe enough to emerge from his grave, hastily dug in desperation the day after the raid by the creatures. As time passed in his near death stupor and morning turned into afternoon, the change occurring within him made the growing sunlight increasingly unbearable. The guns had silenced, but war was waging inside him, worse than any fever he'd ever known. It burned through his veins, the thirst torturous, but the water he lapped from a muddy puddle nearby did nothing to quench it. Eventually he began to dig into the cool earth fuelled by a sheer instinct for survival.

Why hadn't he died when the creature fell upon him? It leapt upon his back and nothing he did could dislodge it. The pain was astonishingly brief as teeth pierced the flesh of his neck and his life's blood was drained from him. The loss of blood and exposure should have killed him, but Narain remained tenaciously alive, in a strange fugue, listening as those soldiers still alive begged for water or death.

That was the true cruelty of war. Soldiers would linger in pain and misery for days before it was safe for stretcher bearers to cross safely into "No Man's Land" or death at last released them.

Digging ferociously, Narain had hollowed out a rut deep enough for him to conceal himself. Then he grabbed three of his fellow soldiers and managed to manoeuvre the corpses on top of him hoping to block out the full effect of the sun. Already the battlefield was heavy with the stench of rotting flesh, but there was also the tang of blood in the air and for some strange reason he took comfort in that.

He was certain he was going mad. He blacked out occasionally and when he awoke he could never fully clear his mind. Nothing made sense. If he had the strength to dig, he had the strength to run, so he should be running to find help. But something deep inside screamed to him to stay put. And the fever continued, sending a fire through him that made his skin crawl.

A few times he awoke noticing that he clutched in his hand a mouse, sometimes a rat, always mangled, blood caking his hands. The last time he noticed it a queer smile lit his face. Locked beneath a canopy of corpses in the grave he dug for himself he was subsisting on rodents.

Then he heard the wolves and caught the scent of fresh blood as they bit into still living soldiers. The wolves' own hearts beating over the excitement of their plunder resonated within him.

One came sniffing around his den. The wolf was young, healthy and Narain could feel the animal's warmth calling to him. "Closer," he whispered, as he carefully moved a soldier's arm to get a better look.

The back of his head began to tingle and soon he could feel a swelling heat in his brain as the wolf came ever closer to the odd pile of bodies. Then, Narain struck, reaching out from under the corpses and grabbing the wolf so fast that all it had time to do was yelp before he snapped its neck. He sensed another on the way and froze. This wolf, however, larger and older, knew better, leaving quickly after a few moments of puzzling out the situation. The pack followed his orders and left the battlefield to the dead and dying.

Narain ripped at the animal's neck with teeth not yet suited for such endeavours until he remembered the army issued knife he wore and slashed into the thick coat. The wolf blood filled his empty stomach and the energy coursed through him, yet he was still in need, so crawling from his hole, he wandered the battlefield. The sentient part of him retreated to allow the feral part to take over and do what was necessary to keep him alive.

He took his knife and slashed at the neck of a nearby corpse, falling upon it and dragging out whatever he could get. Switching tactics on the next corpse, he slashed at the section where the blood had pooled finding the feeding much easier.

Still, his changing body craved nourishment that could not be found in the blood of animals or the cold blood of the dead. Slowly he ran a steely gaze through the field in the hopes of detecting the heat of the living. The sentient mind, buried deeply, rationalised his next move. These soldiers were dying in agony. He would help make the inevitable quick and painless.

The feral mind needed no rationalisation urging him forward. One soldier breathed but was barely conscious. One soldier's eyes were wide and glazed with shock, which made him nearly senseless. Another had been writhing in pain since shrapnel shredded his legs and they were now swollen and infected, the tattered fabric of his uniform glued to them by the blood and pus of his wounds. He called Narain an angel of mercy, smiling as Narain slit his throat. This struck sharply at Narain's sentient mind until his feral mind overruled him and he drank desperately.

He spent the night doing what needed to be done until he had satiated his need and was able to climb back into his hole. By the third night, however, as the fever that had gripped him abated, and the pain of his own wounds was long gone, the true horror of it all struck him. While in his blood lust, he had been able to render faceless his fellow soldiers. His victims. Now, he was haunted by the blood that coursed through him keeping him alive. Their essence taunted him with their agony and fear. He writhed in his grave as the full realisation of what he'd become assaulted him.

The creature that had attacked him with its ghostly sunken features had lifeless eyes, its mouth grizzly with serrated, blood-stained teeth that dripped with the gore of its previous victims. It was a mindless thing and fed mindlessly. The thought of himself, running with those ghouls, ripped at Narain's mind. Climbing out of his trench, he fell to his knees and cursed at the sky. Why had he not fallen completely into the madness that would lead him to feed upon his fellow beings? Did these ghouls remember their crimes? Did they carry their victims with them as he now feared he would?

Rising to his feet, Narain walked slowly toward the forest. He would head east. Instinctively, he knew that when the sun was high enough it would finish him and the nightmare that threatened his world would end. He left the battlefield and its charnel house smell behind him and prepared for the death that should have occurred two days before.

✝

Miles away, the rising sun shone softly through the trees and Narain sought out a clearing where it would not be hindered by them. In the distance, he heard the muffled sounds of mortars being fired; more food for the ghouls. When he found the right spot, he raised his hands to the sun's fatal rays, but the will to survive, heightened now by what he had become, was too strong and it drove him to shun the light. It would not yet destroy him, but it would sicken him beyond all comprehension, if he remained within its rays. He slunk back into the shade of the forest and furiously burrowed deep within the protective earth. Huddled there, panting, he felt the war tearing at his mind. The sentient mind wanted an end to this *unnatural existence. Yet, it was the unnatural existence keeping him alive.*

Narain awoke to the face of a bearded old man gazing down upon him. A candle blazed on the table next to his bed, and two candelabras were placed on the mantle of a currently unused fireplace off to the left. Turning his head slightly, he saw a candelabra on a long dresser. The man stood over him, wiping at his forehead with a damp cloth, then smiled when he noticed that his patient was now conscious.

"Are you awake?" he said in a deep, dry voice.

Narain blinked, his head still fuzzy, and nodded. The bed was soft and warm, a comfort he hadn't experienced in quite some time, and sleep threatened to retake him.

"I am assuming then, that English would be easiest for you." Narain nodded again, noting the French accent that shaded the man's words. "No other languages?"

"Bengali, Hindi, if you are able," Narain croaked.

The old man chuckled and placed the cloth in a pot of water. "Let us count our blessings that we both share English." After a pause, the old man studied his face, saying, "Answer this next question very carefully. What is your name?"

The man asked this with such import, that Narain actually felt nervous about his response. He had never met the man before, he was certain of it, but the man seemed to stare at him with a familiarity that was confusing. Blinking and looking around the room, Narain licked dry lips saying, "Khan. Narain Khan. Private in the Indian Army." He felt it almost necessary to continue to elaborate. "My father is Mohan Khan, my mother is Preity. They live in Bengal."

The man placed a hand on Narain's shoulder. "Well done, son. There will be time for all that."

The man went to a pitcher and poured some water in a metal mug. "You were quite feral when I found you. I had hoped you would come to your senses, but you can never be too sure."

He offered the mug to Narain who took it gratefully and drained it, the liquid quenching the raspiness of his mouth and throat. His whole body felt brittle. Even his eyelids were sticky as he raised a hand to rub them. The water, while it helped, left him strangely unsatisfied.

The old man refilled the mug, offering it to Narain, who refused it politely. Setting it on the table, he stared at his patient, scratching at his grey beard, and commented, "You were involved in quite a battle."

Brows furrowing, Narain acknowledged slowly, "Yes. Yes I was." He had almost, happily, forgotten the battlefield. Even now it seemed like a different life. Rubbing his face, he asked, "How long have I been here?"

"Close to two weeks." Narain's face registered shock and the old man explained, "I found you wandering the forest. I knew the war had crept into the area so, I suppose I was not so surprised to see a soldier wandering in shock. I took you to my estate. My name, by the way, is Alphonse Reno."

"I am Narain Khan."

Alphonse chuckled, "Yes, so you have told me," and Narain returned his smile. "Well, young man, if you are able, I will leave you to freshen up." He pointed to a small room.

"There are facilities in there." He moved over to a chifferobe. "And a change of clothes in here."

Rising carefully to lean on his elbow, Narain said, "I don't know how to thank you for your kindness."

The gentle smile seemed slightly melancholy. "Gratitude is not necessary. When you are ready, come downstairs. We will talk."

After a pause, the man exited leaving Narain to stare after, confused. The man's demeanour was pleasant enough, and yet there was a touch of dread. Like a doctor telling a soldier that the leg must be amputated.

Running his hands through his hair, Narain raised his knees and rested his arms on them. He was only a short time away from the battlefield, but it seemed a whole life time ago. He remembered so little of it all. The fighting itself, the explosions, the cries for help. The blood and dirt spraying everywhere. He knew it had occurred, but it was little more than a nightmare to him now.

Wandering the woods, though, he had no memory of this. Of course, if he had been in shock, he might have blocked it all out. Perhaps talking to the old man would jog his memory.

The room was curious. There were large windows, but they had been boarded up from the outside so that opening the inside shutters would produce no light at all. He had no idea what time it was, whether it was day or night. Night seemed most likely and for some strange reason, the most desirable.

Still a bit stiff, he made his way into the washroom. It was obvious he had already been bathed and he could only imagine how grimy he must have been when he arrived. The dirt and gore of the battlefield had been cleansed from him and even his thick black hair felt cleaner than it had in a long time. It had been so long since he felt warm and clean. From the boat to the trenches to the battlefield he seemed to always feel chilled and filthy. The sun of India had seemed so far away. Narain found Alphonse in a large library/study downstairs tending to a fire in the sizeable fireplace. It seemed to be a large house, several guest rooms upstairs, and downstairs an impressive dining room, living room and kitchen; like the rest of what he'd seen, the heavy velvet drapes of the study were closed, the room well illuminated by candles haphazardly placed around it. Was the man's skin sensitive to light? Narain had heard of rare cases of this. Taking the chance, Narain had lifted one of the drapes he'd seen in the dining room, but his earlier conclusion had been correct. It was deep into the night and the surrounding acreage was practically invisible in the dark. Still, oddly, he thought for certain that he had seen something. Small woodland creatures, eyes glowing, were scuttling about in the dark.

Looking up, the old man smiled in greeting from his chair and motioned Narain to sit in a straight backed but comfortable chair near the fire. "I must say you look a far sight better than when I found you," he said as Narain took the seat.

At last, Narain said softly, "Sir, I don't know how to thank you for your kindness."

"Never mind that," Alphonse assured him. Studying him, he commented, "You are a very long way from home, are you not?" Narain conceded this with a wistful nod and the old man went back to tending his fire, sighing sadly. "My God, what you boys have given up to counter this awful aggression."

The man seemed to be carrying a burden that weighed upon what would normally be a very jovial disposition.

Shrugging, Narain chuckled softly. "Well, I myself have never liked a bully. If I can help in any way to put Germany in its place, I suppose it is worth the sacrifice." The man said nothing, only stared at him as if he had news to impart but couldn't find the words. Blinking, after several moments of silence, Narain cleared his throat saying, "I think I will have to find a way to contact my regiment tomorrow."

This declaration forced the issue and Alphonse took a seat across from Narain, gently saying, "Narain, my boy, I need to explain something to you. It will seem strange and very difficult to hear, but you must listen carefully for your life as you knew it, no longer exists."

Narain stared at him, frowning slightly. What a curiously ominous thing to say. Perhaps the old man was a bit senile. Yet his stomach began to churn a little as flashes began to batter the back of his mind. Strange visions of darkness and pain and a hunger he'd never experienced before. Tensing, Narain's brows furrowed. He would hear the man out. The old man had, after all, saved his life. And after his time in the trenches, it was true, his life would never be the same. "What is it you mean?"

Alphonse looked down at his hands which were clasped together almost as if in prayer. "Bear with me, dear boy. It is a difficult story. It will be difficult for both of us. I only wish I had another to tell you." Narain's brows remained furrowed at the pain the man was obviously experiencing in his memories as he turned his gaze to the fire. Narain had known him only a short time, but he could tell instinctively that he was a good person. A disquieting thought hit him that Alphonse's words were not those of a senile old man, but rather the words of experience.

"I had a son, you see," Alphonse began slowly smiling slightly at the memory of a child long gone. "He would be near your age. Everything a father would hope for. I have a daughter too, she is married and far from here. My wife is long passed. What a woman she was! Beautiful. Full of courage and passion. What a proud man I was. Yet, with my wife gone, my daughter off on her new life, I had only my son left to keep me company. How strong is the bond between fathers and sons?"

"Very strong," Narain said, thinking of his own father so far away.

Alphonse smiled. "His name was Laurent, my son. I had sent him with a friend to town to conduct some simple business. It should have lasted a few days at best, but he did not return." Alphonse's features drooped. "His friend came back leading Laurent's horse, Laurent's body draped across it." The old man's eyes bleared a bit as he looked at Narain. "I ask you now, son, please keep your mind open. It is imperative to understand this story." Pausing, he sighed deeply and began, "I had heard of the folk tales; they abound in this country especially among the uneducated, but they were just that: Tales to frighten the weak of heart. Until my son was brought back to me. His friend needed to stay in town a bit longer, but assured him he would join him on the trail. His friend found Laurent a day later, his body cold and mangled." Alphonse shook his head. "I don't know, perhaps the creatures sensed the war that was on its way. They had been dormant for so long. They follow brutality and bloodshed, you see, dining on fallen soldiers and anyone else that happens to be in their path. Like my son."

Narain leaned forward, curious despite incredulity. "Creatures? What creatures do you refer to, sir? Wolves?"

Alphonse admitted, "I hesitate to use the word for you will think me mad and will shut your mind to all that I have to tell you." Narain indicated his willingness to listen and Alphonse said, "I refer to vampires." To Narain's blinking surprise, he insisted, "Yes, they exist. I was as doubtful as you are, but my eyes have been opened.

"Still, despite the signs, I could not accept what had killed my son. How could I? Obviously some maniac had fallen upon him and had committed some sort of twisted cannibalism. I buried him in our family cemetery, never noticing the shallow breaths or the faintest of pulses.

"A few days later, one of my farm hands told me that he had found a dead pig. It had been dragged from the pen and the throat was torn open. Wolves had not been sighted in the area for quite some time. That night we lost another pig and two days later the remnants of several chickens were found.

"So I decided to stay up one night in the hopes that I could discover the animal prowling around the livestock. I positioned my farm hand at the pig sty while I found a spot at the stables in case the beast had an appetite for larger fare. Then I waited.

"Several hours went by when I heard a shout, then a horrible gurgling scream and the squealing of a pig."

The man became lost in his memories as he continued, "The sound of it chilled me. At last, I forced myself to run, lantern in hand, to the pig sty. There, I saw someone hunched over my hired hand, Jorge, who was lying on the ground, weakly struggling to push off his attacker. I shouted out to him but the man never looked up. I ran toward him, cursing and flailing the lantern. That got his attention. He raised his head, mouth red with gore, and fixed his eyes on me."

Alphonse stopped as if he needed to catch his breath and Narain gently said, "It was your son."

The old man nodded, sighed and rubbed his face as if trying to rub out the grief. "Those eyes that I had once gazed into with such pride and joy now glowed an eerie red in the lamplight. Were it not for that glow they would have been cold and lifeless. There was neither love nor hate. I was simply something disturbing his feed. Something he might go after next should the victim he was working on not quench his thirst. I ran toward him again, swinging the lantern this time as a weapon. My son, filthy with blood and the dirt of his own grave, snarled in fright and darted off into the night with amazing speed."

"He brought down your hand. Why did he run from you?"

Alphonse shrugged. "I have asked that so many times. Was it the slightest recognition that kept him from attacking me? Or, alone, without a pack, did he fear he was no contest for me, despite the fact that he could have ripped me apart. Some of the fiercest predators may back down in a surprise confrontation. And at that point, that is all my son was. A predator.

"Jorge was dead. I testified to seeing a huge creature—a wolf or perhaps a bear, running from the body. I hated to lie, but perhaps that was what people needed to hear since none of the other help or members of the family questioned why there were no animal tracks near the body. They were simple people, people of the land and woods who knew the legends and preferred not to dwell on them too long.

"Those legends whirled around my mind as, two days later, I went to my son's grave and noted the freshly turned earth and the caved-in hole from a body working its way out. I never saw Laurent again. He might be out there right now, hunting with the pack that attacked the soldiers on the battlefield weeks ago."

Narain had found himself transfixed by the old man's story, unable to decide just what he thought of it. Mention of the battlefield stunned him, however and a sickening feeling overcame him. "What is your meaning? I don't understand why you share this story with me."

Carefully, Alphonse said, "My boy, I think you do. And it is vital that you understand and accept it. It is your only choice to accept who you are now."

The words were spoken with such a lid-slamming certainty that Narain was stunned into silence. Images gripped him as the words began to hit home. He looked up at the old man's gentle face, then back down at the floor glowing in the fire light. In his mind, wolves and ghouls danced among the dead and dying on a blood-soaked field, ripping at throats, slurping the gore. And he was right there with them, joyous in the blood that slipped down his throat, fortifying a body that seemed no longer his to command.

The shrapnel! Leaping to his feet, Narain's chair slid back noisily as he clawed at his shirt, ripping it open. The shrapnel had sliced into him on the battlefield, leaving him breathless with pain. It wasn't clear before, but it was only too clear now. Yet, when he looked at his side he saw only the remnants of a long healed scar, the knitting skin thick beneath his fingers. He hadn't remembered the injury earlier in the bath, but he did now and he knew for certain that it had been deep enough not to have healed so quickly in a matter of weeks. His legs buckled as he reached out for the chair. The old man rose quickly and helped him to sit. Looking up at Alphonse, horrified, all he could say was a pleading, "No."

"I am so very sorry, son. I can only imagine how painful the memories are." Narain stared into the fire. He remembered now. The ghoul that pounced on him, bit deeply into him, sucked him nearly dry. He remembered how desperately, painfully, his heart beat as the blood left him and then darkness overtook him. Then, he remembered the pile of bodies he hid beneath. The rodents and wolf and later the forays among wounded soldiers calling for comfort. And the hideous fever transforming him. What he had become now had a name and it was horrible. He had wanted to die. Why hadn't the old man let him?

As if sensing the question, Alphonse explained, "I came upon you digging yourself furiously into the earth. Not far from here. You were raving, desperate to escape the sun, the light of which will only pain you more as time goes on. I gathered you up and took you to my estate, because there was something there that made me think you might be a sentient."

"A sentient?" Narain mumbled dumbly, still staring into the fire.

"The loss of my son," the old man said, "has led me on a quest to understand what I saw that night. I have always considered myself a man of reason, not given to being influenced by superstition and folk tales. But life has a way of challenging devout beliefs. Even the day after I chased my son from his home, I warred with myself. But a man knows his own son. And if a father's grief causes hallucinations, he sees his son clean and whole, not the filthy, broken thing hunched over a hired hand's body. So, my son had become the stuff of legends and according to the legends he was as lost to me as if he were still cold in the ground. He was now little more than a beast, like the other vampires whispered about, capable of no other thoughts beyond the next meal. These beings I have taken to calling "ferals" for that is what they are. Mindless. Living on instinct. Wild."

"But life had another surprise in store for me. One that offered the faintest glimmer of hope. A week later, I found myself staring into the fire so lost in thoughts and memories that I did not hear the scraping at the door until it turned into an erratic pounding. What I saw when I opened it…well I thought for a moment I was losing my mind." He chuckled and poured himself a drink from a stand near the fire.

"Eh, sometimes I think I have gone mad. I wonder sometimes if I'm locked in my own mind and this is all a dream."

Turning his gaze from the fire at last, Narain asked, "What did you see?"

"Jorge. My hired-hand who I had watched being placed in the ground days before. He was as filthy and blood stained as my son had been, but the eyes that met mine were of a different sort. They knew me. The horrible thought that someone might have met their end that night crossed my mind, but judging by the fear and confusion on Jorge's face, I knew it was just as likely that his only victims were pigs and sheep whose bodies would be discovered the next day.

"Jorge was disorientated. He had clawed his way out of the earth and fed and now his human consciousness was returning to him. He came back to my door hoping I could give him some answers. Unfortunately, I had very few to offer him. I told him what had transpired over the past week. That by rights he should still be in the ground. And I offered my theory on why he was not."

Coming out of his stupor slowly, Narain grinned weakly. "I dare say that your technique for imparting this news has improved since then."

The old man laughed heartily. "Yes, well, I have had practice. But Jorge was only the second of the vampire set that I had seen and the first one was heartbreakingly beyond my reach to communicate with. This ultimately led me to take up my mission. Why had my son, the man who had 'killed' Jorge, been unable to progress beyond the creature that I saw that first night? Yes, the other questions were important. What created them? And particularly important to Jorge, what would he actually need to survive? But if I could discover why Jorge, why you, retained humanity, perhaps I could find a way to bring my son back to me."

Anxiously, Narain stared at his hands, finding nothing different about them and yet feeling as though they were very different. As if he was very different from the young man who left India the year before. And of course, he was. This war had taken so much from him but he couldn't reconcile with just how much had been lost. A wave of panicked desperation washed over him again and he exclaimed, "I don't understand. Why do I feel so…normal? Why do I feel like myself? None of this makes sense. I should be dead, I should have died on that field." He turned a helpless gaze to the old man. "Why am I not dead?"

A tear played at the corner of Alphonse's right eye. He closed his eyes to let the emotion pass over him. Then he reached out and touched Narain's hand gently, explaining, "I became an investigator and Jorge my subject and together we came up with plausible theories based on my research and his experience. You, my boy, are sentient. There seem to be two types of vampire. Sentient and feral. The ferals are what may have attacked you on the battlefield. You, and others like you, are sentient. Capable of everyday intellect. Capable of some semblance of your old life.

"We studied the human body, Jorge and I. I travelled abroad, more so than I had ever done before, collecting stories and legends from other cultures. I questioned medical doctors on the possibilities of vampirism—true vampirism as opposed to the legends told of it—and suffered their bemused replies. Most humoured me. Some were downright arrogant. And how could I blame them? It went against everything known about nature. And medical science had never had a specimen to study though, oddly, vampire legends appear in cultures around the world. Even in your own India.

"I told this last point to Jorge and he suggested that he might be that specimen, but I warned against this. We are incredibly cruel to that which we do not understand. I feared even the logic of doctors would not keep them from going too far. Besides, to the outside world, Jorge was now a demon. The undead. A monster. Society would never have accepted the truth."

"And what is the truth?" Narain asked, sadly, his horrible recollections forcing him to accept the awful truth. "Are we not monsters doomed to feed upon humans to survive?"

Alphonse sighed before a bit of passion rose up within him. "You are victims of circumstance. In fact, I believe this condition has a medical, not a supernatural, answer to it. It is beyond us now, but progress never stops and one day the answer will be there. You have a chronic condition. A bizarre one, but one you will have to adjust for. You have something, however, that my son did not. You have the ability to make choices. And it is those choices that prove whether you are a monster or not."

"And what became of Jorge?"

"One thing you will discover is that while this condition has limited you in some ways, it has freed you in a whole host of others. There was a time when his imagination never went further than the boundaries of this estate. Helping me as much as he could with my research, Jorge eventually found himself willing to test those boundaries. Apparently, his constitution has become quite durable. He has the curiosity of youth in a seemingly ageless body. And he still sends me details he feels might be important to my research, including the seamier details of what he must to do survive. From what we can gather, it is possible to survive for a time on animal blood, horse blood being particularly potent, but at some point, human blood is necessary. The others have confirmed this."

"Others?"

The old man paused, and then nodded. "Every so often, I go on… expeditions."

"Searching for your son?"

"Yes. A father never loses hope. As I have said, this stupid war has coaxed the ferals from their hibernation. Occasionally they leave survivors. Newborns as confused as you were. How can I not help them, especially when my son could be the one responsible for their infection? Like Jorge."

"And everything you learn, hopefully brings you closer to bringing back your son."

Alphonse shrugged. "I have only my hope. It is my hope that I will be able to cure my son. To bring him back to me… not only physically but mentally." Alphonse went over to the side of the chair Narain sat in and placed a hand on his shoulder, saying, "You can look upon this as a gift or a curse. Actually, it is probably both. But it is what you make it. My son never got the choice. I will help you if you like and you may stay as long as you wish. I will tell you all I know. Perhaps we can be of help to each other."

It all seemed surreal. Narain could not deny his memories, however. They were real and *vivid and tore at his soul. He watched silently as Alphonse left the room. The old man was right. It was his reality now to make of it what he would. The question was: What could he make of it? He turned his gaze back to the fire, on some level possessing the ridiculous wish that if he stared at it long enough, the fire would burn the memories from his mind, giving him the peace he might never have again.*

Chapter 9

Narain awoke to darkness. It was only after his eyes adjusted to consciousness that he noted the red light of the digital clock beside his bed. He didn't need the glowing numbers to tell him that it was early in the morning, safely before sunrise. He had his inner clock to tell him that. What he didn't know was how long he'd been in bed since Cassie had put him there. The fog slowly subsiding, his mind registered the dull aches in his abdomen and shoulders, and it brought back the memory of Reg's knife slicing into his flesh. He'd never in his life experienced pain such as that, not even on the battlefield. It gripped him completely as if his flesh…was dying.

He raised his hand, rubbing his face, then letting it flop back down next to him. He'd been dreaming of Alphonse and as poignant as the memory was, it felt good to visit the old man again. He had stayed on the estate for a number of years after his transformation, helping in Alphonse's research on vampirism. Later, his niece came to help with his research. Narain's aversion to sunlight did indeed worsen with time and it took some time for him to acquire the skill, not to mention the stomach, for obtaining human blood.

Thankfully, not only was it not consistently necessary, as the years went by, it could be obtained without hurting the victim. Narain had indeed adjusted to his condition with the old man's encouragement and began to feel as if a future was possible. After all, he had, in some sense, made his choice on the battlefield: sentient over feral. Now it was simply a matter of survival, which he really didn't have a choice in.

They parted years later, after Alphonse had convinced him to go back to India to visit his family in the hopes that it might bring the young man some peace. Neither realised how devastating the outcome would prove to be. Narain's attempts to reunite with his family died after a meeting with his brother Aziz, who suggested coldly that it might be best for Narain to remain the fallen war hero his heartbroken parents thought he was.

Leaving Aziz with no idea of what he had become, Narain returned to Europe only to spiral down into despair. He wrote to Alphonse occasionally over the years, but never had the heart to tell him of the depression closing over him. Dead to his family, in a country that was not his either, unable to practice his craft (the very thing that had brought him into the war to begin with), and having to survive in ways that chilled him to think about, anguish turned Narain into something he had struggled not to become.

He wandered the streets at night, waited out the daylight in crypts and abandoned cellars, and tried to swallow his misgivings with the blood he stole from those crossing his path. It was only after he had met Sophie and she helped him out of this pit that he was able to write to his mentor with truth and optimism again. By then, it was too late.

Lucy, Alphonse's niece, wrote back stating that Alphonse had died. She did not go into details, but assured him that it had been quick and that she herself would be continuing his research in the hopes of finding a cure for the disease they were now sure caused both sentient and feral states of vampirism.

The memory caused Narain to squeeze his eyes shut. "I bit the hand that fed me." Reg's words echoed in Narain's mind bringing tears to his eyes. Reginald Jameson, the curse he'd inflicted upon the world. The soldiers that sustained him on the battlefield decades ago remained faceless in his memories and Reg was no exception. But Reg had laid the charge on him with such conviction, that Narain couldn't deny he very likely was responsible for turning his former captain into what he now was. And he brought the beast to Alphonse's doorstep as assuredly as if he himself physically delivered him there.

Narain sighed heavily, wiping at his wet cheeks. Why was Reg in Chicago? He had been truly surprised to see Narain in Cassie's lab, so he didn't believe he'd come for him. What was Reg doing in Cassie's lab?

For that matter, where was Cassie? It had been her invitation that brought him to NewGen that night.

As his senses sharpened again, Narain became aware of another presence in the apartment. His mind still fuzzy, he could not figure out who it was. It took Narain three attempts to sit up and a major effort to throw his legs over the edge of the bed. Standing was another thing entirely. There must have been some organ damage deep within, now repaired, but still tender. Gripping the bed post at the foot of the bed, he pulled himself onto his feet, only to sit back down as a wave of dizziness overtook him. Gently, he inspected the areas where Reg's knife had cut him, noting that someone had removed the sutures. Rope-like scar tissue had formed which would heal to smoothness eventually, but would have been smooth long ago had it not been for the salt that had slowed the process considerably. Taking a breath, he ignored the bruised feeling of his stomach and affected organs within, and tried standing again, this time successfully.

Grabbing his robe on the chair nearby, he eased into it, pulling it tightly closed. Then he made his way out of the room.

The presence was not Cassie's. It was very much male and for a brief moment he feared Reg was back to finish the job. But Reg would have an altogether different presence that Narain would have picked up right away. Pausing, he closed his eyes and tried to focus his still weary mind. Then he smiled and continued down the hall toward the living room. He should have known; Reg would not be lying on his couch snoring.

At some point during the night, Dominic had awoken long enough to turn off the TV he'd been watching, using the remote his hand still clutched. Once that had been accomplished, he let the unit drop from his hand and settled back on the sofa, intent on staying put. He'd been in the condo for a few days, ever since Cassie had contacted him about Narain's condition, and aside from a trip to get fresh clothes and an appointment at the restaurant that he couldn't cancel, he stayed put. The first day had unnerved him. He'd never seen his partner in that much pain. Come to think of it, he'd never seen his partner in any pain. Narain had writhed in agony at whatever was affecting his system yet seemed trapped in some deep slumber. When he offered the vampire a bag of blood as Cassie had suggested he do at some point, Narain reached out without ever regaining consciousness and grabbed it. His movements were instinctual as he sliced into the bag with his fangs and sucked dry the blood. Satiated, his hand fell back to the bed still clutching the empty bag which Dom took carefully from his grasp. He'd never seen his friend in such a state and he found it somewhat unnerving.

Initially, blood oozed out of the awkward suturing that Cassie had performed and Dominic tried to settle Narain down to keep any more from leaking out. Eventually, however, the pain subsided and the wounds that had seemed so reluctant to heal began to knit. Narain's sleep became less troubled until Dom was confident his condition was improving.

So, he himself slept deeper than he had the past few nights when the calls Narain made from his dreaming sent him running. Still, while Dom's reflexes had been dialled down to yellow alert status, they were still tense enough to send him flying over the back of the couch when a hand reached out to shake his shoulder.

"Holy crap!" he called out, landing with a thud on his knees and holding onto the back of the couch. Eyes wide he scanned the utter darkness for anything visible. With the security blinds down he couldn't see a thing except for the displays on the VCR and DVD players and that certainly wasn't enough light for his human eyes to utilise.

"Who's there?"

"It's okay, Dom," Narain's voice said, barely disguising his amusement. "It's me."

"Narain? Why would you sneak up on someone like that…ouch!"

"What happened?"

"I stubbed my toe on the end table."

"Why are the security blinds down? It's complete darkness for you."

"That's all I needed, was for you to come wandering out in a delirium after sunrise and get burnt to a crisp in your own living room."

"Well, I don't think that would happen but I appreciate the concern. Let me put the lights on."

"You find a chair and sit down before you rip something open again. I'll find them."

"How? Your spidey-sense?" Dominic grunted as he nearly tripped and Narain said, "Dom, please."

"Narain sit," he commanded. Now it was a mission. "I have an excellent sense of…

crap!...direction."

Narain eased into a chair teasing, "If you break your neck and die, can I have your blood before it cools?"

"I told you I don't swing that way, so settle down, Nosferatu," Dom said, annoyed not so much by his fruitless search, but by the fact that he knew Narain could clearly see his progress. "Am I at least getting warm?"

"Yes," Narain chuckled. "The wall is in front of you, the switch to your left."

Dominic reached out, felt the wall, then searched for the switch, eventually finding it. The living room brightened by the light of the ceiling fixture. "What the hell time is it?" he asked, checking his watch and whistling. "3:20. I swear Narain I haven't had a normal night's sleep since I joined you." He glanced at the vampire sitting stiffly in the chair. "And may I say you've looked worse. I mean, you've looked better, but you were looking much worse a few days ago." Walking over to him, Dom began to open Narain's robe to look at his wounds.

Clearing his throat, Narain teased, "Now, Dom, you're a very attractive man but I told you I don't swing that way."

"My friend," Dom began matter-of-factly, checking the vampire's injuries, "I think I've seen more of your body the last few days than I've seen of my own, so you better feel lucky I don't swing that way." He patted his back. "I think you're on the mend. It's just nice not to see green, bloody pus oozing out. What the hell did they do to you, anyway?"

"Iodised salt. It retards the healing process and can actually kill the tissue."

"I remember you telling me you had an aversion to it. Now I understand why you're so insistent on sea salt in the restaurant."

A wave of dizziness gripped Narain and he put his head in his hand. He was on the mend but far from whole yet. "You know, Dominic, I have to be honest, I don't understand why you're here. How did you know I was in trouble?"

"Your girlfriend called me."

"My girlfriend?"

"You know, Cassie Lambert. She told me you'd need some monitoring. I couldn't believe how bad you looked that first day I came in here." Walking to the kitchen, Dom grabbed a bag from the refrigerator. "By the way, she left you some dinner." He brought the unit of blood handing it to Narain. "I guess you got around to telling her then."

Narain looked at him, then glanced curiously at the bag of blood, taking it weakly but unwilling to ingest it. Gently, Dom told him, "Look Narain, I've never lied to you. The whole thing weirds me out. But I'm more concerned with your health; so if you need to," he motioned to the blood, "then don't mind me."

Narain stared at the blood, obviously hungry for it, but saying, "Do you realise, 90 years and it still weirds me out, too?"

"There's nothing to be ashamed of, Rain."

Narain smiled gently at him. "My God, Sophie was so very right about you."

Affecting false humility, Dom said, "I know. I am pretty special."

Sincerely, Narain said, "You have no idea just how special." Then he reluctantly put the bag of blood aside on the coffee table. "I'll enjoy it later."

"So you told her, then?" Dom asked anxiously.

Narain pinched the bridge of his nose. "No, actually, I never got the chance."

Confused, Dom told him, "Well, I got a call from Dr. Lambert a few days ago telling me about your condition. She told me that someone would have to be with you. She explained what happened, even stocked your fridge with your favourite food. How did she know all that? And what exactly happened to you?"

Narain explained the incident between Reg and himself and concluded by saying, "I asked her how she knew—but I never got an answer. Perhaps if time had permitted, but I hadn't the energy to pursue it."

"So the question becomes, how did she know?" Dom finished.

Narain nodded. "It's a troubling question."

"Well, on the bright side, she knows and doesn't seem to care. That's one conversation you don't have to have."

Narain turned his bruised eyes to his friend, shaking his head. "I was attacked in her lab by a man who was dangerous before contracting…" he searched for a word never really liking the term vampirism, "…whatever this is. I can't imagine how much more devious he is. She knew about the salt, so she must know much more than the fact that I need blood to survive. How is she mixed up with Reg Jameson?"

"She does a lot of research on biology. That lab is working on a number of cures for blood related diseases. Maybe she stumbled onto something this Reg guy is interested in."

"Or maybe she's working for him. Reg seemed genuinely surprised to see me, but I can't get rid of this feeling that this was a set up."

"Okay, now ask the next question. Why would she save you if she had a part in it?" Narain sighed and put his chin on his hand, staring at the floor. Dom patted his knee, saying, "Rain, you're not going to know until you ask her."

He looked up, curiously. "And she indicated nothing to you?"

Dom shook his head. "Nope. Just called, told me you were in trouble and said there was blood in the fridge. I asked her what had happened, but she said she had to run and hung up." Dom insisted, "Rain, you have to get a hold of her or this thing will eat you alive. She might be able to tell you why this Reg guy is in town and possibly what you can expect next from him. He sounds dangerous."

"He is, Dom. He most definitely is."

†

The Marin Hotel on Michigan Avenue was a five star hotel that boasted rooms with first class accommodations and prices starting well out of most peoples' range. Visiting heads of state often chose the Marin in which to stay as did CEOs of major businesses and celebrities in town promoting their latest projects.

Currently, one of the most dangerous men in the world and his comparatively lethal entourage were calling it base camp. Richard Channing had not been surprised when the calls began. Reginald Jameson was in town and demanding a meeting. Of course he was. The last Channing had heard from Jameson, he was in Europe on an extended business trip, but news of the Los Angeles lab must have reached him by now and he was no doubt hungry for answers. Richard couldn't really understand what made him think he could keep the news from the vampire. Unless a small part of him that hated defeat, produced an unrealistic obstinacy that kept him from calling the man.

It was the same sort of obstinacy that kept him believing he and Cassie could be more than just friends again despite her indications to the contrary.

Or maybe he just didn't want to deal with the arrogant vampire. Jameson hadn't even had a clue about the intricate processes going on in his own body until Channing had illustrated them for him. The vampire might have instigated the project but it was Channing's hard work and research that were yielding results. The most Jameson could contribute was money.

And he never let Channing forget who was funding the project.

The large hotel lobby was done in vigorous shades of blue, red, and grey and teemed with people going to and fro about their business. It advertised, before a prospective guest even made it to the glossy black registration desk, that this hotel was not for the financial faint of heart.

Jameson had left a number of messages for him since the vampire's private plane had touched down at O'Hare Airport but, Channing had ignored them all, until he heard about the little mess that was left at NewGen a few nights ago. Then he could only assume who was responsible for it. Jameson was being clever, though. Days of calls from Channing went unanswered until the vampire finally contacted him and suggested a meeting in his suite at the Marin Hotel. Channing refused immediately. It was doubtful that Jameson would risk dispatching his chief researcher at this point in the game, but Channing wasn't about to meet with the vampire in the privacy of his suite. He suggested the hotel lobby where voices would be kept low and lethal actions would not be attempted. He could imagine Jameson's eyes squinting in irritation, as he reluctantly agreed.

Of course, Channing knew better than to trust the vampire completely, so while he was annoyed, he was hardly shocked to find Jameson missing from the hotel lobby as he walked in at the appointed time. When he stepped up to the polished registration desk, an equally polished young man with a naturally welcoming smile greeted him. "May I help you sir?"

Channing gave the lobby one last scan before saying, "I was supposed to meet someone. I'm wondering if you could ring his suite. His name is Reginald Jameson."

The man's smile grew. "Oh, are you Dr. Channing?" Channing nodded. "Mr. Jameson left a message for you to meet him in the pool room. It's down the hall and to the right."

Now it was Channing's turn to squint in irritation, as he looked in the direction the clerk was pointing. Sighing inwardly, he nodded. "Thank you."

So much for safety in public. Still, there might be some guests interested in a late night swim. When he arrived at the pool room doors, however, he noticed that Jameson had considered that as well. He rolled his eyes at the sign on the door which read "Closed for Private Party."

The humidity of the room grabbed him the moment he stepped in; the sharp tang of chlorine assaulting his nostrils. There were several male figures in the pool, including Jameson and a beautiful, bikini-clad Asian woman sitting on the edge with her feet dangling in the water. The curiously tamed ferals splashed around, indicating enjoyment in their odd grunting way and Jameson affected a beaming smile when he noticed Channing's presence.

"Channing old boy!" he called out, waving his arm across the pool. "Care for a dip? We had guests for dinner. They're sleeping it off in the suite. I'm afraid Marcus made a bit of a pig of himself. I'll have some explaining to do to the escort service." Channing remained silent, still too irritated by the incident at NewGen to play along and Jameson's smile faded slightly as he looked at a feral. "Ooh, I think he's angry." Swimming to the side, Jameson hefted himself out with ease and grabbed a towel from a nearby pool chair. The vampire had the dense muscle tone particular to all his kind, his lack of bulk deceptive, hiding a dangerous strength beyond that of normal men. Strength, grace, endurance; once infected, these beings, especially the ferals, became the perfect hunters, the perfect killers. No matter how civilised Jameson acted, Channing knew how dangerous he could become.

As he dried himself, the vampire looked at the woman, saying, "You know, Piri, I used to be quite the hard ass when I was younger. You should have seen me in the trenches. The decades have taken the edge off considerably."

Unable to contain himself, Channing shot out, "Jameson, that was your doing at NewGen a few nights ago, wasn't it?"

Adopting a look of innocence, the vampire donned a terry cloth robe, saying, "What has you so lathered up, old boy?"

"Early Wednesday morning, I received a call from a lab tech who went into NewGen early and discovered the guard out cold and blood all over the lobby."

"Khan didn't feed," one of the ferals assessed from the pool.

Jameson glanced at him shrugging, "Well you can lead a vampire to a victim, but you can't make him feed."

"Do you think this is funny?" Channing snapped unwisely. "Do you know the damage this could have caused, if I didn't have a very discreet lab tech and an even more discreet clean up service that was able to get rid of the mess before the morning staff came in?"

Jameson's face darkened though his grin remained. "Do I look like a man amused?" His tone actually forced Channing back a few paces. "I come to America and discover my lab in shambles and not only does the director of said lab not return my calls, when he finally does approach me, he whines about some blood splatters on his lobby floor. How amused do you think I am right now?

Chagrined and a bit nervous, Channing lamely offered, "I'm sorry, but I've been busy."

Piri let out a sigh of disbelief, shaking her head. The ferals all turned fascinated gazes on the scene.

Without warning, Jameson charged at Channing, grabbing him and holding him aloft against a pillar. Channing could not help but consider the irony of once again finding his feet dangling above the floor as he stared down into the face of a very angry vampire.

"Oh, that is not going to sit well with me right now," Jameson warned, voice eerily measured. With a slight snarl, his fangs prominent, he said, "When were you going to tell me about the Los Angeles lab?"

His indignation having burnt out, Channing was left to sputter, "I thought I'd have it taken care of by now."

Lowering him back to the floor, Jameson sneered and turned away, fluffing his damp hair with his hand. "Blood splattered NewGen," he spat. "Apparently that was the only way to get your attention."

Stunned, Channing asked, "You did that to get my attention? You drugged my security guard and...what? I mean, what poor victim had to pay for you to bloody up the place?"

"You can rest easy, Channing old chap. No humans were harmed in the making of my statement. Besides, that just happened to be an unexpected benefit to the real purpose of my visit."

Channing grew suspicious, asking, "Why were you there that night?" A good portion of the blood had been in Cassie's lab, which was one reason the incident infuriated him so. Yet, when he spoke to Cassie the next day and after, she said nothing of a break-in and vandalism leading him at first to believe, thankfully, that she knew nothing about it. His cleaning service had indeed been very efficient. Now, as he watched the vampire preening, he couldn't help but wonder what had led him to NewGen labs at all.

Jameson sat casually at a metal table, leaning back with his hands behind his head. He stared at Richard with that infuriating smugness finally saying, "You haven't been completely honest with me, old chap, have you?"

Straightening his suit jacket and tie, Channing said, "What do you mean?"

"Well, lovely Piri did some checking on you, NewGen, and your charming partner Dr. Lambert." Richard stiffened and the vampire continued. "I mean—I blame myself really. I should have asked more questions when I hired you. Delved a little deeper. You didn't seem to have any connection to—well, my sort of people." The ferals snickered. "So what would lead you into doing research on what is considered a mythical condition? Piri's research could find no connection between you and my sort. Your partner, however, now there's another story."

Channing felt the room spin and he clutched the back of one of the chairs by the table. "Oh for God's sake," Jameson said, "do sit down before you fall down."

Channing did so, the implications raging in his brain.

After a few moments, Jameson said, triumphantly, "That wasn't your research that got you the job as my director, was it? It was her research. Of course, no doubt you've added considerably, I'd never take that away from you. The tranqs for example that brought down Blythe. Similar to the ones bulging in the pocket of your suit jacket now. Yes, I felt them. Those were your creation. But it was all based on her research, wasn't it?"

"Alright, you've found me out," Channing said defensively, straightening from the hunched position he had affected. "So?"

"Well, I'm curious," Jameson admitted. "Why not bring her in on the deal? I mean, does she even know how your portion of NewGen labs was financed? With the work she's devoted to this research, how much easier might it be for two of you to work on our little project?"

Guilt shaded his tone as Channing replied, "Honestly, I never brought her in on the Los Angeles project because I didn't want her involved with…"

He paused and Jameson leapt upon it. "Involved with me? Is that what you want to say? You don't want your partner, your former flame, involved with me and mine?" He indicated the ferals who were now out of the water and lounging on the floor next to the pool. Piri remained with her feet in the water, watching the drama unfolding.

"Is that truly the reason, Richard?" Jameson stood and moved behind Channing's chair, leaning forward to speak in his ear. "Or could it be that you don't want Dr. Lambert involved so that you can have all the credit?"

Leaving him to chew on that, Jameson took off his robe throwing it across the table, then went to the end of the pool. "At any rate," he began, preparing for a dive off the edge, "What are we going to do about the latest crisis?" Then he dived smoothly into the water and performed two perfect laps with surprising speed before bursting from the pool and landing squarely on his feet. The ferals clapped and he bowed, then returned to the chair, not bothering with the robe. "Which reminds me—when did you learn of the escape? I have a wager with Piri, you see. I say that you wouldn't have been stupid enough to leave LA, for a benefit of all things, if you knew about this, whereas she says otherwise."

"Piri should give me more credit."

"Oh, see Piri," he called over to her. "I told you."

Piri feigned disappointment telling Jameson, "I'll write you a check later."

Face darkening again, Jameson leaned forward. "So, when did you know that one of the most dangerous creatures around was gorging itself on the American Midwest?" Channing looked up at him, and the vampire nodded, "Oh yes, I know of his rampage. Hungry little bastard, but then that's always been a problem. We could never give him enough."

Wearily, Channing said, "When I returned to Chicago for the benefit, everything was fine. It was a few days later that I discovered it—after the bodies were found. I was contacted by Roger and I arranged to have some retrieval parties sent out."

"And they never returned, did they?" Jameson surmised. Channing shook his head. "No, humans don't seem to have a knack for hunting his sort." He paused, then said, "So, he's here now. Seems to have settled in nicely, judging from the items on the nightly newscasts. Any idea why he's staying here? Why not continue on to the East?"

"I have a theory, yes." Jameson waited, then after Channing's silence, motioned for him to continue, which he did reluctantly. "I think my partner may have something he wants."

He told him of the information about Cassie Lambert and her research that was on his computer in the lab. He explained how the beast was a lot smarter than they gave him credit and that he had managed to hack into the system, obtaining crucial files, including those on Cassie Lambert. "Cassie has been working on a cure, but she stumbled upon something that could have serious consequences for vampires."

Jameson's eyes narrowed. "All vampires?" Channing nodded. "And Boris knows about this?"

"I believe he obtained the information from my files, yes. I believe he intends to eliminate a threat. One of the few things that could threaten him."

"Makes me regret even more that I missed my appointment with Dr. Lambert. We'll have to get that discovery, of course."

Channing grew stone-faced, saying, "No."

"What?"

"No. I don't want her involved in this."

"I want to walk in the sunshine, but we can't have everything. Oh wait, you were supposed to be working on that project for me. How's it coming, eh?"

"This is non-negotiable, Jameson," Channing said, fully realising how little power he had. "I've worked too hard to keep her out of this."

"Yes, I suppose stealing someone else's research is very hard work."

"Think what you will. She's not to be touched by this or I leave the project."

Glancing at his entourage with a grin, Jameson said, "My dear chap, I could kill you now and have it cleaned up before morning."

"I know, but you're not stupid. You kill me, you'd practically have to start from scratch on the project. I don't think you want to waste time like that. Either you leave Cassie out of this or I walk. Or die. Simple as that."

"So, you do have a pair, eh? Piri and I had a bet on that too." He lost his grin and leaned forward on the table, making sure the sharp teeth behind his canines were clearly visible. "I want this discovery, do you hear?"

"I'll figure it out, whether I get it from her or synthesize it, I'll figure it out. But she stays out of this."

"Don't make me regret this, old chap. You've told me that there's something out there can harm me and mine. I don't like the sound of that. You fix this and in the meantime, we'll go hunting for the escapee. And we're probably going to need a supply of tranqs as well."

"Yes, I'd say you'd definitely need a supply of them."

Shaking his head in some sort of victory, Jameson returned to the pool to swim some more laps before the sunrise started peeking through the windows. Knowing how close he'd come, Channing said nothing, simply rose and went to the door. "Oh, and Channing," Jameson called out, splashing slightly to a stop, "make sure you answer your cell next time. Don't want a communications problem like we've had recently."

Channing nodded and left. He felt a level of relief, but it was slight and would be fleeting. Jameson was not the sort of man to desist from going after something he truly wanted. And this was something he wanted. He could see the light in Jameson's eye the moment he brought it up, especially when he mentioned the threat it posed to Jameson's kind. Channing had bought some time, however. Right now, that was all he could ask for.

Chapter 10

Narain cut the courgettes into precise squares, arranging them side by side in a baking dish to be drenched in a sweet ginger sauce and dusted with toasted sesame seeds. It was a new appetiser he'd been toying with, but there seemed to be something missing; a flavour that was stubbornly eluding him and at some point he stopped trying to find it. He was beginning to realise that his inability to capture the flavour had more to do with his preoccupied mind than anything else.

Cooking normally relaxed him, so he decided to stay after the employees had closed down the restaurant for the night. They knew his nocturnal habits well enough not to question this, though they did look at him a bit curiously after he thanked them. It wasn't the fact that he expressed his gratitude—he did that regularly—as much as the ceremonial way he did so.

"I'll finish closing up," he said, gathering all the employees in to the kitchen. "You did marvellously tonight. You know, it's always been a dream to own a restaurant and thanks to all of you, this is a very successful restaurant. I'm grateful to you all."

They smiled, appreciating the words, but confused by the tone. And why wouldn't they be? His words were pleasant, but with a lost melancholy that was out of character.

They had welcomed him back after his few days' absence. "I don't think you've ever been sick," Neil, a waiter, commented.

True. The most time he'd ever spent away from the restaurant was when he and Sophie travelled, or when she was ill and he chose to spend every moment he could with her.

He crushed a few leaves of mint between his palms and inhaled the scent, shaking his head. That wasn't it.

But that comment brought to mind another concern. Many on his staff, such as Neil, had worked there for over ten years. In a business that suffered a high turnover rate, his was one of the few restaurants where people stayed on. He offered them a good salary and excellent benefits, plenty of incentive to stay. Their loyalty would hardly be a problem were it not for one thing. They aged. He didn't. And at some point someone was going to start noticing the absence of wrinkles and grey hair. No family's genes were strong enough to completely erase time.

He pounded three juniper berries in a mortar, sniffed them then pushed the mortar aside.

Narain could mesmer any regular patrons that might begin to notice. It was a curious feature of his condition that he never completely understood himself. A glint of his eyes, internal chemical processes giving off a particular scent with a slight hint of cinnamon, that when exhaled through is mouth, enabled him to convince a person susceptible to it that black was white. It was another ability that aided in a vampire's particular style of hunting. But he couldn't work that magic on an entire staff every day. He would need to start weighing his options, though none he thought of so far were to his liking.

Close the restaurant? Open a new one in another city and send his current staff to it? What of those who didn't wish to leave? He considered moving to another city himself especially after Sophie had died, but there was something about Chicago that held him. It was a comfortable fit. He had travelled to many places but never felt at home in any of them. Not the way he did in Chicago.

He could fire the staff – out of the question.

Narain could tell the staff the truth about himself. Hope that those who didn't run in fear wouldn't run to sell the story to TV tabloid shows. He had indeed been lucky to find Dom, who took his condition in his stride. Could he depend on his entire staff to do so?

He sighed, sitting on a stool and wiping his hands with a rag. One good thing about that dilemma was that it kept his mind off Cassie. He had called her office three times, and left four messages on her cell, but she never returned his calls. She was most definitely avoiding him. He considered going to her office but couldn't bring himself to do so. He had no idea how she had explained away the violence at the lab and wouldn't be surprised if police considered a connection between that incident and the spate of gruesome killings in the city.

Narain couldn't help but wonder if Reg's pet ferals had something to do with the murders. It would a dangerous thing for Jameson to allow considering how they could be traced back to him.

"I say, all these vampiric gifts are wasted on you, old chap."

Narain's gaze shot up, landing on Reg and the two ferals standing behind him in the doorway to the dining room. Jumping off his stool, Narain grabbed the carving knife he'd been using and held it at the ready, backing away from them.

"Reg!" He should have sensed him even before Reg entered the building.

"You see there chaps, I told you he'd be fine. He's resourceful." Reg took off his black gloves and stuffed them into the pocket of his raincoat. "Though, I must say, I've approached deaf old ladies with sharper senses than yours. Oh, I hope you don't mind us letting ourselves in."

"Stay where you are," Narain warned, tensing as one of the ferals took a step closer. They were blocking the dining room doorway and he had no doubt they could get to the back door before he did.

Reg stared at the knife, grinning. "Relax, Khan, we're not here to hurt you."

"It's a bit difficult, Reg. I still sting from our last reunion."

"Look, I apologise for that bit of unpleasantness. Things got a bit out of hand."

"Humility rings false with you, Reg."

Looking around, Reg commented, "Nice place you have here. Quite a popular restaurant from what I understand."

Tightening the grip on his knife, Narain said, "And one well stocked with salt." To prove his point, he stabbed the knife in a nearby bag then pointed it toward Reg. He just hoped that they wouldn't realise that the crystals on the knife were actually sugar, not salt.

"Steady on, Khan," Reg said, holding his hands up in mock concern.

"Easier said than done, Reg," Narain said, heart racing as the two ferals began to reposition themselves alongside him. "Your hounds make me nervous."

Enjoying Narain's anxiety, Reg none the less told the ferals, "Okay, chaps. It's a big city. You two go clubbing while mum and dad here have a chat."

The ferals left, but Narain remained tense and ready, backing away as Reg took a step forward. The memory of that night in Cassie's lab coursed through him and he gripped the knife that much tighter, snarling, "I don't know why I shouldn't kill you now, Reg."

"Because you don't have it in you, so let's waste no more time with that." Grinning slightly, he said, "Khan, I'm really not here to hurt you."

"Then why are you here?"

"Because you and I have a mutual problem and as loath as I am to admit it, I may need your help to deal with it."

"Is that why you tried to kill me last time we met?"

"Well, I thought I could handle it on my own, then." With false camaraderie, he said, "Besides, I knew you'd get out of that mess. You've gotten out of worse scrapes. World War I for example." After a pause, he insisted, "Khan, the stars have aligned and forces have converged upon this very city."

At last feeling a sense of ease, Narain lowered his knife, but remained beyond arm's reach. "You're an ass, Reg," he sneered, but then wondered if this might be a good opportunity to get some answers from him. Like how Reg had managed to tame the ferals. And then there was Alphonse. His hatred for Reg grew even stronger when he thought of him killing the old man.

"How did you get involved with Alphonse, anyway?" he asked. "Did you come tracking me or something?"

"Khan, I was in no shape to track anyone when I crossed paths with that old man. I'd been running with ferals for years, half out of my mind."

"It took you a bit longer than me to come to your senses then, eh?" Narain said with a slight note of triumph.

Reg rolled his eyes and absent-mindedly toyed with a few cups on the counter where he stood. "Well, I didn't have anyone to help me back to my senses, did I? Alphonse didn't come across me days into the incubation period. Oh yes, he told me how he found you in his quest for vampires. The young East Indian soldier he found snarling, digging away from the sun." He appraised Narain, grinning. "You've classed up since those nights, eh?

"No old chap, I crawled my way back to sanity. The ferals were the ones who helped me out of that battlefield. Taught me how to survive. It was only after I was on the road to mental recovery that your friend Alphonse found me. It was the queerest thing: There I was, sitting in his path, my uniform several years tattered, looking like a wild animal and realising for the first time since I fell on the battlefield that I wasn't human. I was more. Alphonse took me in, cleaned me up, and helped me understand the conversion that had taken place. He gave me shelter."

His voice trailed off in an almost haunted way and Narain studied him, curious if a conscience was there after all. "And in gratitude for his kindness," Narain pointed out, "you killed him."

"Oh dear heavens, Khan," Reg threw up his hands, "I'm a vampire, he was there, I was hungry. What do you want?"

"You're a sadist," Narain spat. "You were before and you've carried it over."

"Yes, right, very well. I'm a sadist." Reg began to pace and Narain prepared his body for anything. "I'm a sadist and he was a user." Narain opened his mouth in shock and Reg continued, "Oh please, old chap. Alphonse and that cow of a niece Lucy... We were guinea pigs. Every vampire they helped was a guinea pig in their research to bring his son back to him. I mean how many ferals did they go out and help, huh? Did they even try to make the lives of those lost creatures easier?"

Narain's eyes narrowed as he caught a sincere note of...caring in his foe's voice when Reg spoke of the ferals. It was a note so foreign to the arrogant vampire's voice that it immediately struck Narain.

"That reminds me, Reg," the chef said relaxing again, only slightly. "Those two ferals...How were you able to civilise them?"

Calming down, Reg shrugged. "Yes, well, I hadn't forgotten about them. They were men and women once. You remember the madness gripping your mind during the transformation. Imagine never coming out of that. These people became lost souls. Some had been roaming that forest for centuries. Going dormant when food became scarce. Waking up when idiots decided to build trenches and lob men at each other's cannons. When I became sentient again, I made my way home to my family's estate."

"How did you hide your condition from them?" This truly interested Narain.

"Hide it?" Reg scoffed. "Good lord, I didn't hide it. Told them all about it. My father revelled in it. Said I'd never looked so fit and strong. And he'd never have to worry about the name dying out, because I'd never die out. I mean, we did have to be clever in our dealings with society. My father aged. My sisters aged. I didn't. So I went from his son, to my sister's son, I think I'm a cousin now. Doesn't much matter; money hides many secrets. And all the paper work is in order.

"But once I settled in, I went back to France to find those ferals who had sheltered me and kept me alive. I discovered I could reach them. Their minds were broken, but somewhat repairable. No one bothered to try before so they just continued on as legends. They won't be running corporations or creating gourmet meals, but they don't have to remain in the woods any more, either."

Narain smiled sarcastically. "Rather like the ferals' messiah, eh Reg?" He had to admit though that the news disturbed him somewhat. It was much more comforting to think that a vampire becoming severely feral was inevitable and not simply due to abandonment.

"But all this reminds me of why I'm here." Reg leaned toward Narain, who suddenly felt secure enough to remain where he was. "You and I have a problem."

"So you've mentioned," Narain said, gripping the handle of the knife tighter. "I'm assuming that you're not referring to our mutual hatred of each other."

Reg laughed. "No, actually I don't consider that a problem old chap. No, I mean the fact that there seems to be a third class of vampire."

"Third class?"

He ticked the names off his fingers. "The sentient, the ferals, for lack of a better term, and...well something much, much worse."

"Worse...than a feral?"

"Oh yes. A feral's purpose in life is to feed. This third class of vampire has only one purpose. One joy. To kill. There is a difference, you know. And this third class is stronger than us, faster than us. I think the only saving grace is that, so far, he's not as smart as us." He scanned Narain's face, clarifying, "Well as smart as me, at least."

Suspicious, Narain asked, "You seem fairly intimate with this. Why would that be, Reg? And what could anything you're involved in have to do with me?"

Reg leaned back and waved a hand. "Okay, you're going to laugh." Narain glared impatiently. "No honestly, aside from the blood and destruction, the coincidence is quite amusing. Well, even with the blood and destruction." Narain's glare deepened and Reg's smile lowered to a calculating grin. "The reason I'm intimate with the case is because I'm the one who discovered it and brought it back to the states to study it. It managed to escape."

He reached into his breast jacket pocket and Narain quickly brought the knife up. Holding up a hand, Reg said, "Easy old chap. I just want to show you some literature." He pulled from his raincoat a folded packet of newspaper clippings and after some hesitation, Narain finally set the knife aside to sift through the papers.

Narain scanned the headlines and articles, all detailing some horrific murder or mass murder. "I'm assuming this isn't your doing?"

Reg sneered at him. "No. But do you notice a pattern?" Narain went through them again, then shrugged. Frustrated, Reg pointed out, "It's been making a beeline for Chicago." He pulled out a few more clippings. "And per the two big news dailies in Chicago, it's arrived." He stepped away from the counter and affected the air of a lawyer summing things up. "Now, the boys and I have been tracking it, but it's devilishly hard to pin down. Its trail stopped in Chicago and I couldn't for the life of me figure out why." He turned back to Narain. "Then I saw that picture of you. And it all made sense."

Narain looked at him irritated. "What possible connection could this creature have with me?"

"With us, old chap. With us." He reached into his pocket and withdrew a few pictures of a being in a cage. "It would appear you have another ghost to contend with."

Narain looked down at the pictures, studying the image of a large man in orange coveralls grasping the bars of a cage. Despite the coveralls, there was no mistaking the wildness to his demeanour. It was a wildness no feral had ever possessed for it seemed to have a sense of purpose. This one was thinking. The man's long hair obscured his face in the first picture, so Narain thumbed through two more pictures before the fourth caused him to whip his gaze up to look at Reg. He studied the picture to be sure then looked up again. "This...this can't be..."

"Blythe!" Reg grinned enthusiastically. "Yes, it can and it is. Private Fred Blythe. It seems the night you pigged out in 'No Man's Land' had more repercussions then you might have expected."

Eyes wide, Narain backed away from the photos. He didn't remember. They were all faceless. Blythe? Pointing at the pictures, he said defensively, "That may not be my doing, you know. Your little feral friends were having a feast themselves those horrible nights. I'm here myself because of them."

"Yes, perhaps. I just like to think that it was you because guilt torments you so. But none of that matters now."

Glancing at the photos as if coming to terms with them, compassion for the Blythe he knew became visible on Narain's face. "So tormenting him in the trenches wasn't enough for you," Narain said bitterly then looked Reg straight in the eye. "You have to get your licks in decades later. If he is this caged monster that you say he is, then the seed of it probably lies in what you and the war put him through. A man can only take so much."

"Well you'll be happy to know that he can take a whole lot more now. It took twenty ferals just to bring him down. He killed a number in the process."

"Killed ferals?" It seemed such an incongruous thing.

"This is what I'm telling you. He tore them apart. I don't care how fast they heal you can't put together body parts that were thrown into jumbles three yards from each other. Had to burn the poor blokes after I gathered them just to stop their squirming. This is not our little Blythe any more."

"What were you doing with him anyway?"

"I wanted to see what made him tick. Look, I heard through the grapevine about this mad uber-vamp that suddenly sprang up. This is about two years ago."

"Well, what's he been doing between 1917 and now?"

"He hasn't exactly been forthcoming with answers, you know. The ferals go dormant. Maybe he hoisted a few, then went underground."

Narain considered this sadly. "He wanted an end to it. That day we went over the top, he was on the way to shutting down."

Unsympathetic, Reg continued, "Yeah, well, there have been some changes in that region of France. If they disturbed his little vault with digging, that might have done it. Woken him up, set him off. There was some nasty killing going on suddenly. No one wants to use the 'v' word and quite frankly even ferals aren't that brutal." He pointed at the clippings. "Well you read it all in those. I sent some men to hunt him down. They never came back. Some of the finest hunters mind you. So I went over myself with some ferals. Imagine my surprise and delight when I saw who it was. Once we subdued him, we popped him in the strongest cage possible and shipped him off to one of my labs in California."

"One of your labs?"

Proudly, Reg said, "Oh, I have my teeth into all manner of things. I've increased the family fortune considerably. Another reason I'm the dirty little secret they don't mind keeping. I may have been a crap officer." He noted Narain's look. "Oh yes, I know I wasn't going to rise above the rank of captain. I'm surprised I made it that far. But when it comes to business I can be quite the shark. And now I have the teeth to match the instincts. When I say I'm out for blood, I mean it."

Narain rolled his eyes. "Blythe—how did he escape? Seems to me a good business-man would keep a better watch on his assets."

"Can't plan for everything. The best I can figure is that he mesmered the research-ers."

"Mesmered? Intentionally?"

"Very possibly. Seems like it. I told you, he's beyond feral and sentient. The reason I'm guessing he mesmered them is because he didn't leave them alive, or intact, to ask them how he escaped."

Narain stared down at the newspaper clippings again. "And you think he's here?"

"As I say, I think he's on a mission."

Narain silently went over all this information. Dear God, he thought, Sophie had saved him from his biggest fear. Every time he fed on strangers, even though they survived, Narain was left the next night with his biggest worry: Had he passed the con-dition on? It was why it was so hard to bring himself to feed. Why very often he fought the urge even to his own detriment. Reg was the perfect example of the consequences. Sophie had saved him from creating more like Reg. She passed on her nourishment and once he was sure she hadn't contracted the condition, he could feed in peace.

"I still don't understand," he said, uneasily. "Let's say for sake of argument, that Blythe sensed I was here. What does he want with me?"

"Revenge, hopefully." Narain just sighed in exasperation and Reg said, "Look, this is a fairly new theory, okay. Like I said, old chap, I knew he was heading east with a purpose, but it wasn't until I saw your picture that I realised what that purpose might be."

"And so what is it you hope to accomplish? I know it's not to warn me. Do you hope to enlist my aid?"

"Well, actually, I was hoping we could get your girlfriend involved."

Annoyed Narain said, "Are you mad? What is it you're getting at, Reg?"

"Dr. Lambert. Isn't she your new tasty tid-bit?" He studied Narain, smiling, "Ah, early in the relationship, eh what? She doesn't know about..." he mimed biting his hand.

"No, actually thanks to our last meeting she knows it all."

"Good. Then you need to convince her to give up the serum. It might be the only way to stop him."

"What serum?"

"The cure." Narain blinked, not comprehending and Reg's grin spread wider. "Did she not tell you? I say, that will make for some fascinating pillow talk. And if she hasn't told you, I certainly don't intend to spoil the surprise. I will say this: Coincidence may set us the time and place, but we do the rest. For example, I'm beginning to think our meeting the other night may not have been simply a lucky happenstance. But do ask Dr. Lambert to fill you in on the details. And tell her that her serum might be the only hope in stopping this fiend. For now, I best go hunt my boys down and get them back to shelter before the sun starts getting pushy." Reg grabbed a piece of courgette, savoured it, then spat it out, saying, "Mmm, tasty." He nodded toward the clippings and photos. "You can keep those, old chap. I have more." Then he glanced around the room. "Yes, you've done all right for yourself. I'll be in touch."

The last part, said as he exited, was unnecessary, since Narain was sure he'd hear from Jameson again. At that moment, he was too stunned by the implications going through his head to do little more than stare vacantly at the clippings on the counter. *Coincidence occurs, but we do the rest.*

Cassie. His mind returned to the night of the attack and the one question he'd been in too much pain to push an answer for. How did she know how to treat his wounds? How did she know what nourishment he needed to survive? Before anything was dealt with…Reg, Blythe, any of it…he needed answers from Cassie.

Chapter 11

Cassie Lambert lived in a two-story brick Georgian on a quiet side street within walking distance of the vibrant nightlife surrounding Wrigley Field. As Narain eased down the pavement toward it, he sensed a curious peace which seemed a sharp contrast to the action going on in the bars along nearby Ashland Avenue. A grey cat strode confidently down one of the walkways toward him and he crouched down to stroke its soft fur. Looking around he considered his presence there. Vampire or not, he was not a sneak-thief and prowling around at night made him very uncomfortable. He scratching the cat's ears, and whispered, "I think, my friend, you're better suited for this nocturnal life." Purring, the cat rose and rubbed across Narain's knee before heading off on whatever mission drew him down the street.

It had not been difficult to pick her front door lock. Of the many things Narain had learned in his century and more of life, picking a lock was one of the easiest. Perhaps Reg was right. Vampiric skills were wasted on him. But he could occasionally summon them, and he did this night, skilfully slinking through Cassie's Wrigleyville home and up to her bedroom where she slept peacefully, oblivious to the peace she'd taken from him. She was indeed lovely to look at, he noted as he stood at the foot of her bed studying her sleeping form. Curled on her side, breathing softly, her body was deeply relaxed in slumber under the covers. Narain had always found it therapeutic to watch Sophie sleep. It didn't matter what position she started out in, somehow she always wound up on her stomach. And as she slept, he would rub the small of her back, rewarded with a slight purring moan in gratitude.

Dear Sophie. She'd given up so many sunny days for him, locked away in windowless rooms or behind security blinds, while the world began the day; all to spend time in his arms. Somehow they made it work, but he often regretted the sacrifices she made.

Chasing away thoughts of Sophie, he returned his full attention to the woman sleeping in the bed before him. Sitting in the chair near the window and closing his eyes, Narain calmed his mind then, practically inaudibly, whispered, "Cassie, wake up."

His eyes snapped open. Momentarily, hers followed suit, blinking slightly, as they fought their desire for sleep. With "I think it's just a dream" uncertainty she sat up and looked around the room. Then her breath caught, as she made out the figure sitting in the chair watching her. Faster than he would have expected, she leapt from the bed, ready to run out the door, only to be stopped by Narain whose movements were quicker.

"Take it easy," he said as she struggled in his arms. "It's Narain."

Blinking away the confusion of sleep, Cassie looked up at him, recognition finally on her face. Recognition still tainted by worry. "Narain?" she mumbled uncertainly, backing away. "How did you get in? Why are you here?"

It was more than uncertainty he saw in her eyes—felt in her heartbeat. It was fear. Oh yes, he thought, allowing her to relax. You know exactly what I am, don't you?

Her heartbeat slowed, but not by much. She took her eyes from him for a moment to check the time, then returned her gaze to him, a slight flash of anger in it. "You break into a woman's house at 2:45 AM?"

She was feisty. Anger was definitely warring with fear. "Actually, I broke in at 2:15 AM. I've been sitting there for half an hour."

"Are you insane?" she fumed, anger winning. Stepping over to the night stand, she switched on the lamp, squinting at its glow, until her eyes adjusted. "You jerk! That is every woman's worst nightmare—waking up and finding someone watching them!" She took a sip of water from a glass that was also on the night stand. Lamp, clock, water, tissue, hairbrush, cell phone, lip balm, book…Narain was hard pressed to figure out what wasn't on the night stand.

"I hope you'll forgive me," he said, taking her robe from the doorknob and handing it to her. She was dressed in a very short nightshirt from some exotic resort and while her form was more than pleasing to the eye, he was of an old- fashioned mindset on that sort of thing. "I would have visited earlier but as you know, any-thing before sunset is a bit inconvenient. I would have called but…oh, that's right. I did. Several times, the past few days."

A slight look of guilt crossed her face as she slowly took the robe and slipped into it. Shrugging, she said, "Well, I'm sorry. I've been busy."

"Your research?"

"Yes." Taking a seat on her pillow and leaning against the headboard, she said, "Narain, you're here for a reason."

He stood there, hands behind his back. "I received a visit from an old acquaintance last night. Reginald Jameson, the man who attacked me."

She straightened, true concern in her voice. "Are you alright?"

"Oh yes. This time he just wanted to talk. But our conversation reminded me that I never got an answer to the question I posed to you when last we were to-gether." He moved to the foot of the bed and resumed his stance, expectantly. "So I'd like that answer now."

She began to get fidgety. "What question? A lot happened that night."

"Well, for starters, how did you know to feed me blood? How did you know what salt was doing to my wounds? Why didn't you take a victim of severe blood loss to a hospital?" He paused, and then summed up, "In short, how did you know that I'm a vampire? And for that matter, how long have you known?"

"Look, Narain, it's a long story."

He smiled, then went back to the chair and sat, crossing his legs and steepling his fingers. "Well, I have a few more hours yet before I turn into a burning pumpkin. Spin your tale." At her hesitation, he added, "Because as grateful as I am for your help that night, I can't help but consider that had you not asked me to meet you at your office, I would never have been in that situation to be attacked. Surely you can understand why I smell a whiff of a set up here."

Eyes widening, she said, "Oh no, no Narain, that's not it at all."

"Good. 'Cos I would hate to think that was your plan. Or that you had designs upon using me as some sort of guinea pig on which to test your serum." Her brows furrowed and he said, "Oh yes, Reg told me about it. Supposed to be a cure or something. Reg seems to know you quite well. Funny thing is, I honestly don't think he expected me to show up at your lab that night. Of course, we both expected you to show up. And for that matter, why does a woman make appointments so very late unless she knows the people she's meeting with can't make a meeting during the day? Or am I just being paranoid?"

Once he had finished, he noticed that during his oration she had lost some of her defensiveness and was now sitting with her arms crossed, fixing him with a stubborn gaze. Damn! She was lovely!

"Are you finished?" she said at last. "I mean, I don't have a sun-proof house, so if you want to go on for a few more hours I can stick you in the closet when the sun comes up and we can resume once it goes down."

He fought back the sheepish feeling coming over him. She was actually turning this around on him. "I don't like being a puppet," he said very seriously. "I don't like feeling manipulated."

"Well who does, Narain?" She uncrossed her arms and her face relaxed a bit. "And it was never my intention to manipulate you. I was never going to use you as a guinea pig. And the meeting in the lab was set up, because I knew I was meeting one vampire," she paused, a guilty look crossing her face, "I guess I just wanted a vampire in my corner."

"Really?"

"Yes. Unfortunately, I didn't know that you and Jameson had a history."

Relaxing himself, Narain said, "But I still don't understand. How did you know what I am?"

Brightening a bit, she smiled and stood up. "Okay, let me finally answer that question."

She disappeared into the walk-in closet and he heard her making small grunting noises while rummaging around. Something fell, followed by her "Oh crap!" to which he asked, "Do you need help?"

"I'm fine," she assured him, then let out another exclamation after bumping something to the floor.

"Are you sure I can't help?" he asked, a smile spreading across his face.

"No," she grunted. "It's just in the back, but I…almost…got it!"

She emerged triumphantly with a small dark, wooden box, which she brandished proudly. "See," she said, then cringed as a pile of items tumbled out of her closet. She shrugged, "I'll get those later," and headed back over to the bed where she sat, one leg folded under her. She invited Narain to join her, grinning when she noted him hesitate. "So you're fine with breaking into a woman's bedroom and watching her sleep for a half hour, but sitting on the bed of a conscious and clothed woman while the lights are on—no way, huh?"

Pursing his lips, he said, "I'm sorry, I'm of a different time and place" as he sat down as respectfully as possible on the bed.

"Well, step into 21st Century America and let's play adults here." Composing her thoughts, she said, "Okay, you have to bear with me because it's a bit of a story, and besides, I've always been a fan of dramatic reveals."

Teasing her, he looked at the clock, saying, "Very well."

"Okay, for as long as I can remember I've loved science."

"Oh God," Narain exclaimed, sighing.

She slapped his arm. "Stop it. One of my inspirations was my great aunt who was in her seventies by the time I started to know her, but who had a long career in scientific research, especially biology and blood diseases. For much of her life, she lived in Europe and was looked upon as sort of an odd duck, since she was fiercely independent and never married, which was sort of frowned upon back then. In fact, she lived on her own right up until her death. She came to America not long after I was born and for some reason the two of us just hit it off. She used to tell me that she saw a lot of herself in me. As I grew, I realised how amazing she was. She had been in her early twenties when she devoted her life to science; she went to college when most women were getting married and starting families. Eventually she earned a doctorate and worked with some of the most prominent minds in the field, who actually valued her as more than the girl in the group who got the coffee. It wasn't easy to gain their respect, but she did it.

"Which I think is one reason she took such an interest in my education when I began to show an interest in biology. She encouraged me; loaned me money for school. Apparently she'd been given a large inheritance from an uncle to whom she was close and later I would discover that he'd given her this inheritance not simply out of love but for a purpose. Later, she would instil this purpose in me.

"She told me that she had a cousin who contracted a rare disease and was lost to it. Her uncle, my great, great uncle, whom she used to spend summers with on his estate, developed an obsession with finding a cure for this disease and it seemed that his obsession became hers. She continued the research long after her uncle's death and promised me that when the time was right, she would tell me all about the disease."

"And did she ever explain fully?" Narain asked, enjoying not only the story, but the twinkle in her eyes as she told it.

Cassie nodded. "In a way. As I said, she was active until a year or so before her death. She slowed a bit but nothing overly debilitating, so we were all stunned to find out that one day, she just collapsed and by the time they got her to the hospital, she was dead. It was quite a shock. I still miss her." As Narain reached out and rubbed her forearm Cassie smiled, continuing. "It was also a shock to learn that I was named sole beneficiary of her estate."

"I bet your siblings didn't appreciate that."

"No, not at all, though none really took any interest in her the past few decades. I gave them some of the money, but what they didn't understand was that the reason she gave me her estate was so that I'd have money to further the research."

"But why not just set up a foundation or fund?"

"Well that's what I found so very curious. She actually took quite a risk giving the money to me. I could very well have squandered it. Setting it up specifically as a fund would have kept it safe and secured it for future research. As I considered this, I remembered how secretive she was about her private research. 'This obsession,' as she called it. Perhaps if she had realised the end was near, she would have told me about it. But while she alluded to it in our conversations, she never explained it and often times her demeanour would become...well fearful, I guess is the best way to explain it. Afraid, maybe, of what I'd think of her if she discussed it further.

"It was days after her death that I received a letter from her. She must have made arrangements to have it sent once she was gone. It began simply enough, 'Cassandra my dear, if you are reading this, then it means time ran out before I was able to tell you that which I assured you I would and for that I'm sorry.' She acknowledged my theory by stating that her private research was unusual and she had always feared it would lead others to scoff at it, so she felt it better to go about her business as discreetly as possible. At least until she had concrete proof that it was nothing to scoff at. She gave me the option to either continue the research or to use my inheritance how I saw fit. 'I'm sorry I can't be there to explain it all to you, my dear, and there is just far too much to do so in a letter. So I leave my notes, my journals, my memories, pictures, trinkets. A portion of a family history that would, hopefully, lead to the solace for some that my uncle was denied. Sift through it all, my dear, before you make your decision. Then do what you feel is right.'"

Narain smiled fondly. "You've memorized your last letter from your aunt."

She nodded. "And I did what I thought was right. There were boxes and boxes. A good portion of a woman's life devoted to this. A portion of a man's, my great, great uncle's too, for I found his research in an oak-wood trunk among her effects. Something told me that's where I should start, so I did. And among his journals and photos I found one photo, the memory of which stayed with me. It was nothing incredible and seemed to have no tie to any research. When I first saw it, I thought it was simply a picture of my great, great uncle and a young man. A very handsome young man. Perhaps a friend of his, a stable hand, a neighbour. It's only after I began reading his journals, where he detailed his own research, that I discovered the identity of this man." She handed Narain an old photo that she'd carefully taken from the box. It was brown and curled with age. "This is the photo. Though I didn't know it at the time, it was my introduction to you."

Blinking in surprise, Narain took the picture and studied it, a wistful look slowly spreading across his face. "Alphonse," was all he could say as he looked at the image: He and Alphonse, posing together by the fireplace, in the dining room of Alphonse's grand house.

"There were other photos in there," she told him, as he continued to stare at the photo. "Some of the people who had no connection with the tragedy that befell my great, great uncle's life and led to his...well quest, I guess. But for some reason, this image stuck with me. That face stuck with me. It gave me a face to picture, while I read the entries about the unfortunate World War I soldier who had been affected by what I suddenly understood was the rare blood disease my great aunt spoke of."

"What also affected Alphonse's son," Narain said softly, lost in memories. He gazed up at her. "Lucy? Lucy was your great aunt? I remember her spending summers with Alphonse. She was quite a brilliant woman. She had no compunction about her uncle's research nor did he have any about sharing his research, with her. They made quite a pair."

Cassie nodded. "When I saw you at the benefit, I couldn't believe the resemblance to the man in the picture. And up close it was even more striking. And let's be honest, there weren't many people from India hanging out on French estates back then. So, on a hunch, I went back to that oak-wood trunk, back to the picture, back to the journals, and discovered the name of this young man."

"You mean vampire," he corrected, with a hint of bitterness.

Ignoring this, she said, "His name was Narain Khan. Nine decades and you never changed your name?"

He shrugged. "I like my name. It's all I have left of my family."

"You should like it. As far as my knowing what to do to help you, you can thank Alphonse and Lucy for that. And actually, according to their journals, they were very grateful to you and the others who helped in their research. It helped give them an understanding of the condition and the continued contact, the observations you all would send furthered that research tremendously."

"Grateful to me? I only wish I could have truly showed my gratitude to Alphonse." Narain thought of Reg, left for dead in "No Man's Land," his being transformed all alone. Trapped between the sentient and the feral. At least those who didn't retain their human consciences realised what they had lost. "That could have been me out there," he said quietly.

"What?"

He blinked. "Nothing. I was just remembering how Alphonse took me in. Sheltered me until I was able to accept some form of independence."

She shook her head. "I can't imagine how disorientating it must have all been for you. How frightening. The letters you wrote to him in the 1920s were heartbreaking."

"He kept those?"

"Those two kept everything. Your letters, the letters of a woman named Veronica and another, Jorge."

"Ah yes, the hired hand. He was one of the first Alphonse received."

"You all wrote of loneliness. Uncertainty. Jorge even called himself a fiend."

"Well, what we had...have to do to survive, it's hard not to feel that way. It seemed at first my whole sense of self revolved around that hunger, how to satisfy it while retaining who I was. If done carefully, it does not have to be fatal, but how do you steal something as personal as blood from someone? And what if the hunger is too much one night and death does result?"

Carefully, she asked, "Have you ever killed anyone?" The question sounded so much more blunt than intended.

Narain laid the picture on the bed and rose to his feet stiffly, going over to the dresser mirror and staring as if it wasn't his reflection he saw, but his distant past. Then he blinked it away and turned to her, "Actually, I'd much prefer to talk about this serum Reg says you have. A cure? It would seem Lucy's faith was well placed."

"Well, it took a while but I finally discovered the cause of vampirism. It's caused by a micro-organism passed between vampire and host. That's how it replicates and survives."

"A micro-organism," Narain said, stunned. "Like bacteria."

"Actually, a bit more complex. In fact, symbiotic relationships exist in all facets of life, but I don't know if any researcher has ever seen anything this extreme." Her energy level picked up as she explained, "Once infected and the bugs start to settle in and reproduce, they slowly start to alter a person's basic physiological makeup. They start making a comfortable and safe home for themselves. There are inconveniences. Your ability to process food changes, because what the organism needs for nourishment can only be found in blood, especially human blood."

"Since the process is so delicate, other foods can no longer be ingested unless in very minute amounts, because, well, there's no point to them."

Narain remembered the first time he tested this by sampling a slice of pumpernickel bread still warm from the oven. His body rejected it almost immediately, much to his embarrassment. He tried a few other things—vegetables, fruit, grains—but soon realised that solid food was no longer for him and even liquids could present a problem in too great a quantity.

"The extreme allergy to the sun is another inconvenience. Exposure to the sun causes certain chemical reactions in the body that affect the organisms and can begin to kill them off suddenly.

"Still, there are advantages. The microbes, by their very reproduction, offer the host an extremely efficient cellular repair, unheard of in the study of biology. Hence, the reason for the almost immortal life span of the host."

"And our ability to heal?"

"Exactly. Your increased strength and agility. The longer your time as a vampire, the more efficient that process is, because the microbes have adjusted, their quantities increased. There are a few elements that can harm the microbes. iodised salt, for example. Salt on anyone's wound is aggravating, but for the microbes within your system, it's deadly. With salt in a wound, the microbes die before they can repair the tissue. And, as the blood leaks out, so too does the only source of nourishment the microbes have to gain strength from. They grow weaker. Unable to replicate. Die off. If the infection is severe enough, it can compromise the whole community."

"A community? And how many would you say exist in this community?"

She shrugged. "I don't know exactly. It might be impossible to count. It depends on how long they've inhabited the host. As well as the health of the host. Everything is affected: organs, bone, your very cells." Narain grew pensive and she asked, "What are you thinking?"

Staring at his hands, he considered the bugs crawling around his system, keeping him alive, healing cuts and bruises and the ravages of time. There was something unsettling about the fact that he existed at the behest of billions of microscopic creatures. He looked up at her, grinning feebly. "You've taken all the romance out of it. Somehow, I liked it better when vampires had a metaphysical explanation."

"It's always a matter of finding a way to measure the metaphysical. Then it becomes physical. Alphonse and Aunt Lucy knew there was a scientific explanation, they just didn't have the knowledge and equipment to discover it."

"But the ferals feasted on many soldiers those nights. Why me? Why Reg? Why not all of us?"

Cassie considered her words. "Life is about balance. No organism can be one hundred percent successful or else it would succeed itself out of existence. If everyone succumbed to this, then we'd have nothing but a population of vampires. I've been trying to figure out what the deciding factor is and I have a theory. The answer seems to lie in genes. I believe this organism has been around for millions of years, perhaps mutating occasionally, to better survive the times. This would explain the why legends of vampire-like creatures appear in so many cultures for so many generations. I believe that some humans possess a gene, possibly from ancient times, which lies dormant within them. A super-gene for lack of a better word. Perhaps left over from a time when we had to be physically stronger and hardier to survive the conditions. The gene is not exclusive to race, nationality or gender. If a person without the gene is attacked by a vampire, nothing happens. The wound heals normally, provided the vampire doesn't get greedy and suck the victim dry. Any microbes that are passed into the host find a hostile environment that they can't change and they die. But if a vampire attacks someone with this super-gene, the microbes have a host strong enough to support them, so they replicate vigorously. Once the infection turns on the gene, you have symbiosis."

"Can an infection occur in a dead victim?" He considered Blythe and his possible role in the crazed vampire's creation.

"I think it's a question relative to the corpse. How long since the heart stopped, for example. The heart may stop, but there are still chemical processes going on, albeit shutting down. Are the microbes strong enough to take advantage of this spark of life and utilise it? Are the microbes able to spread fast enough to restart functions? There is an incubation period. Perhaps a victim that has died and been reanimated has a denser amount of microbes within him. I believe most vampires still had beating hearts when they were infected. At least, that's what's been indicated by those who helped in my research. But I can't say the recent dead can't be brought back to life. There's still so much to learn about this condition—what I don't know, I can only speculate on."

"But you knew enough to find a cure."

"You said that earlier. Who told you I had a cure?"

"Reg Jameson. In fact, that's why he was interested in you."

"Jameson, that fool!"

Narain's look turned slightly suspicious. "So, you do know him."

"No. I mean, not really." Sitting back, she explained, "This research is not easy. Until I discovered the microbe I couldn't exactly go to anyone and tell them that there's a whole population of vampires out there. So, a good portion of it was private on my part. It made me understand why Lucy was so evasive, also. Luckily, I was able to use my great aunt's records about many of those vampires who kept in contact with Alphonse, kept in contact with Lucy over the years. I contacted some, some contacted me."

Narain's face darkened. "I lost contact with Alphonse for a while. I wanted to reconnect with him, but by the time I was of a healthy frame of mind, he was dead."

Cassie nodded. "It's understandable. For many it wasn't an easy transition. Most were average people when they contracted the disease. They didn't have castles in Transylvania to flee to. They had to find a way to live in society with what can be a rather unsociable condition."

Narain thought of the ferals and the societies they made for themselves. Not to mention his own nightmarish existence before meeting Sophie.

"Well," Cassie continued, "because these were names that appeared in Alphonse's or Lucy's journals and papers, I felt I could trust them."

"And Jameson was one who contacted you?"

"Not until very recently. I received an e-mail from him explaining that he knew Alphonse and wanted to set up a meeting with me to inquire on my research. I thought it odd that he would be able to track me down, but the name struck me as familiar. I believed he knew Alphonse, because I was certain I'd seen his name in the journals and it's possible that he got my information from some of the other vampires I've dealt with, but something didn't seem right. Before calling the number he gave me, I went back through the journals and discovered that he didn't have a long relationship with Alphonse, and Lucy seemed to suspect that he was a very sinister man. There also had been no contact from him for decades."

"So, why contact you all of a sudden?" Narain said, understanding.

"Exactly. I called him out of curiosity and he really threw me, when he told me he wanted to discuss the research I was working on. Now, it's entirely possible that he heard about me through a vampire grapevine, I don't know. The whole thing just seemed suspicious. Still, I wanted to meet with him, in case my suspicion was unfounded and he could be of help. So...I arranged a meeting in my lab at NewGen."

"The night I was attacked," Narain finished.

She nodded and said with an almost pleading tone, "I wasn't aware you guys knew each other. At that point, I knew what you were and figured that I'd feel safer meeting a vampire with you to back me up. I asked you to meet me there, thinking that I'd have a chance to explain it all to you then. The trouble was that Reg was early, I was delayed, and you were right on time."

He remembered that night only too vividly and the nearly healed scar on his abdomen twisted slightly. "And you've not heard from him since?"

She shook her head then said, "Narain, he's got this wrong about my serum being a cure. It isn't, really. It's more of a toxin. It does kill the microbes, but it kills the host as well. It doesn't give you weeks or even days to get your affairs in order. It's instant. The moment the microbes start dying en masse, you revert back to what you would have been decades ago."

"A corpse."

She nodded. "That's not a cure. That's not at all what my great, great uncle wanted. He wanted a way to bring his son back to him. I kept this formula as part of the research, but I'm still looking for a cure that can save the host and give him at least a few years of...well, normal life."

Narain thought of something. "How is it you know what the effect is on the host? Have you...used it?"

Cassie grew very quiet and he had his answer in this. In her defence, she said, "I never used it on an unwilling subject."

It was his turn to grow quiet, as he tried to wrap his mind around this. Suicide had been a foreign concept to him before the battlefield. Now, it seemed an impossibility, as that part ruled by the creatures within him would never allow it. With what he now understood as the micro-organisms running the show, his body was conditioned to survive and it would no matter what his mind desired.

"They came to you, willingly?" he finally asked. "Was it their attempt to assist in finding a cure, or were they truly looking to die?"

He could see on her face that the thought of testing necessary to gauge the effects of her formula, had left an impact. Calmly, she told him, "Narain, I told you, this is not easy research to do. I do not have access to vampiric lab rats. In the first set of trials," she paused searching for a way to say it delicately "well, we used blood samples. Then, moved on to skin samples. And then, for those consenting, moved on to samples on limbs." His eyes narrowed at the implications. "I had to know what it did to the entire body, intact. Your bodies don't exactly function like normal human bodies any more at least when it comes to research. Those who had given limbs were prepared to do so. It was done with their full consent, whether their reasons were to help find a cure, or simply to end it."

After a pause for this to sink in, she defended, "Narain, you have to understand. This condition is as old as the legends surrounding it. You're a toddler compared to some who have been around for hundreds of years. They experienced a constant cycle of watching loved ones die, of seeing people invent new ways to kill each other, things they cared about fail and fall apart. They wrestled with the same questions you do. Is this the night they decide to kill? What if they create another? How do they hide this from the community? Must they completely lose who they are just to survive? They couldn't kill themselves – something always stopped them. So when this came up, they were willing to try it."

He understood. Yes, he was young and still willing to play the game, but the losses were racking up in his life; Sophie being a particularly painful hit. How long would he be willing to play the game before wishing he could stop? Jameson came to mind suddenly, forcing away any sense of self-pity. No wonder he wanted that toxin. The one who possessed that toxin possessed a great power.

"You said the older a vampire got, the denser the concentration of microbes, the stronger he became, correct?"

"It seems so."

"And most of your test subjects were very old?"

"Well, yes. And I had to consider their age when figuring doses. The higher the concentration of microbes the higher the dosage, though even a little can be effective."

Standing, he began to pace. "I contracted this in 1917 making me only 90 or so years old in vampire years, so I shouldn't be as strong as those much older."

"Theoretically."

"Then what would make a vampire my age strong enough to fight off twenty ferals, some possibly older than him, trying to subdue him?"

Cassie looked at him, surprised. "Kazuhiro is 337 and I don't know if he possesses that much strength. Do you know of someone like this?"

He told her about Blythe from the trenches to the torment Reg had no doubt been putting him through recently. She began to understand why Jameson showed such an interest.

"What could have created this?" he asked her.

Giving it some thought, she said, "Honestly, I don't know. You said Blythe was going through a psychological problem before going into battle?"

"We called it 'shell shock,' but I'm sure it went even deeper. It took all his reserves and bravery to finally follow us over the top."

"All I can imagine, without further study, is that it could be related to stress. Under stress, a body's health is compromised. Chemical processes occur that alter physiology. Perhaps his microbes reacted to this by upping their own production volume. Another answer could be a mutated strain of the microbes. Adrenaline would have been a factor. Perhaps all those years he was dormant, he acted like an incubator for a different form of the disease. Or perhaps he himself has a particular gene that works differently in conjunction with the microbes than yours does. If Jameson is correct though, especially about Blythe's mental state, then he could be very dangerous indeed." She considered this, a concerned look on her face. "Do you think Blythe really came here looking for you?"

He shrugged. "The only thing I know for certain is that I need to be highly suspicious when it comes to anything Reg tells me. Besides, if Blythe is looking for me, it doesn't mean he wants to do me harm. We were not enemies." An inner alarm suddenly went off and he quickly glanced at the clock. Four-twenty-six. "I think I'd better leave. The sun will be up soon."

Climbing off the bed as he rose from the chair he sat in, Cassie walked him downstairs and to the door, an air of romantic nervousness about her stride, as they descended the stairs. The secrets were out now, opening the door to an intimacy they'd been too afraid to explore before.

"You really can sleep in the closet. Once I close the door its completely light proof," she joked.

Narain stared at her, humoured by the note of hopefulness in her voice. "Something tells me closing the door of that closet might be difficult."

"Oh, it cleans up in a snap."

Cassie turned on the downstairs foyer light for her own sake. The house was well lived in and rich with memories. Photos dotted the walls, some, no doubt, taken from the cherry-wood trunk left by her Aunt Lucy. He glanced at a few, smiling as they ignited memories of his own. The house seemed warm and unpretentious. Much like her. He felt comfortable in it.

As they neared the door and he turned to face her, he said, "I'm sorry I was terse with you earlier. It all makes sense now."

"That's okay. It's understandable to be suspicious in your situation." She studied him closer commenting, "You look a bit haggard. You haven't fed since you last had what I left with Dominic for you."

"I feel fine."

"Is this some sort of vampiric eating disorder?"

"It's complicated."

Firmly, she said, "Narain, you suffered a great trauma that night, even for a vampire, and you were already weakened from a lack of nourishment. You'll need to feed a bit more often for a few weeks. I mean, I hate to say it," she stopped a moment, and considered it, "not to mention that it's weird to say it, but you need human blood."

"I'll pounce on the next busboy who cuts his finger."

"This is serious." Both suddenly realised how close they'd drifted to each other as they talked, and he could sense her heart racing. He rather wished she could sense the heightened beat of his own heart. "I'm worried about you. At least let me order a few more units for you. Even with the research as a cover I can't order a vat of it, but a few units will help."

He nodded, looking deeper into her eyes. "Very well. If you insist."

She tilted her head slightly up toward him saying softly, "I do."

With a slight adjustment of his respiration he was able to synch their heartbeats up and it was an exhilarating feeling. If only she could experience it.

He remembered a conversation he had had with Sophie months before her death. Months she had spent preparing him to go on without her. "You'll find someone else."

Almost petulantly, he told her, "I won't. I've had the best. I don't want anyone else."

"You will and you must." Sophie brushed her fingers along his cheek. "And she will make you happy again."

His eyes closed as he savoured the memory. When he opened them slowly it wasn't Sophie, but rather Cassie brushing her fingers along his cheeks. And he did feel happy again.

"I have to go," he whispered, leaning toward her.

"What's stopping you?" she said breathlessly, her eyes receptive.

And with that, they kissed, Narain becoming lost in the warmth of her body as she pressed against him, realising though that every moment in her embrace brought him closer to sunrise. Frustrated, he pulled away. He had to. It was the reality of his life. And yet, he could see in her eyes that she understood and accepted.

"This is not finished," he assured her, planting a few more soft kisses on her nose and forehead.

She smiled. "It better not be."

With an exasperated groan, he opened the door and prepared to leave.

Before he did so, she asked, "Narain what are you going to do? About Blythe, I mean."

He shook his head. "I don't know. I'll have to think on it. I just know I feel he's owed a chance. Be careful and don't have any further contact with Reg. I'll call you soon."

Narain walked down the street feeling lighter than he had in days. There was still the problem of Reg and Blythe to consider, but his main concern had been that Cassie was somehow involved with Jameson and that quandary had been answered.

"Lucy's great niece," he said softly to himself, smiling at the strange interconnection of life. "Alphonse," he said, gazing upward, "may I date your descendent?" He chuckled, but noted the gentle nature of the sky and realised that he'd better get back to his car and home. Traffic would not yet be a concern at that hour, but Chicago's infamously packed neighbourhood side streets meant he had to park a few blocks away.

A noise startled him and he scanned the area to gauge where it came from. It was small; probably a stray cat. Maybe a rat, though he couldn't imagine rats in that area of town. Off in the distance, a car started and pulled away as someone headed off for an early shift.

A curious feeling gripped him and he actually found himself snarling. He turned to see if someone had been following behind, but no one was there. He quickened his steps. Narain had very little to fear from a mugger, but he had no desire to encounter a problem either. Not with sunrise approaching.

Hearing a grunt off to his left, he turned his head in time to see one of Reg's ferals speeding toward him. Ordering his legs in motion, Narain ran with all the speed he could attain. Faster than a human he may be, but it was doubtful he was faster than a feral. An eerie chuckle came from the feral as it altered its course easily and ran on Narain's heels. Its footfalls were almost as loud as his, both unconcerned with breaking the silence of the morning, but then the footfalls of the feral grew still.

Confused, Narain spared a glance back and was instantly body slammed by the second feral he had been unknowingly running toward. Having heard the chase, the second feral had darted out from a gangway between two houses just in time to take down Narain.

Dazed and bruised, the pain didn't last long and Narain struggled to get to his feet, but he wasn't quick enough. The ferals converged upon him, disturbingly quiet as one stuffed a rag in his mouth and they both grabbed hold of his arms.

He struggled and thrashed, but they were strong and efficiently quick. He was dragged into an alley behind a strip mall and while one held him down, the other took a syringe out of his pocket and bit off the protective plastic cap, spitting it down the alley. Narain's eyes widened and his struggles increased. Surely, they knew conventional drugs and poisons didn't work on their kind and all he could imagine was that somehow they had gotten Cassie's toxin; his biggest fear being how they had gotten it. He had left her only minutes ago.

Without further warning, the feral plunged the needle deep into Narain's chest and squeezed down the pump, his exclamation of shock and pain muffled by the rag.

His heart pounded furiously as he felt the drug bursting through his body. Cassie said it worked instantly, the microbes died off and he'd be a desiccated corpse in moments. With a sort of perverse glee on their faces, the ferals released their hold and rose to their feet, staring at him as they backed away. His eyes teared up as they shot from one feral to the other. His breathing became laboured, but something told him that was more from panic than respiratory failure. In fact, while his mind became slightly cottony, his heart still thumped wildly. Surely, his heart would be the first to slow.

Turning over onto his stomach, he spit the rag out and tried to get to his hands and knees but his limbs felt heavy as though he were swimming in mud. No, this wasn't Cassie's drug, but whatever it was, it had succeeded in practically paralysing him. He fell over on his side, glancing up at the sky and noticing a turquoise glow off in the east as the sun slowly intruded.

His heart pounded even faster. The ferals glanced up at the sky as well, but also looked around. He could tell by their stance that they were listening for something, prepared to move when they heard it. The morning was creeping up too fast however, and they'd be as fried as he would be if they stayed longer. Judging by their demeanour, they had miscalculated and their unsuccessful plan had to be aborted.

So with some frustration, they looked at each other, and then ran off down the alley to a safe hold, no doubt scoped out before the attack.

Narain groaned and rolled around fighting as hard as he could against the drug, but fighting a losing battle. If he could at least walk, he might be able to make it back to Cassie's. He laughed bitterly, the laugh barely audible. It was possible that he had miscalculated, too. The sunrise was coming much sooner than he expected. He should have taken Cassie up on the offer of the closet.

Now that he understood the condition, he understood the illness that overcame him when he was exposed to the natural light of day and the microbes began to sicken and die from the poison. It had only happened a few times in the past and only for moments, but it was a horrible all-encompassing feeling and even with this paralytic drug, he knew the last sensation he felt would be excruciating.

Glancing at his left hand, he was stunned to see his fingers scraped and bloody. He realised that instinct had led him to try to dig a hole in the asphalt pavement of the alley, in an effort to hide from the sun. It was as he saw himself trying to do it again, that a shadow fell over him. His vision was blurry, his mind watery, but the figure's outline was large and bulky, with a touch of menace to it as it lurched over him. Without a word or grunt, it picked him up like a puppet and hoisted him over its shoulder, then took off down the street.

Narain was oblivious to everything but the bouncing of his head against the figure's back as they moved with incredible speed. At last, the figure stopped before a manhole cover, reached down and pulled the cover from the street as easy as someone might open a can of soda. The stench of the sewer wafted up as the being eased Narain down into it and followed after, replacing the cover just as easily. Hoisting Narain onto his shoulder again, he splashed through the inches of water and refuse until he found a ledge that was sufficiently shaded from the natural light coming through the storm drains. With a surprising care, he lowered the paralysed vampire onto the ledge in the concrete and arranged him as comfortably as possible.

To Narain this all seemed a dream, his vision hazy, ears registering sound as swollen echoes that thumped through his head. He blinked and continued fighting the effects of the drug, but was losing his stamina as he became overcome with the desire to let oblivion take him.

The figure leaned closer to him and Narain was sure he caught a look at his face, but his brain was sluggish and his vision couldn't clear. The figure said something and patted Narain's cheek, and then it stood up, told him something more, then burst off down the sewer, disappearing into the darkness.

Narain reached out as if to grab him but his arm fell, the movement pulling him forward, where he finally passed out, his head and arm hanging limply.

Chapter 12

Narain opened his condo door, allowing an anxious Dominic to enter. Towelling his still damp hair with a brisk, preoccupied energy, the vampire slammed the door shut and hurried past his friend as if he wasn't there.

"Okay, Rain, what's going on? What is so urgent?" Pausing, Dom sniffed the air, saying, "Hey, no offence but did you know your apartment smells a bit like…"

"A sewer?" Narain spat, sniffing the towel and tossing it in a large garbage bag that contained the rest of his sewer ravaged clothes. He picked up one of the several air fresheners with which he had peppered the place, saying, "And these? Don't work!" and tossed it in the bag with equal venom.

Dominic took a moment to examine him. Dressed in grey tracksuit bottoms, his thick black hair glistening, it was obvious that the vampire had just come out of the shower. Nothing unusual in that. Vampires had to practice hygiene too. But the sewer fragrance in the air, and a garbage bag full of, at one time, good clothes, not to mention the vampire's agitated air, did lend the scene a bit of mystery. He was about to ask what the problem was when Narain cut him off.

"Dom, am I a secret agent?" he asked, pulling on a pair of grey athletic socks.

"No."

"Aside from taking down the occasional purse snatcher or thief who runs past me," he raised a finger, "because I can…I'm not a policeman, am I? I don't go looking for trouble."

Finding his friend's annoyance slightly comical, Dom took a seat and folded his arms, saying, "No, Rain. No you don't."

"I'm a chef. A quiet chef."

"A vampire chef."

"Yes, but a quiet, vampire chef." Going up to the refrigerator, Narain snatched out a unit of blood, gesturing with it. "I want to create my dishes, run my restaurant, and hopefully avoid killing the patrons with food poisoning. I've had strangeness in my ninety vampiric years; have had to avoid scrapes, but my only desire is to…"

"Live a normal life," Dom finished.

Narain smiled. "As normal as possible." Then he lost his smile and began gesturing with the blood again. "So, can you explain to me why, fifteen hours after kissing a woman good night..."

"You kissed her finally."

"Will you listen? Why, fifteen hours after kissing a woman good night and leaving her house, do I find myself waking up in the sewers of Chicago tonight?" He coughed a little and spat something into the sink, running the water. "And let me tell you, the microbes do not like the sewers of Chicago."

"The microbes?"

"Long story."

"Well, hopefully, you can explain it, because I don't have a clue."

Narain bit into the bag with gusto and drank heartily from it until it was drained. Remembering his friend was there though he looked up at Dom, ashamed, and threw the bag in a special container under his sink. Then he rinsed his mouth out.

"Rain, don't worry about that," Dom assured him. "Just tell me what happened."

"That's the problem. I don't really know." He joined Dom in the living room area and sat down in a chair, slicking back his hair with his hands.

Narain recounted his meeting with Cassie; the story she had told him about her family, his condition, and the curious connection they both shared. After describing the strange attack by the ferals, and the pre-dawn rescue, he leaned back, lost in the hazy memories of the few moments before he passed out. "I swear to you, Dom," he said, "I knew that figure. He said something to me but it was so garbled in my mind. Still, he was familiar. So familiar. Of course I can't be sure." He rolled his eyes. "I can't be sure about anything, but I could swear it was Fred Blythe who brought me down into the sewers."

Dom's eyes widened. "Your old army buddy?"

"Yes."

"The monster that Reginald Jameson claims is responsible for the killing going on?"

Narain rose from his chair and raised his hands with a sigh. "I can't explain. I just can't believe Blythe is responsible for..." he looked at the news clippings and pictures Reg had given him that he had spread on the table earlier that night to study, "for that. I would attribute that sort of viciousness more to Reg than Blythe. Blythe was a gentle man. A truck driver in his civilian life. He only wanted to be a good soldier while he had to be."

Dom studied him for a moment, noting the strain on his face from memories washing over him. "Rain, you never really talk much about the war."

Narain sighed, staring at the end table, his eyes acquiring a lost look. "What's to say? The good guys won. It was a long time ago."

Dom said gently, "I'm thinking not all that long for you. At least not lately, with all these reminders cropping up." He chuckled softly, admitting, "You know, when Sophie told me how...when you became...you know..."

"Vampiric?" Narain said grinning with a playful menace.

Dom grinned. "Yeah. Well, I did a little reading about World War I. Watched some documentaries. You know," he hesitated, "that was some nasty shit, Rain. I mean, war is hell, but that one…it was like no one was prepared for it."

Narain stared at him, stunned by the accuracy of the statement. "No, no one was. Really. It was supposed to be over by Christmas, 1914. It lasted four years, involved half the world, and brought into fresh perspective just what complete bastards humans could be to each other."

"So, tell me about Blythe, then." For a moment, he wasn't sure if Narain would speak. Or if he would, Dom wasn't sure if he would simply wave a hand and brush the topic off as he so often did with topics he preferred not to pursue. But he didn't. Looking up at him with an almost resigned look, Narain sighed, allowing the memories to flow unheeded.

✝

The Great War. It would come to be known as World War I. During it, however, it was called "the war to end all wars" by people who never conceived the extent of mankind's cruelty. For four years it sucked country after country into the horrific quagmire. Over 17 million people died. Men, women, children, death didn't discriminate. Whether it was from the terrible new weapons like landmines or mustard gas, or simply starvation, casualties mounted and soldiers returned to their homes maimed physically or mentally. A select few left the war altered in a way unimaginable.

Narain had no idea that Europe was so cold. He'd heard stories, of course. The Viceroy Hotel in Bengal where he had worked as assistant chef had many European visitors staying there and some of the friendlier ones would strike up conversations with the staff. They would tell stories of their various countries, inevitably comparing weather patterns for they were just as struck by India's warmth as he would be by Europe's cold.

He had left India in September 1916, with a battalion of other soldiers, to fight for an empire that looked upon them more as inconveniences than citizens. Each had his reasons for going and all had tearful relatives seeing them off at the dock, after their few weeks of basic training were finished. Narain never realised just how difficult saying goodbye would be until he was holding his weeping mother in his arms, assuring her he'd be fine. Her comments on how handsome he looked in his uniform deteriorated into a list of dos and don'ts that were sobbed out.

Zaheer, who could find rainbows on the cloudiest of days, hid his misgivings in the demand that their first meal upon Narain's return be of French origin. The two brothers chatted warmly, Narain promising to bring back a special recipe and lightly warning his younger sibling to be good for their parents. A warning that he knew was unnecessary considering the boy's gentle disposition.

During this, Aziz had stood several feet away, taking it all in, his face unreadable. Coaxed over by his mother, he stood in front of Narain, his head downcast. To Narain's surprise the young boy eventually wrapped his arms around his big brother's waist and squeezed tightly, never making a sound. Before Narain could respond, however, Aziz released him and ran back to his original position, refusing to gaze any further upon the scene. Narain couldn't help but notice, however, that the boy quickly wiped a tear from his cheek and he sent out a silent prayer that he would have the chance to build a better bond with his brother.

The hardest goodbye was with Ujaali.

Wiping tears from her eyes, all she said was, "But I don't want you to go," the flute-like voice now thick with fear.

Narain crouched down and brushed back her hair. "I'll be back."

Stubbornly she said, "No you won't. You'll leave us forever."

"I will return, I promise. And I'll bring you something from one of those far away countries. Would you like that?"

"Don't go," she insisted, falling into his arms.

He lifted her, hugging her tightly and humming. "You're young now," he told her. "One day you'll understand. I will write you and you can write me. It will be like a game. And when I'm ready to come home, you can plan a big party for me. We'll play all the games you like to play."

She nodded, her cheeks tear-stained, then kissed him on the cheek and held her arms out for her mother. Once in her mother's embrace, she turned her head into the woman's neck and sobbed.

His sister's grief weighed on Narain, heavier than anything he'd ever experienced and he made a silent vow to return to her no matter what.

His father was next and Narain's eyes grew misty again when they embraced. "Your sister has spoken for all of us," his father said, his words hoarse. "Be good. Stay safe. And when your dreams are fulfilled come back to us."

"I will, Baba, I will."

His legs were leaden as he walked up the gang plank to board the ship that would take him so far from home. The voyage would take weeks and having never sailed before, the first week was spent wracked by nausea—much like the rest of the soldiers. The ship's crew had fun with the sea sickness of their charges and once his queasiness had subsided, he recognised it as a form of camaraderie. He would discover later that such camaraderie would be in short supply once the Indian soldiers reached the trenches. They came from all over India, fighting for all sorts of reasons. Some out of patriotism to the crown, some to feed their families. Some like Narain, seeking adventure or opportunity.

By the time he was comfortable on deck, the ship was very far out to sea. They were surrounded by nothing but water and sky and it left him feeling reflective and rather small in this alien environment. The only firm footing was to be found on a ship that swayed at the mercy of the ocean's temperament. When the ocean grew irritable, it tortured them with incessant rocking and the ever present threat that one properly placed wave could sink them. The rain pelted, the sun baked, and the only deliverance from either was below deck where one rolled and swayed and tried to forget the fact that there was still so far to go before touching dry land.

There was beauty in this solitude, though. Cloudless nights revealed jewels in the sky as stars shone their maps above them. During the day, every so often, a glance overboard would reveal pods of dolphins racing alongside the ship. The soldiers and crew would run to the sides and shout greetings to the creatures as they leapt out of the water, almost as if in response. Once, the ship came upon whales in the distance, and the size of their flukes as they slapped the water left even the ship's crew speechless.

The ship finally docked at Liverpool, where the soldiers joined up with another company, before they were ferried to France. Narain handed one of the sailors a packet of letters he had written to his family while on board ship, asking that the sailor see that they make it back to India. The sailor agreed.

"Seems like the least I can do, mate," the sailor said, glancing at the packet. "It's a brave thing you chaps are doing. Besides, you can't half cook. Were it not for your kitchen skills, I might have gone barmy on this run."

Narain smiled. The food on board had been one of the depressing aspects of the trip. Supplies were chosen not for luxury but for duration. He had offered his services to the captain partly for the sake of his fellow soldiers and partly for his own sanity. He hadn't touched a pot in weeks and it was getting to him. So, he did what he could with what he had and the soldiers and crew were happy for the effort.

"I do believe you have a future in this," the captain had said appreciatively after calling him to his quarters one evening after dinner. After the captain's inquiries, Narain explained his culinary hopes and desires. The captain nodded smiling. "Well, India's loss will be Europe's gain. Perhaps once this damned war is over, I might be of some assistance. Keep me in mind, old chap, should you find yourself in need."

Arriving in France, the company marched through the French countryside to the Western Front, where the Allies were bogged down in the trenches, in a campaign that seemed to have reached a permanent stalemate. Narain had to admit that, so far, he had been treated quite well by the British. A few on the ship's crew had a bit of condescension tainting their manner, but nothing unbearable. And there was no overt prejudice from the French, who came to the dock to watch the disembarking of the newest soldiers to join the fray to save this country.

I wonder if they'd be so considerate to us, if a war was not on," Vivek asked as they joined the formation of soldiers preparing to march. Narain and Vivek Bandalar had struck up a friendship on board, growing quite close during the voyage. Vivek was from Nagpur and had enlisted to escape an engagement to a woman he could barely tolerate and who had little regard for him.

"And what will you do when the war is over and you must return?" Narain had asked him.

"Perhaps they will grow tired of waiting and marry her to someone else. Besides, who said I have to return? I can be an ex-patriot in Paris. And maybe once you are a chef, we can open a restaurant and allow Paris to taste what real food is like. Anyway, there's always the chance that the decision will be made for me and I will head off into my next life." He chuckled. "Knowing my luck, she will kill herself just to chase after me."

On board ship, they could joke about war, but marching through the French countryside toward the front, the realities came into sharp focus as they passed caravans of Allied dead and wounded on their way home. Those still breathing looked haunted, with hollow eyes and ashen skin. As they passed these convoys, everything seemed to go in slow motion for Narain. The horrible sights these men had witnessed were etched upon their sunken faces. They were alive and going home, but they were dead to that joy. Worn out. Used up. Eventually, Narain simply averted his eyes and concentrated on the road, praying that the war didn't leave him as hopeless and as dead inside as these men now looked.

Vivek helped keep his spirits up with an irreverent energy that Narain had no choice but to laugh at. He was glad that if he had to be in this cold land, he had a battalion of other Indians marching with him to ease some of the home sickness he was experiencing.

The march to the Western Front took weeks. They marched down country roads, past cottages and farms, where children tending sheep would march along with them for short distances, cheering them on as they had cheered on so many other battalions that passed by.

Occasionally, they marched through villages where people of the town hailed them, shouting in heavily accented English words of encouragement and the names of loved ones to look up once they were on the front.

"Say 'hello' to my father."

"My brother's over there. Please send him my love."

In one village, an old woman surged forward and pressed a letter into Narain's hand. "Please, this is for my son," she said, hurrying alongside the line. "I beg you, see that he gets it. God go with you all."

Wide eyed, all Narain could do was nod and continue the march as the woman fell back. He had learned a little French while at the Viceroy and was able to figure out what the woman was asking, but as he stared at the envelope, thoughts of his own family whirled around his mind. He knew it was unlikely but he could not help but hope that he could somehow fulfil this mother's wish.

In another town, a group of pretty young ladies stood behind a fence, shouting in French and waving at the men who seemed to perk up at the attention. "Namaste girls, namaste," Vivek said, smiling wide and waving back. "We're off to teach the Kaiser a lesson." Then to Narain, he added, "And perhaps on the way back we can teach the lovely ladies a lesson."

Narain blushed knowing his friend was all talk but surprised nonetheless.

With a chuckle, he told Vivek, "You take care or they may not let you back into India."

The air of desperation became deeper, the further they marched into France. The French were fighting for their country and the years had worn them down. The closer the battalion got to the front, the more dour the atmosphere became. Miles from the front, they could hear the constant thump as the warring factions lobbed mortars at each other and even Vivek's ever present grin hardened. Even from afar, they could spot the beating that the forest was taking. Trees that didn't stand like burnt twigs, leafless and blackened by fire, were simply charred stumps blown into splinters. The ground between the two factions, what they'd learn to call "No Man's Land," was chewed up by mortar shells, which left great mounds of dirt and debris and deep muddy craters in their wake.

And there were bodies in the field; Narain could see them. He would learn that they were the bodies of German soldiers, who had been mown down, when they tried to charge into the Allied trenches for a raid. The bodies stayed out there, rotting, for no one dared to go out and retrieve them.

Then there were the trenches: The intricate system that snaked on deeply, far across the Western Front; furrowed wounds that became cities unto themselves. It took months to dig them out and shore them up, before fighting had even been considered. In the trench, British soldiers milled about, slogging through the ever present, ankle-deep water and trying to avoid the occasional strand of barbed wire that had fallen from its place along the lip of the trench, where it protected the trench's inhabitants from night-time attacks *by Germans raiders.*

"Life with my intended is looking better and better," Vivek commented with a hollow tone.

Men moved along the trenches like ants, some darting in and out of little chambers dug into the wall of dirt, where supplies and munitions were stored. Much further back in the trenches, there were even chambers where horses were kept. Other men sat on planks in little indentations, playing cards or checking equipment. Checking equipment, Narain would later learn, was often done more for busy work than concern for safety. Boredom, in fact, was the most tenacious foe for the trench soldier.

As the Indian soldiers climbed down into the trench, the Germans released another barrage of mortar, one hitting nearby, spitting up the dirt which flew at the soldiers. Narain felt something whip into his cheek and swiping at it, he noted the dark blood staining his fingertips.

"Not to worry, mate," one of the British soldiers told him as they settled again. He inspected Narain's face with a practical eye, and then smiled, patting his other cheek. "None too deep. You've just been baptised, that's all." He handed Narain a handkerchief saying, "Keep it. I have another."

Blinking, Narain smiled faintly and thanked him before following after the others.

The Indian soldiers were spread along the trench for a mile. There were several officers, each in charge of a particular section of the trench and Narain, Vivek, and eight others were set somewhere in the middle. Narain was grateful that Vivek was in his unit. It would make the days go faster. He hoped. Narain and Vivek were directed to their section by a soldier who couldn't have been more than twenty. As they slogged their way through the muck another mortar hit nearby, causing all to duck. One of the men answered with some pointless gunfire before everything was quiet again.

Private Fred Blythe, their guide, affected a smile on his young open face, his pale-blue eyes friendly and honest. "Just remember to keep your head low, chaps. Usually, you'll hear a whistle when a shell's on the way, but you can't be too sure."

Narain and Vivek looked at each other, shrugged, then continued to follow him to where two officers were intently playing cards. The pile of cash on the plank between them revealed the reason for the high degree of concentration.

"Come now, Jameson," said one, smoking a pipe and holding his cards in the relaxed manner of a man confident in his hand. "I think I've got you again."

The other, Captain Reginald Jameson, had a tightly wound energy as he debated how much he was willing to put in to see the other man's hand. His brown hair was cut short back and sides, and his bearing had a carefully cultivated military air about it. "Luck turns, Danforth, just remember that."

Blythe halted in front of them, saluting and stamping his foot in military fashion, unwittingly splashing some of the muck on the legs of the men. Lieutenant Danforth remained sitting, but Jameson threw his cards down and burst to his feet. "What is wrong with you, Blythe?"

Slightly oblivious, Blythe held his salute until Jameson returned it with a frustrated gesture. "Private Blythe reporting with new recruits."

"Oh good," Danforth said, playing with his cards, "fresh meat."

Jameson took a look at the Indian soldiers and rolled his eyes, hands on hips. "Oh you must be joking." Glaring at the new recruits he pointed at Blythe, "It's not bad enough they're sending over lower class yabbos like this, who wouldn't know a military manoeuvre from a move in a tiddly winks tournament." He sneered at the soldiers. "What do they think I can do with East Indian apes?"

Narain felt his face burn at the insult, but he knew enough to remain silent. Jameson was a superior officer and rank had its privilege, as abused as that might be.

"Steady on, Reg," Danforth said with a grimace. "There's no call for that. They are here to help us, after all. With no real benefit to their country."

"They'll be hearing a lot worse if the bosch take over everything, which might just happen considering what we have to work with."

"Reg, one question before you attend to the new recruits," Danforth said, looking up at him. "Are you in, or out?"

With a quick movement, Jameson slammed money into the pot leading Danforth to reveal a truly spectacular hand of poker. Irritated, Jameson picked up then tossed his cards on the table, snapping, "It's yours" before turning to military duty. Very well, Blythe, show them the ropes."

Blythe saluted and as he was turning to leave, Jameson stuck a foot out, sending him into the muck at Narain's feet.

"Well, that will boost morale," Danforth said in a blasé tone putting his money in his wallet.

"That's for muddying up my trousers," Jameson told him. "Perhaps, you'll show more care next time."

Try as he might, Narain could not keep the disgust from his eyes. Jameson focused on it immediately, intimidating Blythe to remain in the muck while he went nose to nose with Narain.

"Do you have something you wish to say, Private?"

Narain never blinked, never looked away. Rather, he bore his olive-brown eyes into Jameson's blue and answered, "No, sir."

Picking up on the challenge, Jameson said, "I'm sorry, I didn't quite hear that."

"No, sir, I don't, sir," Narain bellowed.

Backing away, Jameson smiled. "I didn't think so." Looking down at the private in the muck, he asked, "Blythe, is there a reason you're still down there?"

"No, sir," Blythe said, starting to get up.

His eyes never leaving Jameson, Narain crouched down and took hold of Blythe's arm helping him to his feet. That was it. The war had begun and while he was never one to in-stigate trouble, Narain could not restrain himself from firing this first shot. Jameson's face darkened as he said, "Get them out of here."

As Blythe motioned for the soldiers to follow him, Vivek nudged Narain, impressed, whispering, "I didn't know you were tough."

Narain kept his head low as he replied, "I'm not. I just hate bullies."

As the months went by, Narain could not help but remember the conversation he had with his father when the man found the enlistment papers. As his service wore on, he real-ised just how right his father had been. The insanity of this fool's war was matched only by *its cruelty. In his letters home, he made sure to omit details of the horror. He spoke of the scenery, the excitement of learning another language (the few words he picked up in French and German), the rare times the soldiers were relieved and were able to go into the nearby town for a few days, where they were able to bathe and perhaps eat something other than the rations offered in the trenches. Here, he befriended an old woman who allowed him the use of her kitchen, showing him some recipes popular in the countryside. As the other soldiers gravitated to the makeshift canteen where beer and wine were available while rations held out, he visited the old woman to soak up more of her Gallic culinary expertise and share with her a little of his knowledge.*

He wrote of the friendships he was forming with the soldiers he practically lived on top of. That was one of the benefits of the war. Bonds forged in war would never be broken. When one was homesick, he might look to the news sent to another soldier to help him through it. Narain knew who was engaged, who was divorcing, whose wife was expecting and whose parents were having a row with the next door neighbours over escaped dogs, or apples falling in yards or whatever news was fit to print. And they knew of his family and his home. When he showed Ujaali's picture to Private Blythe, the man smiled fondly. "Oh, she's a darlin' isn't she? I bet she misses her big brother."

Narain nodded glumly. "I fear she may."

"Not to worry. You'll be home in no time. They've got to come to their senses soon."

Narain wrote his family much about Blythe, and Vivek and the many others he had befriended. But he couldn't tell them everything. How could he describe the Germans dropping chlorine gas into the trenches, sending everyone running for their gas masks? Those unfortunate enough not to reach the masks in time were left contracting like insects, their exposed skin turning horrid shades of green, then blue. Water seeped into everything. Most times, the trenches had at least an inch of it on the ground, sometimes so much that it had to be bailed out. During heavy rains, one wondered if they would be flooded out completely. During winter it became a horrid slush, threatening the soldiers with frostbite. Dysentery was a frequent visitor, as were lice and vermin and the horrible trench foot.

Narain had studied the art of cooking since he was a little boy and had watched his mother make naan with an infectious exuberance. He got a job at a family friend's restaurant, then as line cook in the Viceroy hotel where he was complimented on his palette-pleasing experiments with styles until he was made assistant chef. Now, he was in a trench, calf deep in water, in a cold country that might not have any restaurants for him to train in, still standing after the war was finally over.

The shell shock was the worst. Many of those men who couldn't switch their focus, found themselves fixating on the sometimes incessant barrage of the mortar guns that the factions fired at each other. A section down the line was destroyed by a mortar that managed to hit its mark, sending body parts flying as wildly as the dirt and debris. Generally, though, it was an exercise in futility for both sides. Still, after a particularly nasty barrage, the thumping that shook the ground often invaded their sleep and left them haunted during the day. Narain was certain that Blythe was succumbing to shell shock, for the poor man seemed to be growing increasingly jittery, with or without bombs, as the months wore on. Of course, Jameson's cruelty didn't help.

That was another thing Narain couldn't write home about. Jameson took great relish in targeting Blythe, especially when Narain was around to watch. Blythe had driven a lorry in London before the war, and possessed not a drop of military blood in his lineage. Despite this, he tried his best to measure up to the likes of Jameson, whose own family had long military careers and who was himself hoping to go much further than Captain in his own career. Narain first truly noticed this sadism one afternoon when Jameson ordered Blythe to fix the barbed wire along twenty yards of the trench. Blythe, the good soldier, saluted, but Narain could see his face blanch at the prospect of carrying out the duty. He was particularly disturbed by the top of the trench, which perhaps a soldier should not be since one day, he might be called upon to go over the top. Narain could see no reason why Blythe had to be the one to perform the duty, however, so he offered to do to it for Blythe, who smiled gratefully. "Are you sure? I don't mind, really."

Narain could see that he did, and smiled, nodding. "It would probably be good for me to do."

Leaning in confidentially, Blythe said, "Well, actually, I'm glad you're willing. Something about up top. Gives me the willies. Don't know what it is."

"Not to worry."

Narain performed the duty and all was fine, until Jameson found out. He roared for Blythe and swiped at him when the soldier came to him. "Did I or did I not, tell you to attend to that barbed wire?" he demanded. Narain stepped up, saying, "Sir, was the work not satisfactory?"

"No it wasn't, Private, because I asked Blythe here to do it, not you.

"But I asked to do it sir."

"That's a damned lie and you know it." Blythe said nothing, simply stood at attention, but with the posture of a whipped dog as Jameson continued, "You're covering for Blythe, because Blythe is too lazy or yellow to carry out the order given to him."

"That's not true," Narain said, ready to step forward, but held back by Vivek who told him in Hindi to restrain himself.

"That's right, jabber on little monkey, and keep your friend in check." He turned again to Blythe and walked around him as best he could in the tight trench. "What you are going to do Blythe, is carry out my order. And if that means tearing it down and starting from scratch, then so be it."

"Would that not be a waste of time, sir?" Narain sneered, holding his fury.

Jameson squinted his eyes at Narain, walking toward him. "Those who are familiar with the military," he began, leaning into Narain's face, "would know that an attitude such as yours can get you in a lot of hot water. So, I suggest you follow your friend's lead and keep quiet."

Narain did so, knowing that anything else he said would be pointless. Blythe glanced at him with a reassuring smile that only made him feel guiltier. It was wasteful, this attitude of Jameson's, and it proved that he wasn't above such pettiness to feel powerful, the consequences be damned. After that, the captain showed his sadism in little slights aimed at Blythe and some of the other Indian soldiers. He never went directly after Narain, though, perhaps realising it would affect him more to see the misery of others. Jameson showed the extremes to which he was willing to take his feud, the night Blythe was left on guard duty and woke the trench up with gunfire and screaming. The moon was nearly full, but even with that light, the trench and beyond it was dark. One could peer into this dark and see all manner of shapes and shadows, never knowing which were real and which a trick of the eyes. It was not unusual for vermin or even the occasional wolf to investigate the top of the trench. Blythe's commotion had sent everyone out to see what was happening and they found him waving his gun around the top of the trench, his face white and eyes wide. Some of the soldiers looked on, irritated, some shook their head sadly.

"Blythe, you fool!" Jameson bellowed, stepping forward. As he did so, he made sure to shove Narain aside. "What are you up to?"

Standing next to Narain, Vivek commented quietly, "Here he goes again. I wouldn't want to be in Blythe's shoes."

"They were everywhere, sir," Blythe said, not bothering to salute, still in a crouched and ready stance.

"Who were everywhere, old boy, Germans?" Danforth said, still as casual as ever.

Blythe seemed surprised by the question. "I don't...I don't know."

Narain could tell by the way he shivered and the quiver in his voice, that this was more than simply seeing a shadow. More than likely, Blythe's shell shock was getting the better of him. Yet, something frightened him terribly, whether or not it was in his mind. Carefully, he walked toward him, ignoring Jameson's irritated glares. To his credit, the captain remained quiet.

"What is it exactly you saw?" Narain said, slowly taking the gun from Blythe's hands.

Relaxing only slightly, the man said, "I don't know."

"Were you sleeping, man?" Jameson demanded.

Narain glared at him, but Blythe said, "No, I swear. I swear. I was keeping an eye peeled. Looking around. It's dark up there. I heard something, like dirt shifting or something and I looked up..."

"And saw..." Narain coaxed.

"Figures." He closed his eyes, trying to envision them. "They were big. Grey, almost sheer white. Ghostly." Jameson sighed, but Blythe continued, "When I turned at the first noise, there was one on the trench staring down at me. Then I looked around and there they were, about seven or so, leaning on the trench looking down. The barbed wire didn't even bother them."

"Tell me, Blythe," Narain said, "Did you see them as well as you see Bolton or McConnel now?"

"Yeah, more than, like."

Narain frowned. Unless Blythe's eyesight was superior to his, in the darkened trench lit by a half moon, it was unlikely he saw these figures very clearly. If he saw them at all.

"This is ridiculous!" Jameson spat. "You were asleep and woke up from a dream."

"A nightmare, more like," someone commented from the back.

"I didn't. I wasn't."

"Could you have been drinking, old fellow?" Danforth suggested.

"Is that so? Were you drinking?" Jameson demanded stepping toward him.

"No. None of us has had anything, since we copped that flask last month. I saw figures up on the trench. They were horrible. And believe me, they were looking to come down here and do us no end of harm."

Clenching and unclenching his fists, Jameson insisted, "You were sleeping on duty, very likely drunk, and you put us all in danger." He was growing calm, and that was never a good sign. "Such actions must be punished. Therefore, since you are so well rested, you won't need any rations tomorrow. You can give your rations for the next two days to Private Khan here."

Narain whipped his head around to face him. "What?"

"Private Khan must be particularly hungry from all the exertion he expends in defending you. So he may have your rations."

As it were, the rations were small, supplies being tight at the moment. The men were already feeling the pinch. And Blythe was not in the best of health to begin with. Narain wanted to lunge at Jameson and hold his face in the mud until he blacked out. A vicious response he would never have had, even against his worst enemies, before sailing to this shattered country. But, the warning look Vivek gave him kept him still. Instead, he simply said, "No. I don't want them."

"What!" Jameson snapped, yet smiled, almost as if that was the statement he was hoping for.

Beginning to shiver himself, Narain said, "I don't know what he saw, but I believe he saw something. It could have been wolves or wild dogs. Or it could have been a pack of Germans who managed to sneak across "no man's land" and who were ready to pounce, were it not for this man's firing. But, whether what he saw was real or his imagination, I will not be a party to this."

Narain was going to leave the scene when Jameson ordered, "Stand at attention, Private." When he was ignored, Jameson reached out to grab his shoulder and Narain whirled around, staring at him. Taken aback, Jameson pointed and walked around him excitedly saying, "You're all witnesses. He was going to strike a superior officer."

Vivek stepped forward, but Narain looked at him and shook his head. The soldiers were grudgingly silent. Rolling his eyes, Danforth resigned himself, sitting on a nearby plank to wait out the inevitable.

"An army," Jameson began, his eyes riveted to Narain, "a proper army, functions on one thing: Discipline. The moment crass insubordination is tolerated, it all crumbles apart. There was a time, Private Khan, when a soldier could be shot for turning on his superior. But we must take into consideration the fact that the British war effort needs everybody they can get—the only reason your rabble was allowed to join. But insubordination cannot be tolerated."

Walking over to Danforth, he held out his hand and sighing, Danforth handed him what he expected. In the dark, it was difficult to see and for a moment, Narain worried that the crazed captain might intend to shoot him anyway. Nodding to two soldiers loyal to him, Jameson stalked closer as the soldiers grabbed Narain forcing him against the wall of the trench.

"Are you mad?" Vivek gasped, but backed off when Jameson stared at him. It was an evil stare, revealing that at that moment pain was his only purpose.

The other soldiers looking on grumbled in confusion, but were silent when Narain said, "Quiet."

This did not sit at all well with Jameson, who loosened his hold on the belt he held and allowed it to extend down so that the buckle was on the giving end. Without a warning, he lashed out, the belt and buckle slamming into Narain's shoulder blade, biting through his uniform shirt. He cried out, the pain slicing into him and he braced for the next blow. Jameson whipped again and again, Narain's fingers digging into the moist dirt of the trench wall as he tried to make as little noise as possible. His knees buckled but the soldiers flanking him held him firmly in place.

"I assure you, I don't enjoy this," Jameson said insincerely, "but an example must be made." He lashed out again, the belt slamming across the left side of Narain's back. "There are choices we must all make. Private Khan could have chosen to allow me to punish Private Blythe, as was fitting, but he chose instead to speak out of turn. Choices have consequences. These are the consequences."

He let loose with a volley of several more whips that cut or left welts all over Narain's bruised back. Gritting his teeth, Narain's muscles contracted with each hit. After the tenth, he was allowed to fall into the muck, moaning softly.

"Now, were we in the Navy," Jameson lectured, rolling up the belt, "That would have been a proper whip and at least thirty more lashes."

"Bully for the navy," Danforth said, a note of tired disgust in his voice, as he methodically lit his pipe.

Narain turned his head and looked at Blythe, cringing at the look of guilt that had spread across the young private's face. For Narain, that was a pain almost as sharp as the fire on his back and he was certain that was exactly what Jameson had planned. Reginald Jameson was an opportunist, who saw a chance to take two people down, and he did so, quite efficiently.

"As for the aforementioned rations," he said, nodding at the two soldiers who had held Narain, "Privates Caldwell and Scott can have both Blythe and Khan's for the next three days. And anyone caught offering their rations to Privates Blythe or Khan will feel the buckle of this belt, as well." He glared at Danforth who rose slowly, and then the two started toward their quarters. Turning, he glowered at the soldiers. "I'll brook no further dissent, be assured of that."

Once the two had left, Vivek hurried over to where Narain was stubbornly trying to pick himself up out of the mud. Every movement brought fresh pain to deep cuts and bruises and part of him wanted to just be still in the mud until the pain went away.

Taking hold of his arm carefully, Vivek and a British solider helped him to his feet. Assessing the injuries on Narain's bloodied back, Vivek hissed, "What sort of animal is this captain?" Then he chided, "Narain, why do you always take that man's bait?" before raising a hand. "I know, I know. You hate bullies."

It was the answer he always gave Vivek after a run in with Jameson. By this time it had become a test of wills between the two and Narain had resigned himself to the possibility that for the duration of the war, Jameson would do everything he could to break him and Narain would do everything he could to keep from breaking.

The climax came weeks later when it was not Narain, but Blythe who finally broke. Narain, perhaps, could have predicted it, but he hoped against hope that Blythe would be able to hold on. The damned stalemate between the sides was lasting forever and there were times when he wondered if the war would ever end; or if rather, it would go on and on, the gaining of ground, the losing of ground, the shelling back and forth, the earth shaking under each bombardment.

It was on a Thursday afternoon that they received the call they'd all been dreading, that at last let loose the insanity of the situation. Jameson called his unit to assembly and they found him looking a little more ashen, and not quite as cocky as he normally looked. His tone was still arrogant and disdainful.

"As you all know there has been a rumour that we are scheduled for a push. Well, the rumour is true. It will be a raid on the German trenches. We are scheduled to go over the top in a matter of moments."

Jaws dropped as the men of the unit gasped collectively. Over the top. Into that bitter acreage that so many had tried and failed to cross. It had been stalemate for years between the two sides, because neither side could figure out a way to send their troops through that hellish territory, without them being mowed down by enemy fire. The push had been a possibility from the first day in the trenches, but it seemed almost sacrilegious to hear it spoken of so bluntly, on a day when the sun was actually shining down on them and the air was unsullied by the sound of German shells.

Still stunned, Vivek nonetheless shrugged saying, "Well, I will be safe from my intended. At least until her death."

"So," Jameson announced after the shock had settled, "you'll need to check your weapons and supplies. Make sure your rifle is in good working order. There will be three blows of the whistle." He gave a soft toot on his. "The first will be a warning to make ready. The second will be a call to assume formation. And the third will be the final order." After a pause, he said, "And remember, we are fighting for a glorious cause. If all goes well we'll be…" the usual saying was that they'd be dining on sausages in the Kaiser's palace by Christmas. But Jameson's tone illustrated that even he was unable to call up that much unrealistic jingoism. Instead a bit quieter, he finished, "Well, with luck we'll be home." He looked around. "Or at least far away from here. Dismissed."

The first whistle warning was heard and Jameson tooted his loudly, sending it on to the next unit who would do the same along the trench.

A chill went through Narain. A part of him felt relief, for he knew one way or another he would be free from that place. It was how he would arrive back on the soil of India that worried him. He looked down at the picture of Ujaali he had taken from his wallet. How will they tell her that her brother is not coming home, he thought.

"Narain," Vivek patted his back. "Let's go. There's not much time."

Nodding, Narain followed him and they readied their gear. When the unit had congregated again, many of the soldiers joked about "old times" while they waited for the second whistle. Danforth looked a bit green, which seemed strange for a man whose temperament was cool even in the worst times. As they exited their quarters, he followed silently behind Jameson, who seemed to review his soldiers with a calculating eye as if already deciding who was likely to make it back.

As if knowing a British charge was imminent, the Germans started their cannons again, to which the Allies readily replied with their own salvoes.

"Captain Jameson, sir," one of the soldiers called out down the trench. "I think there's something wrong with Blythe."

Narain's eyes widened as he saw a malevolent grin cross Jameson's face. A last bit of torture, before the captain left his kingdom. He hurried after, despite Vivek's warning, and saw Blythe huddled in an indentation of the trench that he had seemingly dug by himself, if his scraped and filthy hands were any indication. He held his arms over his head, murmuring into the dirt and Narain was sure that the shell shock had finally taken hold.

Jameson saw only a soldier goldbricking. "Blythe, what the deuce are you doing?" he barked, kicking at the man's leg. "Where's your gun? We're going over to visit Jerry in a few moments." He looked over at Danforth chuckling, but there was no reaction from the other man, not even his usual half-hearted approach. He just watched the scene, almost detached.

"I can't, sir, I can't. I want to go home." Blythe murmured, pitifully.

"Nonsense! This is not a request. This is an order."

"I can't face them. The ghostly things are out there, everywhere."

"They're called Germans, Blythe and it's our job to rid this fair country of them."

Narain recognised the false bravado in Jameson's voice and it was probably the captain's own fear that was leading him to taunt Blythe, who had obviously, finally, suffered a breakdown. "Leave him be, Reg," Narain said. He had long since stopped giving Jameson the respect of calling him by his rank. At first, it was just in references during conversation with the other soldiers. Eventually it was to his face. And oddly, Jameson did not deny him the privilege. "Can't you see he's ill?"

"He's faking, Khan," Jameson insisted. "He doesn't want to go." He kicked Blythe again. "Well guess what, Sonny Jim, none of us do. But that's our fate now, isn't it? So, get on your feet, get your gun and queue up for that whistle."

"No, I don't want to go over the top," Blythe whispered and looked helplessly over at Narain. "I'm useless. They're out there waiting for all of us."

Narain stepped closer. The trench, already tense, was electrified at that point. Deciding play time was over, Jameson scowled and pulled out his service revolver.

"Blythe, this is not a summer holiday," he snarled, his arm ram rod straight as he pointed the gun at the tormented man. "Get on your feet right now."

"Reg, what the devil are you thinking?"

"I am authorized by the British Army to shoot any man for cowardice," he looked around. "Any man who refuses to go over that trench wall. Blythe, you have until the count of five."

"Lieutenant Danforth, stop him," Narain pleaded and some of the other soldiers audibly bristled at the captain's action.

Danforth said nothing.

"One."

Head lowered, Danforth merely walked over to a wooden plank and sat down wearily, staring at his rifle.

"Two."

Narain looked around helplessly. Jameson would do this, he had no doubt. But while the seriousness in Jameson's voice brought Blythe out of his mania somewhat, he couldn't find his legs to stand. Instead, the lorry driver from London looked up at the British gun being aimed at his head.

"Three."

Narain lunged at Jameson pushing the gun out of range of its target. Stunned, Jameson recovered quickly and brought the butt of the gun down toward Narain's skull. Narain was able to deflect it enough so that it only landed a glancing blow and together the combatants fell into the dirt. Concentrating on keeping the gun barrel away from himself Narain was unable to untangle himself from his opponent and soon he found himself pinned underneath as Jameson held the gun to his head. He stared up into the cold, blue eyes, noting the enjoyment that danced within them. Where once the soldiers would have kept quiet during one of these stand-offs, their cannon fodder status now left them uninhibited and they shouted and jeered until the gun was pressed against Narain's temple. Then, silence flowed through the trench.

Showing his teeth, Jameson hissed, "I have enough bullets for both you and Blythe and perhaps a few for your monkey friends, eh what?"

Before he could cock the gun, however, a rifle butt smashed against his back and he fell off Narain, dazed. Blythe stood above them, face still deathly pale and tortured, but cognisant. He kicked Jameson further away and reached out to help Narain up. Relieved, Vivek joined them.

"One good thing about certain death," Vivek told Blythe, "you can taste a bit of revenge and you won't be around to answer for it."

Narain smiled weakly studying Blythe. "Are you with us, Fred?"

Blythe blinked at him. "I think that's the first time anyone has used my Christian name in this whole bloody war. I'd forgotten what it sounded like. My name's not Private Blythe." He sniffed and rubbed his nose with his sleeve. "It's plain old Fred Blythe."

At that moment, the second warning whistle sounded and to their horror, a rifle shot exploded. Ears ringing, they looked toward the sound of the shot and grimaced as they saw Danforth's lifeless body sprawled on the plank, the back of his head blown open, the barrel of the gun still lodged in his mouth.

"I don't want to go," Blythe said as the others lined up near the ladder.

Jameson moaned, waking up and Narain spared him only a moment's notice. Instead he looked at Vivek, whose eyes were misty, his face solemn for the first time in their friendship. "Jameson's right," Vivek said, wiping his eyes and straightening up. "We'll be having sauerkraut by tomorrow tea time."

Hugging him tightly, Narain released him and turned his eyes to Blythe. "You are Fred Blythe, who may very likely be shot for cowardice if he stays behind." He glanced up then back at Blythe. "You may have a better chance up there."

Vivek patted Blythe's shoulder. "And if not, at least you'll be in good company." He looked toward Jameson who was getting to his feet. "Better than the vermin in here."

Still visibly shaken, Blythe nodded, picked up his rifle, and walked with Narain and Vivek toward a ladder. As if out of respect for a new leader, soldiers by the ladder stepped back to allow Narain to be the first up. Not to be the first to fall but to be the one to lead them.

And then, the third whistle blew.

†

Dom caught the tone of melancholy in Narain's voice, as he finished his story. He, himself, found words hard to come by after what he'd just heard. That had been a truncated version of the time Narain had spent in those trenches, during that war. He hadn't even gone into what horror lay in wait beyond the trench. It made perfect sense why the man rarely spoke of it. Who would want to remember it? Finally, gently, Dominic said, "But that was a long time ago, Rain. People change over time, and Blythe has had a long time to change. I mean, you're a gentle man, too, but you can be tough when you need to. Just like with that rapist the night of the benefit." Narain looked up sharply at him and he clarified, "Not that you'd kill," he motioned toward the pictures, "but then again, you would physically be able to do that. Who's to say that this Blythe didn't snap somewhere? You said yourself that he snapped right before going over the top."

Narain considered the words. Of course Dom was right, but he couldn't bring himself to believe it. "No, there's something else going on here. Too many questions. Reg seemed to imply that Blythe gravitated toward Chicago because I'm here…he, of course, is playing up the idea of some vendetta Blythe has against me. But, Blythe had his chance to destroy me. If not let the sun do it, he could have torn me apart in the sewer…I couldn't have run, let alone fight back. So why not take the chance? No, Fred Blythe saved me; I have no doubt about it. But then that leaves the question: Why is Blythe here? Why is all this converging on this town? Reg, Blythe…Cassie."

"Maybe you've been looking at it in the wrong way. Maybe you're not the key. Maybe Cassie is." Narain mulled the idea over. "What do we have here? We have the connection between you, Reg, and Blythe. Reg had Blythe before he escaped. Reg has been in contact with Cassie, she said so herself. You had just left Cassie's when Blythe came across you. Why did Reg have Blythe as a prisoner?"

"He never really told me."

"Exactly. And why did Reg contact Cassie in the first place?"

Narain considered that, and much more. There was a name. Blythe told him something before leaving him in the sewers and while he couldn't remember it all clearly, he remembered quite clearly one statement. "Talk to Channing." The name rang in Narain's mind, from its connection to Cassie and its apparent involvement with Blythe. There was one incongruous figure that might actually be more involved with the drama than initially expected. Perhaps, he was the key to all of this.

Chapter 13

Sasha's Grill on Rush Street had been named "The Number One Steakhouse in the Nation" for three years straight, and if Narain Khan owned a steakhouse, he might be slightly jealous. He owned, however, a restaurant, by nature eclectic, so such distinctions did not concern him. Only the status of the receipts concerned him. He and Gerald Portman, owner of Sasha's, had a friendly competition going, despite what the local cooking world gossip was, so Narain felt no compunction about entering Sasha's in his search for Richard Channing, who he was assured by reliable sources, was having a dinner meeting with the alderman of Chicago's Tenth Ward. Pinning the doctor down had been difficult. He had ignored the messages Narain had left for him and his service seemed unable to ascertain when he would be free for an unscheduled meeting. So, Narain took the meeting to him.

The décor was warm and woody steakhouse chic; dimmed lighting cast a golden glow over the white cloth covered tables, all of which seemed to be full of satisfied patrons. Narain inhaled deeply when he entered, savouring the rich aroma of well-seasoned beef. Portman knew how to cook a steak. The sizzle of the range, in full view of the patrons, made the scent even more enticing as the smoke wafted into the air. Every so often, Narain sacrificed a night of nausea to sample solid food. Ice cream was a particular weakness for him. He might almost be willing tonight, if he didn't have more pressing concerns.

"Will it be one tonight, sir?" A sweet looking hostess in a black blazer asked from behind a podium.

He shook his head, scanning the restaurant. "Actually, I'm here to meet someone. And I see them over there."

Without another word, he hurried into the restaurant and over to the table, where Richard Channing was listening with fake sincerity to the stories being spun by Alderman Stanley Dubcek, one of Chicago's more colourful politicians. The politician leaned back gesturing wildly for a moment, then went back to attacking his steak while Channing chuckled, taking a sip of his drink.

Stepping up to the table, Narain leaned with a hand on the back of Channing's chair, saying, "Dr. Channing, may I have a word with you?"

Channing looked up, stunned. "Mr. Khan, this is a surprise. I understand you've been trying to reach me, but my schedule has been quite tight. How did you find me?" His voice held both annoyance and anxiety.

"I have very good spies," Narain said, nodding as cordially as his preoccupied mind would allow, toward the alderman. "Alderman Dubcek."

"Mr. Khan," the alderman said, putting down his utensils and offering his hand. His Chicago twang was as jowly and robust as the alderman himself as he continued, "Wonderful party you threw a few weeks ago. My wife and her friends were crazy for your spicy cashews."

"They seem to have that effect on women," Narain said absently shaking the alderman's hand. "I'm wondering, Alderman, if I might have a word with Dr. Channing here."

Before the alderman could reply, Gerald Portman came over, a wide smile on his face making the ginger soul patch on his chin look even more ridiculous than normal. Usually Narain would have loved to engage in the phony rivalry between them, but time was not in his favour at the moment. Still, he took the hand offered and offered a charming smile in return. He did not want to panic Channing. "Gerald, good to see you."

"Same here, Khan," Gerald said, flashing his smile across the table. He was always a bit more of a showman than Narain. "Are you here to check out the competition?"

"Oh, I don't see very much competition here, Gerald." Grinning, he said, "Tell me, shouldn't you be off taping a cooking show or something?"

"Well, don't hold it against me because I can cook."

"Yes, but brats at barbecues don't count, Gerald." He couldn't resist a parting shot. Raising a palm, he quickly added, "I hope you don't mind, but I really do need to speak to Dr. Channing here."

Patting his back, Gerald grinned, unoffended. "Come back for a visit any time. We'll discuss barbecue recipes."

Narain nodded and Gerald left. Then he turned back to the table, but Channing spoke first, slightly irritated. "Mr. Khan, can we set up an appointment. I'm having dinner here."

Narain swallowed his own irritation. "No, actually, it is very important and I must talk to you now." He smiled at the other man. "Again, my apologies, Alderman. Hopefully, it won't take long."

The alderman shrugged, pointing toward Narain with a fork full of steak. "Richard, this isn't a problem. I don't mind. Go talk to him." It was more of an order than a concession.

Richard cleared his throat, patted his lips with his linen napkin, and then stood up while taking a last sip of his highball. Swallowing, he waved a hand, "Alright, Mr. Khan. Lead the way."

Noting Gerald at the bar, Narain directed Channing toward him, asking Portman, "Gerald, a favour. I need to discuss something very important with Dr. Channing. Is there some place private we could borrow?"

Gerald shrugged, "Of course." He took them through the kitchen and down a short hallway to his office. Unlocking the door, he said, "Use my office. Just no culinary espionage, eh?"

Practically shoving Channing through the door, Narain quipped, "Don't worry, I want my patrons to return to my restaurant, not leave vomiting."

Gerald chuckled, but noted the stress on the man's face. "Narain, is everything okay?"

Forcing himself to assume a more relaxed posture, he sighed, nodding with a smile. Gerald nodded, saying, "Okay, lock up when you're done."

Blinking, Narain said sincerely, "Gerald, thank you," before entering the office and closing the door.

Channing stood in the middle of it, uncomfortable, hands on hips. When Narain closed the door, he insisted, "Very well, Mr. Khan, we're alone. What is so important?"

Narain studied him. What did Channing know? What didn't he know? About Blythe, about Jameson. About Narain himself.

At last, firmly, he said, "There has been blood spilled in this city. I think you know something about it."

"What?" Channing exclaimed, but his eyes flashed more with guilt than with indignation. "Chef Khan, I have an alderman out there who can be very helpful in a research project I'm working on and you've dragged me away for riddle games?"

"And just what sort of research is it you are doing?" Narain said, folding his arms and making it apparent that Channing would not be leaving.

Resigned, Channing said, "Okay, Mr. Khan. I'm going back to my dinner."

Narain remained firmly planted, eyes squinted slightly. "I had a visit from Fred Blythe," he said coldly, noting how Channing paused and sensing the subtle change in his respiration. "He gave me your name as a reference."

Channing's gaze shot up at him and he realised that his reaction had made it impossible to deny any knowledge of the name. And yet, he tried nonetheless, shrugging and saying defensively, "I don't believe I know the name. I couldn't say why this man gave you my…"

"Don't do this, Channing!" Narain growled, stepping toward him and herding him toward a chair. Channing sat, red-faced, and Narain said, "You are tied into this and I need to know how. For my sake, for Blythe's. For Cassie's sake."

Again, Channing's gaze shot up this time with a bit of fire, but he insisted, "You've been at the ovens too long, Chef Khan. The heat has gotten to you."

Narain realised he would have to force his hand. Noticing a brass letter opener on the desk to his left, he snatched it with lightning speed and leaned over Channing raising the blade to the man's cheek. Channing remained silent, eyes glancing sideways at the letter opener before Narain silently raised his own hand ,slicing open his palm.

Channing burst from the chair, inspecting himself for any blood splatters. "What is wrong with you, Khan?" he sputtered, then looked up staring wide eyed at the palm Narain held up.

Granted it was a calculated cut, but it had bled, tracks of it dripping thin trails down Narain's wrist. The cut itself, however, was already sealing up, the skin knitting together.

"You're one of them!" Channing proclaimed stepping closer. "I would never have guessed." He made a motion to inspect Narain's hand and the vampire impatiently allowed this. Shaking his head, Channing studied the scarring tissue. "This never ceases to amaze me, no matter how often I see it."

After a few moments, Narain pulled his hand back and grabbed some tissues from a box on Gerald's desk. "So, you have dealt with us before," he commented more than questioned, cleaning the blood from his wrist and arm.

Raising his arms, Channing said petulantly, "Okay, your hunch was right, Sherlock." Then he took a seat in the chair.

Narain barely hid his irritation. "Let's not get clever, Richard. Now is not the time for attitude. I need to understand what is going on here. People are dying."

Placing a knuckle against his lips, Channing stared at him, then sighed and lowered his hand. "Alright," he said slowly, "I suppose you should know since you seem to be caught up in it. Probably due to the effort you've put into chasing Cassie."

Narain picked up on the jealous tone to the man's voice and sat on the arm of a sofa against the wall. Bitterly, he tossed the wadded bloody tissue into a garbage can, and rubbed at his nearly healed palm saying, "Oh Richard, I was caught up with Jameson and Fred Blythe long before you and Cassie were even born. That's his name, by the way. Fred Blythe. He drove trucks in London. A gentle man, before he gave his life on the battlefield." Disgusted, he asked, "Did you know any of this? Did Reginald Jameson bother to give you one human detail about the man, before you did whatever you did to him?"

"Very perceptive, Mr. Khan."

"It hardly takes a detective. Jameson tells me Blythe was captured and worked on, Blythe escapes and comes here, Cassie is here doing research on our condition. And you're her partner. 'Dr. Channing.' One of the few things I remember Blythe telling me after he saved my life recently. 'Talk to Channing.' You're involved somehow and I need to know how." Then he added with a sneer, "And I'd like to know how you could involve Cassie in anything that has Reginald Jameson's fingerprints on it."

"You don't understand," Channing snapped. "I tried not to involve her. I didn't want her anywhere near Jameson's operation."

Leaning forward, Narain studied him. "But you needed her research, didn't you?" Standing, he paced back and forth in front of Channing, extrapolating, "It is not a coincidence that a man partnered with a woman secretly investigating vampirism should hook up with Reginald Jameson. As a doctor—as a learned man—you would have laughed in the face of anyone who mentioned the possibility that we existed. Unless you saw the research."

Calmly, Channing commented, "You've given this a lot of thought."

"Yes, well, trying to find one's way home through the Chicago sewer system gives one plenty of time to think."

"What?"

"It doesn't matter."

With a sigh of resignation, Channing began, "I met Cassie in graduate school. She was beautiful, charming, and wickedly funny. She was amazing."

"Still is."

Channing nodded. "Indeed. We were in love. At least, I was in love. I think she felt the same, for a while. But there was always this part of her that was closed off— she wouldn't let me in. We continued the relationship after college, even spoke of a dream to open a research facility. We each had our own reasons, as I realise now. At some point, I suggested we move in together and she insisted that she still needed her space. She wasn't ready for that sort of step. Honestly, I started getting a little jealous. Thought maybe she was seeing someone else. We were both putting in long hours at different facilities. I started envisioning all these scenarios.

"Well, one weekend she asked me to check on her house for her, while she was attending a symposium in Denver. You know, water the plants, feed the fish." He smiled slightly. "She had this room that was always closed. I asked her what was in it once, but she was very evasive. More of that secret part of her she refused to share. I don't think she realised it, but she left the key to that room on the ring of keys she gave me to her apartment. She was in such a hurry packing, she probably forgot to take it off."

Narain's head tilted as he said sarcastically, "And being a good boyfriend you respected her privacy."

"Of course not. I loved her. I was sure I was losing her, so I wanted to know everything. I never expected to find what I found." He paused as he remembered the room. "At first, I was a bit concerned that she had lost it. The room was like a storage locker. Filing cabinets, boxes of files, a few old wooden trunks, papers, medical records, hand written notes, photos. What shocked me more were the books on the supernatural, books on vampires. 'Vampires Around the Globe.' 'Vampires Through History.' That sort of thing. It was an obsessive collection and I just didn't understand.

"I went over to the computer. On the desk were these files with names on them and inside were notes, letters and photos. One had a photo of a pretty Japanese woman posing in front of a Buddhist temple in 1946, according to the date. In another, that same woman was posing in front of the same temple in 1996 according to the time stamp on the back of the photo. It was the same woman. At first I didn't believe it, but it was. Only her hair style and clothes had changed. She still looked to be in her early thirties. Initially, I argued against my eyes. It had to be the daughter of the woman from 1946. A niece. Someone. But according to her file, it was the same woman. And there were other files like that of other people from all over the world. Italy, Australia, Egypt and more. I mean, how many people would be in on this sort of hoax? How many people could find their perfect double to pose for them fifty, sixty, seventy years later?

"Hacking into her computer, I found her medical research and my eyes were fully opened. It made so much sense, what she was going for. She had cracked the code on this mysterious disease, that had been fictionalized for centuries. It wasn't supernatural. It was perfectly natural and Cassie had the evidence…blood and tissue samples, charts, microscopic imaging isolating the microbes themselves. She spelled it all out and it all made perfect sense. She even hinted at having the beginnings of a possible cure."

Narain noted the look of discovery that had crossed Channing's face, while he spoke of his invasion of Cassie's privacy. Shaking his head, he said, "So you stole her research?"

Channing's beaming dimmed. "Yes. Yes I did. Well, copied it really. She never knew. I was hoping that if I could study it closer, I might possibly help her further it. I knew she'd deny it even existed, if I approached her too soon. But there was so much potential there, I couldn't just ignore it."

"How did you get involved with Jameson?"

"I heard through channels that some eccentric British billionaire wanted to gather a team for a special research project."

"Oh, 'eccentric' is far too gentle a term for Reg Jameson."

Channing looked up at him. "Agreed. But hindsight and all." Then he shrugged. "Anyway, I contacted him and we met. He was elusive, at first, about what he was looking for and actually he didn't seem too interested in me. Until I showed him my research." Narain arched an eyebrow. "The research I continued from Cassie's research. Then he told me everything. It was at that point, that I got the impression I had no choice, but to accept the position."

"So you were as much a prisoner as Fred Blythe. Just a different sort of cage." Narain lost the sardonic smile. "What was the project? How did Blythe figure into this?"

"The creature is the project." Narain flashed a dangerously disgusted look and Channing censored himself. "That was our name for him. Blythe has something Jameson wants and he set this project up in the hopes of extracting it." Narain shrugged expectantly and Channing revealed, "Blythe has the ability to survive during the daylight hours."

"Truly?" Narain asked, stunned.

"He can't go sunning in Saint Tropez, but as long as the sun isn't beating down on him for too long, he can function. It's an aberration—well, a positive one, but so far he's the only one who seems to possess the trait."

"And Jameson wants that."

"Can you imagine?"

There were times when Narain could imagine little else. Freedom of movement, day or night. To look upon the sun even as it set or rose. To feel its warmth caressing him, not incinerating him.

"So, when Jameson discovered Blythe's existence in France," Channing continued, "he hunted him down and brought him to Los Angeles to be examined."

"You mean to be experimented on," Narain shot out.

Coldly, Channing said, "Yes. We were trying to figure a way to isolate that ability to survive in the daylight, but it's been extremely difficult. Was it an environmental cause? Did the disease that Blythe contracted mutate, or was it already mutated? Was it Blythe himself who mutated? He had been in hibernation a long time. What was going on during that time? Or was it a perfect combination of both: Blythe's system and that of the microbes? We were trying a number of things to figure it out."

Narain sat wearily on the edge of the sofa cushion, hands clasped and head lowered. He hated the next question. Hated having to ask it. But he needed to know. "What sort of experiments did you perform on him?"

The scientist in Channing took over as he flatly said, "We tried a number of things. The first was testing transference of the microbes from Blythe to ferals."

"And this was done how?"

"We fed ferals to him. We wanted to start by simulating how the disease would be passed in the wild, so to speak, but we also wanted to see what a re-infection would do to the ferals and what the effect might be on Blythe. The microbes already in existence in Blythe and the ferals looked upon the "new" microbes as invaders and killed them. This did little more to Blythe than make him a bit sick. It killed a good portion of the ferals though, making it pretty apparent that the microbes in Blythe had indeed mutated drastically from what infests most other vampires. So, we moved on."

Head still lowered, Narain's gaze bore into the floor. "Moved on to what?"

"To the homeless, mostly. I convinced a few terminal cancer patients to take part. And Jameson brought in a few specimens, that I later found out were business associates who had crossed him."

"You fed him uninfected humans?"

Catching Narain's tone, Channing explained, "We needed to find out what sort of effect Blythe's particular microbes would have on the uninfected. The problem was the specimens wouldn't turn. Only two transformed, but they sickened and died. The microbes Blythe has aren't really capable of transference. Not to mention that we have yet to discover the deciding factor as to which 'normals' will turn. So, we concentrated on the more scientific methods…manipulating blood samples, injecting specimens with a course of treatments. Again, very few became infected and even among those that did, we still couldn't replicate whatever it was that was making Blythe impervious to daylight."

At last, Narain cut him off, head remaining lowered, as he mumbled, "Tell me, Richard, at any point in all this did you ever stop and consider what a twisted, soulless bastard you'd become?" His head shot up, his eyes flashing red, to Channing's wide eyed shock. Calming, Narain stood and began to pace. "Did you not once stop and realise how insane this all was? You kept a being hostage and fed other beings to him."

Slightly uncomfortable, Channing said, "Blythe is not the man you knew. His mind has been destroyed."

Narain laughed bitterly running a hand through his hair. "What you forced upon him is probably the very thing that destroyed his mind. Anyway, I don't believe it is destroyed, but even if that were the case, you were killing people. Conducting experiments on them and killing them. When did you lose your mind? What would possess you to do this?"

Defensively, Channing said, "I don't expect you to understand. Tell me, have you ever heard of a vampire with cancer? With AIDS? Diabetes? How many diseases could be wiped out if we could harness the self-healing abilities you possess? How about tissue regeneration? Reversing paralysis? Blythe is the strongest of your kind, feral or sentient, that I've ever seen and he may hold answers to wiping out a great number of diseases."

"How very noble of you, Dr. Channing."

"Look upon me as a monster, if you like."

"You are more a monster than any feral I've ever run across."

"And tell me, Mr. Khan, how clean are your hands? Do you mean to tell me that in your undoubtedly long life you never overindulged fatally?"

"The difference, Richard, is that any life I may have taken in my life was not done intentionally and I fought very hard to never let it happen again. You have no idea how hard." Sitting back on the couch, Narain leaned his head back and rubbed his face, the full implications of the horror washing over him. Innocent people. Tortured and killed. Blythe tortured. "So you've driven Fred Blythe to madness finally, complete and total madness, and he is now in Chicago butchering people?"

"Well, you'll be happy to know that he isn't responsible for that. In fact, he's out there trying to track down Boris."

"Boris?"

"One of the specimens. Manipulated, man-made. We call him Boris after Karloff, you know? The Frankenstein monster."

Narain raised his head. "You are insane."

Ignoring this, Channing told him, "Boris was a young skateboard punk."

"How young?"

"Seventeen years old." Narain rolled his eyes and Channing continued. "He was a runaway, but a clever kid. Street smart. We manipulated the DNA of Blythe's microbes, let Blythe have him, and then fed him the microbes after. It took nearly two weeks for the kid to turn, but he did, and for a month he was able to withstand sunlight. We thought we had it. But he went through another change and he grew intolerant to the light. There were also physical changes. His face became deformed, his mouth grew three sets of teeth. His hands were more claws than anything else. His eyes were like shark eyes. Cold and black. I could have sworn he was feral. He acted like an animal. But it would seem he was smarter than we gave him credit for. Weeks ago, he escaped, wiped out my weekend staff at the lab. I found out after I came back to Chicago for the benefit. It was a bloodbath. Before he left, however, he stole some computer files."

"Stole computer files?"

Channing nodded. "That's what I mean. No one would have thought, before the tests even, that the kid was capable of hacking. We certainly wouldn't have suspected it after. But he was and he retained that skill. And he took some valuable information."

"And he's been in Chicago committing all those murders? Why is he here? Is he here for you?"

"I don't believe so. Maybe a little. I'm sure he wouldn't mind a bit of revenge. But I think he's got something else in mind. After all, he'd have no reason to know I was here. But the files did mention Cassie."

"Cassie?"

"They were my private files and in them I touched upon the toxin that Cassie has developed. I found out about it myself not too long ago."

"More snooping for love," Narain sneered.

"I didn't have time to find out the formula. The situation only allowed a quick glance. I copied what I could and added it to my files for future research. The bottom line is that I believe he's put two and two together and has come here to track down Cassie and destroy the one thing that can definitely kill him."

"And if Cassie is destroyed in the process…"

"It won't matter a bit to him. He may prefer it. It's a game to him. That's why I brought Blythe here. He may be the only one powerful enough to catch Boris."

"Did you not think it was time now to tell Cassie?"

"I was hoping it wouldn't be necessary."

Shaking his head, Narain sighed, "Oh, the mistakes and missteps in this whole affair astonish me. You didn't think she should know that she's being stalked by some psychotic super vampire of your creation?" Looking at his watch, he put his hand on Channing's shoulder shoving him from the chair. "Come on. Go back to your alderman. We're done."

Channing looked at him nervously as he was led to the door. "What are you planning to do? You aren't going to tell Cassie, are you?"

"About you?" Channing's silence answered that question. Making sure the door was locked, Narain closed it behind them. "I'm going to collect Cassie and bring her some place safe. After that, I'm not sure. I may try to find this beast you set upon the city."

"That beast may be as strong as Blythe. He could literally tear you apart."

"Yes, well, the plan is a work in progress." Stopping their exit down the hall, he shoved Channing against the wall, leaning in close and quietly hissing, "I know why you haven't told Cassie about any of this. You crossed a line that perhaps you yourself never thought you would. Stealing research was bad enough. But how would you tell someone like Cassie that you've committed the sort of crimes you have? Vampires or normals, these are human beings you were working on." He paused, sneering slightly, "For the good of humankind, is it? Imagine her own heartbreak if she found out it was her research that helped inspire this."

With that, Narain left Channing in the hallway and wove his way through the kitchen and restaurant, shooting a look of thanks to Gerald before exiting the building. He walked down Rush Street, past lively bars and eateries, threading through pedestrians enjoying the cool night air of early May, oblivious to the creatures out hunting in the city. Pausing in the doorway of a shop, he affected the demeanour of a tourist, getting his bearings while he allowed the fury coursing through him to cool. It was a dangerous anger, one he hadn't felt in decades; the prime target not so much the situation, but his own helplessness. The sun was setting later and later now. Soon, remnants of daylight would last well near 9 PM. So much of the world was closed off to him during the summer months. As beautiful as it was, spring always left him a bit melancholy. His whole world had come crashing down around him when Sophie took her last breath. For several blissful decades, his condition was little more than a footnote to their life together. Now, the reality of what he had become was being shoved back in his face and he was woefully unprepared to deal with it.

His first priority was getting Cassie some place where the beast couldn't find her. Perhaps his condo, perhaps even out of the city all together. Then, he had to find Fred Blythe and help him track down this man made fiend. Blythe did not deserve the indignity of being sent out like some vampiric hound dog to track this kid down. He deserved peace, though Narain had no clue at that point how to bring it to him.

†

Blythe watched with revulsion as the fiend feasted upon yet more victims. Boris had trapped the two night watchmen in the truck docking bay of the huge tool and die plant and was taking his time with them. So preoccupied with blood was the mutant that he hadn't even sensed his adversary nearby. Blythe desperately wanted to stop him, but knew that there was little he could do. The two vampires had battled a few times—once in a stately graveyard filled with elaborate tombstones and mausoleums, and once in a desolate factory area near the north branch of the Chicago River, but Boris was just too strong for him. Neither could kill the other, but Blythe could not risk a long time of incapacitation if he was to carry out his mission. And Boris' teeth, while not lethal, were nasty, the wounds taking a while to heal; probably another trait bestowed upon the younger vampire from whatever treatment he'd endured at Jameson's laboratory.

Boris liked killing. Blythe had fed a few times already, but tried to do so discreetly. This one relished the act, as well as the blood, ripping out his victims' throats among other things. It was the grizzly business of an unsettled mind. Worse than a feral.

Pulling his head back, Blythe placed it against the cool bricks of the building he leaned against and slid down, his mind weary from the culture shock of the past weeks. The city was made up of canyons of buildings filled with lights, some flashing, some coloured, some brightly blinding. It was filled with continuous noise and constant movement, even in the latest hour. Laughter, music, screaming, crying, gunshots, crashes. Not to mention the sort of vehicles he would never have imagined possible that, when not speeding all over, were trapped in rows on overcrowded streets, able only to inch along slowly. He shied from people, knowing he was no fit sight, but that was difficult to do since people were everywhere. Day and night, no matter what the hour, there were always footsteps and chattering from someone prowling the streets.

It was worse than when he woke up to the sound of huge machinery tearing up his hiding place in the French countryside. He had no desire to kill those workers. He was simply confused and hungry. He wanted to be left alone and dig back down, forgetting it all. But once Reg had trapped him and brought him—by an aeroplane no less—to that private installation on the west coast of America, Blythe's mind had had time to clear. Never had he seen the sort of machines he saw there. The sort they used on him. It was something H.G. Wells might have dreamed up. "High tech," as Reg said one day while taunting him.

Reg had been the one who had explained his condition. Vampirism. That was the realm of Bram Stoker. Not real life. Only, what else would explain Blythe's body, alive, stronger and larger than before, decades after he was sure he had died on the battlefield? And there was that horrible need for blood. His mind was on fire with that need, at times. Why did it have to be Reg who told him that his reward for being a good soldier was to be transformed into a monster? A monster whose blood apparently held some power that Reg was prepared to kill for.

And kill he did. Or rather, allowed Blythe to kill. They starved him until his howls of need became constant, and then they brought in food. The ferals made him sick, but he was so hungry he fed upon them anyway. After that, he was given people to feed on, never realising that they were half drained by the time he got them. There was a woman, ravaged by a life on the street. There was an old black man whose blue jumper and rather rank smell indicated that he had just gotten off from a day of very physical labour when they caught him. There were countless others. All of them dying, never to be reborn as he and Reg had been. He had no idea what was done with the bodies after he fed, but he was certain some horrible sort of treatment was administered. Always to failure if Reg's irritated face when he came to goad him was any indication. After a time, they took samples from Blythe, constantly examining him, draining him and filling him. Reg was only too proud to explain it all to him, even if Blythe only understood a small portion. They toyed with his blood, manipulated it, and eventually decided to try the new super serum on humans.

Jameson liked to reminisce about Blythe's "little Indian monkey" who protected him in the trenches. Blythe knew he spoke of Narain Khan but refused to acknowledge the slur. "He protected you alright," Reg told him, laughing cruelly. "One could say he made you what you are."

Blythe found the comment curious until, after enough visiting from Reg, he realised that Jameson was implying that Khan had been affected by this disease and had given it to him in the horrid way it was passed on. But this couldn't be right. He scanned his memories of their final push over the trench wall, but the memories were so dim, so confused, that he couldn't be sure what had happened. He vaguely remembered the ghouls foraging on the ground. One may have attacked him. Could it have been Narain? He gave it considerable thought recently, after leaving Narain in the sewers, wondering if he had saved the very being that sent him into this torture. Still, Narain had been a friend, often times a saviour, during those dark days in the trenches. Blythe himself understood the need Narain might have had on the battlefield in France, he had it himself when he awoke after the transformation. He fed off anything or anyone he could find before finally digging deep into the earth of France and allowing a swollen mind to go quiet.

Until bulldozers woke him.

There were two more specimens brought to him. One was a dark-skinned woman, Mexican, perhaps, and one was a "skateboard punk," if he had Reg's terminology correct.

Boris was the skateboard punk.

That creature in the empty docking bay feeding on its victims was not the same child they brought to him. What they brought to him was a scraggly blonde boy, no older than seventeen, whose glassy stare revealed just how much they had drained from him, before giving him to Blythe. He barely had enough in him to make it worth Blythe's effort.

They took him away and did…something to him. Blythe couldn't be sure what.

But when he caught a glimpse of him weeks later, heavily sedated, being wheeled to a cell not far from his, the transformation stunned him. That youthful wiriness was still there, but the muscle mass had increased, bulking him up considerably. And when the head lolled to the side Blythe saw the bizarre shape to the boy's mouth packed with dangerous misshapen teeth.

And so it was. Human teeth had fallen out of a mouth now altered to accommodate two rows of long needle sharp teeth. And beneath those teeth were another, smaller set, just as deadly.

Like a shark.

What the devil was Jameson up to? Why would he wish to create a freak that would ultimately be more powerful than him? And what role had Blythe himself played in the creation?

Of course, the boy escaped. He was bound to. What Jameson didn't seem to consider was that along with an increase in strength and endurance would come an increase in cleverness as well. The boy had probably been very intelligent and crafty. Jameson thought he was creating another feral. Far from it. Boris was dazed and confused but he was clever enough to take advantage of it. A survivor before, he was now the ultimate survivor, and the murders he'd committed throughout the western states were not for sustenance alone but also for thrills. This was Jameson's monster and once Boris came to his complete senses he would be a force to be reckoned with.

He was already smart enough to realise that there was something very important in Chicago. Perhaps he overheard a snippet of conversation; perhaps he pulled information out of one of the researchers, before he killed him during the escape. The screams had been horrible, ripping at Blythe who was trapped in his cell and could do nothing. Whatever it was, Boris found something that made Channing turn to the other beast they had, Fred Blythe, for help and in exchange for a promise of peace, Blythe had agreed.

Now, he sat by helplessly watching the little fiend feed off more innocents. Blythe knew he had to bring the kid down, but he hadn't a clue how to go about doing so.

Then he caught sense of approaching vampires and he saw Jameson and his pets arrive on the scene. Moving as closely as he dared without being detected, Blythe listened carefully to what transpired hoping to discover the reason for Reg's presence there.

✝

"There he is, boys, our little lost rogue, found. Took us a while, but I told you we'd find him." Jameson sauntered toward the grizzly scene in the docking bay, grinning, while six ferals fanned around it. Arching an eyebrow toward the two bodies on the ground, he commented, "Bad luck for Chicago, though, that we didn't find him sooner."

Crouched over the mutilated bodies, Boris stared at him, a territorially desperate glare in his eyes. His face caked in blood, he growled, showing his teeth, torn between losing the kill and losing his freedom. With the blood still fresh and ripe, it was a truly difficult decision.

"Oh, settle down," Jameson scoffed. "I've seen your teeth before. You may be stronger with nastier equipment, but I have something you don't have: experience.

I've been around longer than you, my son. Besides, I can walk freely among humans without scaring the living shit out of them. Can you say the same? And, I understand the concept of hygiene." He grimaced waving a hand in front of his nose. "But then, you weren't exactly clean when we hauled you in, were you?"

Boris remained still, coiled and ready to strike if necessary. Licking at the blood on his lips, he mumbled, "I'm not going back," the words coming out partially garbled in his misshapen mouth.

Ignoring the challenge in the young vampire's voice, Jameson said, "Of course you are."

Boris shot up and prepared to battle the ferals who closed rank on him, trapping him against the dock wall.

"Now hang on," Jameson said calmly, stepping closer. "Let's not do anything rash." To Boris, he said, "I have no doubt that you could take us all down in a nasty and violent fashion. This is why I brought this." He reached behind his back producing a tranq gun that had been tucked in his waist-band. "You remember how this works, and how quickly." He touched the tip of the gun to his head. "You see, that's what I mean about experience."

Eyes glued to the gun, Boris' demeanour became more timid. "I don't want to go back."

"You're going back," Jameson insisted darkly, "but how you go back, and as what, depends on how co-operative you are." Boris narrowed his eerie, black eyes and remained expectantly silent. Jameson explained, "I've decided to take a different tack on this situation. You're a smart kid and I like to encourage potential." Glancing at the guards, he said, "If we can get your cravings under control, you might be of use to me. Yes, you're a bit of a freak visually, but tell me, have you ever felt more…alive?"

Boris' wide smile answered the question.

"And who knows, maybe we can do something about the whole freak thing. Straighten out the face a bit." Jameson stared at him with one eye as if imagining what could be done with a pile of clay. "The fact is that life can be a lot more comfortable…a lot more fun, than it is now."

"And what do you get?" Boris asked with growing scepticism. He was perfectly aware that very rarely did someone get something for nothing.

Jameson shrugged. "Well, I get a fine new recruit. And you get what you came here to get." Boris feigned ignorance and Jameson said, "Now, come on, my son. I know exactly what brought you here," again he spared a glance at the bodies, "and it wasn't the legendary food. You want that toxin Channing's old flame has and I have the resources to put it to better use than you do."

"Then you get it," Boris said petulantly, "and leave me alone."

"I've tried," Jameson insisted. "Believe me. I've tried the reasonable way, but that got all cocked up. There are too many old acquaintances converging on this town." Boris grunted at each of the six ferals. "Yes, well indeed I'd love to send them in. They could probably get it from her in no time. But I can't go that route."

"Why not?"

"Because I have to keep my hands clean. I still need Channing and I doubt he'd be very cooperative in future research if we end up hurting this woman. Which would probably end up happening. If we are to carry on the research and find that little secret that will benefit all of us, I'll need Channing to do it."

"You'll need Blythe too."

Jameson smiled. "See, you are a clever little bastard. I don't know what Channing was thinking bringing him here, but extra points to you, if you can bring him in as well. But he is something my ferals can handle. Channing knows full well I intend to recapture him. It's the serum that you have to concentrate on. And I have the information that you haven't been able to obtain yet. I know where the woman lives."

The prospect enticed Boris, but he wasn't sold yet. "And once I have it, I bring it to you?" He began to laugh a creepy, wheezing little laugh.

Jameson was sure he had gotten through to him, despite this outburst of rebellion. "Yes, you bring it to me and then you live the good life. Or you use it on me and continue dining al fresco in docking bays, and hiding in a hole in your filthy, blood soaked clothes as you have been doing for the past several weeks." He leaned closer staring into the soulless eyes. "You remember what it was like on the streets in your old life? Not much different now, is it? Say what you will about the cell, at least you had a soft bed and three squares a day. You behave nicely and I can fix it so that you have a whole lot more, and your freedom. It's your choice."

Boris studied the other ferals. Jameson had a small army of ferals at his disposal, all who could destroy him in an instant if they chose, but none did. He had gained their loyalty by giving them his and making sure their long lives were easy, in a world where hiding places were being dug up and paved over. Blinking, Boris stared down at his misshapen hands crimson with dried blood. Maybe Jameson could fix him, maybe he couldn't. But as time went on, Boris was beginning to realise that as thrilling as it was, there had to be more to life than killing.

At last, looking up, he said, "Once I have it, where do we meet?"

The ferals relaxed noticeably, some even grinned, and Jameson put the tranq back in his waist-band, wrapping an arm around the boy. "I love this boy," he said, handing him a thin cell phone. "The number is pre-programmed." Losing his smile slightly, he added, "And once this is done, you are having a bath. I mean, really, there's a lake the size of an ocean out there, you couldn't have stepped in once?"

Shaking his head, he let the boy get back to his feeding and motioned for the ferals to follow him out of the bay. The next step, of course, was to track down Blythe.

Chapter 14

Cassie woke up with a start, shocked from sleep by continual pounding interspersed with the chiming of the front doorbell and the calling of her name. She shook her head, trying to focus, staring at the snow on the television screen, which cast a bright glow in the darkened living room. The DVD she had popped in must have ended some time ago and the player shut off automatically.

"Damn, did she marry him?" she mumbled regarding the movie's conclusion.

"Cassie!"

The pounding continued and she shook her head again turning on the lamp on the end table, rising off the couch to answer the door before it was beaten off its hinges.

She'd walked to Goose Island Brewery earlier that night to meet an old friend, who was in town, visiting. They hopped to some of the other bars along Addison and it would seem she had been so wrapped up in reminiscing, that she lost track of her cocktail consumption. Pleasantly buzzed, she walked back home, shuffled into the house and fell asleep on the sofa to whatever movie she had managed to put in the DVD player.

She remembered laughing with it. Or was it at it?

The cobwebs clearing, she looked through the peep-hole of the door, noting that Narain's friend, Dominic, had opened the screen door and was giving the storm door a vigorous going over while jabbing his finger at the doorbell.

Concerned, she opened the door saying, "Dominic, what's the matter? Is Narain all right?"

Pushing his way in, he asked forcefully, "Let me ask you, do you ever listen to your phone messages?"

Confused, she blinked the bleariness from her eyes. "I didn't get any phone messages." She couldn't have been that wasted. Walking over to the cell phone on the small hall table, she checked her voice mail and noted that fifteen messages had been left. Looking at Dom regretfully, she said, "Oh my gosh! Is it something important?"

Dom raised an eyebrow, then shoved the question away, saying, "Listen, I need you to go upstairs quick and pack a bag. I'm going to take you over to Narain's condo."

She walked up a few stairs then looked at him curiously. "Wait a minute, why? What's going on?"

Taking out his cell phone, he explained, "You know all those killings that have been on the news lately?" She nodded. "Well, the thing doing them may be coming for you next. Look, go on and I'll explain it on the way to Rain's."

†

"Can I help you, sir?"

Narain hadn't realised how long his eyes had remained fixed on the lobby floor of NewGen Labs. The marble was clean and polished now, but he couldn't help remembering when it was splattered with his blood, which stained the floor, the elevator panel, all leading straight up to Cassie's lab. How had she explained all that? Or did she even have to?

"Sir, do you need some help?"

The insistent voice tore Narain's gaze away and he trained it on the security guard, who'd been watching him. Yes, it was the same guard, looking much healthier than the last time he'd seen him. And luckily, Narain was not quite so hungry.

If the poor guy had only known how close…

"Sir!" This time the tone was sharper.

Narain shook his head, smiling, and walked to the desk. "I'm sorry, allergies. This time of year always makes me a bit hazy."

The name on the guard's badge read "Dennis" and now that he had the visitor's attention, he relaxed his posture slightly. "Are you looking for someone, sir?"

I wonder if he remembers being attacked, Narain thought. Reg had, no doubt, been quick and efficient. What had poor Dennis thought when he woke up? "Uhm, yes, as a matter of fact, I was wondering if Dr. Lambert is here tonight?"

Cordially, the guard said, "Well it's not unusual for her to work late, but," he glanced at the day's sign-in sheet, "no, today it looks like she signed out…early, in fact. About three o'clock. Would you like to leave a message for her?"

Narain shook his head. "No thank you. That won't be necessary."

As he neared the door, his cell phone rang and answering it, he was greeted instantly by Dom saying, "I got her, Rain."

Narain turned back to the guard and held up the phone. "Found her." The guard offered a confused smile in reply. "Where was she?" Narain asked, exiting the building.

"She was at home."

"We both called her home several times."

"Doesn't matter. Look, where are you at?"

"NewGen Labs."

"Okay, she's packing some things. I told her we'd go to your place…"

"Dom, what was that?" Narain heard a distant crash on the other end of the phone. "Dom?"

"Don't worry. Something in her bedroom closet fell."

Narain sighed with relief. "That closet will be the death of her. Okay, I'm on my way home now. Get her to my condo and we can figure out the next step from there."

†

Closing his phone Dominic called up the stairs, "You almost ready?"

Cassie came downstairs quickly, carrying a small back pack and purse and was about to speak, when they heard the sound of the kitchen door being kicked in. A figure in a grungy, red sweatshirt came hurtling down the hall toward Dom. Too stunned to react, Dom was mown down as if by a wave and it was all he could do to keep the thing's hideous mouth away from his throat. He managed to get his feet underneath its sternum, kicking the attacker off him, sending it crashing into the hallway table near the stairs. It was like kicking off a boulder, though, and did little more than slow the creature down. The creature rose with an eerie grace and went after him again, snarls emanating from its deformed mouth. It was apparent on the creature's face, no longer hidden by the hood, that it was enjoying the struggle Dom was putting up and it smiled wide as it lifted Dom up with one arm to send him flying onto the living room floor.

The sickening thud brought Cassie to her senses and she followed the creature as it went after Dom, whacking him aside with the back-pack, then grabbing a nearby vase to slam into the side of the creature's head. Dom began to crawl from the living room and Cassie threw a hefty gargoyle statue at the creature, but she knew it wasn't going to stop the attacker. In fact, judging by the look on its twisted face as it easily batted it away, this was now a game to it that it was thoroughly enjoying.

Suddenly, another figure came crashing through the front window, rolling to his feet to face the first intruder. Dressed in a filthy, orange jumpsuit and covered in cuts from the shattered window that were already starting to heal, his wild hair obscured his features, but the new intruder wasted no time. He grabbed the smaller intruder by the neck, flinging him back against the living room wall with such force, that it left an indentation in the dry wall. Howling in fury, the smaller intruder righted himself and leapt at the larger one. The two wrestled brutally on the floor like pissed off cats until, eventually, the larger threw the smaller off and into a glass coffee table which shattered on impact, the wrought iron fixture twisting from the force.

While the smaller figure untangled himself, the other turned to Cassie and in a deep, raspy voice, growled, "I'm here to help. You need to leave."

The other invader leapt at him again, tackling him to the floor, scratching and clawing at him as they rolled around. He threw him off again, but was having a hard time standing after the third throw.

Cassie turned to Dom, who was still dazed and in great pain, and put an arm around him to help him from the house. Her eyes turned back to the brute, however. Whoever the second one was, she couldn't leave him. Grabbing the purse she'd thrown near the stairs, she rummaged through its contents, until finding what she needed, then she told Dom to stay put while she went closer to the two combatants. He reached out to stop her, but she eluded his grasp.

The second one was on top of the first intruder, smashing his face in, but the first one was able to throw him off and scrabbled on top of his back, wrapping an arm around his throat to choke him. Using all the force she could muster, she kicked at the small attacker, almost succeeding in getting him off the larger man. Enraged by battle, the second intruder leapt off the larger man and straight at Cassie, who held up the taser she'd taken from her purse and fired, sending the paralysing surge of electricity into him, through the wires that were implanted in his neck.

The taser had been given to her by Richard, who worried for her safety, since she insisted on working such late nights. He claimed to have gotten it from a friend and she agreed to carry it, never actually believing it would be very effective. It turned out to be extremely effective. The shock that was capable of incapacitating a normal person, brought the smaller being down, but he would recover soon, so Cassie shocked him a second and then a third time for good measure. The electricity scrambling his system, the figure writhed on the floor, foaming at the mouth.

"This only bought us a few moments," she said breathlessly.

The second figure was regaining his strength, but slowly. "Too strong for me. We must leave."

Shoving him from the room, she grabbed her purse as she heard the creature on the floor stirring to full consciousness. Dom, by this time, had slid, barely conscious, to the floor and the orange suited figure, concerned only with her safety, was ready to lead Cassie from the house when she pleaded, "We have to take him. That thing will kill him."

Nodding sharply, the figure picked up Dom as if he were a child, slinging him over his shoulder, following Cassie out the door.

They heard a howl from the house, as they hurried along the pavement to a Prius several cars down. Lights were on in neighbouring houses as people, disturbed by the commotion, slowly made their way back to consciousness. "Cassie, what's going on?" neighbour Steven Garrity called from his second floor window, to which she shot back, "Nothing, Steve," and rushed to the car.

"The police are on their way," someone else shouted out, making Cassie cringe. Somehow, and she wasn't sure how, she had avoided explaining the break in at NewGen labs to either the police or staff. She was almost sure Richard was behind the clean-up, but she couldn't fathom why and she hadn't known how to broach the topic, without giving her own involvement away. There would be no cover up for this disturbance, waking the neighbours on a street that was usually quiet at this time of night when the Cubs weren't playing a night game, and she was certain that involving the police would do more harm than good.

The strange man slowed as he neared the car she pointed to and she unlocked the back door, instructing him to lay Dom on the back seat. Then, she opened the passenger door for him and hurried around to the driver's side. As she slid behind the wheel, she noticed him staring dumbly at the car.

"Get in," she called. Pointing at the car, he shook his head, oddly fearful and she demanded, "You have to come with us. Get in." He looked down both sides of the street and starting the motor she said, "I won't leave, until you get in."

Screwing up his courage, the figure squeezed into the passenger seat and she eased out of the space, just as their pursuer flew through the front window and rolled onto the grass.

Screeching, Cassie sped forward, noting with concern how easily the attacker was quickly bringing up the rear. Deciding to go on the offensive, she jammed on the brakes and shifted into reverse, gunning the car backwards and ploughing into the figure. The force sent him back and under the car, and he was dragged several feet before Cassie stopped, shifted back into forward gear and sped off down the street.

Her passenger turned, watching without emotion the increasingly small figure of their attacker as he slammed his fist petulantly onto the pavement and dragged himself off the street disappearing between two parked cars.

Cassie drove as fast as she dared to, down quiet side streets, turning left on to Ashland and noting that even at that late time, the street was still well travelled. She was also at the mercy of the stop-lights, which seemed to wait till she neared them to turn red. She could go on the motorway. At least on the Kennedy she could push the speed up to 65 or 70. It was doubtful the thing was still following them but she didn't want to take a chance. An overwhelming urge to put distance between her and her shattered house gripped her. The question was, where would they go?

Speaking was difficult for the being sitting next to her, it was obvious in his cadence. It was also obvious that he was a vampire. No human could withstand the punishment that he took and still be walking. Concentrating on the words, he said urgently, "Jameson and Boris have joined."

Groaning from the back, Dom asked, "Boris? Is that what attacked us?" The passenger nodded. "Is that how it knew where to find Cassie?"

"They spoke tonight," the man explained in a monotone voice that held a trace of a British accent. "Boris is now the errand boy."

"Oh wait," Dominic groaned again, but in recognition of something. "Wait, then you're Fred Blythe, aren't you?"

Cassie's gaze snapped in his direction and the man looked at her, slowly nodding. "Yes."

"My God, Narain was right. There was another." Dom's voice trailed away as pain held him tight.

"We have to get you to a hospital, Dom," Cassie said firmly. "Then we have to get to Narain's."

"No," Blythe said.

Before Cassie could retort, Dom said in a hushed voice, "He's right, Cassie. Rain's is the first place they'll look if Jameson's involved. Remember what he did to him before. We stay away from Rain's, the psycho little bastard won't have a clue where to look. He probably wouldn't have found you tonight if Jameson hadn't gotten involved."

At that moment, realising just how quickly her heart raced, she found it difficult to think further ahead than the car in front of her. "Then let's concentrate on getting you to a hospital."

"Get me to the nearest critical care."

Looking back, she noticed him squirming around as if searching for something, but his movements brought spasms of pain from what could very well be internal injuries. "A hospital is better."

He swiped at the sweat and blood on his forehead with the back of his sleeve exclaiming, "Damn, I've lost my cell."

"I have mine. What about the hospital?"

"Look, we're a bit pressed for time here. Sun's going to come up and we have to find some place for our friend here to roost." Blythe shook his head but Dom continued, "Plus that creep is still out there and you have to get somewhere safe at least until we can figure the next step." Wincing in silence, as a spasm of pain went through him, he finally forced out, "Drop me at a critical care and get the hell out of here."

"Drop you..."

"At the front door. I'll go in, say I was mugged, then try to contact Rain later. In the meantime, you get some place safe."

"Dominic, you could be seriously injured. I'm not dumping you on a doorstep."

"My God you're stubborn, woman!" He winced again. "You don't have time to hang out with me in an emergency room. Jameson has resources and who knows how well that creep can track. Hospital or critical care, whichever comes first, do a drive by and get some place safe. Jeez!"

Cassie was prepared to protest, but cautiously, Blythe reached out and touched her arm as if to nudge her to humour the injured man. Brows furrowed, she looked at him, yet nodded subtly swallowing the response. St. Athanasius was about twenty minutes north and Cassie wove through the traffic, praying there were no cops around, just waiting for drivers like her.

Pulling up at the entrance to Emergency, Cassie parked the car as out of the way as possible, without being too far from the door.

"What are you doing?" Dom grumbled, opening the car door and easing himself out. "Let me get out, then split."

"Dom, shut up," Cassie ordered, exiting the driver's side. She was surprised to see the hulking figure of Blythe, now standing at the back waiting for the injured man to exit. Once Dom eased out, Blythe scooped him up and carried him toward the entrance. Cassie quickly closed the car doors and followed.

The waiting area of the St. Athanasius emergency room was normally swollen with a variety of desperate, late-night injuries. This night had proven to be a rare, quiet one and only five cases were waiting, when the trio entered. Noting one man with a thin rod sticking clean through his shoulder, Dominic did not feel quite so badly off. Still, his energy was depleted and he couldn't help but feel grateful that the stranger known as Blythe had taken the initiative to carry him. Cassie went off to find a nurse, while Blythe placed Dom carefully in one of the hard, plastic seats. He was astonished by the being's gentleness and concern that Dom was as comfortable as possible, and he noticed for the first time Blythe's own injuries from the battle with Boris. Most had healed, despite the look of the bloody and ripped coveralls he wore, but he could see through the rips that some of the wounds were still open and oozed slightly.

Patting his shoulder, Dom said weakly, "Rain was right about you. You're a good man." Then he nodded toward Cassie, who was still trying to grab a nurse's attention, saying, "Get her out of here."

Nodding, Blythe took hold of Cassie and gently forced her from the nurse's station. "What are you doing?" she asked, as they passed Dom.

"I'll be fine," Dom assured her and Blythe continued the march to the exit.

Responding to her reluctance, Blythe finally stared at her, pointing back at him, saying, "Safe," then pointing between the two of them, "Far from it."

Rolling her eyes, she acknowledged the truth of this and hurried out to the car with him.

†

Narain eased the car down Cassie's street, noting with dread the flashing blue lights of squad cards that had blocked it off. Double parking, he sat silently behind the wheel, raising his eyes to the sky in a quick pleading prayer, before turning off the motor and exiting the vehicle. He had been on the Kennedy, nearing the Ohio Street exit, when the flash came over the local news radio station about a violent home invasion in the Wrigleyville area. It was far too coincidental. He'd ended his call with Dom earlier that night, thinking all was well, and a short while later came this news story.

He, of all people, knew how quickly fortunes could change.

Walking toward the crowd gathering just beyond the yellow police tape, he heard snippets of neighbourly speculation. It was a double suicide/homicide. A drug deal had gone wrong. The woman had been abducted by an obsessive ex-boyfriend. Narain knew enough not to believe any of it. If they only knew the true horror that had likely invaded their neat little neighbourhood.

Frustrated, Narain retrieved his cell phone and dialled Dom again, as he had earlier that night, to find out the estimated time of arrival at his apartment. There had been no answer then, just as there was none now, but this time he heard the majestic strains of the "Imperial March" from "Star Wars" that Dom had downloaded as his ring tone, unconcerned with how unprofessional it sounded.

"That movie came at a pivotal time in my life," Dom had insisted when Narain questioned the choice.

"That explains so much," Narain had replied.

The music came from inside Cassie's house and Narain quickly cancelled the call, not wanting to attract the crowd's or the cops' attention. There was little damage to the outside of the house, save for the ruined front window. Approaching one of the policemen monitoring the crowd, Narain resorted to his own version of a Jedi mind trick and began mesmerising the cops with the tone of his voice and the warm scent of cinnamon he produced.

"Officer, would you tell me what happened?"

The cop stared at him, uncertain at first, before blinking saying, "Home invasion. At least that's what we think. But the owner isn't here. In fact, neighbours report her speeding off in a car. There are some signs of forced entry in the back and a struggle ensued, mainly in the living room, but no one was in the house when the first unit arrived on the scene."

"May I take a look inside?" he asked politely.

Again, there was the slightest of hesitation before the cop broke policy and raised the tape saying, "I don't see why not."

Narain walked with a careful grace across the lawn, his demeanour projecting determination as if he was supposed to be there. He nodded to a few uniformed officers coming from around the back and they returned the nod, assuming he was a plain clothes detective.

Inside the front door, splatters of blood speckled the carpet and Narain noted the hall table smashed to pieces, and a small table lamp resting on top of the sad pile of wood. Scanning the floor, he found one of the things that brought him in here; Dom's cell phone lay where it had skidded in the corner, just behind the bottom stair. Walking over to it carefully, he picked it up inspecting it, then setting it to vibrate, he pocketed it. Under any other circumstances, he would never dream of disturbing a crime scene; he wouldn't even be trespassing on one. But he also wanted to limit evidence of Dom's involvement in that night as much as possible. Besides, the cops could probably do little to capture the being behind the destruction in this house and it might be safer for them if they didn't try.

Stepping into the living room, he was stunned by the violence that had taken place in it. What had happened to Dom; to Cassie? The struggle had been fierce, judging by the broken furniture. He prayed it hadn't been Dom's body that made the indentation in the wall. As in the entranceway, but to a much larger degree, blood splattered the floor, only here, shards of glass from the window and coffee table twinkled among it. He crouched down, inspecting the skeletal remains of the glass and metal coffee table. Strange, he thought. A body would have to have fallen on it with great force to twist the metal the way it was and if it was Dom's body, he doubted the man would have survived the impact. Equally doubtful, however, was that Dom would have the strength to throw his attacker with that sort of force. Weak as his skills were, he could still sense the two strange signatures that mingled with those of Cassie and Dom. Dipping fingers in one of the stains of blood, he raised it to his nose and sniffed at it, blinking. It wasn't the normal smell of blood. Or rather the smell of blood untainted by vampiric microbes. That had a different scent altogether.

Narain felt a presence nearing the room and froze in his crouch, eyes staring intently at the wide doorway. He relaxed only slightly when he saw that it was a plain clothed detective passing the doorway, followed by two more. They had come from the direction of the kitchen and as the parade passed by, one said, "Both doors are beat up, but I'm almost sure the invader came in from the kitchen. At least one of them did."

"Yeah, that front window was crashed into, not out of."

The first cop glanced in the living then paused, searching the room with an odd expression on his face.

"What's the matter?" one said, glancing around as well.

"I don't know. My eyes are playing tricks on me. I thought I saw something. You smell spice?"

Narain could feel the slow and steady pulses of the other two, but the pulse of the first one was stubborn in its heightened thump of possible discovery, so he increased his concentration, hoping no one else would enter the scene, as the room became ripe with the scent of cinnamon. Sweat beaded his forehead as he gazed squarely at the cop, whose own gaze squinted with the need to catch a glimpse of something. Eventually though, the cop's features relaxed and he shrugged. "I don't know," he said, a chuckle in his voice. "This whole case is weird. I got the chills."

"What are you, a rookie?" one of the others jibed good-naturedly. "The chills."

The other patted his shoulder. "Come on, let's go get a cup of coffee and settle down your chills."

Once the three had left, Narain's eyes rolled up and he fell to his left leg. The glass on the floor gave quick cuts to the palms he laid flat to brace himself, but the cuts healed just as quickly and he slowly stood up. That had been too close. Mesmering was much easier up close and one-on-one. Of course, the very thing that made that cop difficult to mesmer, is what made him a good cop. He had to get out of there before he came upon someone he couldn't mesmer.

Standing, Narain took one last look around. He had really just entered the house in the hopes of gaining some clue as to what had transpired and where his friends were now. He had no doubt that Boris had struck here. Was the mad little beast capable of taking prisoners? There was something heartening in the fact that both Cassie and Dom were missing, since, needing only Cassie, if the beast was the one behind their disappearance, he would have sucked Dom dry and left him a husk on the floor.

Unless he drank a little, then stored the rest for later. Narain shivered at the thought. He had heard of some ferals doing that, saving for a bloodless day.

He had no idea what had happened and what state Cassie and Dom were in and it ate at his mind. But there had been another. Was that Blythe? Sighing, he stepped carefully out of the living room and left the house, again adopting the air of a professional. All he needed was to be spotted by the cop who'd nearly discovered him and have his dimmed memory sharpened.

On the lawn next door, a man was standing in the spotlight of a local news station, as they interviewed him on the strange disappearance of his neighbour. Ducking under the crime tape, Narain joined the crowd watching this spectacle and zeroed his hearing in on what the neighbour was saying.

"...in the window upstairs. I saw the guy come through the window of the house and run after the car. I think Cassie was driving. By the time I got out to the front lawn, I saw the car down the block stop, then it backed over the guy and sped off."

"What happened to the assailant pursuing the car?" The interviewer asked, then directed the microphone toward the man's face.

The neighbour's face grew blank. "You know, I don't know. I tell you, it sounded pretty bad, the thud and all. But maybe it looked and sounded worse than it was. I mean, I know Cassie wouldn't purposely hurt anyone."

Looking down the street, Narain noticed that section had been blocked off as well, and a few policemen were squatting in the street no doubt inspecting skid marks. He rolled his eyes with some level of relief, certain that Cassie and Dom had gotten away. His concern now was to figure out, before Reg did, just where they had gone.

Chapter 15

Cassie hit the floor with a soft plunk, her right butt cheek taking the brunt of the fall. The birds chirping in the soft, morning light outside sounded like snickering children as she blinked the sleep from her eyes, gazing up confused at the sofa from which she'd fallen. She had a perfectly comfortable and much wider bed upstairs. Why was she camping on the sofa? Then she remembered the drama of only hours before which offered a possible explanation. It all came back to her—the crazed attacker, dropping Dom off at St. Athanasius, and the long ride up I-294 with her quiet, dishevelled protector; a vampire capable of savage brutality who sat in the passenger seat quietly watching, as city congestion turned to new subdivisions that turned to clean farm land and forest preserves. There was little traffic that time of night as they exited onto Route 120 and drove through the far north-western towns of Illinois. His face was unreadable in the shadows of the car interior, especially with his beard and long hair that fell haphazardly across his features. He had said very little after leaving Dom at the hospital and for that matter, neither did she. There was too much going on in her head. With the sun still down, she had still felt vulnerable in the city, even though their attacker might be miles across town. The fiend was called Boris, or so her companion had told her.

And the name of her protector was Blythe. He grew silent after reasserting how dangerous this Boris was, leaving her to jabber on nervously more for her own benefit about needing a place to hide, about her drained cell phone battery, about needing to call Narain. It was Narain's name that seemed to elicit a reaction from Blythe, but it was quick and she was too preoccupied to deeply analyse it. She had noticed how he kneaded his hands resting in his lap, his fingernails hard, stained and dangerous, thick, yet chipped from battles.

The country house was about two hours away from Chicago, in McHenry. It rested in a clearing, half a mile down a service road off Route 120. The area had yet to succumb to the suburban sprawl that had claimed so much of the rural areas of Northern Illinois and the service road cut through thick forest until a clearing opened up at its end where a two story cottage stood. As she eased out from behind the steering wheel she scanned the area as best she could in the rural darkness. Were it not for the cement driveway and pavement reflecting what moonlight there was, it might be difficult for her eyes to pick up any walkable path. This wasn't the first time she had arrived at the house in the dark, but it was a rarity. Motion sensor lights on the corners of the garage would provide sufficient light but the switches were in the house and not knowing when she'd be up there next, she turned them off the last time she stayed at the house.

"I think we'll be safe here," she said, tracing one hand along the car, as she stepped carefully around the front of it. "At least long enough to catch our breath and figure our next move."

Blythe said nothing as he exited the car, coming around beside her. Raising the keys, she squinted to find the right house key. When she located it, she moved up the pavement to wooden porch stairs that *thunked* hollowly, as she stepped on them. "Now watch your step. It's dark." As she spoke, she tripped over a branch that had found its way onto the steps and Blythe reached out, catching her with ease. She thought she saw a smile playing at his lips, then realised how ridiculous it was for her to warn a vampire to watch his step in the dark. As she opened the screen door, inserting the key into the deadbolt on the storm door, she said, "I'll have you know I have the night vision of a cat," then quietly added, "that's gone blind," as she opened the door.

She was certain she heard a chuckle this time from the hulking figure that followed her and she felt a bit more at ease. Cassie was well aware that, if she weren't the great grandniece of Alphonse and the grandniece of Lucy, if she hadn't read the journals and investigated the disease, she would not feel nearly as comfortable as she did being in the same room with the vampire. She knew the truth, however. And Blythe while obviously possessing a wildness and great strength, had also revealed himself to be incredibly caring and rather gentle. A good thing since she was finding her own stamina weakening, as the adrenaline that had fuelled her from Chicago quickly evaporated in the quiet of the country. There was an almost vacuum-like silence so far from the constant whir of traffic and city congestion. Without a word, she went over and turned a lamp on near the couch, falling onto the soft cushions, sitting there with her head back. After a few moments she sighed, saying, "If you'd like to have a seat, Mr. Blythe, we have to figure out the next course of action, but I just want to sit here for a moment and rest my eyes."

And that was that. Thoughts of crazed vampires and secret toxins all drifted away, as sleep overtook her.

The next thing she knew, she was laying on the floor looking up at the ceiling, her legs tangled in the afghan she hadn't remembered using. Blythe must have placed it over her. Where was Blythe? Then she noted the sunlight brightening the living room and her heart seized. It was a soft light from a partly cloudy sky, but it would be enough to poison a vampire. Perhaps he had been able to bury himself in the woods before sunrise.

Struggling from the afghan, she got to her feet, ignoring the kinks in her neck and back, then realised she had no idea what to do next. Where did a vampire dig in to escape the sun? Did he do it near the house, or in the thick woods surrounding? It was as she moved around the sofa, that she glanced out the now open drapes of the backyard window, seeing a figure on the deck out back. She stared in surprise, not ready to believe it, but the tattered bright orange jumpsuit and the long unruly hair would not allow her to deny her own eyes.

Blythe did not need to look back when Cassie stepped onto the porch from the house, he sensed her presence immediately. At that moment, he was wrapped up in watching a bird. Something he hadn't done for a long time. He'd seen birds, mostly crows and sparrows grabbing whatever crumbs they could from the curbs of Chicago, but he didn't really watch them. Didn't really see them. This one he saw and couldn't take his eyes off it. It was bright red and sat in a tree branch of a conifer, like a Christmas ornament. There were two others somewhere in the trees as well, their calls, mixing in with the other early morning bird song, making him realise how little he'd heard prowling the alleys of Chicago. There was so much noise in that city, the sounds melding into each other drowning out anything of distinction.

A bit of sun escaped the clouds and fell upon him. It felt good for the brief moment, but if it happened more often, he would have to go in to shelter. He couldn't risk too much exposure; his ability simply gave him a better freedom of movement.

The sunlight landing on him amazed Cassie, who gasped as she came forward. "Didn't that hurt you?" she asked, standing next to him as he leaned against the deck railing. He shook his head. "So, you're able to be out in the daylight?"

He nodded. "Not long. Small duration."

It could have been the amount of talking he'd had to do the past day, more than he'd done in quite some time, but his voice was sounding much smoother, the words more natural to his tongue. The act of talking still seemed difficult, though, and the British accent he carried over took some getting used to.

Staring at him as if he were a specimen, Cassie exclaimed, "This is incredible. I've never come across anything like this. I don't think anyone has. I mean, since the aversion to sunlight rests primarily with the microbes, yours could be another species altogether. Which could be dangerous, I guess." Her face brightened. "Or, it could be a real break-through. Maybe a clue to a true cure."

Turning his head, he stared at her, blinking, then moved away a bit and she realised how that must have all sounded to a being who'd spent the past few years being experimented on. "Oh, I'm sorry. I would never…I just got overly enthusiastic…I mean, you have to admit it is pretty incredible."

He stared at her. For a moment, she noted that tiny smile he'd given her before and she was relieved her fumbling had put him at ease.

"Look, I'm sorry I fell asleep. I didn't mean to. I was only going to…"

"Rest your eyes."

She chuckled. "Yes. Are you hungry?" Catching herself, she said, "Well, you probably are, but I don't think I have your brand of juice in the fridge." He eyed her hungrily, then smiled a bit looking away as her anxiety over his intentions crossed her face. Softly slapping his arm, she said, "Oh, very funny," then grew concerned by a small wound still festering. "Hey, did you get this last night?"

He looked at his right forearm and said nonchalantly, "Yes. Boris bit me."

She could see through the tatter of his jumpsuit that there were other bite marks still red and swollen. "Why haven't they healed right?"

"Boris Bites," he said, stretching his back, "take a while to heal."

She inspected his forearm, the scientist taking over again. "This is interesting." The wound oozed a bit, but whether it was not painful, or Blythe had a high tolerance, he didn't react to her touch. Of course, it must have been worse last night. "And you say they do heal?" He nodded. "Hmm, reminds me a bit of Komodo dragons. They bite their prey and bacteria in their saliva infect the wounds. Usually, that's what brings the animal down. Though in this case it's apparently not fatal. Boris must have something in his saliva that keeps the wound from healing, but not permanently. Could be why he can outlast you in a fight."

"Quite a Petri dish, aren't I?" Blythe said, in what she was sure was his first straight out quip, though it was spoken with a touch of weariness.

Clearing her throat, she judiciously said, "I was thinking, and I'm not passing judgement here, but if you'd like to get cleaned up…maybe take a shower—I mean you're a bit road worn and your clothes have certainly seen better days. I have nothing in the house to fit you, but I can at least wash the uniform."

She spoke her words so carefully not to give offence, that he saw the wisdom of taking the chance when he could. He nodded and she led him upstairs to a tidy bathroom. She showed him the shower, the soap, and the soft, fluffy towels in the linen closet. A far cry from bathing in Lake Michigan.

With a finger on her chin, she said after some consideration, "Until your clothes are dry, I think the best I can offer is a sheet. You can wrap it around yourself. You'll look a bit like a Roman senator, but it shouldn't take too long."

He shrugged, willing to accept it. It was hard to worry about modesty when he'd been living like an animal for so long.

She left a queen-sized flannel sheet on the floor outside the door while he showered, then went downstairs to throw his clothes in the small washer in the kitchen, going over in her mind the next move she should make, all the while flashing back on the sad figure in her shower upstairs. What sort of man had he been before? What brought him to this state? He was obviously not feral, though strong feral tendencies existed in him. They seemed there more out of necessity. Was this how it had been for her great uncle Alphonse as he scoured the countryside aiding newborn vampires hoping to find and help his son? He had been able to lead many back to humanity, assuring them they did not have to give their humanity up because of their condition.

Could she do the same for Blythe?

There was also the current situation to consider. She felt fairly confident they were safe. There'd be no reason for Jameson to suspect a hideaway in the McHenry countryside and as wild as Boris might be, she doubted he'd be able to track them miles from where they left him, crawling off the street in Wrigleyville.

Still, she'd feel better once she could contact Narain. She had tried to call him once while still in Chicago, but the connection had been bad and the call hadn't gone through. When she had the chance to call again, she had noticed with dismay that her battery was too low. She'd have to recharge the phone, which she was going to do when they arrived at the house, but sleep had taken hold.

After throwing the clothes in the dryer, she was going to go upstairs to check on her guest/bodyguard/whatever, when she saw a shadow of movement in the room downstairs that she was converting into an office. Cautiously moving to the doorway, she peered in seeing a newly scrubbed Blythe, the blue flannel sheet wrapped carefully around him, gazing around at the bookshelves and boxes that were scattered in the room. He was holding an old journal, one of Lucy's, the brown leather binding slightly weathered. Occasionally he would glance at it, scanning a few lines, and then go back to investigating the file folders on the top of the file cabinets.

He knew she was in the doorway and she knew he knew. She stepped in slowly, not wanting to snap the mood. "There's a lot of stuff here," she commented, studying it all herself. "A couple of lifetimes—well Alphonse, Lucy and me. You wouldn't know them, I guess." Sighing, she went over to a box, fingering through all the photographs inside. "I'm not sure if it was smart to bring it all up here. I'm not sure how secure it all is. I come here as often as I can. My parents bought this property as a vacation spot when they were first married. Built the house. There's a lake not too far from here. We had some great summers up here. When Mom died, my siblings and I...well, we couldn't part with it. We each took a share of the tax bill and kept it. They've all moved out of state now, so I figured I'd buy it from them. I'm in the process of doing that right now." She stared at a few of the photos. "I guess I just wanted to separate all this from my other work. Bring it some place where I could concentrate solely on it."

Turning to her, he held up the journal and waved it around. "Is this all about..."

"Good portions of it are files detailing the experience of other people like you. People who've had a much easier time dealing with the condition."

He looked at the journal. "Reg told me some of it. I don't completely understand."

His freshly washed hair was still damp and slicked back, leaving his face more visible then she'd ever seen. There was no major disfigurement as with the ferals. It was a nice face. An honest, if rather melancholy face.

"I've been researching the condition for well over a decade and I don't completely understand it. I just know for sure that you're not a monster." He looked down again. "It has a cause and I believe it has a cure. I'm hoping to find it." One of the photos caught her eye and she smiled, bringing it to him. "Hey, look at this. You might recognise this guy."

Blythe took the photograph, studying it, then glanced up at her, face a bit brighter. "Narain."

She nodded, tilting her head to look at the photo. "I don't know who the other person is. Might be another vampire my great grand uncle helped. Narain's in a number of photos I've come across."

His brows furrowed. "'Vampire.' You say the word as if it's natural."

She shrugged. "I suppose after all this time researching it, it kind of is for me."

"Narain is your friend?" She blushed, sighing, giving him some indication of the degree of friendship. "He was a good man. Helped me more than he should have had to."

"You must have gone through hell in that war. I think that would knock the emotional wind out of anyone."

He said nothing, simply gave the photo back to her and stood stoically near the computer desk. Placing the photo carefully back in the box, she asked, "Are you familiar with computers?"

He gave her a look, saying, "I don't understand half the contraptions in this house."

She pursed her lips. "Yeah, that'd make sense." Then she went over to the computer, turning it on and dragging the cursor onto a particular file on the desk top. "Okay, it's really not that hard, once I get you started. Then you can look at it. "

Reluctantly curious, he moved around the chair and watched her. "Look at what?"

"Well, there's a whole lot of medical research connected with all this. Much of it gets pretty technical. What I started doing was recording a journal that's a bit more accessible to people without doctorates in medicine." She clicked, then clicked again. Then she motioned for him to sit and after he did so, she showed him how to scroll down using the mouse. "You don't have to read it all, but I thought it might help better explain what's happened to you and some of the theories I have on how to reverse it."

He said nothing, but his focus on the screen indicated that he was interested in the text. She had to admit he was pretty adaptable. There had been no huge reaction to the very modern appliances in the house, but then considering what he had already seen as a prisoner of Jameson's, very little would surprise him.

"Okay, you do that while I try to call Narain." He nodded and she left him to his task.

†

Narain growled and put his fist into the wall next to the window, leaving behind a significant dent and yet one more section of his condo that would need repairing. Besides the shower stall, still damaged after his run-in with Jameson, there was a kitchen cabinet that had been angrily yanked off its hinges, when he got home that morning. Rubbing his hand, he glared at the security shades that kept out the sun, sat on the arm of the sofa for a few seconds, and then went back to the pacing he'd been doing all morning.

Cassie was out there somewhere, mad creatures hunting her, and he was trapped in the apartment until the sun was safely down. Narain's one assurance was that the sun kept the hunters as much at bay as he was, but Reg was resourceful and was not about to let a slight inconvenience like solar incineration keep him from tracking his prey. He, no doubt, had specialists with untainted blood doing his leg work.

All Narain could do was wait for contact from his friends. He'd called Cassie's cell phone, but an automated message stated that it wasn't in service. He had toyed with the idea of contacting Channing to see if he had a clue as to where Cassie may have gone, but despite the researcher's professions of love for Cassie, his allegiance was highly suspect.

The phone rang and he scowled at it. So far that morning, he'd been offered free satellite hookup, the latest in cell phone technology, and the chance to consolidate his bills into one easy payment with a low interest rate and affordable monthly payments. If he had to listen to one more robotically charming voice congratulate him on being pre-selected, he was going to throw the phone through the window, sunlight be damned.

The voice he heard when he picked up the phone, however, was the voice he'd desperately been waiting to hear. Taken aback by his snarled greeting, Cassie said, uncertainly, "Uhm, Narain, is that you? It's Cassie."

His anger faded instantly, his heart racing with a nervous excitement as he said, "Cassie? Cassie my love, where are you? I'm nearly frantic."

There was a pause then a playfulness to her tone when she asked, "Your love?"

"Yes," he said, ignoring the implications. "Where are you? What happened? Your house is a mess."

As if this jogged loose a repressed memory, her voice became hoarse and sticky as she pined, "Oh, my house. That whole window is gone. God knows what he did to the back door. I doubt I have anything left inside."

"No, no, don't worry. I've arranged a board up service. Once the police have finished their investigation, the service will take care of it. It will be secure."

Still upset, she said, "Oh Narain, I couldn't believe it. It all happened so fast. Dom came to get me…oh, Dom. God I almost forgot. He's in the hospital, St. Athanasius."

"Calm yourself, I know."

"You do?"

"Dominic's mother called me this morning to tell me. Apparently, he was mugged," he said knowingly. "He's doing fine. They had to take him into surgery for some internal bleeding but he's doing well."

Cassie gave an audible sigh, her voice sounding much calmer. "It was just amazing, Narain." She recounted the fight between the two vampires, much of which he'd surmised from the look of the living room. Then she detailed their escape. "I mean, I backed over that creature and dragged him for yards. Yet as I sped away, he was crawling his way to the side of the street. Any broken bones have mended by now. I just can't believe…you know it's not just Boris' strength it's also…well determination. It's like he has an insane need to attack. Blythe did his best to hold him off, but Boris was wearing him down."

That was another problem. According to Cassie's story, Blythe had saved her, at great risk to himself, and was now sitting in a room examining computer files. This bit of chivalry would be in keeping with the Blythe Narain had once known. But Blythe was no longer the man Narain knew. Not completely, and while he wanted passionately to believe he could trust her being in the hands of his old friend, he also couldn't help but remember those pictures, recall what Jameson had told him, and remember the fact that Channing had brought Blythe to Chicago, because he believed Blythe was capable of hunting down and destroying an even deadlier beast.

Was Cassie safe in his old friend's hands or would the feral nature he must be fighting win out and see her as little more than a food source?

As if tipped off by his silence, she said, "Narain, are you concerned about Fred?"

"Fred?"

"Fred Blythe?"

Narain blinked. "Fred. Yes, yes, of course." It had been far too easy to think of him as a one-named creature. A "Blythe"; half mad killer. He was Fred Blythe. Maybe all he needed was to be reminded of who he was. "Well, to be honest…"

"Narain, don't. I don't know if it's the quiet of this place or what, but…well let's just say that he's had ample opportunity to hurt me if he wanted to, and he hasn't. I trust him as much as I trust you."

This struck Narain, though he couldn't grasp why. He wondered if his concerns were unfounded after all. "Listen, tell me where you are? I'll leave as soon as the sun goes down."

After giving him the directions, she paused and Narain grew concerned. "Cassie, what is it?" The playfulness returned to her voice as she said, "What you said earlier. Am I really your love?"

Grinning wide, enjoying the chance for a quick flirt, he shrugged, switching the phone to his other ear and feigned indifference. "Well, I'm quite fond of you, yes. Love, of course, is all a matter of perspective and one needs to tread very carefully before jumping into such matters. It is a most serious thing, not to be taken too lightly."

She giggled saying, unconvinced, "Uh huh. You keep telling yourself that, pal."

He chuckled before his smile faded. "Cassie," he said seriously, a slight desperation in his voice, "be careful. Don't tell anyone else where you are and be vigilant. I'll get there as soon as I can."

"I will. And Narain."

"Yes?"

"I'm quite fond of you, too."

He smiled, refusing to say goodbye, preferring instead to let that sentence be the last words he heard from her, before seeing her again. Hanging up the phone, he kept his hand resting on it, as he turned his head and glared again at the window.

†

Cassie snapped her cell shut, clutching it tightly. Sighing, she stared out the window at the sunlit yard, as if the glow was a protective force field surrounding the house. She looked at her watch. Sundown was over nine hours away. She had a few hours to put aside the worry. Meandering down the hall, she entered the room where Blythe was sitting, his eyes glued to the computer screen. Stepping beside the desk, she held up the phone, saying, "I just called Narain."

Turning his attention to the device in her hand, he said, "Called Narain?"

"Yes on my cell." Blythe's brows furrowed. "My cell phone."

Shaking his head, Blythe commented, "The last telephone I used weighed about five stone and was the size of a corgi." Leaning back, he ran a hand through his hair, then waved it around. "I just simply can't believe this. I feel like I've strolled into a Jules Verne book."

"It's a lot to take in."

Staring away, he said, "You know, when Channing let me loose in the city, I was stunned by it all. I remember staring up at this huge building," he moved his hands to indicate a tapered shape. "Meaty and tall. Stood there for a good 20 minutes staring at it. And that's not even the tallest."

"Wait…did you say Channing? Richard Channing?"

The look of stunned surprise on her face telegraphed clearly that this was a name that carried strong resonance for her. "Do you know him?" he asked, looking away and regretting that the information had slipped out in so awkward a fashion.

Her eyes scanned the floor as she considered the implications. "He is my partner." Blythe's eyes widened and she quickly added, "I had no idea that he was mixed up in all this." She paused, considering it all, asking, "But how is he mixed up in all of this?"

Blythe related every detail he had to offer. His capture, his captivity, what he could remember of the experiments; the poisons they tested on him and the blood they took from him. He told her of Boris' creation and how once he had escaped, Channing had sent for him to protect her. That's why he had showed up at her Wrigleyville home the night before. Sentences were becoming easier for him to speak, but exposition of a longer length was still a chore. That, plus the fact that he had still been half mad early in his captivity, left the story choppy. But Cassie found herself sitting cross legged on the floor in front of him, listening to the ordeal he'd been put through, and feeling as if she had just heard news of Richard's death, for the man responsible for this torture was not the man she once loved. Or thought she had loved.

Once Blythe had finished, silence hung between them until Cassie began to shake her head slowly, saying, "I don't know what to say. I'm at a loss...I never once suspected that he even knew about my research, let alone that he was involved with someone like Reginald Jameson. I could not, for the life of me, understand how Jameson found out about the toxin."

"You shouldn't blame yourself." Her feelings of responsibility were evident in the way she avoided his gaze. He glanced at the computer indicating what he read. "I see what you've done and what you're trying to do. It is not your fault that he's taken that and turned it into something it was never meant to be."

At last able to look up at him, her face softened as she said, "You've been through so much." She reached up to touch his hand, which was resting on his knee.

Shrugging, he looked back at the computer screen, saying nothing.

Studying him, her face brightened. "I have an idea." Then she hurried from the room, returning with a towel, comb, scissors and a pink razor. She pointed at the screen. "You can continue to read, if you like," before spreading the towel at the floor behind him.

Oddly trusting, he allowed her to work behind him, perhaps realising that even with scissors there was very little she could do to hurt him. She grabbed his hair and pulled it into a pony-tail, saying, "I'm assuming you won't miss this."

Understanding, he grinned, saying, "Well, it could be the source of my strength."

"Believe me, this is not the source of your strength."

He waved a hand. "Then chop away. Not quite the fashion in my day."

"I can just imagine." Using the scissors, she made her way through the pony-tail. While the hair was now clean, it was still a mass of tangles and took a bit of effort to cut. "Should have brought garden shears," she joked and actually heard him give a low chuckle. Once the tail was amputated, she brushed through his hair with her fingers. "I'll work on the snarls and cut a bit more. Then we'll go after that beard."

She placed the pink razor on the desk next to him, and he picked it up, fascinated, before flashing her a disbelieving look. "I know it doesn't look like much, but it's the latest technology in ladies' shaving. It won't be the smoothest shave you'll ever have, but it'll get the job done."

Blythe read a few more paragraphs of the journal, but the truth was his mind was wandering. He found her intriguing. She had no fear of him, his strangeness, and the touch warmed him. It wasn't a sensual pleasure. It was the warmth of human contact which he had been denied for so long that made his skin tingle. It was the breezy way she combed his hair, laughing at herself as she tripped over the leg of the desk and recovering herself gracefully. He closed his eyes. It had been so long since he'd been alone with a woman's voice. That sweet tinkle of the tender pipes. Female voices could be heard all over the city, but to be alone with one, to converse with one, he had not done that for a long time. Not since before the trenches when Mary, the neighbour girl, stopped by to send him off proper with a hug and a kiss, and the hope that perhaps there'd be more, when he returned. Or his sister, Rose, chatting on with their mum about how smart he looked in his uniform. Then, there were the girls down the docks, who sang a chorus of *bon voyage!* to all the brave lads heading off to fight the Hun.

At some point, Cassie told him to follow her to the bathroom upstairs, where the soap and water would soften his beard for easier shaving. She had trimmed it closely as she could with the scissors, now it was up to the pink razor. He repeated his look of scepticism and she repeated her look of "just you wait."

Closing the toilet lid, she indicated that he should sit and he did so, then she lathered up his face with suds produced from a small dollop of flowery scented gel and began to shave his chin. The last time he'd had someone shave him was before the war, when he visited a barber before taking Mary out for a day at a travelling circus that had arrived in town. There hadn't been anything serious between him and the neighbour girl; just a connection from childhood that had grown along with them. But he fancied there could have been something serious. If he had come back from the trenches.

"There now."

Relaxed by the ministrations, Blythe had found himself actually half dozing, and his eyes drifted open as the rhythmic strokes of the razor turned into the gentle wiping from the towel. He looked at Cassie, who smiled back at him, giving his hair one last going over.

"Well, I'm not a stylist," she said, "but I have to say, this is not bad at all. Take a look." She pulled him up, turning him to face the mirror over the sink, and he actually found himself gasping.

It was almost the face he saw in the mirror the day he left for France. Outside of reflections in windows or water, he hadn't seen himself in a long time. And even then, he avoided looking rather than be reminded of the wild-haired caveman he'd become. But groomed and beardless, it was if time had melted away.

"Quite a good looking guy," Cassie said studying his reflection. On the mirror, she indicated his eyebrow ridge with the comb. "I'm guessing the brows are more prominent than they were." She moved the comb around the reflection to his lips. "And the mouth has had to accommodate a new dental anatomy. But it's not terribly deformed. Especially when one considers the walking shark tooth that Boris is."

A grin exploded into a smile on his face and he lowered his head, laughing. That's what he found so refreshing: Her honesty. She pointed out the positive, but she was not about to sugarcoat the negative either.

"What?" she asked, as he laughed harder than he had yet in her presence. He looked up at her, gnashing his teeth, and she began to get it. Grimacing she said, "Oh no, did I go all science geek again. I'm sorry. I wasn't saying you look bad. Just the opposite. I just tend to get really clinical, when I'm fascinated by something. I am a scientist after all."

Reaching out, he grabbed her and embraced her, relieved when her guilt relaxed.

"Thank you," he said, mindful not to squeeze too hard. She had brought back a sense of himself. She had reminded him of what he had been, before this thing he had become, and no matter what was heading his way, he felt good to let it go for that moment and get reacquainted with himself.

Chapter 16

Patrillo Surveillance had an excellent reputation. Two brothers, Mark and Jay Patrillo from Schiller Park, had started out as repo men, and in a matter of seven years, thanks to Jay's knack with the latest gadgetry, had become one of the most successful detective firms in the country. They eventually opened branches in Florida, California, and Las Vegas and their good name reached even into Asia, thanks to some high profile cases. The brothers, themselves, remained in their Chicago home base. They were savvy, able to cope with an increasingly high tech world, and most importantly, they weren't interested in a client's motives. Their only concern was that the checks cleared at the end of the case. And heaven protect those whose checks didn't clear. The brothers were able to work both sides of the law with acrobatic agility and having used them a few times before, Reg Jameson was confident they would be able to assist him in his current concern.

As he listened over the comm while they executed their assignment, he became even more impressed with their professionalism.

"Mark, I have rabbit leaving hole, left on Grand, heading west," Jay's voice said briskly.

"I'm in pursuit."

"Copy that Jay," Mark's voice was equally officious, shades of the cop he almost was. "Will double round and meet you cross State Street, unless he turns off before then."

Jameson shifted in his seat behind the wheel of the van he was driving, a smile crossing his face. It was like listening to a police drama on the radio. They had a bit of the theatre about them, but never enough to risk the case they were working on. They loved the money too much for that.

Dr. Cassie Lambert had, indeed, posed him with a challenge and after Boris' failure of the previous night, Jameson was forced to get involved, no matter what Channing might think. Especially now that Blythe was involved. If he were lucky, he could kill two birds with one stone, and get the experiments back on track.

He thought of Boris, sitting in the back of the van with the ten ferals. The group's

Inactivity, since the sun had set, was probably eating away at that vicious little ball of Energy, but the wait was necessary.

When Boris had phoned him, legs still twisted, but mending, from his mishap with the back of the good doctor's car, Reg was both furious and concerned. After all, Boris was a valuable asset he didn't want to lose; one he might still be able to use. But it had become a matter of tracking down three people in a car, in a very big city bustling with cars.

His dear little Piri was the one who offered a suggestion. "They're bound to contact Khan at some point. If they haven't already. Keep an eye on him and he may lead us straight to them."

He loved how she used the word "us." She would have absolutely no part in the recovery operation, but she liked to feel included in the general play.

Mark and Jay Patrillo didn't mind being awoken in the middle of the night, as long as it involved a lucrative case. And the Jameson name chased away any misgivings they may have had, for they knew how lucrative his cases had been in the past. He explained his objective, careful to leave out the vampiric end of it, and indicated that a portion of the sizeable fee had already been wire transferred into a special account for them. They readily agreed and began their surveillance.

A well placed packet of money given to the night-time security guard at Lake Point Towers was enough to garner them the information that Khan had gone out several hours before and had not been back since. Mark Patrillo took a stakeout position near Khan's regular parking spot, while Jay went to make arrangements should it be necessary to institute a plan B. Khan pulled his silver Lexus into his space at approximately 4:20 AM., his demeanour quick and preoccupied. He got out of the car alone and did not return until after sundown that night, leaving the brothers to suspect that he remained alone in his condo throughout the day. He carried with him a gym bag that he placed in the trunk before entering the car and backing out of the space. Mark thought for a moment that he'd been made when the car stopped and the subject scanned the parking structure, a curious look on Khan's face, but eventually the subject pulled away. That's when Mark alerted Jay who had taken a position on the street outside the garage entrance. Mark himself pulled out of the garage and with his brother began double tailing Khan as he rode through the city. Both were excellent at tailing a subject alone but having the two car system enabled one to back off before the subject became suspicious.

†

It was an intricate dance and Reg would have enjoyed taking part in it, but one problem kept him sitting parked on the side of the street, waiting for the okay to proceed from the brothers.

Khan's vampiric skills were weak, there was no doubt about that. He seemed to ignore them rather than cultivate them, but then, to be fair, one hardly needed much skill of any sort to dish out overpriced curries in an overrated cow town. Not to mention that having a cow to milk for most of the century meant Khan wouldn't need to put his skills to the test. Yet, the skills were a part of his makeup and a vampire never really lost them. Reg couldn't gauge how weak Khan's skills were and preferred not to risk it. If Reg had been waiting for him to drive out of his parking garage, it was very possible Khan could sense him. And tailing him, with a van full of ferals, especially in the stop and go of downtown traffic, might put him on Khan's radar. Having two private detectives to do the task was the logical choice. They would keep him apprised of the route Khan was taking and help Jameson track him to Lambert. Once they found the hidey-hole, the ferals could take it from there.

The receiver on the dash hissed a bit and Jay said, "Okay Mr. Jameson…" another reason he liked them; they insisted on calling him Mister, "I think it's safe for you to start out but keep at a slow pace initially. We're about five minutes going north from your location."

Another voice chimed in. "Jay, I think he's heading for the Kennedy," there was a pause. "Yeah, we're going for the Kennedy west bound."

"Copy that," Jay said then directed his attention to Reg. "Okay, Mr. Jameson, head to State, make a right, then a left on Ontario. Eventually you'll get to the entrance ramp to the I-94. We may hit the last bit of rush hour, but I don't think it'll be too bad."

"You know Mark, if we hit the tail end of rush hour we'll have to be careful. He starts changing lanes and we may lose him."

As much as Reg enjoyed listening to the interplay, he was growing anxious to get going so when Jay gave him the green light, he was only too happy to ease the van into traffic and judging by the excited whoop from the back, Boris was, too. The feral in the passenger seat kept an eye on the map read out on the dashboard computer screen and indicated when to turn and which direction.

As the Patrillos suspected, Khan did go onto the Kennedy Expressway which was slightly backed up, though nowhere nearly as bad as it would have been a few hours before. Rush hour in Chicago tended to last from 7 AM. to 10 PM. Skilled in their jobs, though, the brothers were able to keep their target in their sights and Khan's consistent driving implied that he hadn't discovered the tail. As they neared the Cumberland interchange near O'Hare where I-90 branched out into the various directions of the 290-294 Tollway, Khan's car veered into the lane merging onto 294 North.

"If he's meeting this doctor," Mark commented, "It doesn't look like she's in the city any more."

"He wouldn't have made you," Reg asked "and is now leading you on a chase?"

"Nah!" Mark replied. This was not over-confidence. It was experience. "I've been made before and the first thing they do, even the casual ones, is try to lose the tail. Unless they're extreme professionals, it's obvious what they're doing. Besides, I don't think he'd have made both Jay and me."

"Well, where is he headed?"

"I-294 takes you out to the northern suburbs. Goes up to Wisconsin. We won't have an idea where until he gets off the toll way."

The northern suburbs? Jameson thought. If she was squirrelled away there then she was very clever. He wouldn't have thought she'd leave the city. He checked the dashboard clock. They'd been on the road for an hour and who knows how much longer before Khan alighted. Sunrise was scheduled for 4:38 AM. He'd have to keep the time in mind. Always keep the time in mind. The importance of recapturing Blythe was making itself felt again. This game had lasted too long. It would be finished tonight. Then he could get back to the business of finding his ticket to the daylight world.

✝

Pulling up the darkened driveway slowly, Narain parked the car behind Cassie's and eased from behind the wheel, looking around the clearing. His eyes and ears were alert for any sights and sounds that seemed out of place. The snap of a twig, the rustling of branches. His gaze penetrated deep into the woods surrounding the house, deeper than normal vision would, but he saw nothing out of the ordinary for a rural area. Everything appeared fine.

A nervous sensation had been burrowing into him since he left the city, but he couldn't explain it for there didn't appear to be anyone following him. Of course it could be that he had become too much a city man. There was something unsettling about the silence of the country. Well, near silence. He could still pick up the flap of a night bird's wings as it moved from one branch to another. Or the scuttling of a raccoon or opossum as it foraged on the forest floor. He had lived too long choreographing his nights to the music of a metropolis.

This nervousness was much more than a man being out of his element, however. It had been many decades since he had needed the sort of skills he would need to go up against his own kind and he wasn't sure if he'd be up to the task, should it be required. He noted that the soft yellow lights on two front corners of the attached garage were on and lights brightening the interior of the house. Stepping with cat-like grace across the lawn, even his footfalls were silent as he stepped on the wooden porch and peered into the front of the window. The living room beyond the gauzy curtain was empty and he noted a staircase just before the entrance to a small hallway. Moving back, he noted the lights out upstairs so it was doubtful anyone was up there. In fact, the living room seemed to be the only room illuminated. When he walked around the side of the house, however, he saw that a hood light above the stove in the empty kitchen was on. The storm door was wide open and the screen door was unlocked, making Narain's heart skip a beat when he opened it. She was near and he focused on the sense of her.

Sliding inside, he was at odds with his next course of action. His calling out might garner him a reassuring response from Cassie or serve to make his presence known to any of Jameson's people who may have gotten there first. Of course any ferals in the area most likely knew about his presence at that point.

Craning his head around the kitchen door frame, he studied the darkened dining room, catching sight of the door leading to the back deck where a figure stood illuminated by the light over the sliding door. He sighed, swallowing hard. It was Cassie, as relaxed as if the insanity of the past few days had never occurred and she was simply enjoying the night air before retiring.

Hurrying through the dining room, he slid the screen door open wide and sped out to the deck to embrace her. She turned, a smile brightening her face which disappeared quickly as steel bands wrapped themselves around Narain's upper chest and midsection, pinning his arms down. One of the bands moved up, encasing his neck and he realised that what held him fast were not bands, but the arms of the being that now stood behind him.

"Oh no, Fred," Cassie said, raising her arms. "It's okay. It's Narain."

Fred? Blythe? This was Fred Blythe holding him so firmly that he was having trouble breathing. Pressure increased on his windpipe, feeling like a python was strangling him. If he put up a struggle he might at least slip out of the grip and jog somewhere outside Blythe's reach, but this would only work if Blythe's guard was down and he loosened the hold. Narain would never be able to break free of the hold Blythe currently had on him.

So, he let Cassie work her charm hoping that she would get Blythe to release him before his windpipe was crushed. That would be incredibly inconvenient since they took a long time to repair.

"Fred, please," Cassie implored, sliding over to him and placing a hand on his thick arm. "Remember Narain? He served with you in the war and I called him to come help us."

Narain felt Blythe's chest heaving against his back as if trying to break through the confusion, then at last there was relief as he let his arms drop and Narain fell to his knees, wheezing life back into his chest and throat. Cassie knelt down beside him, rubbing his back while he caught his breath. Then, as if realising for the first time why he was there, Narain looked up at Cassie and pulled her to him in a fierce embrace. Visions of her Wrigleyville house slammed into his mind, as well as thoughts of what he might have found if she hadn't escaped and he held her tighter, occasionally pulling away to hold her face in his hands and kiss her deeply before pulling him to her again.

At first stunned, her embrace tightened around him and she clung to him, allowing the reality of the situation to truly hit her.

At last, when they were able to stand, she wiped a bit of moisture from her eye and turned Narain toward Blythe. "Narain, I believe you know this gentleman."

Narain's eyes widened slightly. The last time he'd clearly seen that face was when Blythe was lying on the battlefield watching Narain as he crawled away desperately to escape the ghouls that would change his life.

Both their lives.

It was indeed Fred Blythe. He was several inches taller and bulkier with sheer muscle, but the face was still the same. Smooth shaven, hair short, clean and groomed. Innocently handsome, he was not the mad man in the pictures Jameson had shown him.

Near speechless, Narain cleared his throat, put out his hand and said, "Fred, my God! It's good to see you."

"Narain, my friend," Blythe said, disregarding the hand and embracing him in a much gentler bear hug.

When they parted, Narain looked at him and noticed that while it was Blythe, there was still an unsettling distance in his blue eyes. His mind was indeed very wounded, understandably so.

"Well…welcome to the 21st century," Narain quipped, smiling as the ice was broken with chuckles.

"It has been a long time," Blythe observed.

Narain studied him closely, eventually losing his smile and looking down. "Fred," he began, uncertain how to say what he needed to say. "I'm so sorry. This should never have happened to you." He raised his arms. "None of this should have happened."

Blythe's eyes crinkled in confusion for a moment, before he realised what was bothering his old comrade in arms. "So, you don't remember what I told you?" he began. "The sewer?"

Blinking, Narain said, "A little. I remember you telling me about Channing." He shot a concerned glance at Cassie after the slip, but she nodded.

"He explained Richard's involvement," she said sadly. "I can't believe what he's done. I would never have thought him capable of it."

Narain rubbed her shoulder and Blythe told him, "You're not at fault...for me. So many ferals feeding. Jameson tried to convince me you were the one, but I don't believe you were."

A weight was being lifted from Narain's conscience, but he was having difficulty letting it go. He remembered Blythe staring at him as he crawled by, the look in the young private's blue eyes, a cry for help. Shaking his head, he said, "I should have done something. I left you in the field."

Blythe looked at Cassie, a slight wave of humoured frustration crossing his face. "Why do the innocent always drag guilt to themselves?"

Sensing Blythe searching for the words, Cassie elaborated, "Narain, none of this is your fault. If anything, it was the fault of the ferals and even they were in a situation not of their making. You can't keep looking for ways to bear responsibility." She considered this, saying, "I mean, then maybe you should apologise for not standing over Fred and fending off the ferals. And while you're at it, you can apologise for helping to start the war in the first place, 'cos I'm sure you had a hand in that somehow if we back track and over-analyse." She took his hand. "The bottom line is, we can't accept blame for everything—only what we're truly responsible for. Sometimes...well shit happens."

A chuckle exploded from Narain and even Blythe smiled appreciatively. Then Narain looked up asking, "Has she explained everything to you? What we are?" he waved a hand around his body, "What all this is."

Blythe nodded. "I understand, slightly. There's much to" he tapped his forehead, "comprehend."

"You're right about that, my friend," Narain agreed before a slight pleading element entered his tone. "So you understand that this is not...this doesn't have to be a horror. It can be managed. Not always conveniently, but it is manageable. A normal life is possible. And you—you can move about during the day. You would have a freedom of movement I only dream of."

"You dream of moving freely during the day, yet you feel it is manageable?"

Narain glanced at Cassie, caught by the logic of the question, but insisted, "Yes, yes I do. It required making adjustments, but it is manageable."

"And what about the blood, Narain?" Blythe's question was spoken with such flatness that it chilled Narain. "What about the blood we must take, must have? Can one make adjustments for what we must do to survive? What we have done?"

Narain realised that his friend's pain was not driven by fear, but rather by guilt. That's what blocked his acceptance of his situation and what kept him distant and occasionally disorientated. Narain could understand wanting to give over to the madness and let the feral nature take control to wash away the memories. He remembered the lost years after his visit to India. Before Sophie. Before he discovered just how full his life could be despite what he was. He had given over to the feral then and there had been a bit of peace but it was a peace that required the surrender of all sensation, good and bad.

The fact was though, that Narain had no idea what to say to assure Blythe that this life could be just as full.

Still, it was Cassie who finally spoke. "Fred," she said softly, "my great, great uncle and great aunt devoted their lives partly to prove exactly what Narain is saying. You've only learned a small portion. There so much more to understand."

"I think I know all there is to know."

"I thought so, too," Narain said.

"And I believe there is a cure," Cassie assured him. "Perhaps I won't find it in my life time." She looked at Narain. "Alphonse and Lucy didn't. But it's there and I plan to keep looking."

Before his old friend could rebut, Narain said, "I think what we need to do now is concentrate on…well, what we need to do now. If Jameson has recruited Boris, then he's even more dangerous than he was before."

"Who, Boris or Jameson?" Cassie asked.

"Take your pick. We may be safe here for a while, but Jameson has a lot of resources at his disposal. He may be able to track us down here and he doesn't have to only rely on the ferals to do the job. He can send others out during the day."

"He tried that with me before," Blythe said ominously. "They didn't get far."

"Fred, my friend," Narain patted his back, "as strong as you are, you can't take on an army. Besides, Reg has been studying you. He knows your strengths and weaknesses and what he'll need to overcome you."

Cassie threw up her hands, exclaiming, "This is ridiculous! He has Richard working for him. Richard apparently has a good deal of my research and is actually very talented. He'll more than likely stumble onto the toxin I've developed. Perhaps he'll even come up with something better. Why expend all this effort on a formula that was actually a mistake? It certainly isn't what I wanted. I might have pitched it out myself, if it weren't for the chance that it may lead me on to the path of an actual cure. One that doesn't kill the patient."

Narain and Blythe exchanged knowing glances fully understanding what was driving Jameson. "I don't believe it's about the toxin any more," Narain explained. "Were it not for other factors, he'd probably simply contact you, try to convince you to give or sell him the toxin, maybe even try to steal it from you and when that failed, he'd walk away planning to make another overture in the future. That's the businessman side of him. But so much has happened that he's losing control. And the more he loses control of a situation, the more sadistic he becomes."

"Like the trenches," Blythe added.

"Very much so," Narain agreed, then raised his index finger considering this. "Yes, but then like the trenches, the more sadistic he gets, the sloppier he gets. The more foolish his decisions. We could use that to our advantage."

"We may have to soon," Cassie and Narain both looked at Blythe, who had stalked toward the porch railing and was now staring out into the darkness. "They're out there."

"What?" Brows furrowed, Narain joined him, gazing deeply into the forest. "Are you sure?"

Blythe turned to him and tapped his temple. "Quiet yourself."

Understanding, Narain stilled his mind letting the sensations of the night come to him. He'd never been very good at it and it took concentration, but the sensations were there. He could sense ferals fanning out in the forest and he realised that this had to be what was plucking at his nerves earlier. "How many do you think?"

"Six, eight. And Boris is out there, too." Boris had a sensation uniquely his own.

Turning back to Cassie, Narain grabbed her hand, saying to his friend, "Come on, Blythe. We're leaving." But Blythe remained where he was, his head swivelling from side to side as he used all his senses to gauge the position of the ferals. "Blythe, come to the car." Narain insisted.

"You take her and leave," Blythe growled.

"I won't let you be our decoy," Narain shot out.

"Go," was all Blythe said before leaping over the deck railing and racing into the night.

Narain was ready to run after him when Cassie held him back. "I can't leave him to them," Narain insisted as the scenario of 90 years ago seemed to be playing out again. Then he looked at Cassie, realising that he couldn't leave her either. In fact, Blythe was right. Between the two, Cassie was the one with the least defence against what was out there and both had to do what they could to make sure she was safe.

Nodding quickly, he followed her into the house.

His intention was to run through to the front door, but she directed him toward the kitchen. "What are you doing?" he asked hurriedly.

"I have to get something," she said, escaping his grasp and jogging toward the refrigerator.

"Are you mad?"

Rummaging in the lettuce crisper, she pulled out a half carton of eggs and put it on the counter. "No," she snapped, opening the carton, apparently empty save for an egg-sized vial of translucent liquid. She showed it to him. "This is what all the fuss is about?"

"That's the…"

She nodded, taking a box out of a cabinet drawer and retrieving a syringe. "This is a recent batch I made for further testing." Inserting the needled into the vial, she filled it and replaced the needle cap. "I figure we'd better not leave it here for them to find. Besides, you guys have your weapons," she raised the needle, "I better have a weapon too."

She put the vial in the pocket of her jeans and capped the syringe, carefully placed the syringe in the other pocket then took his hand as they fled from the house.

Outside by his car, he tried to gain a sense of where the ferals might be at that point, but while he could sense them he couldn't judge their positions clearly. It was a subtle skill and he had not used it, not needed to use it, for so long that it had atrophied. Narain stared at the house, remembering the sight of Blythe running into the woods, buying them time to escape. Frustration gripped him. He was leaving Blythe behind again, abandoning him again to the mercy of those things as he had done in the fields of France.

Cassie's voice broke the spell, "Narain, he'll be alright."

He looked across the top of the car at her. She had no way of being sure on this point. The ferals had taken Blythe down once before. But Blythe was out there to protect Cassie and his efforts would be wasted if Narain didn't get her out of the area. He nodded and they both entered the car.

†

Blythe knew speed, not surprise, would be the tool to use in this battle. The ferals knew he was here and would be able to sense any direction he came from, so an ambush would prove useless. These creatures, however, were geared for the hunt. They were used to stalking their prey and didn't expect their prey to turn on them. That's how he had beaten them in France. He hadn't wanted to kill even those soulless creatures; he simply wanted to be left alone. They had given him no choice, however. Just as their mindless allegiance to Jameson would get this new pack killed. And this time he had more than his freedom to fight for.

Blythe paused, assessed the situation, then swerved slightly, lunging toward the feral directly in his path. Not expecting the attack, the feral was bowled over by Blythe, who gave him little time to react. He was able to squeak out some feral signal to the others in the area before Blythe dug his nails into his captive's neck, ripping the head from his shoulders. Letting the body fall, he pivoted to take on the other feral crashing through the trees toward him. He caught him mid-leap, tossing him easily into the branches of a tree, but the feral just as easily grabbed hold of a branch to stop the momentum. Then he dropped, rolling without injury and getting to his feet.

He snarled at Blythe, releasing the woody mesmer scent particular to ferals that helped in stunning their prey. It was wasted on Blythe who studied the creature's movements. Something seemed off. By now, the creature would have scanned for an opening and taken advantage of it. Whether the effort was successful was another story. Crouched low, this one merely stalked around him just beyond Blythe's reach, occasionally feigning attack, but never going through with it. As Blythe watched him, fascinated, something whipped past his neck, cutting the flesh slightly as it passed. Turning his gaze, his eyes followed the movement of the small missile until it embedded into the trunk of a tree.

Returning his gaze to the feral, he moved to the tree then risked a quick look at the object. A dart! This time he heard the snap of the silencer as another dart came his way and with careful concentration he was able to knock it away with little more than a prick of his thumb.

His downfall in France came back to him and he realised why Jameson had the gall to bring only eight to fight this battle. Jameson's dogs were armed with more than their natural weapons and it was why the feral in front of him didn't attack. The mesmer scent hadn't worked, but his movements had held Blythe's attention just as sharply, enabling the other feral to take him with a tranq gun.

Another dart whipped past him and he ran in the direction from which they were fired, the other feral hot on his heels. Stopping dead, he rounded on the feral behind him, bracing himself for the impact as the feral crashed into him. Using the feral's shock against him, Blythe threw him to the ground, snapping his neck. Then he dug his fingers into the feral's chest cavity and ripped out his heart, tossing it aside. It would beat until the sun fried it, the body quivering until the microbes that powered it at last lost their own struggle for life. Without the heart to power it, though, it was a useless thing.

Now he would need to find the feral with the gun. Leave it to Jameson to entrust the tranq gun to a feral with poor aim. Of course, it was possible that the other ferals had tranq guns as well, so he would need to be careful for the tiny missiles could come from any direction. Blythe would not be taken like he was in France: Mad, helpless, shipped to some alien world. He sensed movements several yards to his right. The ferals were beginning to understand that this would be one prey animal that wouldn't go down easily for the pack and were adjusting their methods.

They were powerful alone, but even better as a pack and their skills relied on that, sometimes to their detriment. See one, expect another, Blythe thought as he went in search of the figure ahead of him to at last put an end to this game.

Chapter 17

Narain's night vision made headlights unnecessary and he wanted to do everything he could not to attract attention. So, he drove the car carefully down the service road in the dark. Cassie's hands fidgeted and her head moved continuously as she scanned the dark wall of forest bordering the service road. It must be nerve-wracking for her, Narain thought. She could probably see very little beyond a few feet. He reached over and touched her hand, assuring her, "We'll be on the highway soon."

She looked at him, returning his smile, then hers vanished as shock washed over his face. "Hang on!" he shouted.

Two ferals came charging toward the car, appearing off to his left out of the darkness like ghosts, and Narain swerved to avoid them. Using their combined power, however, they slammed into the front of the car as it passed, forcing the turn to be wider than he intended. The car drove off the road, its right front end slamming into a tree.

The force stunned Narain, as did the bump from his head hitting the steering wheel, but the effects of the concussion lasted only moments. Shaking his head, he looked over at Cassie who was rubbing her chest where the seat belt strap had bit into it when they crashed. Otherwise, thankfully, she seemed unharmed.

"Are you okay?" he asked quickly, reaching out to touch her shoulder.

She mumbled, "Uhm, yeah, just shaken."

It was then that his instinct kicked in.

Narain glanced around, instructing quickly, "Something is about to happen. When it does you climb through the driver's side, get back on the road and head back to the house. Lock yourself up as best as you can and call whoever you need to."

"What are you..."

Before the question was out, the driver's door flew open and Narain was dragged from the car. Not expecting the sort of force his attackers possessed, Narain allowed the two ferals to take him from the car, but turned the tables and used the momentum against them. The three tumbled to the ground a few feet from the door as he held them there as best as he could while he heard Cassie scramble from the door, the only sound she made being the grunts from the exertion of climbing over the steering wheel before she ran down the road. "Keep to the road!" he called after. She was nearly blind in the night, but if she could keep the smoothness of the service road beneath her feet, she'd find her way back to the house. He just prayed no one but Blythe would be waiting for her.

One of the ferals squirmed under him, freed an arm and slammed a fist into Narain's head. He saw stars, but was able to reach out and grab the feral's pant cuff as it was standing. It would have been difficult to hold one feral down let alone two, but retaining a grip on them might buy Cassie some time.

Narain had shifted his position to lying on top of the one, so when the feral standing kicked at him to dislodge his grasp, it only took a slight shift on Narain's part to manage a kick which landed in the other ferals' rib cage. The feral on the ground snarled in pain and with tremendous force rose quickly to his hands and knees. The force knocked Narain back and consequently pulled the leg of the other feral out from under him. The once upright feral now wriggled like a turtle on his back, momentarily stunned, and Narain took the opportunity to leap on him, repeatedly slamming his fist into him. He did what he could to scramble the creature's brains before a pair of hands grabbed him and yanked him off the first feral.

Going slack Narain was able to slip out of the feral's grip, then reaching up, he grabbed the feral's shirt and threw him on top of the other, punching his face as many times as he could before being tossed off and thrown clear a few feet.

Crouched, head lowered, gaze unwavering, Narain sensed the hopelessness of the situation as he watched the two ferals come to their senses. So far, any success he'd had was due to surprise and, perhaps, the ferals' own arrogant expectations that he wouldn't put up much of a fight. No matter how fast he was, they were faster; their power of recovery was probably better; and no matter how much strength his desperation for Cassie's safety gave him, they possessed more.

The fact was that they were going to beat him. The question was should he stay and fight or run while he was still able in the hopes of making it back to Cassie in some sort of useful condition?

He was torn, though. His eyes narrowed, his fingers clawing the dirt. The desire to fight was there. He wanted to run, but he couldn't ignore the thrill of his own feral instincts, brought on by the stress of the fight firing his body. It reached down to something primal buried deep within and resonated through a body not completely his to rule. Like a junkie, he had been given a fix that he hadn't had in a very long time and he wanted another. For a moment, he even snarled.

His rational mind, however, beat through the feral instinct gripping him. Survival in this case did not mean hunting prey. It meant running, so diverting the crazed energy into his legs, Narain darted into the forest, using the fight he would have given the ferals to leap over fallen branches and dodge small trees. He could hear the strange, pig-like grunts of the ferals who took only seconds to recover from their confusion before running after him and crashing through the forest. Unconcerned with stealth, Narain increased his speed knowing that ultimately it would do little good. He could sense them splitting up and knew that they more than likely planned on racing ahead and ambushing him. No matter what instincts he possessed, this was their world, not his. They knew what moves to make to survive in it.

He could still sense their presence behind him, when a new presence entered his mind, but by the time it did, it was too late. Something came hurtling at him from the woods off to his side, snarling and squirming viciously as the force of the impact and his momentum sent them tumbling along the forest floor. Briefly, Narain felt as if the ribs on his left side had been caved in, but that was the least of his concerns. As the two rolled to a stop, he was pinned underneath the flailing creature that had ploughed into him. He forced it as far away from his body as he could, but the creature was massively strong and equally determined. Narain had only a brief glimpse of the twisted mouth and the soulless black eyes before Boris slipped from his grip and drove his teeth deeply into Narain's left shoulder.

The pain was mind-numbing, made more so by his attacker's attempts to rip away the chunk of flesh in his mouth. Screaming, Narain reached out and grabbed Boris' lower jaw and neck, desperately trying to detach the crazed vampire, snarling himself as he did so. Like a mad dog, Boris switched his attention from Narain's shoulder to his right forearm, clamping his rows of teeth around it and tugging with equal ferocity. Narain howled again and punched at the kid, even resorting to snapping at the kid's neck with his teeth though it didn't have a third of the impact that Boris was having on him.

Through the pain ripping into his mind, Narain thought he heard a shout, then suddenly the vampire on top of him reluctantly released his hold as he was dragged from his victim. Narain shifted quickly to his hands and knees, the best defensive position he could take at that moment with the throbbing fire possessing his shoulder and arm. He had fought other ferals before, had been bitten by them before, but the agony of the wounds never felt like that. He could feel the blood still oozing from raw wounds that should have begun to knit.

"Stings a bit, doesn't it?"

Blinking the sweat from his eyes, Narain looked up to see Reginald Jameson staring down at him, holding the hood of Boris' filthy sweat shirt while the younger vampire hissed in irritation. Narain squinted, fascinated. It wasn't strength enabling Jameson to hold Boris at bay. It was allegiance. Jameson had gained the crazed vampire's allegiance.

"Something in his saliva, we think," Jameson explained. "We're not quite sure what. The wounds heal, but it takes a painfully long time for them to do so. Another curiosity of bioengineering." Directing his attention to Boris, Reg told him, "And where are Blythe and the woman while you're playing with him?"

As if remembering his original mission, Boris hissed at Narain, then disappeared into the forest in the direction of the house.

"Kids," Jameson commented. "You have to keep on them constantly."

Narain called up his reserves to chase after the fiend when Jameson said, "Don't do that old chap." The two ferals came crashing through the forest to join them. "You'd never make it."

Panting, Narain rose to his feet, gasping, "How did you find her?"

"By following you." Noting the look of guilty astonishment cross Narain's face, Jameson said, "Oh please, there are people who do that for a living. Don't feel so bad. How could you have known? You've grown soft all these years playing life as normal."

Narain sighed. The sense of unease he'd had earlier. That's what that was: An instinctual knowledge that he ignored, because he denied being a part of a world he was mired in.

"Reg, don't hurt her," he pleaded, the pain in his wounds decreasing, but only slightly. "None of this is worth it."

"Of course it is," Jameson scoffed. "My God Khan, what's wrong with you? What your girlfriend discovered is far too big for her to keep safe."

"And it would be safer in your hands?"

"A darn sight safer. I'll be honest, I'm protecting my own on this. I could lock that formula up where no one can get it. All vampires will benefit from that, including you."

"Provided you don't decide to use it at your will."

Smiling slyly, Reg shrugged. "Well, nothing in life is certain."

"And what about Cassie?"

"I'll offer her a job." Anticipating the next question, Jameson said, "And if she doesn't accept, well I don't know."

"Reg please," Narain said desperately, "she's never tried to do anything but help us."

"I understand that," Reg assured him. "As well-intentioned as your girlfriend's efforts have been, she has nonetheless stumbled onto something that could prove very dangerous to all of us. When Channing told me the toxin existed, all I wanted was the formula or a sample of the toxin to ascertain the formula. Then Channing would, hopefully, be able to create an antidote for this poison. Perhaps even a serum that would make us immune to it. I certainly don't want a poison that powerful simply floating around without a way to fight it. I think tonight illustrates it isn't safe in her hands."

Pointing into the forest, Narain insisted, "Reg, that thing will kill her."

"No, I don't think so."

"She's the only human in the vicinity with nourishing, untainted blood. You think he can control his urges?"

"Yes, I do. I've told him to bring her to me and he will."

Narain was stunned. "Oh dear God Reg, how naive are you! This isn't one of your pet ferals we're talking about here. This one is psychopathic. He loves to kill. What good will Cassie be to you dead?"

Jameson gave no indication that he agreed except to look at one of the ferals and order, "Go keep an eye on things."

The feral took off quickly in the direction that Boris ran giving Narain some consolation as it proved that Jameson truly wasn't after Cassie's life. Voice a little more controlled, he asked, "And what about Blythe?"

"Well, that's a horse of a different colour," Jameson said, aimlessly stamping his heel into the earth to dislodge a small branch that had been buried there. "He carries the secret to something very useful."

"He has no idea why he can withstand daylight."

Jameson looked at him eyebrows arched. "Ah, so you know. Then you understand just how important it is. He may not know why he can, but the secret is in him somewhere and I intend to locate it."

"You can't do that, Reg. You can't keep him locked up like a rat."

"I can and will. He was absolutely worthless in the trenches, but I've finally found a use for him."

"Private Fred Blythe was more of a hero than you could ever hope to be," Narain fumed. "Besides, he's not the same young soldier you tormented in the trenches and he'll probably tear your ferals apart tonight."

Jameson laughed cruelly. "All I need is for my ferals to keep him busy, keep him away from Dr. Lambert." He presented the tranq gun he had concealed in a holster behind his back. "This will take care of the rest. You see, I've learned from my mistakes. Channing can prove quite useful." Grinning, he stalked closer to Narain, waving the gun around his head. "You've had a taste of this stuff, haven't you? Of course, what they gave you was nowhere near as potent as what's in here. It'd probably take you two months to get movement back from this."

Sweat broke out on Narain's forehead as he remembered the morning he was attacked by the ferals and injected with the poison that paralysed his body. It was the morning Blythe had saved him from the incinerating rays of the sun as Narain felt his muscles rebelling, becoming useless.

"For Blythe," Jameson shrugged, "I don't know, maybe a day. Two at the most."

"Don't do this, Reg." Narain growled, his heart racing. The still open wounds on his shoulder and arm throbbed in rhythm with his heart and he remembered the teeth marks on Blythe's body from his battle with Boris the night before. The night he saved Cassie and Dom.

"Whatever time, it'll be enough to get him back in a cage." Jameson held the gun barrel against Narain's cheek, tracing it down to press underneath his chin.

Blythe had not left him. "Reg let him be. Give him peace."

The other feral, hearing the deepening tone to Narain's voice, tensed slightly, but Jameson was too lost in the joy of his sadism to care.

"I'll give him a roof over his head. Plenty to eat. There are homeless people all over L.A. All I'll ask in return is the chance to cut him open once in a while and see what makes him tick."

Flashes came to Narain of the photographs with Blythe in a cage looking more like an animal. Jameson drew out his words, his slithering, taunting tone that of a man with too much power trying to pierce the hearts of those with too little.

"And I'm thinking now," Jameson said, the point of the gun falling to Narain's chest. "Perhaps Dr. Lambert would be willing to work on the project."

Standing stock still, Narain closed his eyes, remembering the trenches. The dirt. The incessant thunder of mortars. The screaming agony of the wounded and dying. And always Captain Reginald Jameson's vicious cruelty, and the pride that every soldier under his command had to swallow to placate him.

"What do you say, eh Khan?" Jameson said, his tone oily. "I'll set you up in a cage next to Blythe. He'll have his little monkey friend back. If Dr. Lambert is good and co-operative I'll treat you well. If she isn't, I'll flail you alive and make her watch as your skin grows back."

Eyes snapping open, Narain's hands shot up, grabbing the gun and forcing Jameson to shoot at the feral running toward them before taking it from him and tossing it into the underbrush. The dart lodged directly in the chest, and the feral fell to his knees, then to his stomach, desperately fighting the effects.

Stunned by his adversary's forcefulness, Jameson nonetheless recovered quickly, tensing as he backed a few steps away. Sneering, he said, "I forget old boy, sometimes you are capable of showing your teeth. Shall we resume what the war interrupted all those decades ago?"

"I can think of nothing I'd like better," Narain hissed as he ran toward Jameson. Before he got to him, however, Jameson executed a perfect roundhouse kick and connected with Narain's sternum, sending him sprawling backwards.

"I'm afraid I've learned a few new tricks since those days, old chap," he said arrogantly, lowering his leg and standing at the ready.

Rubbing the pain from his stomach, Narain decided upon a slower approach, leaning forward as he circled Reg. "I beat you last time; it's understandable you would need more training."

"If I remember correctly, I was on top of you when someone knocked me in the head."

"It's all perspective," Narain growled, fangs lowered, eyes flashing red as he searched for an opening.

"I say, Khan, is that a touch of the feral finally coming out in you? Are you finally embracing the gifts given to you decades ago?"

That's when Narain decided upon his next move. Ego would be Jameson's downfall as it had been before. He ran at him again, and Jameson successfully used a forward kick to send him flying.

Arms outstretched, he said, "Dear God, Khan, give me some competition."

Narain charged forward again, but this time stopped short and when Jameson's leg stretched out he caught it, dragging Jameson forward and to the ground. Knowing seconds counted, Narain fell on the dazed vampire punching him in the side of the head and struggled to keep in charge of Jameson's flailing arms. They rolled along the forest floor, Narain realising he could not let Jameson stand. Jameson, for his part, was bucking wildly to try to get Narain off him so he could right himself. At some point, Narain found himself underneath and looked up to see a truly evil glint in Jameson's eye before Jameson grabbed a nearby stick jamming it deeply into the meat of Narain's still open shoulder wound.

Narain let out a howl, loosening, but not relieving his grip.

"What do you think this will solve, Khan?" Jameson said, punctuating the words with punches to Narain's injured shoulder. "The only way you'll win tonight is if you kill me and we both know that's unlikely."

With every blow Narain receded into the pain, allowing it to bring out the base instincts that always came forward in desperate times. Instincts he hadn't needed for a long time. Summoning all his strength, he grabbed Jameson's shirt and with a roar, threw him to his side. Then, before Jameson could react, he fell upon him, burrowing into his shoulder with teeth unused to such violence.

Screaming in agony, Jameson beat at his adversary's back, writhing violently and trying to get him off him but Narain was unconscious of anything but his objective. Blood slipped down his throat as it dribbled down his chin, his teeth connecting with the elastic tendons and finally, the stone hard bone. Then, getting to his feet, he held Jameson down with one leg while he braced himself with the other and with manic strength ripped Jameson's arm from his body.

The shock of the unexpected violence silenced them both as they stared at each other, Jameson's face a horrified mask; Narain brandishing his trophy over him. Seconds passed as their gazes melded into each other's. Then without another word, Narain darted into the woods, Jameson's agonized curses of "You bastard!" chasing after him. When he felt he had run far enough, Narain whipped the still squirming appendage deeper into the underbrush and turned back to Reg.

His mind was heated with fever, his body felt brilliantly alive as he sprinted through the foliage. For a brief moment he felt like running forever. The rational mind persisted however and he sprang back into the clearing where Reg was leaning against a tree clutching at his empty shoulder socket, blood leaking through his fingers. Narain crouched by him leaning in to look at the wound, then flashing the man a smile that chilled even Reg's heart.

Shaking, Reg refused to give in to fear or pain, instead he laughed and panted, "I never…knew…you had it…in you, Khan. All these years…trying to…deny who you are." He inhaled sharply. "Who knew you…were so…fabulously…demented?"

Narain's voice was low and menacing as he growled, "I'm protecting me and mine, Reg. You know the arm can be reattached" He looked at the wound, the edges already sealing up, "but this is going to take a long time of keeping the arm still and quiet. Not to mention," he looked up into the night sky and sniffed a little, "it won't be long before sunrise. So you get to choose which is more important to you now—gathering your specimen or having the use of two arms throughout the rest of a long life." Patting his cheek, Narain stood suggesting, "If I were you, Captain, *sir,* I would recall your troops and have them help locate your missing limb."

"Khan!" As Narain hurried back into the woods, Jameson screamed out, "You've only bought some time, you bastard! It's not over!"

†

Cassie saw the garage security lights in the distance and allowed herself a few gasps of air before sprinting toward the house. Her right elbow and left knee throbbed from the skid she had taken after a nocturnal critter skittered across her path, but she had to stay focused on the house, not on her scrapes, or what was happening to Narain. Or what might be following close behind her. She had known, as well as he had, how risky her running back to the house was, but it was the least risky of the options they had.

Reaching the car, she gave herself a few moments to allow the stitch in her side to untie before looking up at the house and realising the pure folly of the plan. Dawn wouldn't come for hours. Where could she hide for hours from beings that could smell the scent of her desperate perspiration, or hear the thudding of her terrified heart? And how could she stay out of reach of beings who could rip doors off their hinges?

She reached down and felt the somewhat reassuring outline of the syringe in her pocket. It would provide some safety. She could scrounge up other weapons, too. It wouldn't kill a feral, but a cleaver to the gut would certainly slow it down. All too briefly. She left the support of the car and made it a few steps toward the porch, when a crashing through the trees alerted her to something that was approaching her with dangerous speed.

She was able to side step in time for it to miss her, but with the skill of a cheetah, the creature stopped, pivoted and charged back at her, knocking her down with such force that she was left breathless underneath it. His hot breath, rank from the odour of past meals, washed over her face, making her gag, and his black marble eyes scanned her eerily. As they struggled, she tried to hold his face away from her, but it was obvious that he had the strength to break her grip if he wanted to. He didn't. His enjoyment of the struggle was evident in the horrid grin he gave as his tongue flicked out and lingered by her cheek. She grimaced, shivering, as it traced a path along her jaw line and down her neck.

"You have something I want," Boris hissed in her ear.

Unable to hide her fear, "I have nothing," was all she could squeeze out.

He was straddling her now and she wished she could reach into her pocket and retrieve the syringe, but he now held her hands in a firm grip, pushed together in front of him as if she were honouring him with a prayer. Whether or not he picked up on an unconscious tell she may have broadcast, or he sensed a subtle change in body chemistry, his smile grew wide and he realised that she was hiding something. "You have it here, don't you?" he asked, moving down and with one hand patting at her abdomen, her stomach, her hips. Triumphantly he looked at her, "I think I found it!"

Holding her one arm, he pulled her to her feet and dragged her to the garage door, pinning her against it. She kicked at him but he laughed, unaffected by the blows. Staring at her, head tilting from side to side, he said, "I've been told to take you back intact." He lowered his head to her chest and listened to her heart beat before adding, "but you sound so tasty. I don't think he'll really care."

Boris reared back as she let out a scream and was diving in to rip out her throat, when he was suddenly yanked away from her. Cassie recovered herself, looking up and noting that Boris was in a crouch position about a yard away snarling with venom at Blythe, who stood in front of her.

"Fred, be careful!" she said, reaching in her pocket for the syringe as Boris charged at Blythe.

The two connected in a flurry of growls, grunts and groans and Cassie tried her best to stay clear of the battle, but just as she was popping the cap off the needle of the syringe, the combatants knocked into her and the syringe flew from her hand, landing in the grass. She debated which would be more expedient: Going into the house and getting another syringe to fill, or hunting in the dark grass for the one that had slipped from her grasp. She decided on the latter, getting to her hands and knees and crawling around carefully, gently patting the grass for the familiar feel of the syringe.

With a howl of pain from Boris' teeth sinking into his bicep, Blythe threw the younger vampire hard to the ground, then leapt on him, the two rolling, nearly steam-rolling over Cassie, who managed to move away just in time. She hissed again in frustration as they came back the same way and moved out of their path.

"I'm going to rip your throat out," she heard Boris coo in an oddly sing song way, "then I'll have dessert."

She looked up to see Boris pinning a severely worn and winded Blythe to the ground. She wasn't worried however, because she had finally discovered the syringe and as fast as humanly possibly she ran to the two just as Boris was about ready to make good on his threat. So wrapped up was he in his conquest, that he didn't sense her come up behind him.

He only barely reacted to the needle she plunged into the base of his neck.

His reaction began to grow however, as the toxin caused the microbes that had reanimated him to die off. A frightful keen of agony escaped Boris' lips as he reached behind his head in hope of getting to the reason for the excruciating sensation.

Eyes wide, Blythe threw the younger vampire off him and ran to Cassie, staring at the needle she held, then back at the dying fiend.

Refusing to go easily, Boris got his feet and hissed at the pair, his mouth a horri-ble grimace. His charge, however, was cut short by the cramps taking over his body, sending him to the pavement of the driveway as the poison spread through his body.

"Bitch!" he screamed at the sky, falling backward as his body convulsed. His skin became mottled, leathery, shrinking on his bones, his hair falling out in clumps onto the pavement. His eyes, the soulless black marbles they were, shrank as well, drying in their sockets and snapping off from their now dried stalks. Like pebbles, they fell down the sides of his face and landed on the pavement beside him.

Boris' convulsions had long since ceased, the only movement being his stub-born and futile gasping for breath as his respiratory system began to shut down. At last, his mouth open wide, he breathed a last ragged breath and was still, his body contorted and stiff like a well preserved mummy.

Cassie had known what to expect, almost. She had seen the effects of the toxin before but on much older vampires whose bodies and bones dried to dust once the microbes were dead. In vampire years, Boris had been an infant, possibly a year from the date of his death approximately. The microbes had given him strength and healing power, but they had not had time to infest as completely as they did the vampires who had agreed to be the guinea pigs for her serum.

Blythe had not been prepared, at first, and when they walked over to the body, seemed more disgusted than horrified. But she noticed a slightly detached quality come over him as he crouched down prodding the corpse to make sure it was truly dead.

"Worked quickly," he commented dryly. "Does it always?"

Her eyes remained fixated on Boris' hideous mouth which, it seemed like only moments ago, had been poised above her throat ready to tear her apart. Sighing, she answered, "On the test subjects I've used, yes."

The term "test subject" understandably unnerved him and he shot her a glance. "They agreed to it," she assured him. "They were willing to help me test the toxin in exchange for the chance to find peace."

Blinking, Blythe returned his gaze to Boris and sighed, "Peace."

Chapter 18

Narain sped through the trees out-distancing Jameson's curses until Jameson himself gave up and went silent. Then nausea sent Narain to his hands and knees as he retched up the remnant of Jameson's blood that had slipped down his gullet. The feral that had gripped him during his battle was releasing him and the blood caked on his face, the taste of it that remained in his mouth, the memory of the texture of Jameson's flesh as he gnawed off the arm, sickened Narain to near distraction. What he had become for a moment, despite the reasons, terrified him, for it had been far too easy to take on that role.

His stomach empty, he rolled onto his back, gasping until his breathing finally relaxed. Then he got to his feet. He had to get to Cassie.

He was sure that for that night Reg was taken care of. Now there was only Jameson's mad dog to deal with. Grabbing the end of the stick still embedded in his shoulder, he winced as he pulled it out. Then he unbuttoned his shirt, removing it and using it to wipe the blood and gore from his face before tossing it aside. He looked over at the tear in his undershirt and the wound it exposed. It was better; not much, but better, as was the wound on his arm. Leaning forward, hands on knees, he lowered his head, gathered his strength, then shot off again in the direction of the house.

Reaching the clearing, he could sense one more feral skulking around the house. This time Narain could sense him clearly and he blinked, scanning the direction from which he felt the presence emanating. There it was, crouching down in the driveway, studying something, then rising and heading toward the side of the house where the kitchen door was. Narain sprinted at top speed across the clearing, reaching him before the feral could near the corner of the house, and taking him down. He quickly rolled out of reach of the thing's hands and crouched low, staring at him. Deciding subtlety was really not a feral's strong suit, Narain hissed, "I chewed Jameson's arm off and threw it in the forest. He needs you to help find it before sunrise."

The declaration stunned the feral, who took a step back, yet stared at Narain as if waiting for the punch line. Rolling his eyes, Narain pointed out, "Would I be here if this weren't so?"

Even a feral couldn't deny the logic and this one wasn't about to try. Whipping around, he ran back to the forest, disappearing within seconds.

Narain could sense only Cassie and Blythe. What about Boris? Was that another bioengineered talent the creature had: Being able to remain camouflaged from a vampire's radar? Surely as weak as Narain's was, he would have picked up something if the little maniac was running around nearby. Rubbing his face, Narain straightened then looked ahead toward the driveway, squinting to make out what exactly the feral had been so interested in.

Walking over to the form slowly, he grimaced at the sight of the mummified creature in the red hooded sweatshirt as it stared up at him from empty eye sockets. Even in death, the face seemed cold and vicious, any traces of the boy Boris might have been long gone.

"Death most definitely does not become you," he said softly, "but then life didn't exactly either."

The hinges of the screen door protested with creaky squeals as Cassie flew down the steps, the door slamming with a *thwap* behind her. She threw herself into his arms, holding tight as if afraid he'd disappear. He held her with just as much determination.

"Narain, is it over?" she asked, her voice strained. "Please tell me it's over."

"Reg won't be bothering us for a while," he assured her, rubbing her back. Then he pulled away to look at the corpse on the driveway. "It looks like you and Blythe took care of the real threat." Keeping an arm around her waist, he squeezed her to him. "Did you use the toxin?"

She nodded. "He was young; otherwise he'd be in worse shape. Narain, listen." Turning away from the corpse, she put her hands on his chest. "You have to talk to Blythe." His brows furrowed as she explained, "He says he's tired. He says he wants to rest."

The words she couldn't say were clearly in her tone and he looked back at Boris. "Blythe was here when…" Cassie nodded and Narain lowered his head. Without another word, he accompanied her back into the house.

Blythe was standing on the backyard deck, head raised to the sky, breathing in deeply as if analysing the air that filled his lungs. He very likely was, Narain thought. It was air very different from the air that hung over the battlefield of 1917 France when they were in trenches, gazing up into the sky talking about the lives waiting for them when the war was over. Yet, Narain sensed a peace about Blythe that hadn't been there earlier. It made Narain's throat constrict.

Swallowing, he walked up to his old friend as Cassie hung back near the door. Leaning on the railing as Blythe did, he raised his gaze to the stars as well. "You don't see them as clearly downtown," he commented. "The stars."

"A canvas of light over the city," Blythe told him. "Remember the stars over the trenches?"

Narain nodded. "On a clear night, when the shelling had stopped, the stars were gorgeous."

Blythe scanned the forest. "No more left," he pronounced. "Ferals, I mean. Reg?"

Narain smiled slightly. "He offered to lend a hand but I took the whole arm." Blythe looked him up and down and Narain told him, "I think he's gone for a while. They have more pressing concerns than you right now."

"For now."

"Forever as far as I'm concerned. You'll never go back to that place."

"You always were an optimist."

Narain blinked, surprised by the sincerity of the assessment, for he never really considered himself as such. Of course what one projects to the other might not be what he sees himself.

Blythe continued. "Going on about 'When I become a cook,' 'When I see my family,' 'When I can see Ujaali again.'" He paused. "'When the war is over.'" Gently, he asked, "And Ujaali? Did you see her again?"

Narain smiled wanly, touched that Blythe remembered his sister's name. "You can't have everything in life."

"Shame," Blythe said. "She was a darlin'. She missed her brother, I'm sure." He paused. "I had a sister. Rose her name was. And a brother Daniel. They were older than me. Long gone by now." He seemed proud to have remembered the information as if it had been lost to him for a long time. "Think I'd like to go and see them now."

A chill went through Narain. "If they are gone…"

"Narain, you were always good to me. Couldn't have been a better comrade, a better friend. Now I need your help again."

"No." The word was sharp and Narain prayed final but he knew better.

"I'd never ask if I didn't need to." Blythe turned and looked at Narain, straight in his eyes. "Can't do it myself, you know that. Tried it before. Now I understand," he waved a hand in front of his body, "they'd never let me."

Narain's throat ached, tears threatening his eyes, but he still said, "No."

"It's time," Blythe insisted. "Long past. I shouldn't be here, mate."

"None of us should. We do what we need to do."

"You're fine. You fit. Found a way. I can't. Won't be able to." He pounded his head lightly. "Not all there, you see."

Paying close attention to the exchange, Cassie stepped up to Blythe, telling him, "We can help you. How could you have fit in when you've been in a cage most of the time you've been 'awake?' Let us help you."

Blythe reached out and gently touched her cheek. "You're a good woman." He looked at Narain, winking. "She's a good woman."

Narain smiled. "I know." He thought for a moment, for the slightest of seconds, that his friend would rescind his, as of yet, unspoken request. He didn't and pain gripped Narain's heart as he realised Blythe never would. He studied the larger vampire's form. His clothes were ripped from battle, scars still lining the skin visible in the rips. Like Narain's own wounds served to him by Boris, Blythe had wounds that were still raw. All the wounds would heal. The skin would knit. The pain would fade. Physical, that was. There were wounds deep inside Blythe, however, that would never heal. So many were left over from that horrible war, and Narain finally saw this clearly. At last, after a moment of silence, he pursed his lips, and turned to Cassie, saying, "Cassie, please get the vial and syringe."

"Narain, no," Cassie pleaded, her voice thick with emotion.

Narain's eyes never left Blythe's gaze as he repeated, "Please Cassie. Get the toxin."

She ran a hand across her mouth, then balled it into a fist letting it fall to her side. She then walked slowly into the house to retrieve the toxin from the refrigerator where she had replaced it.

Narain squinted, raising a chastising finger. "You know you are being very unfair to me."

Blythe smiled and looked down knowing that Narain was only half joking. "You have a good lady. You have good friends."

Narain knew he meant Dom but told him, "You are my friend."

Blythe smiled, considering this. "I have good friends also. Friends who will bury me properly as I should have been so many years ago. Friends who will see to it that I'm not forgotten." Cassie walked up and reluctantly handed the vial and needle to Narain. The larger vampire touched her cheek again. "Friends who will understand more clearly as grief eases."

Cassie reached up gripping his wrist trying to create the impression of a lifeline that all he needed to do was hold and she would pull him back. But in his mind, it was more a shackle to a life he didn't want. She knew this and let him go at last, kissing him gently on the cheek, his eyes closing slowly to savour the experience.

Narain's tone turned steely as he poked the needle into the vial's membrane asking, "Cassie, how much is necessary?"

"Two CC's," she told him, voice quavering as she showed him the lines on the syringe. "More won't matter, but that's all that's necessary." She raised a shaking hand to rest between her breasts. "It's best to do it here. Over the heart. It will go quicker. And Narain be careful. Don't prick yourself by accident."

He studied the needle in his hand, amazed that the clear liquid, as little as there was, could take down something with the power that Blythe possessed. The syringe felt like a lead weight. Inhaling, Narain nodded, saying, "We should go inside. Maybe light candles or something."

Blythe shook his head. "No. Here." He pointed to the stars. "Those are all the candles I need."

Standing before him, Narain readied the needle. "Are you sure?" he asked, hoping against hope. Blythe nodded. "Absolutely? You don't want to give it another day? See what the future brings?"

Blythe grabbed Narain's shoulders, saying, "My future died in 'No Man's Land.' I simply wish to join it."

Swallowing hard, Narain went cold, his eyes flashing red as he summoned as much killing instinct as he dared to carry the task out.

Cassie gasped. The needle went straight into Blythe's chest and she could tell on the man's face that the burning was beginning as Narain pushed down the plunger. Blythe shook violently, howling as the microbes running his body began reacting to the poison invading their world and Narain reached out to him, grabbing him. They sank to their knees as Blythe's legs gave out on him, Narain holding him tighter, repeating over and over, "You are not alone."

Cassie could see that organs were shutting down as a blue tinge came over Blythe's skin followed by a sickly grey pallor. Raising the head that had fallen on Narain's shoulders, the larger man looked up at Cassie, hoarsely saying, "Thank you."

Narain held him tighter, feeling his skin changing texture beneath the jumpsuit. It became tighter, pulling against the bones as if Blythe were shrinking in his arms. Blythe's arms went limp, followed by his body and at some point Narain realised that he was completely supporting his friend, but the man's substantial mass had decreased and the burden became lighter and lighter.

He was drying up. His recently groomed hair fell like chaffed wheat, his lips thinned, pulling away in a grimace, the shape of his skull becoming more prominent as the now leathery skin dried further. The microbes that had kept him alive for so long were dying, drying up, his cells following suit. Before Narain was prepared; before he could say a proper goodbye, Blythe's body became a husk that slipped out of Narain's arms and onto the deck floor.

"No!" Narain sobbed, caught by surprise. The jumpsuit kept the skeleton intact but the skin had finally turned to ash. Narain stared down at the bones which had yellowed as the microbes service of them had ceased. Jaw open, Blythe's empty eye sockets gazed upward toward the sky.

Cassie stared at the scene, her cheeks wet from the tears she shed not only for Blythe, but for Narain's heartache. Placing a gentle hand on his shoulder, after some moments, she quietly said, "I'm sorry."

"No," he said, never looking up. "It's as it should be. As it should have been."

After a moment, she said, "Uh, we should find a container to put…the remains in." Narain said nothing, hands at his sides, gaze fixated on the pile of ash, bones and jumpsuit that had been his friend. His silence made her nervous as she asked, "Narain, what are you thinking?"

Narain remained silent for a few moments then finally, softly, said, "I was just thinking: My affairs are in order." He paused, sighing. "Dom will get the restaurant, that's taken care of."

Unable to find her voice for a moment, she noted that the vial was still in his hands and she understood fully the knife edge they stood on. At last, she asked, "Narain, what are you saying?" as if trying to reason with a sleep walker.

He blinked away a few tears that escaped his eyes, and sighed again. "I'm thinking that it would be nice to see my parents again. My brothers. Old friends left behind long ago. Sophie."

Cassie felt her knees weaken and she found herself leaning on him. "Blythe did not want you to think that way," she insisted. "He couldn't handle this, but he didn't want you to follow him."

Narain said nothing, caught up in the weight of his options. He didn't move, nor make a sound and she realised what it had been that led him to ask her for the syringe earlier; what had helped him plunge the serum into his friend's heart. The decision had been Blythe's to make, just as it was now Narain's and it was based on love and loss, joy and pain, and it was uniquely theirs. She could never understand his world completely, no matter how extensive her research. It had to be Narain's decision.

Tears fell as Cassie understood that, short of wrestling the vial from his hand, there was nothing she could do. It was yet one more battle he had to fight. Crouching down beside him, she gripped his face forcing him to look at her. "To some this is a gift," she told him firmly, anger staining her words, "to others it's a curse. You have to decide what this is for you. But I'm sorry, I can't stay and watch. I know what it is to me and I know that I don't want to lose you nor can I watch as you're taken from me. If that's selfish, I don't know what to say. I don't have your strength." She kissed his forehead, saying, "I'm sorry," her lips lingering for seconds just below his hairline.

With that she stood, walking back into the house, unable to look back at the sad figure kneeling so straight-backed and still by the remains of his friend. Walking into the living room, she sat on the arm of the sofa, but a claustrophobic feeling came over her already swollen mind and she felt as if the house was slowly caving in. Standing stiffly, she walked with uncertain strides to the front door and beyond.

The air was so clean up there, the night silent save for the sodden sound her footsteps made in the night-dampened grass. Cassie stood a few feet in front of the porch, staring into the darkness beyond the range of the security lights. She'd have to find a container for Blythe. Unfortunately, though she'd like something a little more solemn, it might have to be a box or crate if she could find one in the garage.

Taking a quick glance toward the drive way, she grimaced realising that she had something else to worry about tomorrow. Perhaps the sun would incinerate the remains of Boris, but it seemed unlikely. As with the toxin, he had been too new a vampire to be affected that way. The sun could kill him, but not erase his existence the way it could with older vampires. The microbes had not had enough time to take over as completely as they had with the older vampires. Like Narain.

Tears welled in her eyes again and as much as she tried to concentrate on anything else, all she could think about was that lone figure on the deck. No, she was not brave. She could not jab the needle into him knowing what it would do to him. She could not hold him while he dried into bones in her arms. How could she tell him not to do it, though? What right did she have?

What right? The fact that she loved him. That was her right. Because she was selfish and wanted him to stay with her. Blythe had not tasted what life could offer and after all his suffering couldn't bring himself to believe that it offered anything better.

She realised with pure dread that she should have fought harder for Narain rather than leave him alone on that deck searching for his own lifeline. Heart pounding frantically, she turned to run back to the house, intending to talk Narain back to life but found herself running into his chest instead.

Stunned, she backed away a few paces, relief slowly wresting away her shock. Narain said nothing, his face unreadable, but he raised his hand offering her the vial he held. She took it, gratefully, then let out a cross between a laugh and a sob and fell into his outstretched arms. Pulling him closer, she gripped him tightly, unwilling to let him go again.

He embraced her just as fiercely, clinging to her, his face buried in her neck. "I had a dear love," he whispered. "Her name was Sophie. She sacrificed a great deal for me to continue. She had a long life, yet when it was her time, I know she didn't want to go. She had no choice in the matter. How could I throw away the life she valued so highly when I have a choice?" He pulled Cassie away and studied her face, combing her hair from her face and smiling. "And how could I give up when life suddenly seems worth living again?"

Enfolding her in his arms, he again relished the warmth of her body and the giggles of relief that she released, letting her scold him for scaring her so terribly. In a way, he guessed that he wasn't ready to give up quite yet, that, there was still some hope to hold onto in this world Suicide, release, had finally been a possibility, and the fact that, after all the loss and gief that had been visited on him through the decades, he had been willing to continue, heartened him.

Perhaps the glass was half full after all.

Chapter 19

A solemn hush fell over the crowd gathered in All Souls Memorial Cemetery. The last of the 21-gun-salute had just fired and the casket was lowered into the ground, as a lone bagpiper began to play in the distance. Cassie looked out over the faces of the crowd, mostly old men, grey and craggy, many from the generation that served in the war after the war to supposedly end all wars. They were paying their respects to a fellow soldier. It didn't matter that they'd never met him. He had been a veteran and that made him one of theirs. When asked, they agreed to serve again by attending this fellow's funeral.

"It's very gripping," Cassie said softly, trying to be as inconspicuous as possible with the thin cell phone up to her ear. "Some of the old guys are even crying. Blythe would be proud."

Dressed in a navy blue trouser suit, she found herself bending down to pick up a handkerchief that one of the old vets had dropped in the grass. He thanked her, his eyes watery, though she couldn't be sure if that was from age or emotion. "My grand-dad fought in the big war," he said with a sniffle, his words musical with the remains of a brogue brought over from Ireland long ago. "They never found his body. Lost at sea." He waved the handkerchief toward the grave. "I'd like to think I'm honouring him a little bit here. Honouring all of them."

She smiled softly patting his back before he moved off to join some friends. Returning to her conversation with Narain who had remained safe from the sun in his apartment, she told him, "This is a wonderful thing you've arranged for him, Narain."

"I wish I could have done it in England, but that would be pushing it." He held the phone closely to his ear. Very dimly in the distance he heard the mournful bagpiper playing. Money had greased most of the mechanism here. Official documentation was needed for so much in a circumstance like this. He hated dealing with forged papers and under-the-table favours, but this was important and long overdue for a man who had helped to save his country.

"Were the limos comfortable enough?" he asked.

"I think the old gents found them quite comfortable. Oh, and I think Blythe's 'grandson' will work out perfectly. He had what you told him down pat and seems very good at thinking on his feet. I think the stories passed down from his grandfather's days in World War I will be quite convincing."

"Dom's doing, really. He's got a knack for finding the right people when necessary. I just know Dom was relieved not to have to impersonate the grandson and that his only role was to get Khan's ready for our guests after the funeral."

There was a moment of silence before Cassie said, "I wish you could be there. You should be the one telling those stories."

Narain sighed, for he wished he could, too. But it wasn't the all-encompassing frustration he had felt being trapped in the apartment during Sophie's mid-morning funeral. He had been with Blythe when it counted and had seen Blythe off on his journey. This was all just a bit of icing on the cake for his old comrade.

At last, he said, "Cassie, will you stop by after the memorial?"

There was a smile in her voice. "Of course."

And if he was uncertain before, Narain knew at that moment that Sophie had been right. He had found love again and it would be as fulfilling as it had been with her. He would be broken-hearted again; Cassie was, after all, only mortal, but that would not be for a long time. In the meantime, he would be reminded just what a gift he'd been given. It was, after all, a matter of perspective.

Epilogue

She looked to be resting comfortably. The diminutive Indian woman, having experienced many decades of life, now lay quietly in the bed of her room in the assisted living complex into which she had been moved a year previously. A nasal cannula provided oxygen to lungs overtaxed by age and the machine made a slight hissing sound as it provided its relief. Was this the sound that had replaced that sweet tinkle of a laugh from so long ago?

Narain blinked at the moisture forming in his eyes looking down at the old woman lying so still in the bed. He mouthed her name, "Ujaali." The little girl he had lifted so easily. The little girl he had left behind. She had grown, married, raised a family, spoiled her grandchildren, and rejoiced in the birth of two great-grandchildren before her vibrancy began to dim. She was 97 and time was very quickly running out.

It had taken two and a half years to track her down using a variety of methods, including detectives on two continents. Narain hadn't even been sure what he would say to her if he found her or, for that matter, why he had initiated the search. He just couldn't shake the pressing need to find her. He needed to know if she still lived and if so, if she had had a good life. He had been relieved to find out that the answer to both questions was yes. He discovered that she had married a truly loving man who predeceased her a few years before. They had moved to the states not long after the wedding where he was a respected engineer and teacher and they produced six wonderful children who had placed her in one of the best senior care centres once her time was nearing its end. Her life had been rich with joy and that's all Narain ever wanted for her.

Then why was he standing before her bed, fighting the urge to disturb her slumber, desperate to hear her call his name? It would not be the voice Narain remembered. The voice of the little sister he left behind. Ujaali was a woman now. She had grieved for her brother and moved on, living a life that would have flavoured her voice.

He knew why he was there. The experience with Jameson and Blythe months before had shaken Narain more than he cared to admit. It had opened up wounds that he thought he had dealt with decades before. She was the last link to the family that had been ripped away from him and with her so close to death, his resurrection would no longer have an impact on her life. When he had discovered she was still alive, he wanted to see her desperately. Yet now, standing by her bedside, he felt like an intruder. To her he had died a very long time ago; what right had this ghost to disturb this myth at the end of her life?

Before he could convince himself to leave, however, Ujaali's eyes opened and her gaze drifted slowly up to him, a smile chasing the slumber from her face.

"Narain," she softly exclaimed and he needed no other urging. Quickly he sat next to her, grasping the hand she reached out to him.

She displayed no shock, no fear. Simply pure joy as tears glistened in her eyes. Still, her soft voice was slightly chiding as she pointed out, "You never returned. You told me you would, but you didn't."

Narain found himself speechless, lowering his head and squeezing back tears. He felt her still soft hand reach out and brush back his hair as she gently asked, "Why didn't you come back?"

A sob caught in his throat as visions of his sister clinging to his neck on the day he left India gripped him. At last, he found his voice. "I wasn't able to," he told her, raising his gaze to hers and trying to regain his composure. She was on the threshold of death; seeing the young brother who went off and died in a foreign land, yet accepting his presence next to her without question. Swallowing, he said, "I had something else I had to do. I couldn't return."

"Cooking?" she asked, innocently enthusiastic, sounding very much like the five-year-old he had left. "Did you become a famous chef?"

He smiled, offering only, "I did all right for myself. But I thought of you so often."

Ujaali rubbed his hand, hers cold yet curiously soft. "You haven't changed." She shifted slightly and he pressed the button to raise the head of the bed up. "So many years and you're still my handsome brother. Just like Aziz."

His brows furrowed. "Aziz?"

"He visits also. He tells me I would be seeing our family again soon. I will see them all very soon." Narain nodded, understanding the dream that brought Aziz to her. Or perhaps their dead brother had come to her in a vision to prepare her for death.

"He told me I would see Rohit as well." She motioned to a family portrait on the table next to her bed. Pointing to the handsome man posed next to her in the picture, she said, "My husband Rohit. Your brother-in-law. And my children. Your nieces and nephews. I told them so very much about their brave Uncle Narain." A slight coughing spasm caught her and he waited patiently for her to finish. "My brother who won the war."

Ujaali chuckled though emotion made Narain's throat tighten as he stared down at the photograph he held, studying the smiling faces of the family. His family. Nieces and nephews who would never know their Uncle Narain. "They are lovely children," he said finally. "And they are good to you?"

She clucked her tongue. "Oh, 'good' does not describe the love they've shown me. I am so proud of them. I will miss them so." A thoughtful silence fell over her before she admitted, "Still, it will be good to see the family again. Oh, and my darling Rohit. How I've missed him these past years." Narain smiled in understanding, but then looked away, the smile fading. Reaching up she took his chin turning his face toward her again. Staring into his eyes, she sensed the sadness hiding just beyond them. Pursing her lips, she asked, "You don't belong here, do you?"

Narain was trying so hard to be strong yet failing miserably as tears spilled down his cheeks. A veil had lifted slightly during the conversation offering her a clarity that she might not be able retain long in her current physical state. She saw him for the anomaly that he was: Her brother, 20 years her senior, looking 70 years younger than she.

Still, there was no fear or concern. Just a gratefulness at their reunion mixed with regret that it would be so brief. Quietly she said, "When I go to meet our family again, you won't be there, will you?"

He sighed, shaking his head, "No, I must stay here."

The guilt in his voice touched his sister deeply and she rubbed his cheek. "That's okay, bhai. You returned. Soon it will be my turn to leave but we'll meet again." Her eyelids grew heavy as sleep crept up on her. "Just be happy."

"I will, my dear little sister." Narain allowed her to slip away from him into the sleep her body craved. He didn't know when her last breath would be taken but it would be soon. He could sense it in the great effort her age-weakened heart was putting into beating. He could hear it in the wheeze of her shallow inhalation. He could feel it in the coolness of her skin.

But the body had its own time and would cease when it was ready. He had learned that with Sophie which was why every moment he had spent with her was a gift from the heavens and more precious than gold. Ujaali may have days or weeks, perhaps months. This however would be their last meeting. It was difficult enough sneaking into the hospital at so late an hour. Even if he could withstand the daylight hours, he could never explain his presence to those who had been told he had died in battle so long ago.

Allowing himself a few more moments to gaze upon her, Narain finally sighed, leaned forward and kissed Ujaali softly on the forehead, softly humming a verse from the children's song they had sung together so often when she was a child. When he closed his eyes, he was certain that he could see the path back home and hear the sweet laugh of a five year old girl coming to meet him. Then he forced himself from her side and walked out of the room, never once turning back. He had become quite good at not turning back.

†

"Ujaali."

Ujaali's eyes drifted open again and she coughed from a bit of the congestion that had settled in her chest. She had been having such a wonderful dream about Narain. How she had missed him all these years. How she missed her family. How she had wished it hadn't been a dream.

"Ujaali, wake up."

She looked up and a smile spread across her lips. "Bhai," she whispered reaching out to the figure sitting on her bed. Her eyes were cloudy from sleep but she knew he was there. "My brother, you came back. I've missed you so."

"I'm here, Ujaali, to help you. Then we can be together again."

She nodded. Yes. Her bhai would help her pass. He would take her to see her family again. The last few months had been so tiring. She just wanted to rest. Nodding again and smiling, she reached out to him and he enveloped her in his arms. Her big brother. Protecting her. He was so strong and handsome with a scent of cinnamon that warmed her entire being and distracted her from feeling the set of fangs that punctured her neck.

THE END

Acknowledgements

I'm grateful to Reg Davey and Dagda Publishing for giving my vampires a chance to see the light of the day (so to speak). I'm also grateful to my friends and family who encouraged and inspired me to keep going with the novel and the series.

Above all, I'm grateful to my nephew Eric McCreary who is and always will be the greatest joy in my life.

About the author

A resident of Chicago, Laura is the author of "Chicago's Most Wanted™ The Top 10 Book of Murderous Mobsters, Midway Monsters, and Windy City Oddities", "Vampires' Most Wanted: The Top 10 Book of Bloodthirsty Biters, Stake-wielding Slayers, and Other Undead Oddities", and "Trouble" a science fiction comedy with western overtones. She is interested in any number of things, far too many for her limited free time to accommodate. Never the less, she remains a giggling idiot for the ages and encourages the world to follow suit. She likes cats, and even thinks she owns a few, when in reality they own her.

"To Touch The Sun" is her first full-length horror novel.

Made in the USA
Charleston, SC
10 March 2014